The
Sisters Club

a novel

LAUREN BARATZ-LOGSTED

DIVERSIONBOOKS

Also by Lauren Baratz-Logsted

Jane Taylor Novels
The Thin Pink Line
Crossing the Line

Johnny Smith Novels
The Bro-Magnet
Isn't It Bro-Mantic?

Diversion Books
A Division of Diversion Publishing Corp.
443 Park Avenue South, Suite 1008
New York, New York 10016
www.DiversionBooks.com

This is a work of fiction. Names, characters, places and incidents either are the product of the author's imagination or are used fictitiously. Any resemblance to actual persons, living or dead, events or locales is entirely coincidental.

For more information, email info@diversionbooks.com

First Diversion Books edition August 2015.
Print ISBN: 978-1-62681-705-0
eBook ISBN: 978-1-62681-704-3

NEW CLUB!

Looking for like-minded women who love books to talk about same, and could use some feminine support in their lives to help each other become our best selves. Interested parties should contact Diana Taylor at…

Sylvia

I burned the inside of my arm taking the double chocolate-chip muffins out of the oven.

Crap.

Forty-six years I've been cooking, ever since Minnie and I were four and our aunt used to let us stand on one of the scarlet, vinyl-covered chairs in her kitchen to help roll the dough for the rugelach. You'd think I'd learn how to cook one single thing without burning myself.

But there was no time for self-pity tears, no time to run for the first-aid kit in my small office, because the phone was ringing.

"Sylvia's Supper," I answered.

"I'm having a dinner for four tomorrow night," an expensive woman's voice said, breathlessly, "and the caterer I always use just called and canceled at the last minute. Said something ridiculous about a fire."

She definitely sounded like the kind of woman for whom someone else's fire constituted "something ridiculous."

"That wouldn't be Kate Bakes, by any chance, would it?" I'd seen the story on the midday news on the little TV I kept on all day in my back office to check on the news and my soap operas between customers and cooking. Kate was my biggest competitor, and while I'd always dreamed of besting her, arson had never been in my plans, nor was this the way I wanted to win.

"Yes," the woman said hurriedly, "but I have no time for that now. My husband will be arriving here tomorrow night with his boss and the boss's wife. The holiday bonuses were delayed until January this year—right now! I've only got this one chance to make it a decent one. I need this dinner to be spectacular."

Far be it for me to say, *Then why don't you put on an apron and try cooking something yourself?* So instead, I said, "What do you need?"

"What have you got?" she countered.

"Lady," I said, having grown quickly tired of all of her breathlessness and angst, "I can make anything you want."

We reviewed menu options, finally settling on clams casino and a field greens salad for starters, homemade parmesan bread, side dishes of lemon-drizzled asparagus and rosemary roasted potatoes, a main course of a crown roast with the little white booties left on— booties being her word—and for dessert a frozen chocolate praline layer cake. None of it combined to make a menu I'd ever want to eat all at once, but it seemed to satisfy her. I could hear her anxiety level subsiding as we settled on each item, until…

"And you'll have it here by seven thirty," she said, sounding as though her blood pressure was going through the roof again, "won't you? And you'll supply all the heating dishes and what have you—yes?"

"You want this delivered?"

"Don't you do deliveries? You *are* a caterer."

Actually, I did do deliveries. But I usually tried to avoid them because for the past year it was just me there, alone, every day. Plus, I hated that she thought she could just call at the last minute and expect me to dance to her tune.

"My delivery boy left five years ago," I said, "and I don't think he's coming back."

"I can't believe you wasted my time like this," she said. "All this while I could have been calling other caterers. I won't have time to come pick it up myself. I'll be too busy getting dressed. Plus, what if grease dripped onto the seats of my car?"

Well, that is a hazard.

"I can't be—"

I cut her off. "I'll deliver it personally," I said. "Heating dishes, what have you, booties, and everything." What the hell, I could use the money. Business had been slow, despite what the political analysts on the news programs kept saying about the economy recovering just fine. Probably just their own personal economies were fine. "Just give me the name and address," I said, holding my lucky pen ready to write it at the top of the yellow order form.

Once she gave me the necessary information, she surprised me by saying something nice.

"You've really saved my life," she said. Then she added, "Thank you, sir, thank you so much."

"Sir?" I snorted. "It's not sir. It's ma'am. You've been talking to Sylvia."

Click. I hung up.

But I didn't really hold it against her. I get that all the time. We may have been twins, but Minnie had inherited Mom's speaking voice while I somehow wound up with Dad's. If I had a nickel for every phone-in customer who mistook me for a man, I could have afforded a sex change operation.

I placed the order to one side, figuring I'd start what prep work I could do for it that day: check what supplies I had on hand, what supplies I still had to pick up, set the sides and first layer of homemade chocolate ice cream in the springform pan, and toss the pralines with sugar and set the mixture out on sheets of wax paper. Then I went into the office and got out some aloe from the first-aid kit, put it on the burn stripe on my forearm, and then went back out front and took a cooled double chocolate-chip muffin from the tray. I leaned against the counter and surveyed the business my sister and I had built.

Before opening Sylvia's Supper, my sister and I were accountants. For twenty-five years we crunched numbers, trying not to scare shifty-eyed people into thinking we'd turn them over to the IRS. Yeah, our lives were exciting. I took a bite of the muffin.

It was a good muffin. My sister would have loved that muffin.

I miss my sister, dammit, I thought. *I miss her every damned day.*

But how many times can you cry when there's no one there to hear?

I polished off the muffin and went back to business.

On the way home from work, I decided I would stop off at the bookstore. *No matter what goes wrong in life,* I thought, *the bookstore is always the best place to go.*

Cindy

Climbing onto the bus, I slid on the steps, icy from the boot leavings of previous passengers. If Eddie were with me, he'd say it was my fault for wearing those boots: four-inch heels, narrow toes, black suede, coming to mid-calf with a couple of inches of soft black fur at the top. Of course Eddie would have been totally right to say that. But I loved those boots. They were one of the few things that made me feel like an individual. Besides, after telling me it was my fault that I slid for wearing the boots, Eddie would tell me they made me look hot.

I teetered down the aisle, found a seat nearly at the back, sat down, and right away pulled out of my brown suede satchel a copy of *Swept Away By Desire*, the romance novel I'd been reading. When I bought it a few days ago, I'd stripped off the jacket like I always did with a new book, stripped away the picture of the hero and heroine rolling around half clothed in the surf, because I didn't want to hear other people's snotty comments about my reading habits. It's been my experience that if you have a book in your hands, and you keep your nose in it the whole time, even the most die-hard talker that sits down next to you will eventually get the message and shut up. It's not that I'm antisocial, as a rule, but there are times when you just do not want to talk endlessly to strangers about the weather.

As the bus pulled away from the curb, I felt a strong chill. Even with the heat on, the cold windows always retained their own brand of weather. I pulled my patched, tan, suede full-length coat with the blond fur trim tighter around myself. If Eddie were with me, he'd say a lot of animals had died to keep me pretty. He'd say it even though he was the one who bought me the coat. Then he'd smile and tell me I did look pretty in it, that it was worth a hundred animals dying if necessary.

But none of that mattered. The coat covered my hated uniform, the black polyester pantsuit I had to wear to work in the lingerie store. And I didn't care about anything right then. I was just glad the bus was taking me away from the mall and all those obese ladies my manager was always pressuring me to get to buy thongs. Let me tell you, "one size fits all" is *not* truth in advertising.

Still, within the rose-colored walls of Midnight Scandals, the lingerie store, I was the blithe spirit; the one my manager, Marlene, was convinced could sell G-strings to an Eskimo. And I smiled, always smiled, convincing myself at least half the time that I really was the blithe spirit everyone thought they saw.

The bus chugged up the hill, depositing me at the stop outside the hospital. On the way down the stairs, book safely back in my satchel, I slipped again in my heels. Of all the things you can say about me—and Eddie always had plenty, good and bad—at least I was consistent.

If Eddie were with me, he'd have said, "Why do you have to come here every day, Cin? Give it a rest." I knew he just said those things because he worried about me. He worried that if I spent too much time at the hospital it would depress me. But Eddie wasn't there and it was my time, the magic purple-blue time between afternoon and evening; and for one whole hour I could do what I liked.

As big a place as the hospital was, it felt like everyone knew me. Not surprising, really. And when I got off the elevator, the nurse on Douglas buzzed me right through.

In her room, my sister was where she always was when I came to visit, in a chair by the window, looking out.

"Hey, Carly," I said, putting my arms around her, embracing her in a hug she didn't return. "How's it going today?" As I settled down on the edge of the bed just a couple of feet from her, I tried to think of something perky to say. "Any new cars come and go in that lot out there?"

No answer. Not that I expected any.

I reached out slowly so my movement wouldn't startle her,

replacing a hair gone wild behind her ear. My mom always said that seeing us side by side was like looking at a carbon copy of the same person. But growing up, I could never see it. Carly was the super pretty one, while I was the paler version of her. Still, as I smoothed her hair with my hand, in profile I could see the basic resemblances: the same long and straight honey-blond hair, the same slightly darker sweep of brow over gray-blue eyes, and the same lips we used to joke were made for kissing. Of course there were obvious differences: I had my work makeup on while she was scrubbed beyond clean, as though someone would be wheeling her off to the lobotomy chamber any second. Plus, there was that lifelessness in her eyes, and the lack of conversation. Me, on the other hand, I was nothing but chatter.

I told her about every blessed thing I'd done at work that day, about the 38D customers trying to cram their way into 34Bs, about the 32As stuffing their way into Cs, about all the damn endless thongs, and Marlene being such an eternal bitch.

"I swear," I said, forcing a laugh like she might actually for once laugh along with me, "if I could afford to quit, I'd start some kind of thong bonfire in the store. Or maybe just threaten to strangle Marlene with one."

No returning laugh. Not that I'd expected one.

And then, all of a sudden, I was full stop out of happy chatter. The only other thing to talk about in my life was Eddie. And I'd made a pact with myself from the day Carly landed herself in there, never to talk to her about Eddie if I could avoid it. When Carly had still been full of life, she'd hated the topic of Eddie, which was a bit of a big problem, since I loved Eddie so much. I swear, I loved that man *to death*.

With nothing left to say, but with time still remaining on the clock, I pulled *Swept Away By Love* out of my satchel.

"Let me read you some of this," I said, sounding falsely excited in my own ears. "I really think you'll like it." I found the page I'd turned over into a triangle to mark where I'd left off. Funny, I hadn't noticed before, I only had one short chapter left. Holding the book open with one hand, I gently covered the clasped hands in Carly's lap with my other. When her fingers didn't resist, I increased the grip, holding on tight. I was never quite sure who I was holding on tight for: her or me.

"Do you remember when we were small," I said, really smiling now at the memory, picturing us as little towheads full of girlish hopes and dreams, "and we used to read comics to each other under the sheets with the flashlight?"

• • •

Outside, cold had turned to colder. And the true light was gone, leaving just the light from the city.

I pulled the fur collar of my coat up around my neck and thought of the night ahead. If I went home right now, Eddie would be there, on the couch waiting. He'd want to know what I'd planned for dinner, which was absolutely nothing. He'd already know that, since there was nothing really in the house to eat, nor would there be any grocery bags in my hands if I walked through the door now. Then Eddie'd say, even if he laughed when he said it, "How do you expect me to watch *Idol* with an empty stomach?"

And Eddie would be right, of course; he'd be completely justified to say those things. I was a failure. I was a failure as a girlfriend. I was a failure as a sister. Hell, if you listened to Marlene talk on the days she was off her meds, I was even a failure at selling thongs.

Lise

"Don't you think you're being a little hard on Danitra?" I asked John, forcing a smile in the hope of taking the sting out of my criticizing words.

It was always hard not to be critical of John, who was always so critical of everyone else.

But John was not to be condescended to, even if his professor was smiling while doing so.

I sometimes wondered what I looked like to my students, perched as I was then on the edge of my desk: spiky black hair streaked with auburn highlights, brown eyes behind dark horn-rimmed glasses, my white Oxford shirt beneath a brown tweed jacket, jeans like any of them might have worn, and the pump at the end of my foot every now and then swinging with the motion of my leg as I danced the occasional nervous twitch. Did they find me formidable? Did they, perhaps, laugh behind my back?

"No," John said, clearly taking himself at least as seriously as any twenty-year-old intent on writing the "Great American Novel" ever has. "I don't. Isn't the saying 'show, don't tell'? Did you hear the section she read? She told everything!"

The sheer outrage of it. Still, it wouldn't be proper to laugh at him.

"Well," I said, considering, "Danitra did tell an awful lot. But here's something you need to keep in mind: you write drama, Danitra writes comedy. They are, at the end of the day, two very different animals. If your goal is to create the first, you need to create fully developed characters and draw scenes in much the same way you'd paint a picture. Usually. But with the latter? Your goal is to make people laugh, and sometimes the quickest way to do that is by telling a few things, skipping the reader along to the funny bits. Neither way is superior," I shrugged, "just different."

It was a good thing John was looking at me, because he missed it when Danitra stuck out her tongue at his profile. I stifled a laugh. In the short time since the winter semester had started, I'd already noticed what a resilient creature Danitra was. She was the classmate John most criticized—well, they all criticized her—but she just took it with good humor, making appropriate revisions, vastly improving the work each time, and discarding without malice the suggestions that didn't make sense to her. She had a good editorial ear. She would go far. And John? John might go far too, if his ego didn't stumble him up. John never took criticisms graciously, including mine; he was always certain the way he'd written it first was best.

"Oh, come on," John scoffed. "How can you even suggest comedy is as good as drama? You must know one is superior. And which one."

"*Basta*," I said, hopping down off my perch. "Enough. I want you to finish the chapters you've been working on and polish them to the best of your ability—and that means you too, John; none of this 'It was perfect the first time I wrote it'—and have it ready to read next Tuesday. I haven't decided yet who's to go first, so you'd better *all* be ready."

Twenty faces met the news with dismay and groans about "But there's a football game on Saturday!"—as if any of my budding writers cared about football; besides which, our team sucked—and "There's an all-weekend party in Kent Quad!"

It didn't matter that they were all in college and taking their writing seriously enough that they were actually bothering to take Writing Workshop, an advanced single-genre course with the focus on either poetry, fiction, or creative nonfiction—in my class it was straight fiction, and students in the know knew that if they were ambitious enough, I'd actually let them attempt novels—they were still all just kids.

"I'm not concerned about your social lives," I said with no mercy. "You want to be published writers, right?"

Twenty heads nodded.

"Well, if you are ever lucky enough to land a publishing contract—we won't even talk about talent—you'll be expected to meet deadlines. So you can consider this your first deadline. Now, shoo, get out there and write."

• • •

I hurried from the classroom to my office, hurrying not because I wanted to get there quickly but because I just wanted to get out of the damn cold. The campus would be pretty enough in a few months, when the flowers sprang up around the lake and it was finally warm enough again to sit on the benches and feed the ducks, but for now I was sick of winter.

The plaque outside my office door read "PROFESSOR LISE BARRETT, MFA." I never looked at it without a feeling of pride: pride at what I did for a living, followed hard by a feeling of imposture.

Fifteen years ago, I'd been a student at the Iowa Writers' Workshop, where I'd received my MFA with much fanfare. I was supposed to be the Next Great Thing. In truth, I was much as John was now: all sound and a lot of fury, signifying not much. Oh, sure, I'd placed the odd story in increasingly less prominent publications, starting out with the *Paris Review* and *Esquire* before the precipitous fall that had landed my last story in some last-chance publication named the *Last Chance Review*. Seriously. I think maybe they paid me two dollars and a contributor's copy. And I may be being optimistic about those two dollars.

At least the MFA at Iowa earned me the right to teach writing at the university level. And when I'd started here right after receiving that MFA, I'd been greeted with open arms. The dean was sure I'd earn prodigious renown, earning some for the university as well. But if the name of the game was publish or perish, then I was perishing here. I'd never set out to write short stories—I was a novelist at heart—but between teaching classes and tutoring others on how to write, somehow there never seemed time to write anything in my beloved long form.

Before you know it, a decade and a half have slipped by, and you've got nothing to show for it but a dollar from the *Last Chance Review* and a handful of students who will probably succeed where you failed.

I draped my winter coat over the back of my chair, rubbed my hands together in the north-facing tiny office that was never warm enough, even in spring, and turned on my computer.

Funny, but when I first started out teaching, office hours, which I was supposedly there for right now, were always filled with students stopping by. We'd get into debates about what was going on in the classroom or about what Art with a capital A should/shouldn't be. We'd talk about life. But now everyone relied so heavily on computers as a form of communication, nearly no one ever stopped by. They just e-mailed. My colleagues complained relentlessly about this. They said students were always making the most outrageous, not to mention stupid, requests through e-mail: "Will you read my essay now and tell me what you think before it's due on Friday so I can perfect it before the due date?" "What notebook should I buy for your class?" "I'm not going to be in class on Friday—big kegger the night before—so do you think you could loan me *your* notes?" Me, I couldn't see what they were complaining about; answering e-mails, even a whole slew of them, took less time than talking face-to-face with students for ninety minutes two days a week. Me, I had a whole file of stock answers to plug in because students did predictably ask the same questions over and over again. Me, I missed the contact of talking to other human beings, even much younger ones looking for a good grade, face-to-face.

The computer was warmed up; my e-mail was on.

There were several e-mails involving departmental bullshit plus the usual assortment of spam the university's supposedly strong spam-filter never quite managed to keep out. There were also three other e-mails: one from student John, one from my sister, and one from Tony. I opened John's first.

> From: JohnQuayle@yahoo.com
> To: Lise.Barrett@ctubiversity.edu
> I'm attaching my chapter for your early review.

Since you *did* say even I wasn't exempt from revisions, perhaps you could read it now and tell me what you think I ought to change.

I pulled out one of my stock replies from the folder I'd created just for such purposes.

From: Lise.Barrett@ctuniversity.edu
To: JohnQuayle@yahoo.com
'Fraid not. If I read your chapter today, it would give you an unfair advantage over the others. The only way to make it fair would be if we declared your due date to be today instead of next week and graded you accordingly. Are you sure that's what you want?

I was sure it wasn't. With John out of the way, I could concentrate on Sara.

From: sarabarrett@peacers.net
To: Lise.Barrett@ctuniversity.edu
Sis-tuh!
You would not *believe* how amazing it is here! We've moved east and it's much better than the last village we were in. Of course, I got diarrhea right off the bat, but I recovered nicely and am still just loving everything about Africa. The people! The animals!
How is the novel going?
Love

Several months ago, Sara had thrown over a safe and respectable job at a relocation agency, plus the full benefits and retirement plan that came with it, to follow her dream of working in a Peace Corps type of organization. It was a move that our parents, security-oriented workers right down to their own 401Ks, were appalled at. As far as I was concerned, in their eyes, they were glad I'd seemingly given up my dream of writing novels and were even more so now that Sara had done a bunker on them. On some level it was galling to think my younger sister was braver than I. But it was tough to resent Sara. In sympathy and solidarity, then, and in part not wanting to be out-adventured by my younger sister, I'd recently told Sara I'd started working, finally, on a novel, in earnest and in secret. Our secret. Of course, I hadn't done anything of the kind.

I wrote back, telling her what I thought she wanted to hear— that the secret novel was going well—and imploring her to keep on top of her malaria pills. Then I opened the last e-mail.

From: Antony.DiCaprio@ctuniversity.edu
To: Lise.Barrett@ctuniversity.edu
Do you have any idea how good you look in those jeans? And how much I'd like to see you out of them? But, alas and alack, I promised Dean Jones I'd pop by for some of his wretched sherry this evening. Rain check on those jeans?

Tony was in the same department as I am, but he taught only dead authors, while I'd committed myself to live ones. Hey, at least we both loved to read. Tony was also the kind of rangy, long-limbed, blond-and-blue-eyed man who could make tweed look trendy, and he was my other big secret. Not that we'd get fired if people learned of our on-again, off-again affair—I mean, it wasn't like he was a student, after all—but it would be frowned upon, particularly when each of us came up for peer review.

We'd been together for three years. At the end of the first year, he'd asked me to marry him. Not realizing how serious he was, I'd all but laughed in his face.

"Who gets married these days after just one year together?" I'd said. "And why? I'm not even ready to have kids yet."

A year later, following a pregnancy scare of Sara's, I thought I had the childbearing itch and asked him to marry me. It was his turn to laugh.

"You're still not ready to have kids. You're not ready to be married," he'd said. "Don't be ridiculous. Ask me again someday when you understand what it is you're saying."

I had a hunch that his "no" was a defensive reaction to my earlier "no," but even I could see he was right: I wasn't ready, neither for marriage nor kids.

Since then, we'd just continued on in our off-again, on-again way, neither of us ready for anything more, both content to remain what we were—at least for the time being—a man and a woman who enjoyed each other's company more than we did anyone else's. Oh, and the sex was still good.

I wrote him back that he could have as many rain checks as he needed, provided he had some power over the universe and could make it warm enough to turn the oddly persistent snow into rain.

Then I shut down the computer and declared office hours over early for once. No one was going to show, and if John Quayle wrote back again, well, I could always deal with him tomorrow.

Diana

The early-morning sun streaming through the mini blinds cast zebra-striped, tan shadows diagonally across my naked body. Too bad the body thus illuminated wasn't a better one. Put it this way: Rubens would have placed me on a diet.

"Come on, Diana," Dan said, his voice husky, "roll on top. Please. You know you come better that way."

It was true, of course. But I always hesitated, fearful I would crush my husband of one month. Not that I weighed that much more than Dan. Not that much. The high-tech scale in our enormous bathroom put his weight at two hundred pounds—he was very tall, so he could carry it easily—while it put my own at two seventy-five. It had taken me a while to get used to the American system of weights and measures, but really, whatever language you were putting the numbers up in, it was a lot.

As gingerly as I could, feeling something like an elephant in a rose garden, I did as Dan asked. I spread my thighs around him and he entered me, his hands on my buttocks pulling me closer to him. It felt so good.

I could never look down at my husband from this position without marveling at my incredible good fortune. He was so beautiful with that jet-black hair, startling blue eyes, straight nose, determined jaw, and those perfect lips that never minded taking the dive down between my legs.

I'd met Dan early the previous year. My girlfriends from work had insisted I accompany them to a private club to celebrate one of their birthdays. I didn't normally like to go to places like that, because there was too much risk of someone saying something hurtful, but it seemed churlish to opt out of someone else's birthday celebration.

Not in the door a half hour, Dan made his move on me. At first, I thought it was some kind of put-up job. Surely, it was a joke, this American man in London on business taking an interest in pathetic me. But Dan was so determined to talk to me, dance with me, get to know me better—he said I was charming, funny, and beautiful—and I started to believe maybe fairy tales really do come true.

We'd been standing at the bar, winded from dancing three dances in a row, waiting for our drinks. Dan had his arm possessively around my shoulders when some sot sat down on a stool next to him and, leaning in with bleary eyes, tapped Dan on the arm.

"What's this?" said the sot. "Fancy a bit o' the lard, do you?"

And then Dan did something disgusting; a truly and wonderfully disgusting thing I'd never seen him do before or since. He put his finger up his nose, took out a snot, and examined it as though puzzled.

"What's this?" he said, echoing the sot's own words. Then, as though discovering the answer to the sphinx, knowledge dawned on his face and he looked at the sot with a cold gleam in his eyes. "Oh, that's right. It's *your brain.*" Then he wiped it on the sot's sleeve. "Now fuck off."

It was a vulgar thing to do, of course, but Dan was so refined in every other way, it made it OK. Plus, he'd done it in defense of me. No one had ever done such a thing on my behalf before.

I suppose if Dan hadn't been so much stronger looking than the sot, the sot might have fought him, but instead he slinked off, ashamed.

But I no longer cared. There was no one else in the club any longer as far as I was concerned. Because if it hadn't been love at first sight earlier, it certainly was then.

We were married on New Year's Eve.

And now I was back in the present, and Dan was squeezing his hand between our jointure, as he liked to do, placing two fingers on my clit and rubbing until he was sure we'd come at the same time.

"I love you," he said afterward, a bead of sweat above his gorgeous brow as he strained upward to kiss me on the lips, "so very much."

Dan rolled me off of him and slapped me on the thigh. "I wish I could stay here like this with you all day," he said with an easy smile, "but someone has to work around here." The words might sound it, but there was no criticism in his voice. Then he rose from the bed, looking like a Greek god, and headed off to the bathroom. A moment later, I heard the shower. Already, I knew his habits. The shower would take no more than five minutes, another five to do whatever it is men do in the bathroom, then he'd be into his expensive dark-gray suit like a light, and, briefcase in hand, he'd head downstairs for a quick exit. I'd offer to make him breakfast, but he'd insist I wasn't to move one beautiful limb, that he'd have the limo driver stop on the way into the city.

And then he was gone. Dan Taylor, CEO.

Alone, I did what I did most days since Dan had moved me there: lived the life of a lady of leisure, tidying up a bit before the cleaning lady came. Mostly, I thought about my life.

A long time ago I had taken the words of the Duchess of Windsor to heart. I'd wanted nothing more than to be rich and thin. And loved, of course, but that had always seemed like an impossible dream until Dan came along. Now, thanks to Dan, I had that as well as the first item in the duchess's dictum. I lived in a house that could only be termed a modern mansion, made of red brick with white trim and black shutters framing the long windows, not far from one of the best golf courses in the country. Dan always said that, come the warm weather, he'd teach me how to play. I thought it was great that he'd want me there, part of his own private oasis of sanity; but even though I smiled whenever he suggested it, I knew I'd never say yes. The idea was sheer madness; there were too many possible sand traps of embarrassment there. For whatever else I was, whatever Dan had enabled me to become—a rich woman who was loved—I'd never have the other half of the duchess's equation: I would never be too thin.

Of all the men I'd been with in my forty-two years, and I had been with several, Dan was the only one who never asked me to lose weight for him.

"You have such a pretty face." I'd heard those words all my

life. And it was true. I also had thick blond hair I usually wore up in a French braid, soft brown eyes, naturally clear skin that any spotty actress would envy, a cupid mouth revealing even white teeth. I did have a pretty face. And yet even Fat Frank, who would have outweighed me on that bathroom scale by at least a hundred American pounds, had always said, "If only you'd lose a bit of that weight, Di, you'd be such a looker."

As if he was one to talk.

But Dan never said that. Oh, he did tell me I had a pretty face, often. But he also told me the rest of me was pretty too.

The phone rang and when I looked at caller ID, I saw it was London calling. It was my sister, Artemis. Well, it was already afternoon there.

I let it ring for a few times, debating whether or not to pick up. Even reviewing the hurtful things men had said to me in the past was sometimes preferable to talking to Artemis; if I were a bunny rabbit, I often thought, Artemis would be both my carrot and my stick. But I knew if I didn't pick up, she'd only keep calling. Artemis knew I rarely left the house.

"How's Connecticut treating you?" she said in plummy tones as soon as I answered. "Are you ready to pack it in and come home yet?"

"No," I said, not for the first time. "I like it here. Dan's here." Well, the second part was true, at any rate.

"Just give it a little time," she said. "Before you know it, Dan's being there won't feel like enough."

She was always such a ray of sunshine, my sister, Artemis.

Four years my junior, Artemis had received every good thing and gene the Richards family had to offer, plus she got all the love; I just got the food. Whenever I was sad about something, or angry or hurt or even happy, my mother would just give me another piece of cake. Before I knew it, my body was something like cake.

"How is that possible?" Artemis said, after I'd assured her Dan was enough. "You don't go out anywhere. You don't see anybody. You haven't made any new friends there yet, have you?"

All of this was true.

I tried to tell myself that her words only *sounded* bitchy, that in reality she was merely worried I'd wind up hurt. Still, those words of hers did rankle.

"It's only been a month," I pointed out. "Technically, I'm still on my honeymoon." I was starting to feel angry. "*You* give it time."

"Now, now," she laughed. "There's no need to get shirty."

"I've got to go," I said.

"Brunch date?" she said sharply, suspiciously.

"Yes," I said firmly, thinking of the cleaning lady, Consuela, due soon to arrive. Well, it did qualify as a date. Sort of.

"Is it with a man?" she said. "Does Dan know?"

"No," I said. "It's with a Brazilian...dignitary."

"Oh. Well. La-di-da. Be sure to shoot me out an e-mail later and tell me how brunch went with your dignitary."

"Give Mum my love," I said.

"Will do. But perhaps you might call her sometime yourself?"

Here's the thing about Artemis: she could be a bitch to the hilt, but sometimes she had a valid point.

She rang off.

Things hadn't always been quite this way between Artemis and me—her being unpleasant, me parrying the unpleasantness. When we were very young, we even shared a pair of friends, Sally and Samantha, who were themselves sisters, same ages as we were. I always envied the way Samantha stood up for Sally when the boys at school picked on her for being too puny to be any good at sports, and I envied the way they liked to wear the same clothes, despite the difference in their ages; it was as though they admired each other so much, they liked looking the same. I longed to have what they had—sisters, loving and supporting one another—and was grateful for their friendship. I was grateful that our friendship with them brought Artemis and me just a little closer together. But then they moved away and Artemis and I drifted apart.

Of course, despite Artemis's propensity toward the bitchy *bon mot*, there was an underlying truth to what she'd said on the phone: I *was* lonely in Connecticut. There was nothing for me to do there. When Dan wasn't around, there was no one for me to be.

I was grateful that Dan found me beautiful, and I was grateful he married me; I was grateful he stood up for me to the sot once upon a time, and I was grateful he never asked me to lose weight. But none of that was why I married him. I married him because I loved him. Still, sometimes it was lonely being Mrs. Dan Taylor, CEO.

. . .

Dan called on the mobile to say he wouldn't be home in time for dinner, again, and something about working late with a client. I might've been resentful if I didn't recognize the truth in what he'd said earlier: one of us *did* need to work around here. Not wanting to eat alone, yet again, although I did need to eat, I decided to go to the bookstore. Maybe I'd have a sandwich or two in the café area while cracking the spine on a new thriller.

When I went to pay at the cash register, I saw they had out new copies of the store newsletter. I picked one up, perusing the contents while I ate my smoked turkey with roasted red peppers and fresh mozzarella on focaccia bread.

The newsletter listed notices of upcoming store events, story times in the children's department, author appearances, that sort of thing. On the flip side, there were schedules for groups meeting in the bookstore: book-discussion groups, writers groups, even Scrabble groups. As I glanced around the crowded café, I realized that must be the Scrabble group meeting in the corner right over there. I recognized the colorful board and the wooden tiles, even though I'd never played the game myself. There were also two women who looked remarkably similar to one another sitting at a corner table, laughing over their coffee and cake as though they truly enjoyed one another's company; I envied them, sure they were sisters.

Then the thought occurred to me: If other people could place ads in the store newsletter for all these other clubs, why couldn't someone place an ad for something different, for a sisters club? Certainly, there must be other women in the area who had a sister they were missing who, for one reason or another, was not physically on the scene. Sure, in the modern era, a sister need only be a phone call or mouse click away, but you can't hug a telephone when you're feeling lonely. You can't hug a computer. And maybe, like me, there were others whose relationships with their sisters were not all books and TV would have you believe they are, and yet they wanted that sister-like bond, dreamed of it.

Yes, I thought, a sisters club. Why had no one else ever thought of it? Of course I knew I couldn't just blatantly call it that from the start—other women would think I was balmy—but it's what it would be nonetheless.

In my excitement, in my haste to find the store manager, I forgot all about my smoked turkey with roasted red peppers and fresh mozzarella on focaccia.

I had more important things to do.

I was going to find some sisters. Whether they knew it or not, it was what they were going to be.

Four Women

"This is the stupidest idea I've ever heard in my life!"

It didn't start out that bad, but it was awkward.

Diana was the first to arrive at the bookstore, getting there at six forty-five, fifteen minutes early. Since she was the one to organize the whole thing, she felt a responsibility to be there to greet everybody else. Plus, still getting used to the horrors of driving on the wrong side of the road, she always allotted herself extra time to get anywhere.

She sat at the table for four in the café with a gigantic cinnamon bun on the white plate before her, filling up the time with nervous nibbles and taking in the familiar room around her: the cone-shaped light fixtures hanging down over the square and round tables, the soothing periwinkle walls, some amateur photographer's work displayed on them—she liked the one of the cat on the windowsill, at least—and the people at the other tables. The ones in groups of two or more all looked like easy friends with fun or important things to discuss. The loners looked content to be so. Next to the cinnamon bun, Diana had a copy of a bestseller from a few years back with an Oprah's Book Club sticker on it; since the ad she'd placed said she was looking for women who were also book lovers, she'd figured it would be prudent to arrive with a book.

Diana's gaze shifted back and forth between the round analog clock on the wall, the hands of which seemed to sweep so slowly, and the front entrance. Perhaps no one would come? Even though three people had RSVP'd to her plea in the newsletter, maybe they were all just having her on. With just two minutes remaining before seven o'clock, Diana thought of getting up and giving up. Her first serious attempt to make new friends in her new country, and already it was an obvious failure.

Sylvia walked into the bookstore at exactly two minutes to seven and went straight to the café, scanning the faces there. When she saw a large woman with gorgeous, thick blond hair wearing a pants ensemble all in winter white starting to gather her things as though she might be leaving, Sylvia approached her. On the phone, Diana had said, with a self-deprecating laugh, "I'll be easy to spot. I'm a bit bigger than most people."

As Diana shook Sylvia's offered hand, she took in the other woman's appearance. Sylvia, obviously older by a handful or more of years, had a natural thinness to her, like she'd never had to worry about a calorie in her life. She was petite but with a hard edge, as though you wouldn't want to cross her in an alley; her taut body was clad in jeans and a long-sleeve yellow T-shirt you'd expect to see on a younger woman. Sylvia had red hair that had to be a dye job, but it was cropped in the neat short cut of someone who couldn't be bothered with much fuss. Her brown eyes, encased with lines, looked as though she'd laughed a lot at one point; but the steely expression on her face said that had been a long time ago and she saw nothing funny about life right now.

And when she talked, she sounded more like a man.

In short, she was nothing like Diana.

"So, you're a fan of Oprah?" Sylvia observed as soon as they were seated.

"Well," Diana laughed nervously, "everything can't be Dostoevsky and Dickens, can it? What kind of books do you favor?"

"Everything," Sylvia said, "I read everything." She drummed her hand on the table. "Crap, this is awkward."

"Excuse me?" Diana said politely. But she never got an answer, because just then, at seven on the dot, Lise walked in.

Lise strode with purpose up to the other two, still wearing her usual teaching outfit of tweed and denim. She didn't offer to shake hands, claiming she thought she'd caught a cold from one of her students, someone named John. Instead, she just took a seat next to Diana, across from Sylvia, Diana looking like the warmer of the two.

"That's three of the four of us, then," Diana said brightly. "I suppose we could start telling a little bit about ourselves, although it doesn't seem quite fair to do so before the fourth arrives. After all," she laughed nervously, "we wouldn't want her to think we'd been talking about her."

"We don't even know her to talk about her," Sylvia said. "And anyway, I hate people who are late. If you're late, you deserve to go to bed with no supper."

"Perhaps we should just wait a few more minutes?" Lise offered Diana helpfully. "After all, the roads aren't all that great tonight."

Lise and Sylvia went and ordered cups of coffee. When they returned, Diana addressed Lise. "Sylvia says she reads everything, while I," she lifted her paperback and waved it ruefully, "favor popular fiction. What sort of books do you like?"

"Oh," Lise said with an easy smile, "I suppose you could put me down in the everything camp too."

"That's wonderful!" Diana said. "The two of you have something in common already."

Lise tried to smile again encouragingly, but Sylvia just scowled and the conversation thumped into awkward silence as the three watched the clock tick together.

"This is—" Sylvia started to say at seven fifteen, but she never got to finish her thought, at least not then.

"Omigosh, I am *so* sorry!" Cindy threw her brown suede satchel down on the table in a move so sudden, the coffee cups would have flown if the other women hadn't moved quickly to grab them out of the way. Then Cindy shrugged out of her patched, tan, suede coat, letting it fall onto the chair behind her. She rooted in her satchel, pulling out a brand-new red spiral notebook and a cheap pen, flipped the notebook open to the first pristine blue-lined page, and then, pen in hand, looked up at the others expectantly. "What did I miss?"

"Introductions, for starters," Sylvia snorted. "By the way, you're not really going to take *notes*, are you?"

Cindy blushed, dropping her pen as though it had burned her. "I guess I've never done anything like this before."

"Who has?" Sylvia snorted again.

"Perhaps we could just talk a little bit about ourselves first?" Diana suggested. "It would probably be a little bit easier to have a conversation if we actually knew who we were talking to."

The others looked at her.

"So talk," Sylvia finally challenged Diana. "This was all your idea, after all."

"Oh, no," Diana said. "I mean, it was my idea, but I couldn't possibly go first. I'd feel as though I were hogging the limelight. But," she added, "I do think it would be nice if whoever does go first tells us a little bit about what she wants out of life, what her goals are. You know, if we're going to become, um, *close*, it's important that we help each other achieve our best selves."

As Diana spoke her last sentence, Sylvia rolled her eyes. "Don't you think that's forcing things a bit?"

"I don't mind going first," Lise said with an easy confidence. "I'm Lise Barrett. I'm thirty-seven years old. I work at the university, teaching writing. I have a younger sister who threw over her job to do peace work in Africa. I envy her. Most days, I love my job. Most days, I also love one of my colleagues, who I've been dating secretly for the past three years. But this was never what I wanted out of life. Oh, the romance part of it is fine, just not the work. What do I really want? I want to write a novel."

"A novel?" Diana gushed. "Oh, my. I *love* reading novels so much, I can't imagine anything more wonderful than writing one."

"I just can't imagine being *smart* enough to write a novel," Cindy said. "All those words!"

Sylvia said nothing.

Cindy picked up her pen, rolled it between her fingers.

"I'm Cindy Cox," she said, taking a deep breath and following

Lise's lead. "I'm twenty-three. I work in a lingerie store, which I absolutely *hate*. I live with my boyfriend, Eddie, who I absolutely *love*. He's a musician and singer. My sister Carly just got out of the hospital. Again. She has a problem with drugs, only this time she tried to kill herself. She wouldn't talk afterward for the longest time and was put on suicide watch. Now she's back living with our parents. I wish I could talk to her—we used to talk so much! But now I never feel it's right to burden her with my problems. She's got too many of her own. Plus, I don't really have any problems. Well, except for the job. But other than that, everything's just great. What do I want?" She screwed up her face, as though considering the question for the first time, ever. Then her eyes lit up as though the thought had just occurred to her. "I want a baby."

"A baby!" Diana said warmly. "You know, I've never been at a place in my life where I thought it was the right time to have a baby."

"I know what you mean," Lise said. "I've often thought it would be wonderful to have a baby, but the timing was never right."

Sylvia said nothing.

Diana looked at her expectantly, but when no words were forthcoming from the other woman, Diana shrugged. "Well," she said, "I guess it must be my turn. I'm forty-two and on New Year's Eve I was married to the man of my dreams." As Diana spoke, she picked up breathless speed, like a prisoner encountering a priest after a month in solitary confinement. "Dan is everything I ever fantasized about wanting in a man but never imagined I'd have, not in this lifetime. Our wedding ceremony was magical! Well, except for the fact that the bride looked like something of a white whale in all that white satin, while her sister—that would be my sister, Artemis—looked like a sylph standing at the altar beside her. And then there were all the nasty bees Artemis kept putting in the bride's ear that Dan couldn't possibly love her, not really."

Diana looked embarrassed. "I suppose it's silly, isn't it, talking about oneself in the third person like that."

"That too," Sylvia said.

"I beg your pardon?" Diana asked.

"Well, it's also a bit silly to be telling so much about your wedding to three women you've only just met."

"Diana did indicate in the ad she put in the newsletter," Lise said, rising to Diana's defense, "that she wanted to meet other women who loved books to talk about that as well as their lives."

"Huh," Sylvia said. "Except for mentioning Oprah and 'everything,' not much has been said about books."

"Well, I did say I wanted to write one," Lisa said pointedly before turning to Diana with an encouraging look. "Go on."

Diana took a nibble off her cinnamon bun. "OK, then. Everything for me this past month has been wonderful. There's just one problem."

The others looked at her.

"Well, look at me!" Diana said. "I'm *huge*! You know it's funny, or maybe it's not funny at all, but when I lived in London I couldn't wait to get out of there. You know, Londoners make fun of Americans all the time. They see the pictures in the newspapers and on the telly, and they just think everyone over here is so fat. Back home, I always felt like this anomaly. Not that everyone is thin there, but nothing like the obese Americans you see on the news. Back home, I always felt as though I'd done something wrong. I just figured it would be so much different here. And it is different here, in many ways. I have Dan. I have this great house. But everyone here seems to be either obese or too thin. There's no happy middle! I still get disgusted looks from people, and some days I feel as though I can't take it anymore. So what do I want? Isn't it obvious? I want to be thin."

Lise gave Diana a sad and sympathetic smile.

"That must be so hard," Cindy said. "I just can't imagine—"

"You people think you have problems?" Sylvia cut her off. When she spoke again, she spoke with authority, like a drill sergeant barking out orders. "You want to know how to solve your problems?" She pointed at Lise. "You, write a book." She pointed at Cindy. "You, have a baby." She pointed at Diana. "And you, go on a diet." She brushed her hands against each other as though getting rid of annoying crumbs that weren't there. "Problems solved."

"*You're* the one who doesn't understand anything!" Diana was angry. "Do you think I like being like this? Do you think it's my choice?" She paused, gathering momentum. "You ever watch the celebrity shows on TV or leaf through the gossip mags, and you see some gorgeous man with some woman on his arm who looks like she doesn't quite fit in the picture? Maybe she's older, or she doesn't dye her hair. Or maybe she's even fat. Or, what about that first Bush president of yours and his Barbara? People were always making cracks about her looking like his mother. Everyone laughs, snickers. How would you like to be that woman? Hmm? How would you like to be that woman who the airlines demand pays for two seats on the plane unless that woman is flying first class? How would you like to be that woman who *never* fits in the picture, who people are *always* laughing at, looking from her gorgeous husband to her, and people's eyes always saying, 'God, what could he possibly see in her?'"

At last, Diana ran out of steam.

Sylvia had been looking straight at Diana the entire time the other woman was speaking. She eyed her a moment longer. Then: "But he loves you, doesn't he, this *Dan*? And you're sure of that?"

Still visibly angry, Diana nodded.

"Then what's it to you," Sylvia said, "what anyone else thinks? Seems to me, that what they think says more about them than it does about you. Fuck 'em if they can't take a joke."

Diana opened her mouth to speak, then shut it again. In her own peculiar way, it seemed as though Sylvia was sticking up for her.

"Crap," Sylvia said. "And *this* is why I never bother with other women. My mother raised me not to be a joiner, and she was right."

Sylvia got up and put on her coat.

"You're not leaving already?" Diana said. "But you never told us about yourself."

"Of course I'm leaving," Sylvia said. "This won't work. It *can't* work. This is the stupidest thing I've ever heard in my life. Whoever heard of such a thing? You can't just *decide* to be close to other people. It doesn't work that way."

"If that's your attitude, then why did you ever come here anyway?" Diana called out to her as the other woman walked away.

But Sylvia never turned. Instead, she walked right out the door.

Diana

Well, that went well.

Oh, it wasn't totally horrible, not after Sylvia left, never having answered my challenge about why she'd come in the first place. Why *had* she come? She was like some surly person showing up at an AA meeting with every intention to go out drinking afterward. But in a way, I could see she was right: it was damned awkward trying to forge a bond with people one didn't even really know. Still, at least Lise and Cindy were making the attempt. In fact, Lise and Cindy had been quite comforting.

"You know," I'd said, "it's not like I haven't done everything under the sun to lose weight, but nothing ever lasts for more than just a little bit."

"Some people," Lise had said, clearly referring to Sylvia, "just don't understand that weight isn't always a choice for other people. It's a medical condition, just like so many things."

"Exactly," Cindy had added eagerly. "A lot of it's genetics, just like with substance abuse. I think sometimes, because my sister's a druggie, if I even take two pain-killers for cramps, I'll follow in her footsteps. Is it like that for you? Were your parents really big too?"

I was sure she was trying to be helpful, but it didn't help, not really. And no, my parents weren't big too. Everyone else in the Richards family was normal size. I was always the lone fatty.

Despite the efforts of Lise and Cindy to make me feel better, the next morning Sylvia's words still rang in my head: "And you, go on a diet."

As if it was that easy. As if I hadn't already tried the no-fat diet, the no-carbohydrate diet, the nothing-but-vitamin-water diet. The weight always came back. Still, maybe there was something drastic I hadn't tried yet?

"Do you think I should lose weight?" I asked Dan as he was leaving for work.

Funnily enough, it was a question we'd never addressed, not directly.

"No." He looked at me puzzled. "Why do you ask?"

"I don't know," I hedged. "I just thought maybe it would make you happier with me, that's all."

"I don't need you to lose weight for me to be happier with you," he said, touching my face with his fingers. "But I do wish you were happier here."

"I am happy here!" I protested.

"But you never see anyone but me," he pointed out, echoing Artemis's words about my status here. "Except for the bookstore, you never see anyone. It can't be much fun for you, me being gone all day."

"It's fine. Really."

"I know!" he said. "We could have some people in from work, or maybe some of my golf buddies and their wives."

I pictured what such an evening would be like: the inevitable stares of "What's he doing with her?" from each person who came through the front door.

I'd not met many of the people in Dan's world yet. Since we'd been married in London, and during the holidays no less, the only people to make it across the pond had been Dan's parents and sister, plus her family. They'd been pleasant enough—they'd surprised me by not judging me at all—but they all lived in Michigan where Dan had grown up, so they were hardly within calling distance.

Yes, they had been very pleasant, even when Artemis had made everyone uncomfortable by grilling Dan at the pre-wedding party. She'd made everyone uncomfortable except for Dan, of course.

"Isn't it odd," Artemis had said, winding one of her pretty golden locks around her manicured finger, "that a man should reach the age of forty-four, a successful man, and not have been married at least once?" I know that sounds awful, but in her own way, Artemis was only giving voice to what everyone else in my family was obviously thinking. "Don't you American moguls usually have at least three families by your age? You're not covering up for something, are you? Like one of those Hollywood actors who marry and adopt a few kids just to prove to everyone he's not gay, when of course everyone knows otherwise?"

If Artemis had been that sot in the private club, Dan might've picked another snot out of his nose to prove a point about her. But it was supposed to be a nice family gathering and he dealt with her inferences with equanimity.

"Hmm," he said, his expression cloudy as though considering the issue. "Why haven't I been married before?" Then he brightened. "I know!" He took my hand, looked me in the eyes, and then kissed me full on the lips before turning back to Artemis with an easy smile. "It's because I've never been in love before."

Dan was always so good to me, that even though the suggestion of having people from his work life or golf life in for an evening sent all kinds of insecure worry raging through me every time he mentioned it, I couldn't deny him.

"Sure." I forced an easy smile. "Whenever you like."

Once he was gone, though, I got busy doing research, Sylvia's words goading me on. She may have had a crass way of putting it, "You, lose weight," and I'd reacted negatively to her negativity at the time. But just like a hurtful truth in Artemis's clothing could still be a truth nonetheless, I saw a glimmer of validity in the terse words Sylvia had spoken. Sure I'd tried a lot of things to lose weight before, but had I really tried *everything*?

I went online, first looking under weight loss. But nearly everything there, I'd tried before. Some of the things more than once. I was just about to give it up when I saw a link for surgical solutions and there it was:

Gastric bypass surgery.

Surgery. It was an option I'd always assumed was reserved for the truly desperate, and I'd never thought myself to be one of those people before, but now I saw that I was.

It said it was only recommended for people one hundred pounds overweight or more. I certainly qualified for that. It listed other conditions: patients needed to have been obese for over five years, should not have a history of alcohol abuse, should not have untreated depression or other major psychiatric disorders, and should be between the ages of eighteen to sixty-five. I fit in perfectly. Well, except for the part about depression. But who in the world that weighs two hundred and seventy-five pounds doesn't get depressed occasionally? As for "other major psychiatric disorders," it was possible I had a few of those, but none that had been formally diagnosed as such, thank God.

The website described the procedure: how gastric bypass surgery makes the stomach smaller and allows food to bypass part of the small intestine; and how the patient would feel full more quickly than when the stomach was its original size, which would in turn reduce the amount of food eaten and thus the calories consumed. Bypassing part of the intestine would also result in fewer calories being absorbed. This would inevitably lead to weight loss.

There were even before and after photographs of celebrities who'd had the procedure done. I had to admit, the celebrities looked abnormally unlike their before pictures in their after shots, as though they'd had part of themselves sucked away through a giant straw, and they were still trying to get used to their new state—but no one could deny they were now half the people they used to be. And in a good way.

The website also outlined risks, but I didn't pay any attention to that part. I was too busy focusing on one particular line:

The average patient will lose two-thirds of their body weight within the first two years.

I wondered if that held true no matter what the starting weight. If so, someone starting at one fifty would weigh fifty just two years later. But that couldn't be right. And then I remembered: they only performed this surgery on the truly obese.

I did the math. Not that I'd ever been terribly good at math, but I did it anyway.

If my calculations were correct, in two years' time I'd lose one hundred and eighty-three pounds. I'd weigh ninety-two pounds!

I reined in my enthusiasm. Even I could see that ninety-two

was just too small. But imagine, I thought, the difference I could see in just one year! In just a few months!

Going to the online Yellow Pages, I began searching for surgeons.

. . .

It's amazing, in America, how quickly you can get a surgeon to see you when you tell him or her your husband has an insurance policy that insures you to the hilt.

"Mrs. Taylor?" the nurse called into the posh waiting room, chart in hand. "Dr. Rich will see you now."

Dr. Rich turned out to look very, well, *rich*. He had steel-colored hair that looked as though it cost two hundred dollars a pop to maintain. He was also naturally lean, and I got the impression when he looked at me sternly, that he didn't have much patience for his obese patients. Oh, well. So much for bedside manner.

"You certainly are a perfect candidate for the surgery," he announced forty-five minutes later, having given me a complete exam. "Your blood pressure is high. You're at grave risk for type two diabetes. The question is: Do you really want it?"

I thought about my life thus far. I knew, on an intellectual level, that it was foolish to wholly define oneself by one's weight. And I didn't define myself wholly that way. But to say it didn't make up a large portion of the equation, given the life I'd led, would be a lie. Perhaps, if I had the surgery, I could go on to live life like a normal person.

"I definitely want it," I said with conviction.

"Terrific," he said. "Then there's just one question."

"And that is?"

"How do you intend to pay for this?"

"I assumed my husband's insurance company would cover it."

He laughed, a vaguely nasty sound as though I were the stupidest twit who ever lived. "Mrs. Taylor, I'm afraid gastric bypass is considered to be, roughly, akin to cosmetic surgery. I highly doubt your husband's insurance would cover it. And, even if they might, you'd need to jump through an awful lot of hoops first. For starters, you'd need a documented history at previous, unsuccessful weight-loss attempts."

"I'm two hundred and seventy-five pounds," I said tartly. "How much more documentation do they need?"

"You'd also need to prove that your obesity is an imminent threat to your health, which, however much I might believe that to be true, in the long run, they'd never believe it is imminent. You'd need documented attempts at exercise and/or pharmacological efforts, et cetera, and even if you were able to jump through all those hoops, at the other end of the line, after the operation, you'd still have a devil of a time getting the insurance agency to pay up."

He made it all sound so hopeless. And long. It sounded like I'd have to wait a long time to get what I wanted when I wanted results now. Hell, I wanted results *yesterday*. I sighed. "What other alternatives are there?"

"Have you ever heard of, 'In God we trust; all others pay cash'?"

"Excuse me?"

"Cash, Mrs. Taylor, twenty thousand dollars of it, to be exact. Can you pay cash?"

It was a startling notion. I'd assumed I could get this taken care of with insurance and get it done before Dan could talk me out of it, figuring by the time the claim was made to the insurance company the surgery would be over with, a done deal. But I couldn't just take twenty thousand dollars out of our joint savings account without saying anything first. That would feel too much like stealing from my own husband. Then I remembered the savings I had from my job in the days before I became Mrs. Dan Taylor, CEO. Yes, I could just pay for it. I said as much.

"Great," Dr. Rich said. "In that case, I think we can speed through the extensive history and psych eval. When shall we schedule you in for? Did you want to do it next week sometime?"

I hadn't imagined it would suddenly be that easy after the hoops he'd made such a fuss about before. But then, I supposed, the idea of twenty thousand dollars in cash must have made my two hundred and seventy-five pounds look awfully attractive to him just then.

"How long will I need to be in hospital?" I asked, thinking I should have thought to ask questions like that earlier.

"Four to six days." He shrugged as if it were nothing. "Recovery time? Typically you should be able to return to normal activities in three to five weeks."

Three to five weeks? It sounded like an incredibly long time to me. But then I thought about how I'd always been a fast healer. Even the time I'd needed extensive oral surgery, I'd been back at work the same afternoon. Surely I'd be up and around sooner than his prediction.

Then I thought about the hospital stay.

"Could we wait a bit and do it the week after next instead?" I asked. "My husband will be going to Japan then for two weeks on business."

"And you thought to surprise him by being *thin* upon his return?" He smiled, but it wasn't what you might call a friendly smile.

I could feel my cheeks redden.

"No, of course I didn't think it would happen *that* quickly," I said. "I just want it to be a...surprise."

What I was really thinking was, if I told Dan about it in advance, he'd surely try to talk me out of it, tell me I didn't need it, tell me I was fine the way I was.

"A surprise?" Dr. Rich raised his eyebrows. "Very well."

"And you did say my obesity was life-threatening," I said, seizing onto something he'd said earlier, "didn't you?"

"Oh, yes," he said in all seriousness. "If you don't do something drastic about all that excess baggage you've been carting around, you could very well die. Someday, at any rate."

There it was. Surely even Dan would come to realize in time that what I was doing was merely taking a necessary step to ensure my well-being. Once the initial shock was over, he'd understand it was all for health reasons.

It was for the best.

Lise

"What are you doing?"

I didn't answer right away. I was too busy staring at the half-blank page on the screen in the blood-colored alcove that constituted my home office, trying to figure out how to introduce a physical description of my protagonist. I didn't want to do anything so trite as have her look in the mirror. Then it occurred to me: I didn't need to tell the reader what she looked like right off the bat. I could let that information emerge organically, perhaps through a comparison with another character or maybe through dialogue. That settled, I went back to crafting the setting.

"What are you doing?" The question came again and with it, an accompanying nuzzle at the base of my neck.

I swiveled in my chair, one pajama-clad leg still tucked under the other; the pajama bottoms were light-blue flannel with a cloud pattern on them, and, over the matching T-shirt, I'd donned an old gray and maroon university sweatshirt, protection against the creeping chill in the cottage located just off campus.

There was Tony, in all his naked glory, the thatch of dark-blond hair surrounding a penis that was already rising to the occasion. It was very tempting but...

I tucked my pencil behind my ear, readjusted my glasses, and then turned back to the computer screen.

"I'm writing the Great American Novel," I said, clacking away again, as if I spoke such sentences every day. But even I could hear the ironic half quotes I mentally placed around the words. After all, internally I treated my student John's aspirations to do the same with irony, didn't I?

"Oh, of course," he said. More nuzzling. "Anyone can see that."

Nuzzle. "What's it about?"

"It's called *Messia*. It's a contemporary literary retelling of *Romeo and Juliet* only in my version it's about an Israeli girl and a Palestinian boy."

"Sounds intriguing. I hope they don't die in the end." More emphatic nuzzling.

God, it was tempting. But how was I ever going to make any progress if...

"Come on," he said, grabbing my typing hand. A little known fact that probably would have made my students laugh at me was that I always typed with only one hand, resting my head on the clenched fist of the other as I clacked along. "In another half hour we'd only both have to get up anyway to make eight o'clock classes. I'll even make you breakfast afterward."

"You mean *you'll* put the toast in the toaster this time?"

"If you're really good, I'll even turn on the coffee machine. Come on." Taking both my hands now, he gently tugged me up off the swivel chair. He kissed my neck and whispered into my ear. "At the end of the day I'll be off to that stupid Shakespeare conference in Toronto. I won't see you for three whole days. *Three whole days* with no sex."

He had a point. What would be the harm in a little morning sex? Once he was gone, I'd probably get plenty of work done.

I let him lead me back through to the semi dark bedroom, the illumination from the bathroom off to the side casting a beam of light against the rumpled sheets. It wasn't as though we hadn't just made love the night before, but we were always good at making love, Tony and me.

He laid me down on the bed, pulled my pajama bottoms and panties off in one go, leaving my fuzzy socks, T-shirt, and sweatshirt on as he placed his tongue between my legs. Tony well knew how I hated to be cold and that it was always worse for me in the early morning. He'd only remove my twin tops when he was done down below and was ready to do other things. As for the fuzzy socks, he'd let me keep them on for the duration.

There was something eternally wonderful about making love

with someone I knew as well as I knew myself.

As Tony trailed feather kisses on the insides of my thighs, teasing me by playing the sexual version of the children's game Too Hot/Too Cold, my mind tiptoed its way back to the computer still on in the other room. What would be an important enough tale to tell? What could I do with my characters that would make readers say, "I'm glad I took this journey"? Perhaps more importantly, what could I do with those pages that would make me say such a thing?

"So, what's going on in the book now?"

"Huh?" I propped myself up on my elbows and saw that Tony had ceased doing what he'd been doing and rolled off to the side, his right cheek resting on his open palm.

"You'd gone back to work," he said. He jerked his head backward toward my office. "You're back with your magnum opus, aren't you?"

One of the truly awful things about making love with someone I knew so well was that he knew me sometimes even better than I knew myself.

I at least had the good grace to be embarrassed.

"No worries," Tony said, inching up beside me and nudging my chin up with his knuckle before deep-throating me with a kiss. "Just for being a particularly bad girl," he said with a smile, "I'll let you make it up to me."

. . .

The phone rang.

Tony and I were in the kitchen gulping our way through toast and coffee. I had never been a late person by nature, but sometimes Tony's nurturing had a tendency to make me so.

Before I picked up the phone, I looked at the caller ID, but it wasn't any number I recognized.

"Lise?" I knew that British accent. There were plenty of professors at the university who affected faux-British accents, as if teaching English to the point of tenure somehow conferred a new nationality on people who originally came from Nebraska or

California or even Connecticut, but there was only one person in my fairly small world that spoke that way with authenticity. Immediately, she had my full attention.

"Diana?" We'd spoken a few times on the phone since that somewhat misguided night at the bookstore two weeks before.

What an odd night that had been. Diana had been so overly eager, almost desperate for things to work out. Cindy had been very eager too, for that matter, but she had been a different kind of eager, perhaps because of her youth. And then there'd been Sylvia, the hostile one; the one who made everyone else wonder just what the hell she was doing there.

I'd been giving Sylvia a lot of thought since that meeting. Well, I would, wouldn't I? Given that she was in a real sense responsible for me finally getting serious about writing a book. And what I'd been thinking was that her hard shell was just a cover-up, like a turtle. There had to have been a lot of pain in her life, not just recent pain but nearly life-long pain, to create a shell that thick. I wondered what those pains were.

And then, whenever I thought about the "book" aspect of the club, I had to laugh. Diana's ad in the newsletter had said she was specifically looking for women who loved books "to talk about same"…as well as other stuff. The funny part was, I'd tried to join many clubs over the years where the ostensible purpose was to discuss books, only not much book discussing ever got done. Instead, the other women in those clubs mostly talked about their relationships, or their kids if they had any, after a mere cursory discussion of the book in question, sometimes lasting no more than five minutes. It was frustrating, really, when I'd put several hours into reading some book—often lousy—I wouldn't normally be interested in, only to not really discuss it. But I could see where those other women were coming from: they wanted to make a human connection with other women and books were as good an excuse as any to get out of the house. The only problem was, those women I'd been in groups with before I hadn't been able to connect with them. But I did want to make a connection. Then I saw Diana's ad, and, in a way, it seemed the perfect compromise: women getting together who loved books but without a specific agenda as to what had to be read. I could almost see Diana saying, in her overeager but pleasant way, "So what if we didn't really talk about any books specifically? At least we all know we *like* books!"

In the few times we'd spoken since, it had just been superficial stuff and as yet we'd made no plans to get together again. I liked Diana well enough; I'd just been too busy with work. As for the other two, that night at the bookstore had been awkward, and, despite my instant liking of sweet Cindy and my curiosity about tart Sylvia, a part of me had begun to think I never would hear from them again.

"Is something wrong?" I asked Diana now.

"I hate to impose," she said, sounding as though she really meant it, "but I'm going in for a bit of surgery later on this morning."

"A bit of surgery?" How casual she made it sound. "What's wrong?"

"Nothing's really wrong, per se. I've just decided to take Sylvia's advice."

"How do you mean?"

"Well, I'm going to have this gastric bypass surgery you read about all the time and—"

"Diana, have you thought this out?"

"Of course I have. I'm not a child. Anyway, it was stupid of me to call. I'll just have to find someone else. Bye."

She was obviously hanging up.

"Diana!" I screamed loud enough so she'd hear me even if she'd nearly put the phone down.

"Yes?" she said.

"Just tell me what you need."

"Well, it says here on the pre-admittance form that I need to put someone's name down for them to contact in case of an emergency. You know, if something should go wrong."

My head instantly filled with images of all sorts of things that might go horribly wrong.

"What about your husband?" I said, voicing the obvious.

"Oh, Dan's in Japan this week, next week too." She gave a laugh that was more tin than tinkle. "And I don't really know anyone else here. I mean, I suppose I could ask Cindy. But she does seem to have so many of her own problems, what with her sister and everything. Perhaps Sylvia…"

Putting Sylvia down would be disastrous. If there was any kind of emergency, Sylvia would only make Diana feel worse by telling her it was all somehow her own fault.

"What about your own family?" I asked.

"Well, of course my sister, Artemis, and my parents are my next of kin, but they can't very well pop over here to handle an emergency should one arise, can they? Not that there will be any— emergencies, that is."

I grasped at other options, any other option. "And there's really no one else?"

She laughed, a rueful sound. "Unless you include the mailman, I'm afraid the answer is no. I really don't know anyone else here."

It was sad to think I was the closest person to her. "Of course you can put me down," I said impulsively.

"You won't regret it," she said, as though she'd just sold me something. "I'm sure nothing will go wrong. This is all just a formality; you know, one of the hoops they make you jump through."

"I'm sure you're right. But please have the hospital call if they need me for anything at all." I gave her my cell number so the hospital could reach me even in class, even in the bathroom, praying all the while nothing would go wrong. "And please call me yourself, just as soon as you're able, and let me know how it goes. If you give me the name of the hospital, I'll come by after work."

"What was that all about?" Tony asked a moment later, as soon as I'd hung up. He rose and knocked back one more swig of coffee before shrugging into his coat.

"I'm not sure," I said, feeling a bit stunned. Then I looked up at him. "But I think I just became someone's next of kin."

Cindy

I'd barely had time to set the grocery bags down on the counter when I felt arms snake around me from behind, squeezing me tight. The pressure of the hands against my belly felt funny somehow, and I looked down to see one was holding a stuffed bear. The hand moved upward till I was face-to-face with the bear, and I saw that it was white plush and holding a red satin heart with white stitching on it that said *I love you.*

Then it was as though the bear was talking. I heard, in a voice that I guess was meant to sound like a bear, but a nice bear, "I'm sorry, Cindy. I'm sorry I was in a bad mood last night. You know I love you, right? You know I love you more than anything in the world and that I'd die without you, don't you? You forgive me—"

"Of course," I said, turning around in Eddie's arms, looking into those eyes I loved so much, and seeing love looking right back at me. "Of course. It was nothing."

Eddie kissed my neck till my knees went weak then he perched the bear on my shoulder. I looked to my side, caught the bear's eye. "Damn, that thing's cute."

* * *

"Is dinner ready yet, babe?" Eddie opened the cabinet under the sink, tossed an empty beer bottle in the trash, and left the cabinet open. Then he reached for the chipped chrome handle of the fridge, the constant hum it always made getting louder as he opened the door, and pulled out another beer then walked out of the room without waiting for an answer. Then came the clicking sound of the remote, followed by music and raucous laughter. It was probably

MTV or VH1.

I stood in the small kitchen adding more onions and peppers to the oil sizzling in the pan. I'd forgotten to pick up any meat on the way home from work and figured I'd make up for the lack of meat with extra vegetables. If I was lucky, by the time dinner was served, Eddie would have drunk enough beer that maybe he'd mistake the eight ounces of mushrooms I was planning to add at the last minute for the missing meat. But who could blame him if he was upset? I should have remembered the meat. And even if he noticed, the mutual oral sex we'd had in the kitchen after he gave me the bear had been hot enough he probably wouldn't mind.

The kitchen was a yellowed-tile and cheap-cabinet disaster, not that I had much love for cooking. It was the smallest room outside of the bathroom in our rental, which also had a living room and bedroom. The apartment was on the second floor, above the florist we paid rent to, and you could hear the sounds from the street at all hours of the day and night, even with the windows shut in winter. The windows themselves were old—Victorian, I think it's called—and double-hung with two long rectangular panes over a single water-shimmery sheet of glass. When the train came through, you could hear them shuddering in their frames.

"Dinner!" I announced, carrying two plates into the other room, the smell of the soy sauce and red wine I'd added to the mix tickling my nose. I moved to place everything down on the round table, which was at the far end of the living room from the TV and covered with a cream-colored crocheted cloth I'd bought at Sears.

"Smells good," Eddie called over. "But why so fancy?"

"I just thought—"

"Come on," he said, smiling an invitation, flashing a brilliant smile as he took his feet off the low coffee table and moved newspapers and magazines out of the way. "Show's about to start."

I didn't bother asking what show he meant as I set down both plates on the coffee table before settling on the floor across from him, half my ass on the lumpy area rug, the other half on the hardwood. Whatever it was, it would no doubt have something to do with people beating each other up to become the last person standing and that last person standing would no doubt win something grand, like a ton of cash or a recording contract or something like that.

Eddie's eyes were on the screen and my eyes were on Eddie as he raised the first forkful to his mouth. I waited to eat myself, all the time wondering: Would he like the dinner? Would he notice anything was missing? Would it go on being a good night or would it turn into a bad night?

I saw his Adam's apple move as he swallowed.

"What do you think?" I asked.

"I think that guy is totally fucked," he said. "Look at him! How does someone with so little talent get on TV anyway?"

"I meant the food," I said.

"Oh," he answered, leaning across the table briefly to kiss me on the tip of the nose, flashing another smile. Then, without even looking down at his plate, he forked up some more. "It's great, Cin. You're an awesome cook."

I let out the breath I hadn't even known I'd been holding and lifted my own fork.

Maybe if Eddie managed to stay in an OK mood for the rest of the night, we'd have sex later. Even if he didn't, we'd probably still have sex later. It just might not be so much fun. Taking Sylvia's advice from the one night I'd met her, I'd thrown my birth control pill for the day down the toilet that morning. It was strange taking the advice of a woman I'd only met once, and a nasty woman at that, but she'd spoken like the Voice of God. And, really, she had a point: If there was something I wanted, more than anything else in the world, why just sit here wanting? Why not just go for it?

As I ate, I watched Eddie watching the TV.

Eddie had long wavy brown hair—chestnut, I think you'd call it—that my mother always referred to as Jesus hair. He had green eyes flecked with brown that had a certain animal quality to them. His body was thin, and he didn't gain weight no matter how much food he ate—which may have been because of the coke he snorted on weekends—and he usually dressed in torn jeans and T-shirts with band names or political slogans on them. Eddie always said it was a cool look for a rock star to have. A rock star. That's what

Eddie wanted to be, even though thirty had come and gone for him recently. Eddie still thought it would happen someday. Most days, I believed that too.

Some days, and nights, it felt like I could just go on looking at Eddie forever.

The night I'd met the other women at the bookstore, we'd spent some time after Sylvia left talking a little bit more about ourselves. Diana talked about her husband. Lise talked about that guy she was seeing secretly from work. When it came my turn, I told them about Eddie. Right before coming out that night, Eddie and I had gotten into a big fight.

"What do you mean you're going out?" he'd demanded. "What do you need to go sit with some strange women in a bookstore for when I'm right here?"

I couldn't really blame him for being upset. Except for nights he was with his band, practicing or playing gigs, we were always together. And if the shoe was reversed? If he just wanted to go hang out with some guys I didn't know? I'd have felt the same way he did: abandoned, like maybe the great thing we had together—this thing where each of us was the other's whole world, or most important world, where we got lost in each other so much of the time to the exclusion of all else—just wasn't enough for him anymore.

But for once I didn't listen. This was something I wanted to do, *for me*. With Carly sick again, I wanted to make a connection with other women who could fill that particular emptiness. So I'd ducked under his arm and out the door, promising I'd only be gone an hour or two, promising I'd give him the blowjob of his life when I returned.

As it turned out, I was gone three hours and Eddie was very angry. As it turned out, it took more than one stinking little blowjob to make him forget my three-hour defection.

But as I'd sat in the bookstore café with those nice women, Diana and Lise, I just couldn't bring myself to tell them dark stuff, like how mad Eddie'd been about my leaving, so I told them good things instead.

"When I first met Eddie eight years ago," I'd said, warming

to my subject, "I was a sophomore in high school and he was just out of technical college. He was so cool, so mature compared to the other guys I knew! He wanted to go on the road with his band right away, but his mom insisted he at least work at a real job for a bit first. She thought he should know what it is to work for a regular paycheck. But the economy was bad and any job he went for, there were always like a million other applicants too. Then he saw an ad in the paper for a used-car salesman job. If you ever meet Eddie you'll know Eddie could sell anything to anybody! But when he went to fill out the application, there were like sixty other people already there. Eddie said it wasn't just like a regular application, where you fill out references and stuff like that, but that there was also a long test that went with it. There were questions like, 'Are you willing to do accounting work'?"

"Ah," Diana had interrupted. "They were doing a psychological profile on your Eddie."

"That kind of question is meant to filter out people who aren't really interested in the particular job," Lise had added. "If you say 'yes,' they think: If you want to do accounting work, then why are you applying for a job selling cars?"

"Exactly," I'd said. "And of course, as Eddie told me later, he was too smart to fall for that trick. He put down 'no,' he did not want to do accounting work. But then came another odd question, 'Do you like blind people?' "

"Ha!" Diana'd laughed. "A blind question about blind people. That's very clever."

"Huh?" I'd said. "A blind question?" I mean, it was obvious to me that it *was* a blind question, because it was about blind people obviously, but I didn't get what she was getting at.

"A blind question," Lise had kindly explained, "is one that profilers put in as a control. They expect one hundred percent of people to answer the question the same way. In this instance, they'd expect everyone to answer, 'Yes, I like blind people.'"

I still hadn't been sure what she was talking about, but I certainly understood the last sentence.

"But that's exactly it!" I'd said. "That's where Eddie's so brilliant!

Eddie wrote, 'No, I don't like blind people.'"

"Huh?" Now it was Lise's turn to be surprised. "Who doesn't like blind people?"

"That's exactly what the interviewer wanted to know," I'd said, getting excited in the telling, "when he called Eddie in for a follow-up interview. 'Mr. Haven,' Eddie told me the interviewer said, 'your application looks quite good. We really like the fact that rebuilding cars is something you do as a hobby, it shows you have a real attachment to the product. But one thing has been puzzling us. Out of sixty applicants, you were the only one who put down, 'No, I don't like blind people.' Could you tell us why that is, Mr. Haven?' Now it was Eddie's turn to look at the interviewer like *he* was the one causing the puzzle. Eddie told me he spread his arms wide, looked the interviewer straight in the eyes, and said, 'Because they can't drive cars!' Eddie was hired on the spot. Course, he didn't stay at that job very long, but I still love that story."

The other two women had loved the story too. Maybe they were seeing right along with me the possibilities that were Eddie. And I'd only been telling the truth: I *still* loved that story.

Crash! The TV never knew what hit it as the remote slammed into its center, courtesy of Eddie's hand. "Goddamn fucking idiots," Eddie said now. "I don't even know why I watch that stupid program."

My hand had stopped midair with my fork halfway to my mouth. I wasn't sure what my next move should be: go on eating, or lock myself in the bathroom, claiming diarrhea. If there is one thing that will get you out of almost anything in life, it's diarrhea. I mean, who wants to risk finding out you're lying?

"Babe," Eddie said, his eyes had gone dark, "get over here."

Oops. It was too late to claim the diarrhea defense. It's been my experience that it only works if you plan ahead for it. If, on the other hand, you try to just announce it spur of the moment, no one ever listens to you.

I set my fork down, obeyed. And maybe, I thought, it'd be good. Even when things were really bad, in its own way it was always also kind of good.

Eddie spread his arms wide over the back of the couch behind him and thrust upward with his hips, his cock clearly straining against the fly of his jeans.

"Take care of me, babe," he said, his voice husky with wanting, but it was more of a command than a plea.

I knew it was safer to obey than to resist. And anyway, I didn't really want to resist. Seeing Eddie like that had me feeling pretty horny too.

I undid the button of his jeans and then the zipper, tugging and tugging until I had them down around his ankles; Eddie never wore underwear, so whenever he wore the jeans that were slightly worn through in the back, you'd get a little glimpse of butt cheek peeking out at you. It was definitely a good rock-star look.

My hand was around the width of him, and I'd already started licking when the thought occurred to me: If I brought Eddie off like this, how would we ever make a baby tonight?

I dropped his cock like it was some utensil from the kitchen I was temporarily putting aside.

"What the fuck, Cin?" Eddie said, half rising. The jeans around his ankles made the move less threatening than it might have otherwise been. "Don't stop now."

"I'm not stopping," I said, kicking off my boots and sliding out of my own jeans and panties. I didn't even bother removing my top and bra, not wanting to waste time during which Eddie's cock might lose its momentum. If Eddie wanted them off, he could take them off once I was securely astride him. Then I smiled, letting my hair fall against his face as I spread my thighs around him. "I'm not stopping at all. I'm just flipping over the tape."

Eddie was like a rounded-off brick moving inside me. It would've been nice to have been just a tad bit wetter first but experience told me my body would get accustomed.

His words came out between thrusts like they were keeping their own beat. "I…just…can't…believe…all…those…idiots… on…TV."

"I know, baby, I know," I said, riding him for all I was worth, praying he'd come soon so I could start making that baby.

At the bookstore that night, Diana and Lise had wondered *why* I wanted a baby right now. These days, they said, if given the choice most women waited till they were older than I was. Not wanting to be rude, I didn't point out that they'd both waited so long, they were almost at the point of *too* old. But I did tell them the truth about myself: how I'd never had anything that was my own, how with a job I hated and a sister I worried about I was hoping to have just one tiny person in the world who I could love and take care of. If I waited till the time was right, I'd probably wait forever. And, anyway, I'd told them, I loved Eddie so much, I knew I'd never love another man like I loved him, so why *not* make a baby with him now?

"I…love…you," he panted, thrusting harder now.

When Eddie spoke to me like that, when he looked at me with that wide smile of his that could have charmed the pants off any groupie, when he looked deep into me like it was only me he loved and only me he ever would love, I felt like the luckiest girl in the world. Eddie's face looked so beautiful, framed as it was by my hair falling all around it like a curtain. "I love you t—"

"Fuck," Eddie said when the phone rang.

"Let it ring," I said. "If it's important they'll call back later."

"Yeah, but what if it's Joe? Joe was supposed to call me about that gig this weekend." Eddie reached for the phone on the small table by the couch, even as he kept thrusting up into me. "Yo?" A pause. "No, she's busy right now. Who is this?" Pause. "Sure, I'll tell her." He hung up, thrust some more.

I stopped riding. "Who was that?" I asked.

"Someone named Lise. Said it was some kind of emergency." He shrugged, and then grabbed my ass tight with both his hands as though trying to jump-start me. "Come *on*."

But I was off him like a light, running bare-assed to my satchel where I found the crumpled sheet of paper on which I'd written all the other women's numbers; Diana'd had them from when all of us first called her. After that odd night at the bookstore, I'd never expected to talk to any of them again. They were older than I was; what did we have in common? But for some reason I'd taken all their numbers down and never thrown out the sheet of paper. I punched in Lise's number, all the while Eddie was shouting in the background, "What the fuck?"

"Shh, shh," I begged. "Please. Just give me one second."

Lise answered on the first ring. "Cindy?" she said. Well, I thought, I guess everyone except us has caller ID these days.

"What's wrong?" I said. "What's the emergency?"

"I'm sorry," she said, sounding a bit embarrassed. "I guess it's not exactly an emergency. It's just that Diana had that gastric bypass surgery, you know, the one that's supposed to make people lose lots of weight immediately."

"What?"

"I know, I know. But she wanted to do it. I guess that thing Sylvia said to her about just losing weight put the idea in her head. She realized she'd tried almost everything before, but never surgery. She thought it was going to be easier than having a tooth pulled. But I just came from visiting her in the hospital. I guess it was a lot harder than she thought. She's in a really bad way. Anyway," and here she coughed, like a stranger who has just gotten too personal with you and now thinks maybe they've gone too far, "I just thought you might want to know. It's just that she doesn't really know anyone else here but us. She's all alone in the hospital, and if we don't visit her—"

"Of course I want to know. Thank you…"

Then I heard a sound that wasn't coming from the phone, wasn't coming from Lise. I looked up in time to see Eddie shake the jeans off from his ankles, something like a growl coming out of him as he kicked the jeans away.

I only had enough time to say, "Thank you so much for calling" and "I'll look in on her tomorrow," before Eddie was on me.

Sylvia

After I'd walked out of the bookstore that night, I'd been so angry I hadn't been able to see straight. The nerve of those women, thinking *they* had problems!

First there was that Diana, whose sister might sound like a bit of a jerk, but at least she was still alive. And hey, if she was a jerk, at least she was doing it from far, far away.

Then there was Lise, whose sister was also far away, but who sounded pretty nice to me, except for the whole competition thing. But wasn't that Lise's fault more than the sister's, for allowing herself to get jealous of someone she obviously loved so much, for not being as brave as her sister in truly going after what she wanted out of life?

Finally, there was Cindy. True, her situation did strike even me as sad, having a druggie/depressed person for a sister. But here's the thing: Her sister was still *alive*. So no matter how bad Cindy might think things were right then, there was still time to set it right. And that was the same thing with all of those women: their sisters were still alive, while mine was…mine was…

My sister, Minnie, was my twin, just five minutes younger than me. We used to joke that, because of our huge age discrepancy, I was sure to die first.

Whenever I looked at Minnie, it was like looking in the mirror.

We lived together all our lives: growing up, then in college, finally in the little two-bedroom condo I still lived in. Neither of us ever got married. Neither of us ever had kids. When people would ask us how we could stand to be around each other so much, Minnie would always say, "We're just like those Delaney Sisters. You know, the ones who wrote those books? Except we're fifty years younger and we're not black and neither of us is a dentist; we're accountants instead. But other than that? It's exactly the same."

Minnie always did the talking for both of us. Me, believe it or not, I was the quiet one, the shy one, at least by comparison.

But then Minnie got breast cancer last year, and she started forcing me to come out of my shell. And oh had I come out! It was like all the nasty things I used to only *think* in my head suddenly came flying out of my mouth without thought. Or maybe it was that, with Minnie dying and then dead, I didn't care what the world thought anymore. Life was short; I'd say whatever I wanted to.

"I won't be around to stick up for you forever," Minnie'd said one day when I was sitting next to her, holding her hand while they gave her the chemo. "You always said you wanted to run your own catering business, that as much fun as it was making Thanksgiving dinner for just me, what a thrill it would be to have total strangers paying for your cooking."

So Minnie took out her life's savings, helped me open Sylvia's Supper, helped me hang up the hand-painted sign over the front door, and helped me set everything up just perfect.

And then she died.

* * *

I stood in the doorway of the back entrance to Sylvia's Supper. It was near to closing time, but I figured I'd give it another fifteen minutes to see if any last-minute stragglers, maybe needing an immediate dinner, would stop in. I had one arm wrapped tightly around my waist in a vain attempt to keep warm, the other hand holding a cigarette as I stared up at the stars of the late February night sky.

I know, I know. I shouldn't have been smoking. Funny thing was, right after Minnie died, I started up again. I'd been without a cigarette for twenty years, we both had, but no sooner did Minnie go in the ground from cancer than I realized the thing I was missing in my life most, besides her, was a smoke.

But I should have quit. If I hadn't quit again before, I should have quit after what I'd found that morning. While doing a routine breast exam in the shower, I'd found something: a lump. It was my biggest fear in life—that the awful way Minnie went was the way I was going to go too, because we were twins—and it was coming true.

Of course I hadn't made an appointment with the doctor. Why go, only to get told the obvious? And I knew I wouldn't be strong enough to go through what Minnie had: the chemo, the cutting, all for nothing, all for just a few more months of pain. Of course I'd wanted her with me a little longer, even just another day. I'd wanted her with me forever. But not like that. Not in so much pain.

Minnie was so brave. And I knew that, whatever else I might have been in this life, I was no brave soldier. I'd just let things run their course on their own. If I were lucky, maybe I'd just die in my sleep.

"If that's your attitude, then why did you ever come here anyway?" Diana had called after me, that night last month at the bookstore.

I knew I'd made it hard on the other three women, coming in there with my crossed-arms attitude as if to say, "Entertain me. Convert me. I *dare* you." But so what?

"Because," I could have told her when she called out to me, "I loved my sister more than anyone else in the world, and I miss loving someone that much. I want someone to be close to again. Even if we're just meeting to talk about books or to 'help each other become our best selves' like you said in your ad in the newsletter, I need other human beings to be close to again."

But I couldn't say that. I couldn't say that to those women who were strangers.

Crap. The phone was ringing. And I hadn't even finished my cigarette yet.

I tossed the cigarette on the pavement, ground out the business end with my toe, made sure all the sparks were out, and then went back inside.

"Sylvia's Supper," I answered the phone.

"Um, Sylvia?" The voice was gnawingly familiar, but I couldn't quite place it. It had that stuttering quality to it, but without an actual stutter, as though the speaker wasn't confident she had the right to interrupt.

"Yes, this is Sylvia," I said patiently. "I make supper."

Well, *I* thought it was funny.

"This is Cindy," the voice said, gaining in strength, "Cindy Cox. We met at the bookstore a couple of weeks ago?"

And of course I knew who she was then, even if she hadn't added the part about the bookstore.

"What—" I started to say, but she cut me off.

"I hope you're satisfied."

"Ex*cuse* me?"

"We all took your advice," she said. "I'm trying to get pregnant, I'm pretty sure Lise is writing a book—"

"Lise is writing a book?"

"That's not the worst part. Actually, come to think of it, that's not bad at all."

"So what's the worst part?" I asked, not sure I really wanted to know.

"It's Diana." I heard an intake of breath. "She took your advice to just lose weight, and it's all gone just horribly, horribly wrong. She had that gastric bypass surgery—"

"I never told her to do that!" I was more than willing to take responsibility for my own sins. But I was not willing to take responsibility for someone else's idiocy.

"Does it really matter what your exact words were?" she said. "You said something to Diana, she heard what you said in a different way than you said it, and now this has happened."

"This? What's the this?"

"Never mind that now. Diana's back home. Lise and I are meeting there tomorrow night, and I decided you'd better be there too. After all, you started this."

"Whoa! Hey, just because you all made some choices to do some things, you can't put the responsibility off on me."

But she didn't respond to my outrage. Instead, she was rattling off Diana's address. And, not knowing why I was even obeying this annoying little twit, I was scrambling for a pen so I could get the address down before I forgot it.

"Just be there," she said, hanging up.

I'll say this for Cindy Cox: she sure knew how to get other people to do things.

Four Women

RECOMMENDED READING:
Diana: *In Her Shoes*, Jennifer Weiner
Lise: *Writing Down the Bones*, Natalie Goldberg
Cindy: *Suzanne's Diary for Nicholas*, James Patterson
Sylvia: *Talk Before Sleep*, Elizabeth Berg

"What ever possessed you to do such a stupid thing?" Sylvia asked.

Diana was lying propped up by down pillows, on the gold-and-white couch in the large living room off the cathedral-ceiling foyer. She shrugged. "It seemed like a good idea at the time."

Lise had been the first to arrive, bearing a tray of finger foods: spinach in phyllo pastry, mini quiches, and a few blander options selected with Diana in mind. "I figured you probably couldn't get up to do any cooking yourself," she'd said, placing the tray down on the marble-top table in front of the couch.

Cindy, walking in next, a cab having dropped her off, looked around stunned, as though she'd just stepped into an old episode of *Lifestyles of the Rich and Famous*. "I bought a chocolate cream pie," she'd said. "I got it at Stop & Shop." She shrugged, looking embarrassed at her offering when compared to the grand surroundings she found herself in. The pie pan with its clear plastic dome still had the black-and-white label with its UPC on it. "Mom always says never to go anywhere empty-handed."

Sylvia had come in last, late, carrying a large pot.

"Aren't you the one who said," Diana had laughed, "that people who are late should be tarred and feathered?"

"I don't recall those as being my *exact* words," Sylvia had grumbled. Then she'd surveyed the selection of food lined up on the table. "What's all this?" she'd said.

On Cindy's face was the look of someone who suspected she'd done something wrong, even if she wasn't quite sure what that something was. "Lise and I were trying to do a good thing," she'd said defensively. "We figured she couldn't do any cooking."

Diana had neglected to point out that she was wealthy enough to order in anything she liked or to hire the best caterers to cook something for her. The truth was, food was not Diana's favorite topic at the moment, not when the mere ingestion of any of her old favorites—rich, fatty foods like spinach phyllo and chocolate cream pie—sent her running, as best she could in her postsurgical condition, for the bathroom.

"Diana can't eat things like that!" Sylvia had snorted. "What are you two trying to do—kill her?"

"Hey," Lise said defensively, indicating the blander options, "I did at least bring other healthy choices."

Sylvia ignored her, lifting the lid off the pot she was holding and letting the aroma of Jewish penicillin fill the air. "It's why I was late," she muttered under her breath. "I figured you could use something easy on the stomach but with lots of vitamins in it, so I brewed up a pot at the last minute."

Diana looked at the other woman. "I'm touched," she said gently. "I can't believe you took the time—"

"Well, don't let it get to your head," Sylvia cut her off. "It's just soup."

Lise had taken her tray and Cindy's aluminum plate off the table and then located the kitchen, big enough to run a catering business from, where she deposited the offending items on the counter before rooting around in the unfamiliar cabinets and drawers until she found four Chinese soup bowls and matching soup spoons. If Diana couldn't eat rich foods, none of them would.

Then they'd all found places to sit in the living room—Lise sat at the other end of the couch down by Diana's feet, Sylvia dragged over a side chair, and Cindy settled down on the floor—while Lise ladled up Sylvia's soup.

"Thanks," Diana said, accepting a plate. "I think I can just manage this without dumping. Dumping—that seems to be all my body can do since that wretched surgery."

"Dumping?" Sylvia said. "That is definitely more than I want to know."

"Dumping Syndrome, actually," Diana said, as though the other woman hadn't spoken. "It's when the stomach contents move too rapidly through the small intestines. The symptoms are bloody awful, and when I tried to eat just one chocolate kiss the other day, my intestines immediately said to me, 'Hel-*lo*! Don't you remember what you just put us through?' That's why it's so great you brought this soup. I'm pretty sure you didn't put any chocolate in it." She tried to laugh at the absurdity of it all. "You didn't, did you?"

"Of course I didn't," Sylvia said. "What do you think I am— stupid? And I'll tell you something else, if my intestines were having conversations with me, I'd be worried."

Diana colored.

"Don't worry about it," Sylvia said dismissively. "As a matter of fact, I think you look thinner already."

Diana brightened at that. Then she said, "But you know, it's not fair for us to talk about just me. We should talk about everyone else too, you know, if we're to be kind of like sisters."

"Sheesh," Sylvia said, "you're still stuck on that? And whoever said anything about being like sisters? Give it a rest. Why do we have to be *like* something? Why can't we just be four women eating soup?"

"I don't know," Lise said. "I think it's kind of nice to have a theme. Maybe we should even have a group title," she laughed, "like a book?"

"Oh, that's right," Sylvia said. "Cindy said something on the phone about you starting to write a book."

Lise leaned forward, immediately caught up in the topic shift. "It's amazing," she said. "All those years I spent putting off trying to write a novel, I think I was putting it off because I imagined it would be very difficult."

"And it's not?" Cindy said. "I can't imagine writing anything more involved than a grocery list."

"I don't mean to say it's easy," Lise said, "and I'm sure it's not the same with everyone. It's probably not even the same for individual writers from one book to the next. I guess it's just that the idea of the novel has been living for so many years in my head, taking its shape, developing its own tentacles of subplots, once I finally sat down to write it, it's just all spilling out. In just three weeks, I've racked up over two hundred pages."

"What's it about?" Cindy asked. "Is it a romance? I love romances."

"Yes, it does have romantic elements—it's a contemporary retelling of one of Shakespeare's plays—but it's not strictly a romance," Lise said. "I guess you could call it a literary novel."

"About?" Diana prompted.

"It's about a pair of star-crossed lovers," Lise said.

"Well, that's descriptive," Sylvia snorted. "I don't think anyone's ever read one of those before."

Diana sat up straighter against her pillows. Ignoring Sylvia, she spoke directly to Lise. "You know," she said, "my sister, Artemis, works for a gossip magazine, and she knows lots of literary agents and editor types. Of course, they're all in London, so maybe you wouldn't want that, but I'm sure she could find someone to look at your book if you'd like that, perhaps help you out."

"Do you really think it's going to be that easy?" Sylvia said. "You write a book one month, and the next someone buys it? Whatever happened to artists needing to struggle first?"

"Of course she's right," Lise acknowledged. "Almost no one makes it right away as an author. As a matter of fact, anytime you read about an overnight success story, chances are that person has a half dozen or more unsold books in a cedar chest at home. I've heard that. Still," she smiled at Diana and shrugged, "I guess there's no harm in talking to your sister."

"I'll call Artemis tomorrow," Diana said, obviously pleased. Then she looked expectantly from Cindy to Sylvia. "Who's going to talk next?"

"Don't look at me," Sylvia said with such outraged vehemence that Diana started to laugh.

"Stop being so funny," Diana begged, holding her midsection. "You're going to make my staples pop."

Sylvia looked at the others. "I'm funny?"

"Are you kidding?" Cindy said. "You're the funniest one here."

"I am?" Sylvia said.

"As some of you already know," Cindy said, "or at least Sylvia sort of does…I'm trying to have a baby!"

"Oh, that's terrific news!" Diana said. "If I weren't so sore, I'd jump up and hug you."

"Here's what I don't get," Sylvia said.

The other three looked at her, puzzled.

"I told the three of you to write a book, have a baby, and lose weight, pretty much in that order, and you listened to me. What were you all, *crazy*?"

"It's not like I never tried to lose weight before," Diana said. "I tried, many, many times. You just made me want to look for one last method."

"For me," Lise said, "it was like an epiphany. All those years feeling like I should be writing a novel and feeling guilty all the time but never really doing anything about it. Talking to you I suddenly realized: Why *not* now? So I take a chance on myself and maybe I fail. But at least I should try."

Cindy laughed. "Are you kidding me?" she said to Sylvia. "That night, you were like the Voice of God. You were like Morgan Freeman, doing a voice-over! 'You, do this. You, do that.' I'd have been scared to *not* listen to you. Besides," she shrugged, "it's like Lise says: Life is short, and if you really want something, why not at least try?"

"I don't think those were my exact words," Lise said.

Cindy shrugged. "They might have been."

"You really are all crazy," Sylvia said.

"What does Eddie say about it?" Lise turned to Cindy. "About the baby."

"You know, it's funny," Cindy said, "Eddie usually has a lot to say about everything." She paused, looked up at the ceiling as though the answer to her perplexity might be found there. "But he hasn't said much about this."

"Oh, I'm sure he must be thrilled," Diana said. "I'm sure you both are."

"Well," Cindy said, "it hasn't happened…yet. But enough about me." She turned to Sylvia. "You know," she said, "that night at the bookstore, you left before you had a chance to tell us about your sister, or anything really. What's she like?"

Life is short. Sylvia heard the words in her head, the words Cindy claimed Lise had said, even if she hadn't. *And if you really want something, why not at least try?*

And suddenly, in a big rush of words, like a dam had broken, in more words than she'd spoken in one sitting in an entire year, Sylvia told them about Minnie. She told them about the lump. She told them everything.

· · ·

Dan Taylor opened the front door to his house and dropped his suitcase on the glossy black-tiled floor of the foyer.

"Diana!" he called.

As soon as he'd realized that the business part of his trip was done, and all that remained was to go on client dinners to girly bars and karaoke clubs, he'd hopped the first plane that would let him overpay to fly on it, figuring on surprising his bride by coming home several days early. He couldn't wait to see her.

"In here!" Diana called.

Dan Taylor followed her voice and walked into his own living room, finding his wife lying on the couch with a comforter over her lower body as though she'd been ill, surrounded by three women he'd never seen before. All the women had tears in their eyes, as though they'd just received some sad news.

"Dan!" Diana smiled through the tears. "You're home early!"

"I couldn't wait to get back to you," he said. "What's going on?"

"Funny you should ask," Diana said with a nervous smile. "I have a little something to tell you."

Cindy

"I can't believe you're smoking that thing!" I said.

"What?" Even in the dark confines of the catering van, I could see the surprise on Sylvia's face.

Back at Diana's house, after her husband walked in on us, we'd all made ourselves scarce pretty quickly. Well, except for Diana, of course. Lise said she had some student papers to go over and left first. Then Sylvia and I walked out at the same time. I said good-bye to her and started walking down the long driveway.

"What are you doing?" Sylvia had asked. I think it was then that she looked around the Taylors' driveway and must have realized the only cars there, outside of her van, belonged to people who lived in the house.

"Walking," I'd shrugged. "It's too much money to take the cab both ways. I figured I'd just walk until I find a stop on the bus route." Not that I really thought there would be one close by. There was no need for the bus to stop anywhere near Diana's neighborhood.

"Don't be ridiculous," Sylvia had said. "Hop in."

"I don't want to inconvenience you any," I'd said. "Don't you have somewhere you need to be?"

"Don't be ridiculous," she'd said again. And in that instant, I realized she really did find me ridiculous. But now she was the one behaving ridiculously.

"That cigarette," I said. "You just told us all you found a lump in your breast and now you're *smoking?*"

"It calms my nerves," she said. "Besides, I didn't feel right about lighting up back there." She gestured with her head back toward Diana's house. I could see what she meant: Diana's house was so perfect, no way would you want to smell it up with smoke.

"If it bothers you so much, I can put it out," she offered. But she didn't make a move to put it out. The cigarette dangled free out of the corner of her mouth as she shifted gears to pull out into traffic.

"It doesn't bother *me*," I said. But I was lying. There was something, a secret I hadn't told the others back at Diana's house. Eddie and I'd had sex the night before and I woke up that morning certain I was pregnant. I know you can't get pregnant that quickly—or at least I think you can't, or maybe it's that the symptoms don't start that quickly—but I was almost sure that I was. And, being almost sure of that, I was sure Sylvia's cigarette smoking was making me nauseous. "It just bothers me because I don't think you should be doing that right now." "First you say it doesn't bother you, then you say it does bother you. I wish you'd make up your mind," she said, rolling down her window and tossing the lit cigarette out into the night. "Fine. I'll smoke when you're gone."

The drive from Diana's house to my apartment, even though both were within city limits of the same small city, took time—a slow, sliding progression from the wealthiest area of the city to an area that was, well, substantially less so. As we drove, the mansions disappeared and became just regular big houses, then condos, then strip malls as we drew closer to my neck of the woods.

"Wow," I said, looking for something to talk to Sylvia about. She seemed like such a hard person to talk to. We'd only talked twice in person, once on the phone, and yet every word seemed to be its own potential minefield. "This van doesn't stink at all."

"What did you expect?" she barked a laugh. "Did you think it would smell like garlic and onions?"

"I don't know," I said. "I guess I did think it would smell like food."

"Insulated door," she said, gesturing with her head at the barrier between where we sat and the back of the van.

"Ah," I said, feeling stupid even as I said it. What kind of jerk says, "Ah"? Something about Sylvia made me feel stupid.

Maybe she somehow sensed that and took pity on me, because

for once she asked me some questions. I'd noticed that before about Sylvia: Diana and Lise asked other people things, but not Sylvia. I just figured maybe she didn't care to know.

"So," she coughed, but it wasn't like a cough from the cigarette she'd been smoking. Rather, it seemed like a cough of nervousness and it occurred to me, not for the first time, that maybe Sylvia wasn't so good at talking to people. Not that I was all that great at it myself. When you get right down to it, some days, it's amazing human beings are able to communicate with each other at all, like each of us is a play with our own programs and no one knows the songs in anyone else's plays.

"So," Sylvia said again, "I guess I missed a lot of that, um, *girl talk* the night we all met at the bookstore. But after tonight, I know about Lise's writing and I know about Diana's foolish attempt to lose weight."

I didn't think what Diana had done was foolish, just desperate, but I didn't feel brave enough to say that to Sylvia. Getting her to throw her cigarette away seemed to suck up all the bravery I had in me for one night, at least where she was concerned.

"But what's your story?" she said. "I mean, outside of wanting to have a baby."

So I told her about Eddie. And, since I wanted her to think the best of Eddie, I told her my best Eddie story: the one about blind people and cars. When I was done, she didn't laugh like the others had.

"Eddie sounds real, er, *interesting*," she said.

"He is," I said. "He's the most interesting person I've ever known." It was true. Unlike the high-school jerks I'd gone out with before meeting him, Eddie had big dreams, even if they hadn't come true yet.

"Must be nice," she said, "to be in love."

We were almost at my street. Just a few more turns and we'd be there. A few minutes ago, I thought I'd summoned up all the bravery I had where Sylvia was concerned for one night, but I knew I was going to have to summon up some more. And quickly.

"Look," I said, "it's just dumb of you not to go get that lump checked out."

"You're calling me dumb?" Sylvia said. I could feel the anger coming off of her in an instant wave, like one of those tsunamis. But I was determined not to let her wash me away.

"No, I'm not calling *you* dumb," I said. "I'm calling what you're *doing* dumb. It is dumb not to get a thing like that checked out."

"I know what they'll find," she said grimly.

"No, you don't know that," I said. "Maybe they'll find it's nothing. Or maybe they'll find it's a little something they can take care of."

"Or maybe they'll find that it's a big something that'll just kill me anyway," she said.

"But you don't know that," I said, feeling exasperated with her. For a woman who was smarter than me, she wasn't being very smart. "That's the whole problem," I said, "you don't know anything."

"Thanks a fucking lot."

"But I mean it." Now that I was standing my ground with Sylvia, I found I couldn't back down. "You're in the worst place you can possibly be in: not knowing. At least once you do know, even if it's really bad, you'll be able to make choices about how you want to deal with it. You'll know."

She didn't say anything.

"I'm going with you," I announced, making the decision right while I was saying the words.

"What?"

"You make the appointment," I said, "you tell me when it is, and I'll go with you. I'll take you. Even if I have to take the day off from work, I'll take you."

"But you don't have a car," she snorted. Sylvia was big on snorting.

"Of course I have a car. Or I should say, *we* have a car. The only thing, I like to keep it free for Eddie to use it."

She didn't say anything about that. Then: "So, what? I'll have to pick you up, and then you'll come with me?"

It did sound kind of silly in a way and convoluted when she put it like that. Still...

"Once you pick me up," I said, "I'll do the rest of the driving. That way, you won't have to worry about that part of it at all, and you can just think healing thoughts. I *can* drive," I sniffed. "Sort of."

"And you think you can drive this van? Because, you know, it's not like a regular car."

"Piece of cake."

"Fine," she said. "I guess it's a deal."

Sylvia pulled into a parking space on the street across from the apartment. She looked at me with her hands on the wheel, like she expected me to get out right away, but I didn't. Not caring if she thought I was the oddest woman who ever lived, I stretched across her, craning my neck so I could see our apartment over the florist. There, silhouetted in the window against the drapes, was Eddie, pacing back and forth. Was he pacing because he was eager to have me come home or was he pacing because he was mad I'd been gone so long?

"What the hell are you doing?" Sylvia said.

I ignored her question.

"Could you just drive me around the block," I said, "and drop me somewhere on the next street over?"

"But isn't this where you live?" she said.

"Yes, but…" I had to think of something quick. I patted my belly. "All that soup from before." I forced a laugh. "You know—sodium. I thought maybe I should just walk it off."

Diana

"Diana, are you OK?" Artemis asked, naked concern in her voice.

"Of course I am."

"Thank *God*. It's just that I was so worried after getting your e-mail saying you'd gone and done something drastic like having surgery, and then when I couldn't raise you on the phone."

"Well, as you can see—or at least hear—I'm totally fine now, or mostly, at any rate. The first few days, even weeks, were damned awful—nothing you read in the literature can prepare you for it. But now that I've mostly healed and have gotten used to a new way of eating—"

"I can't believe you had major surgery without consulting me first!"

Artemis's scream was so loud, I held the phone away from my ear.

"I'm sorry," I said, "if you're bothered by it, but it was a rather sudden decision."

"How could you decide to do something so major so suddenly? And why didn't you tell anyone about it first? God, Diana, you told me about it in *an e-mail!* Do you have any idea how you've made us all feel over here?"

I walked the phone from the kitchen to the living room. When we'd first moved in, the kitchen—with its wide-open spaces, central island, and the skylight overhead, all that black marble and the hanging array of copper pots and pans and the Sub-Zero fridge—had been my favorite room in the house. Except for the bedroom I shared with Dan, of course. But now the kitchen felt like a mockery. I could no longer make the huge meals I used to love to, and the only appliance I still used regularly was the Cuisinart to pulverize vegetables and fruits and wheat germ into health shakes.

"I just didn't see the point in telling you before," I said. "After all, you're there, I'm here. I could hardly put you down as an emergency contact in case something went wrong. I mean, you are a bit far away."

"Yes, but to wait a whole month to tell us—and then to do it in an e-mail!"

She had a point: I should have told my family what I was doing before I did it, even if they'd given me grief over my decision. Still, my insides hurt, as they did occasionally since the surgery, and I was in no mood to concede her point, so instead I said, "I believe you've said that already."

"What does Dan think about it all? No, wait. I don't know why I didn't think of this sooner. *He* put you up to it, didn't he? That rat bastard. I knew he was too good to be true."

"Of course *Dan* didn't put me up to it! As a matter of fact, his reaction wasn't much different than your own."

"You mean you didn't tell Dan in advance either? But why ever not?"

"Because I wanted to surprise him. He was away on business in Japan when I had it done."

"And you say he was just as upset about it as we are?"

It was true. That night he'd returned from Japan, Dan had been very upset with me.

"Why didn't you tell me you wanted to do this?" he'd said.

"Because I knew you'd only try to talk me out of it," I'd said, trying to convince myself I was in the right when I knew, deep down inside, I was in the wrong.

"Perhaps," he'd admitted with a nod. "But isn't that what marriage is about? Talking through major issues together before reaching a decision both parties can live with?"

I'd shrugged.

"You wanted this so badly you went through this alone?" Dan had pressed.

"Not exactly," I'd admitted. "I put Lise—she's the one you just met with the auburn-streaked black hair and the tweed jacket—down as the person to contact in case of emergency. And you should have seen her," I added, smiling. "Every time the slightest thing went wrong, she'd sweep in, setting the hospital staff straight in no time."

"You had a *stranger*, some woman you've only met a handful of times, put down as your emergency contact instead of me, your own husband?"

Dan's sense of betrayal had been profound, despite my explaining how the people I'd normally put down as next of kin, he and my family, were all on different continents at the time. Still, he had a point. If the roles had been reversed, I would have felt so betrayed I'd have hit him with my copper pots.

"Yes," I told Artemis now, hating to give her the satisfaction, "Dan was beyond upset. But when I explained to him what the surgeon told me—that I was morbidly obese and that to go on being so presented a potentially deadly health risk, which I guess is why they call it *morbidly* obese—he came around." This was true as well.

"Of course I don't want you to *die*, Diana," Dan had said. "I just wish you'd trusted me enough to tell me first. And, anyway, aren't there potential health risks *with* the surgery as well? You could have died on the table while I was in Japan, and I would have only learned about it in a phone call from some complete stranger."

"I'm sorry," I'd said. "I'm so sorry. I promise I'll never do anything like that again."

And then Dan, in an instant going back to the wonderful man I'd fell in love with, laughed.

"I should hope not," he'd said. "I'd like to think that if there are any more secret surgeries in your future, you'll keep me in the loop." Then he'd reached for me with the passion in his eyes that always telegraphed his desire to make love, perhaps more than once since he'd been gone so long. But I'd had to disappoint him: my staples still hurt.

"So how much have you lost so far?" Artemis asked. It was a sneering sort of question, as though she expected my response to indicate that I'd yet again failed, even after taking such a drastic measure. But maybe that was just my own insecurities talking. Maybe she was merely trying to be encouraging, and I was only imagining the sneer. It was always so hard to tell with Artemis. She either tried to protect me or made me feel worse. It was as though she'd invented carrot/stick. Sometimes I wondered why I still bothered with her. But the answer was obvious: she was my sister. So even if our relationship had its flaws—OK, major fault lines—I always hoped that *this* time would be different, that one day she'd lay down the stick and finally become carrot through and through.

"Twenty-five pounds." I spoke the words proudly.

"Can you convert that into British weight, please? Some of us haven't renounced our citizenship yet."

I converted it for her.

"That's insane!" she said. "It's just too much."

"What do you want me to do," I said, "put it back on?"

"No." Even when she said it, I wondered if she was telling the truth. "No, of course not." She was protesting too much. "But what does your surgeon say? Surely, he can't approve of such a fast weight loss."

"On the contrary. He says it's perfectly normal in the first month. He says it will slow down to a more normal rate very soon, which makes sense, since if I kept up at that rate, by the end of the year I'd weigh zero. He did also say that what I'd read about losing two-thirds my weight was inaccurate and it would probably be closer to one-third. He said that's the problem with the Internet, that too many people try to become their own doctors and that sometimes the information you read on those sites is laughably false. Oh, and of course I've started exercising. That makes a difference too."

"*You? Exercising?*"

"Just walking every day. My first goal is to make it all the way down the driveway and back up to the house again without getting out of breath."

"Oh," she scoffed, "the driveway."

"It's a very long driveway, Artemis." My voice was steely. "You haven't seen the house, but I can assure you, the driveway is very long. And once I conquer that, I'll go farther."

She digested that for a moment. Then: "Twenty-five pounds? Mother will be livid! She'll be worried you're turning into one of those anorexic actresses. It's all she'll talk about."

"Hardly." I laughed at the idea of me giving anorexics a run for their money. "I've got a long way to go before anything like that happens. But," I added, suddenly wanting to share one of my first triumphs with my sister, "when the postman came up the drive the other day with a large package for Dan that wouldn't fit in the box, he said, 'My God, Mrs. Taylor, you look wonderful! I swear, one of your chins is completely gone!'"

"And you're proud of that?" Artemis said. "How rude."

"Of course I realize it was crudely put, but you had to be there to see the look on his face. He meant it kindly." I sighed. Why had I ever thought Artemis would be happy about someone, even if it were only the postman, paying me a compliment? "Never mind all that," I said. "I've been meaning to ask you, do you think one of the literary agents or editors you know over there would be willing to look at a manuscript a friend of mine over here is working on?"

"You've made a friend? But that's wonderful news!" she said, and I could almost see her smiling through the phone, and it wasn't a sneering smile at all; this was a genuine smile. She was all carrot for once.

"Three friends, actually." I smiled, feeling encouraged. Even though Sylvia was rarely what one would call "friendly," it would have felt churlish to leave her out.

"And one of these three spanking-new friends has written a book? And you think that—what?—I can just call up one of my pals and, boom, lickety-split she'll be snapped up by a publisher and become an overnight smashing success?"

And now she was back to being stick.

I might have known better than to ask Artemis.

I said as much.

"Don't be so hasty," she said, sounding carrot again. "I've got the perfect person for your friend to talk to about her little book. I'll shoot you out an e-mail with his contact info in it." And suddenly it was almost as though I could hear her smiling again through the transatlantic phone lines, although this time, I couldn't quite make out what that smile looked like. "His name is Dirk Peters."

"Are you sure he's any good?" I asked. I was skeptical.

"Oh, come on, Diana. You and I may have our...*issues*, but you sell me short if you think I'd refer your new friend to anyone who wasn't on the up and up. After all, I am a professional. And if you still have any doubts, you can look Dirk up on the Internet."

. . .

As soon as Artemis rang off, I punched in Lise's number. I couldn't wait to tell her the great news. She'd told me a bit about her schedule and I thought she might be on lunch break just then. Ah, lunch. I remembered lunch.

"But what does this Dirk Peters do?" she asked, quite sensibly, making me wish I'd thought to ask Artemis that question. "Is he a literary agent? An editor?"

"I honestly don't know," I admitted. "Shall I ask Artemis when she e-mails?"

"No, that's OK," she said. "I trust you. I'll let it be a surprise to me. Just the idea that a publishing insider is going to be looking at the words I've written..."

We both let that dream hang in the air for a moment.

"Anyway," Lise said, being the first to puncture the dream, "I wonder how Sylvia is doing. When I talked to Cindy, she told me she was taking Sylvia to see the doctor on Thursday, that she had insisted Sylvia make the appointment."

"Oh, that's so kind of Cindy," I said. For all of Cindy's youth and peculiar fashion sense—so much suede all the time—she was a good person. "Can you imagine trying to talk Sylvia into anything?"

"That must have been some talk," Lise agreed with a laugh.

Suddenly I was embarrassed over what I'd said. "It's not really very charitable of us, is it?" I said. "Here Sylvia has this dreadful problem—or perhaps she has a dreadful problem; none of us really knows—and you and I are laughing at her."

"Oh, come on," Lise laughed. "You have a sister, don't you? If we can't laugh at each other's foibles, who can?"

I supposed Lise was right. There was a definite difference

between the way Artemis laughed at me and the way we were talking about Sylvia. Sylvia was hard to talk to, let alone talk *into* anything. It was simply a fact. I liked to think that if Cindy hadn't thought of it first, either Lise or I, both probably, would have done the same thing.

"I suppose you're right," I said. "Still, the not knowing must be so hard. Can you imagine what Sylvia must be going through?"

Sylvia

I'll tell you one thing. It didn't take a brain surgeon, or a mammographer, to figure out, no matter how attached Cindy was to that I- don't-like-blind-people-because-they-can't-drive-cars story, that that Eddie character of hers was no great shakes.

But there might as well have been a blind person driving the Sylvia's Supper van from Cindy's apartment to the surgeon's office on Federal Road.

"Watch with the shifts!" I said. "I'd hate to survive breast cancer only to have to spring for a new engine or something."

She stared out the windshield grimly, her hands at ten and two on the wheel whenever she wasn't stripping my gears. "Just shut up and let me drive," she said.

Whoa, that girl had some kind of balls on her when she wanted to.

I stared out the window too, watching the spring rain fall. It wasn't much more than a drizzle, but, having the soul of a cat, I hated the idea of getting out into it. Beyond the gray and white of the sky, there was a kind of glow, like maybe the sun was thinking about fighting its way through.

"Hey, I've got a great idea," I announced, as she took the sharp turn from White Street onto Federal. "Why don't we just drive right by the doctor's office? We could go to lunch instead. My treat. It could be like a caterer's holiday or something."

"We're not blowing off this appointment," she said, pulling into the parking lot. "If you want to buy me lunch so bad, you can do it afterward."

Like I'd be hungry then.

We went inside. The waiting room was windows on three sides, which made me suddenly glad the sun hadn't won the war with the rain clouds yet. It'd have been a bitch to die of the greenhouse effect before finding out I was dying of breast cancer.

While I filled out a bunch of forms, Cindy, sitting at my side, pulled a paperback out of her giant purse. The book didn't have a front cover.

Huh, I thought. Maybe Cindy was even poorer than I thought, if she had to buy used books with the covers torn off.

"What are you reading?" I asked.

"Just a book," she said, moving her hand so it covered the title.

"Yeah, but what kind of book?" I said, moving her hand out of the way: *Love's Exploding Embers*. "Hey, you like romances?" I was just trying to be friendly.

But she reddened. "It's just a book," she said, shoving it back in her purse. Then she got up and picked something from the selection of magazines on the glass table: *People* magazine. Everyone in the waiting room was reading magazines.

When in Rome, do what the Romans do and read magazines.

I got up and got a magazine too: *Martha Stewart's Living*. Might as well see what the competition was up to, heh. As they say, as if.

"Sylvia Goldsmith?" the nurse called from the doorway separating the waiting room from the examining area.

I tossed Martha back on the table. It was do-or-die time. Probably die.

Cindy tossed *People* down on top of Martha.

"What are you doing?" I said as she got up and started to follow me.

"You don't think I'm letting you do this alone, do you?" she said. On another day, I might have given her a fight; but I could see there was little point to it. Besides which, I was so scared, there was little fight in me.

We went to the examining room where I exchanged my light sweater and bra for a hospital gown, and then sat on the edge of the examining table, waiting, waiting.

The surgeon was about forty years old or so with coffee skin and black hair. I hated it that most of my doctors were now younger than me. His name was Dr. Gupta.

"How's things in India?" I asked.

"Fine, I suppose," he said, "but I am from Pakistan. Things are not always so good there these days, but some of us are surviving."

Cindy sat on a swivel stool in the corner while Dr. Gupta felt up my breast. If I weren't so scared, I'd have probably laughed at the absurdity of it all.

"Ah, yes," he said, looking up at the ceiling as he gently moved his cool fingers around. It was like he was a blind person who could only divine the future through touch. "This pea-sized marble over here? This is what you were feeling, yes?"

He didn't have to make it sound so small, but yeah, I nodded, that was it.

"Well," he said, "I could, of course, do a needle biopsy on it, but I see little point. It is so small and hard, I doubt I would be able to draw any fluid from it."

"Great," I said, pulling the Johnny coat back around my breasts and moving to jump back off the table. "I guess that's that then."

"Not so fast," he said. "When was your last mammogram?"

I thought about it. "About two years ago," I finally said.

"Tut-tut," he tut-tutted. "A woman your age, Ms. Goldsmith, you should be getting them done every year."

"Yeah, well."

"This is your lucky day," he said. "We have a mammography machine right here in the office. You know, a lot of us surgeons are one-stop shopping these days." He laughed at his own joke. On another day I might have laughed too, but it wasn't a laughing day for me. "I will get the technician, and once she has done the test, we will go over the results together in my office."

When the technician came, a burly Brunhilda if I ever saw one, I started to follow her. And Cindy started to follow me.

"What are you doing?" I said. This make-way-for-ducklings act was getting old. Was I to be allowed no privacy?

"Just keep moving," Cindy said, putting her hand on my back and pressing me forward.

Great. This was just what I always wanted: to have Cindy, with her perky young breasts, see my fifty-year-old breasts get flattened like a pancake in a vise.

"Will I be exposed to a lot of radiation just by being in here?" Cindy asked Brunhilda once we were all in the mammography room.

Brunhilda looked at Cindy just as oddly as I did.

"Uh, no, dear," she said.

Then she made the machine come together so that my right breast, the offending one, was as thin as cookie dough after the rolling pin's been at it. Afterward, for good measure and since maybe this wasn't a total day at the carnival yet, she flattened the left side as well.

"Inconclusive," Dr. Gupta announced, as we all sat in his office a short time later. "You see these shadows here?" I nodded, but really, it all looked the same to me. "It is so hard to tell. There could be something there," he said, then he shrugged, "or it could be nothing."

"I guess that's it then," I said again, starting to rise.

"Next step," he said, "is a surgical biopsy."

"You want to *cut* me?" I said.

"It will just be a small incision." He shrugged, held his thumb and forefinger about an inch apart. "Whoever looks at it will barely see it afterward."

Funny man. He thought I was worried all my sexual suitors would find me less attractive.

"And I suppose you're just going to do the surgery right now too?" I said. I looked around the office, as though he might be hiding a surgical table under his desk or something. "I didn't see an operating theatre anywhere when I walked in."

"Oh, no," he smiled. "We may be one-stop shopping, but we are not one-stop cutting. We will be doing the surgery at the hospital. Next week."

Lise

I was supposed to be teaching a class, but my mind was on everything but. Instead of teaching, my mind was worrying if my novel was good enough and worrying about Sylvia in the operating room. Hell, I was even fantasizing about Tony.

"Ms. Barrett?"

Was the ending of my novel the right one? To have everyone die just seemed too obvious and yet a happy outcome wouldn't have fit. And what was going on in the operating room right now? What were they finding?

I may not have known Sylvia all that long, in the greater scheme of things, but her circumstances touched me deeply. She presented herself to the world as a prickly pear, but anyone could see that what she was going through was deeply frightening to her and that part of the reason for her prickliness was as a defensive gesture against disaster. Not that I was certain the surgery would reveal anything deadly—lumps turned out to be nothing all the time—but with her twin's medical history it *was* worrying. And, if nothing else, even if she were a complete stranger whose story I'd only been told, hey, I was a woman, I had breasts; I could empathize with her greatest fears.

"Ms. Barrett?" It was then I realized I'd missed something.

"What is it, Danitra?" I said.

Danitra's black hair, usually kinky, was braided into seemingly a hundred tiny braids held together loosely at the base of her neck by one more braid. She'd taken the marginally improved weather to heart and was prematurely wearing a yellow sundress with spaghetti straps.

"We were talking about John's story," she said. "I was saying that it was fine to know a lot of big words, and even use them occasionally, but that if readers had to keep running for their dictionaries every five minutes they'd feel dumb, not to mention pissed."

John, his own brown military hair looking as though it'd been freshly trimmed just prior to walking through the door, his dark eyes glowering, scowled at her.

"John said I was totally wrong," she continued, "but everyone else was agreeing with me, so we were all looking to you to arbitrate but—knock, knock!—you don't seem to be home today."

She was right. There was a lot on my mind. Not only was I worried about Sylvia, but I'd also e-mailed the first draft of my novel to Dirk Peters, Diana's sister's friend. He'd said it was OK to send it as an attachment file, and I'd done so two nights ago. I knew it was unrealistic to think he'd read it already. He was a busy literary agent, after all. I hadn't known who he was when Diana first called, but I'd started to read the publishing trade magazines like they were bibles for a new religion and knew now: Dirk Peters was a modern legend who was known for his mane of blond hair and his seven-figure deals, and who was called, but not to his face, the "Jaguar." Still, I obsessively checked my e-mail anytime a computer was within spitting distance, as though even if he didn't really have time to read my work, and he probably hadn't, it might have leaked into his brain on its miraculous own, like poison filling Hamlet's father's ear.

I looked at my students' expectant faces.

I didn't care right then about yet another petty skirmish between Danitra and John, always more petty on John's part than Danitra's. All I cared about doing right then was: first, verifying that Sylvia would be all right; second, checking my e-mail again. If everything were fine with both, then I'd hunt Tony down and have some sex.

"Danitra and the others have a point," I spoke severely to John.

"How would you know?" he sneered. "You weren't even listening when I read from my chapter."

He was right, of course. I hadn't been listening.

But by then, a few months into the spring semester, I was all too familiar with John's work.

"Look," I said to him, running out of patience, "if your hope is to someday have more than just a few literary snobs read and appreciate your work, you're going to need to change a few things."

"What are you suggesting I do? Talk *down* to my readers?" he said.

"Of course not! But there's a vast sea of difference between talking down to readers and walking on a cloud of such rarefied air that no one really *gets* your work but you. Is that what you want? To be your own audience of one?"

It was a mistake to say that. I knew it even as the words were flying out of my mouth, like the little girl in the story who opens her mouth only to have toads hop out. And if I didn't know it then, I certainly knew it when John hastily gathered up his things and nearly tripped in his rush to get out of his chair.

"What do *you* know anyway?" he said, getting so close to my face I could see the tears in his eyes. He was only twenty. He would hate me for this. "When was the last time *you* wrote a novel?"

I could have told him I'd just finished one and that I was hoping it was a good one, but it hardly seemed like the time. Besides, he didn't give me a chance because, in an instant, he was gone.

The other nineteen students had the grace to keep their eyes on their desks, but somehow this averting of their eyes, as though embarrassed for my sake, was worse than John challenging me head-on. Were they embarrassed for me because of what I'd said to John? Or because of what he'd said to me?

Danitra was the first to look at me again.

"Ignore him, Ms. Barrett," she said. "You know John. He's just mad because he couldn't think of a comeback that used the words 'ineluctable' or 'gravitas.'"

She was right, of course, to a certain extent. But I knew that what had just happened wasn't good, not at all.

. . .

I'd ended class early, telling the students that it was always good to write when the passion was high and that they should all go back to their dorms and write me essays about conflict. They could handle the material anyway they wanted to, they could even fictionalize it, but I wanted the theme to be what happens when irresistible force meets up with immovable object.

"Shouldn't we *all* write it as fiction," Danitra had pointed out, "since this *is* supposed to be a *fiction*-writing class?"

"Of course you're right," I'd laughed at myself, adding, "Duh-me," which made them laugh too.

Now I was racing across the campus to my office, barely noticing the more determined leaves insisting upon appearing on the branches of the mostly stark trees or the trickling sound of water rushing downhill into the gutters, the sun rapidly melting the snow remaining from the end-of-season New England storm we'd been sucker-punched with earlier in the week.

But once I was there, the LISE BARRETT, MFA plaque mocking louder than ever after John's words, neither of the things I'd been racing toward were waiting for me. Cindy hadn't called with news about Sylvia, and there were no e-mail messages from Dirk Peters. Declaring the day a total loss, I decided to cancel office hours for the afternoon. But I didn't bother to put up a sign before heading off to faculty parking to retrieve my car. No one ever came anyway.

• • •

Back at the cottage, I paced the afternoon away, waiting on e-mail, waiting on the phone to ring.

I thought to call Cindy, but then I remembered she didn't own a cell phone. Even if she had one, she'd probably have to turn it off at the hospital.

At four o'clock, the phone rang.

"Lise?"

"Cindy?" It was very loud wherever she was.

"Believe it or not," she shouted, as though trying to hear herself, "we're at the mall. After the surgery, Sylvia insisted we come here."

That sounded promising.

"It went well then?" I said.

"We don't have the results yet," she said. "First they need to send what they took out off to the lab to do a biopsy. But Sylvia came through it like a champ. And, for some reason, afterward she just felt like going shopping."

"I need some new shoes," I heard Sylvia growl. She must have been standing right next to Cindy. "I figure, if it's good news, new shoes would be a good thing to have. And if it's bad news? New shoes couldn't hurt."

"Sounds like a plan," I laughed.

"The surgeon said he should get the test results back on Thursday," Cindy said. "And Sylvia wants us all to meet her that night at Sylvia's Supper."

"I can issue my own invitations, thank you!" Sylvia shouted. "I'm not dead yet."

"I think we'd better go," Cindy said. "See you Thursday!"

She hung up.

I felt somewhat relieved, as though someone had mercifully poked a nice tiny hole in the anxiety ball I'd been carrying around in my chest. Even if they had no solid news yet, at least their spirits sounded high.

Feeling as though maybe their high spirits might overflow into a positive effect on my life, I checked my e-mail one more time. And there it was: a message from Dirk Peters. Feeling like I was opening Pandora's box, but then telling myself it must be good news if he'd written back so quickly, with trembling finger I pressed READ on Dirk's e-mail.

> From: dirk.peters@dirkliterary.uk
> To: Lise.Barrett@ctuniversity.edu
> Dear Ms. Barrett,
> I've had the chance to review your pages. I must say, this is the most unmitigating pile of overwritten shite it's ever been my displeasure to read. Sorry I can't be more encouraging. You did indicate you have a day job. You still do, don't you?
> Cheers!
> Dirk

• • •

Two hours later, I was sitting in front of the fireplace when Tony let himself in the door with his key. When he'd phoned a short time earlier, asking if I wanted to catch a movie and then a late dinner, I'd said no, I was too busy working. But he must have heard the cry in my voice, for here he was.

"What are you doing?" he asked quietly, settling down on the floor behind me, stretching his legs out around my hips and putting his arms around my neck.

I shrugged off his arms, picked up a few more sheets of paper from the stack beside me, and fed the pages into the flames.

"I'm burning my book, of course," I said.

The Women

RECOMMENDED READING:
Cindy: *The Girlfriends' Guide to Pregnancy*, Vicki Iovine
Diana: *The Reading Group*, Elizabeth Noble
Sylvia: *Crazy about Cupcakes*, Krystina Castella
Lise: *Jeff Herman's Guide to Book Publishers, Editors and Literary Agents*, Jeff Herman

"You should have seen her," Sylvia said to Diana and Lise, champagne bottle in hand, nodding her chin to indicate Cindy. "We were just driving around in the van, killing time, waiting for Dr. Gupta to call with the results. My cell rings, I answer it, she hears me say, 'You mean everything's OK?' and she whips the cigarette right out of my fingers and tosses it out the window."

Then Sylvia popped the cork on the champagne.

Sylvia's Supper boasted two tables for two. One was next to one of the display cases and Sylvia often used it at the end of the workday to go over the day's receipts. The other was for people who stopped in for lunch or a snack and then felt like eating there instead of taking the food back to work or eating in their cars. On the odd warm days, which would come more often now as spring arrived in earnest, Sylvia carried the tables outside so that customers could eat on the sidewalk, enjoying the sun and the sound of traffic. That night, Sylvia had pushed the two tables together in the middle of the room, covering them with a linen tablecloth and hanging up the hand-painted CLOSED sign an hour early.

Diana and Lise looked at Cindy as though she might be

certifiable. Who would have the nerve to take a cigarette away from Sylvia?

"You should have seen the look on her face!" Cindy said, laughing. "You'd think I kicked her cat or something."

"You're lucky she didn't kick you," Lise said, laughing too.

"I just told her what I thought," Cindy said. "That it was dumb for her to keep on smoking after what she'd just been through."

"She was right," Sylvia acknowledged, pouring the champagne. Cindy put her hand over her glass to indicate she didn't want any. "It was dumb," Sylvia continued. "So I quit right then and there, not that it's been easy."

"Then everything really is all right?" Diana said. "There's no cancer?"

"No," Sylvia said, breathing a sigh of relief as she set down platters of stuffed mushrooms, mini empanadas, and fresh vegetables with low-fat dip, the latter items prepared with Diana in mind. "But Dr. Gupta said I was lucky this time. He said that with my family medical history, it'll always be a concern."

"Still," Diana said, "you must be incredibly relieved. I know I am."

"Of course I'm relieved," Sylvia said. "But I'm something else too."

"Explain," Lise said, reaching for a mushroom and popping it into her mouth.

"It's just that, when I thought I was dying," Sylvia said, taking her time framing the thought, "I guess I just kind of figured, 'OK, fine, crap, but still, game over, nothing I can do to change things now.' But as soon as Dr. Gupta told me the news, I started thinking about the life I've lived so far. And I started realizing that I haven't hardly lived at all. I'm not saying I didn't love my sister—I loved Minnie tremendously, still do—but all the time she was alive, we were too busy being twins for me to let much else enter my life and hardly anything in the way of romance. And since she died? I've been a shell. But now I feel as though I've been given a second chance and maybe I ought to do something with it."

"Like what?" Diana prompted.

"I'm not sure yet," Sylvia shrugged. "Live. Now that I know I'm not going to die, *yet*, I feel like what I'm supposed to do is live, really live."

"I'm going to do something too," Diana announced.

The others looked at her.

"I'm going to go back to London for a bit soon," she answered the question in their eyes. "Artemis and my mother have been after me to visit—far be it for them to come here—and Dan's been so busy with business trips lately, I thought I'd pop across the ocean."

"They'll be thrilled when they see you," Lise said. "How much have you lost so far?"

"Forty pounds," Diana said, proudly displaying the loose waistband on her pants for all to see. "It's been coming off so rapidly, I've promised myself only to go shopping for new clothes once a month. My size keeps changing so much, although I do think it's starting to taper off. But no, somehow I don't think *thrilled* is the right word for what Artemis and Mother will be." She looked directly at Lise. "Did you ever hear back from Dirk Peters?"

Lise made a face. "And how," she said.

Then she told them about Dirk's e-mail.

"That's the cruelest thing I've ever heard," Cindy said.

"Dirk sounds like a dick," Sylvia said.

"The funny thing is," Lise said, "as soon as I read his words, I realized he was right. I don't know about unmitigating, but the novel I'd written *was* overwritten crap."

"Still," Diana said, "I feel so responsible. I think I'll look this Dirk up when I'm over there and give him a piece of my mind. Maybe he was in a bad mood that day. Perhaps he'll reconsider and ask to see it again."

"I doubt it," Lise said, "and it wouldn't matter if he did."

"Why do you say that?" Diana said.

"Because I burned it, every last page of the manuscript," Lise said. "I fed it to the fireplace. For good measure, I deleted the file, threw away the disc."

"Oh, no!" Cindy said, clearly distressed.

"I think it's sad too," Sylvia said to Cindy, "but don't you think you're taking this a bit too hard? After all, it's not *your* book she burned."

"No, I'm not taking it too hard!" Cindy said. "And what's with the crack about it not being my book? We all know *I* could never do anything like write a book. Look at all of you: you all do such grand things." She looked at Sylvia. "You're going to do something, even if you don't know what it is yet." She turned to Lise. "And you've written a whole book, even if you turned around and burned it." She turned to Diana. "And you, you've got…*London* and new pants every month." She looked down at her champagneless glass. "But what do I have? Nothing. I never even finished school."

"You never finished school?" Sylvia asked.

Cindy shook her head.

"It's not too late," Lise said. "You could start taking classes."

"It's the middle of the semester, isn't it?" Cindy sniffled. "What school starts new classes at the end of March? I'd have to wait until summer. Or fall."

"So take online classes," Lise advised. "Take classes on a computer."

"That'd be perfect," Cindy said, "if I *had* a computer."

"So take mine," Sylvia said suddenly.

"Don't you need it for work?" Cindy said.

"Not the one in the office here," Sylvia said. "The one I have at home. When Minnie got sick, she bought a new laptop. She wanted to be able to participate in message boards devoted to spiritual healing, and she wanted to be able to do it from any room in the condo, so that once she got sicker, she could do it on the couch or even lying in bed. Me, I used to go online when she was sleeping, look for new cures." She paused. "But I don't need it now. Honest. The thing's just sitting there, gathering dust."

"But I wouldn't even know how to set a computer up," Cindy said. "I'd probably electrocute the building or set myself on fire or something."

"It's not that hard," Lise said, "and I'll help you. Once you've got the laptop from Sylvia, just give me a call and we'll work out a time for me to come over and set everything up for you and teach you how to use it."

"It's not too late," Diana said, reiterating the message Sylvia and Lise were trying to communicate. "Look at me: I'm changing—at least my body is; the jury's still out on the head—and I'm nearly a decade and a half older than you. Why, I'm practically old enough to be your very young mother."

At that, Cindy's eyes welled up.

"What did I say?" Diana asked, perplexed.

"I think I'm pregnant!" Cindy blurted out.

"But that's wonderful news," Diana said, "isn't it? Isn't this what you wanted?"

Just then, they were interrupted by an insistent pounding on the door. The woman on the other side of the glass was wearing sunglasses, even though it was almost dark, and a yellow raincoat. Tying back her dark hair was the unmistakable pattern of a Hermes scarf.

The pounding continued as Sylvia rose and went to the door, where she pointed at the sign: CLOSED.

Cindy came hustling up behind Sylvia, wiping at her eyes with one hand as she reached for the lock with the other and turned the key that was hanging from it.

"Don't mind Sylvia," Cindy said with an apologetic smile. "She's very ornery, but she's the best cook in Connecticut. What do you need?"

"I've got a very important person who knows food coming to my house in an hour," said the woman in the yellow raincoat, "and I haven't got anything to give her, certainly not anything impressive."

"Well, I'm sure Sylvia will be only too happy to help you out," Cindy said, ignoring the dark look Sylvia shot at her. "Hmm…let's see…what do we have here?" Cindy walked the length of one of the display cases.

"Give her the veal," Lise suggested. "Veal always impresses."

"Oh, yes," Diana agreed. "And that veal looks like it has artichokes and red peppers and all sorts of wonderful things around it."

"But don't they treat those baby veals awful bad?" Cindy said.

"No true foodie cares about that," Sylvia said. "Do you think Julia Child cared about that? Julia'd toss a lobster into a pot or slaughter a calf without even blinking." Sylvia looked at the woman in the yellow raincoat. "You did say your dinner guest knows food, didn't you?"

The woman nodded.

"Ooh, you've got shrimps here!" Cindy said. "Give her the shrimps too!"

Ten minutes later, the woman in the yellow raincoat was gone, Sylvia's three friends having helped her load up her car with covered dishes containing chilled shrimp that had been boiled in chardonnay butter, the veal with artichokes, a charlotte russe for dessert, and a dozen designer cupcakes.

"I never did cupcakes before," Sylvia'd told the woman, delicately packing up the cakes, each one a work of art. "I always figured, you know, if people want cake, they'll want a real cake, not some miniature thing. But then I was reading a magazine while waiting in the doctor's office and realized they were all the rage— some people even prefer them for weddings—so I figured I'd better expand my culinary horizons. Anyway, here you go." She handed over the bag. "Your rinky-dink cakes."

To make up for Sylvia, Cindy handed the customer a bottle of Veuve Clicquot, twin to the one the women had been drinking, at no extra charge.

"See?" Cindy said to Sylvia. "You need us. We keep you from doing dumb things like smoking cigarettes and getting into trouble by being rude to your own customers. That only took us all ten minutes and that lady gave you two hundred dollars."

"You really think you're pregnant?" Sylvia said.

Cindy nodded.

"And now you're not sure what you want to do about it?" Sylvia asked.

Cindy nodded again.

"Crap," Sylvia said. Then she reached out and, gently, folded the younger woman into her arms.

Lise

Cindy had Tuesdays off from work, and since I had no morning classes on Tuesdays, I picked up the laptop from Sylvia the night before. I'd offered to bring it over to her right away that night, figuring she'd be eager for it, but Cindy said it would be better to wait until Eddie was out and that he was going to meet with one of his band mates the next morning to work on writing some new songs.

"I just want it to be a surprise for him," she said brightly. "We've never owned a computer before."

Their apartment, when I arrived, was not what I expected. Of course, I can't say I expected anything specific, per se, and it's not as though my cottage was all that much bigger than the space she and Eddie were sharing. But her apartment looked like the kind of place that people only inhabit temporarily, as a weigh station to something bigger or more permanent. And yet, Cindy and Eddie had been there for six years, ever since her dad kicked her out. And when the train passed through down the street, the windows open to catch the early spring air, it was damn loud.

"Where do you want it?" I asked.

"Right over there," she said, indicating a round table that I guessed passed for the dining room table at the far end from the living room.

I set the laptop down, hooked her up, and explained her Internet options.

Once the setup was complete, she smiled widely, like a kid on her birthday.

"Say, do you still have a little time left?" She looked suddenly shy and hurried to say, "I don't want to keep you if you have to go."

"I have at least another hour. What's up?"

"Do you know how to download songs? I just know Eddie'll be more excited about the computer if when he comes home I have some new music waiting for him."

So that's what we did with the next hour: checked out bands and downloaded a sampling of the free music people were giving away.

"This is like a whole other world!" Cindy said at one point.

Before leaving for class, I showed her how to check her e-mail.

"Hey, look!" she said. "I've got e-mail already! Who could possibly be writing to me?"

She opened her mailbox and, as my last good deed of the day, I showed her how to use the delete button to get rid of spam.

* * *

From: Dean.Jones@ctuniversity.edu
To: Lise.Barrett@ctuniversity.edu
Lise,
I regret to inform you that I've received a complaint about your teaching from one of your students. I'm sure it's just a mix-up that we'll be able to clear up in no time, but I'd still like you to call my secretary to set up a meeting as soon as possible.
Yours,
Dean

His name really was Dean, making him Dean Dean Jones, a thing everyone in the department laughed at, but still I stared at the e-mail in perplexity: Why would one of my students complain about me? My students loved me. All anyone had to do was look at the letters they sent me after graduation to see that: letters when they placed their first stories with the *Atlantic* or the *New Yorker*, letters when they secured their first agent or publishing contract. They all credited my classroom as the chief reason for their success, although I must admit, proud as their letters made me feel, for them *and* for me, I'd always felt a certain envy too. Was I forever destined to be the publishing bridesmaid but never the bride?

I looked at the date on Dean's e-mail, suspecting some kind of prank. Was it April Fool's Day? But no. April Fool's Day had passed a few days ago.

My hand was on the phone, ready to give Dean's secretary a ring to schedule that meeting, when I changed my mind. Dean's secretary, Martha, was a huge chatterbox. If I so much as called and said "Hello," she'd be filling my ear for the next half hour with news about her grandchildren and gossip about the other professors in the department. Not that I usually minded hearing about how her granddaughter was on her way to becoming the National Spelling Bee champ if only she could master the *S* section of her Oxford dictionary, nor did I mind hearing gossip about how Sally Markham, the poetry professor, had gotten drunk at the dean's latest sherry soiree and made a pass at Phillip Exeter, the classics professor who was older than Homer. But I didn't have time for all of that right now. I had more important things to do. The only reason I'd even checked e-mail in the first place was as a palate cleanser.

The first time I'd tried writing a novel, the one Dirk Peters hated so much, I'd immersed myself in it entirely, shutting myself up in the blood-colored room of my cottage for hours at a time with no more stimulation than the constant mental knitting of creativity and the white screen pages to be filled in front of me. But now that I was well into my second novel, I'd discovered it was best for me to work in short super bursts of energy, blasting out a page or a page and a half as quickly as the words came, rather than agonizing over each one to get the perfect metaphor or image. Between bursts, I distracted myself by checking e-mail or by checking on the rising Amazon ranking of Annabeth Todd, a debut novelist who had written the sort of book I was now writing. Hers was a satire, as was mine—mine being about a loveless schoolteacher who somehow gets tapped to be ambassador to Switzerland, only to find herself entangled with both the US and Swiss presidents. When she sleeps with both within a twenty-four-hour period, dramatically and enthusiastically making up for her years of lovelessness, the paternity of the baby comes into question. Oh, and there was also going to be a Clare Booth Luce style of arsenic poisoning, a subplot involving Nazi gold and a tense shootout on the Matterhorn. At least that's how I thought it was going to go.

If I was at home, I'd step outside for a cigarette break. I hadn't told anyone except Tony I'd taken up smoking again; if I was at school, not wanting to set a bad example by smoking in front of the students, I'd walk across to the playing fields and just watch them killing each other at rugby for as long as it would have taken me to smoke that cigarette I so badly wanted. Once I got back to work, it was as though the words were ready to pour out of me again.

It was odd, but as it turned out, as devastating as Dirk Peters's words to me had been at the time, he was right: my first effort *was* an unmitigated pile of overwritten crap. I'd made all the same mistakes I usually found in my student John's writing. It was as though I'd followed every trite piece of writing-school advice to the letter: show, don't tell; write what you know; no backstory dumps. The problem was, I'd been so busy obeying the letter of the law that I'd forsaken the spirit entirely! And what had I wound up with for my misguided efforts? A present-tense derivative lump, the whole being all show and no telling to such an extent, that when I recalled certain passages in my mind, I wanted to scream at myself, "Stop showing us the character's clenched teeth, narrow eyes, and metaphorical steam coming out of her ears! Why can't you just say 'I was angry'?"

But now, this time it was different. It was as though the unseen Dirk Peters had become a mentor for me. Before, with the first novel, I'd written as though writing for the world—writing for history, for posterity, the phrase "Great American Novel" constantly dancing in my head, even if what I was writing was more like the "Great Middle Eastern Novel" only by an American. Now all that had changed. It was as though I was writing for an audience of one: Dirk Peters. Having seen pictures of him in the publishing trade magazines, whenever I wrote now I envisioned a miniature version of him perched, legs crossed, a European cigarette dangling from one elegant hand, a snifter of Armagnac in the other, atop my computer in the office or my laptop at home. He goaded me on, employing that sexy accent I'd heard him use on Book TV. "Come on, Lise, luv, this is great stuff you're writing here. But don't you think you should let your heroine show a little more leg in this scene?"

What can I say? If I had to pick a muse, Dirk Peters was certainly a raunchy muse to have picked. But he was also right on the money with the editorial advice I imagined him giving. "Pace, Lise, pace! And by 'pace' here, I'm not talking about what you do back and forth across the floor, nor am I speaking Latin to you, although I could. I'm talking about the flow of your story. Take me to the far edge of excitement and draw me back, let me live with it for a while before bringing me back to that edge. You know those old cliffhanger movies that used to be so popular? Why do you think they were so popular? People love being teased." Was it just me, or did Dirk just grab his crotch? "Tease me, Lise! If we were making love, would you want me to shoot my whole wad in the first five minutes? Then don't you do it either! But also, don't keep me too long in a lull phase. Excite me."

"That sounds rather commercial, though," I'd object in my head, "doesn't it? I thought you were a *literary* agent."

"Look in your Webster's, luv," Dirk would say. "*Literary* mostly means 'of or relating to books,' which is me. Sure, I sell literary books with all the highbrow loftiness that word has been forced to bear, but I also sell commercial too. Really, anything the market wants and will pay a lot for. I swing both ways."

What else can I say? Dirk was also a chatty muse.

The first novel I'd written had been agony from start to finish. But this time I was having—dare I say it?—fun. The Dirk in my head kept prompting me, "If the writer isn't having fun with her creation, how can she expect the reader to?" The Dirk in my head said, lighting another cigarette, replenishing his Armagnac. "Screw that Great American Novel crap! For one thing, the rest of the world *isn't* America, now is it?"

And he was right. Screw that Great American Novel crap. The new book I was writing was—dare I say *this?*—commercial, even if it was a political satire, because it could also be read as a romantic comedy. *And what's so wrong with writing something commercially viable?* I asked myself. If I was going to keep writing, for Dirk *and* for me, I might as well write something that had at least a snowball's chance—instead of *no* chance—of getting published and making some money.

Even though his advice thus far was serving me well, he could still be annoying, and I promised myself I'd hit him in his insufferably priggish face, handsome as it was, for all the anguish his rejection e-mail had caused me if I ever met him face-to-face; not that *that* was ever going to happen.

"Fine," I answered aloud, mildly exasperated with the relentless Dirk in my head. Good thing no one was in the office to hear me. Obeying him nonetheless, I closed the computer file with my manuscript in it. Then, before leaving for the day, I checked e-mail one last time. There was something from Sara. Seeing her name there made me realize how long it had been since I'd heard from my sister.

> From: sarabarrett@peacers.net
> To: Lise.Barrett@ctuniversity.edu
> You'll probably ready to kill me for not getting in touch sooner. But then, you haven't exactly kept in touch lately either, have you?
>
> Now, I don't want you to go all ballistic on me—and please, *please* don't say anything to Mom and Dad!—but remember that little diarrhea bug I told you about a few months ago? Well, it never did completely go away. I'm really OK! I'm just, you know, not *totally* OK. So I might be going into the hospital here for a bit. Like, maybe, tomorrow.
>
> But enough of that. Hey, how's that novel going?
> Love

Diana

When Artemis met me at the gate at Heathrow, the shock on her face was visible.

"My *God*, Di, look at you! You must be four-fifths of the girl you were when you left!"

Artemis, for her part, was still a sylph. When I was younger, I used to imagine that Artemis was what I'd look like, if only I were thin.

"Not quite," I said, unable to keep the smile from coming to my face as I did a model's twirl for her. "But I'm down fifty American now, so I'm getting there. What do you think?"

It was probably a mistake asking her that question—she'd probably say something like "Four-fifths of a cow is still a large farm animal"—but somehow I couldn't help myself.

"It's just...it's just..."

It was a moment for the ages: Artemis out of words.

"Yes?" I prompted tentatively, preparing myself for the stick that was sure to follow.

"It's just that...you don't look like you anymore." And then she surprised me, reaching out to place one of her elegant manicured hands over one of my slightly larger ones as she smiled warmly. "I think it's just great."

Impulsively, I threw my arms around her.

"Hey, don't get carried away!" she said, peeling me off after allowing me my moment of sisterly bonding. "And don't get carried away with the weight loss either. You know, just because you look good now is no reason to think if you go further you'll look better. Some people lose a lot of weight only to wind up looking like a great big sack of empty skin."

Artemis. Stick.

"Well," she said, all business now, "let's gather your things."

I'd brought two large suitcases with me. Even though the trip was just for a week, I'd gone on a shopping spree ahead of time, buying all new outfits with which to impress my family.

"They're *huge*," Artemis balked, taking in the size of the two suitcases. Then she shrugged. "I suppose large people's clothes do take up much more space."

Fucking Artemis.

As the plane had landed, it'd been pouring buckets out, a typical London day in April; but as we stepped out of Heathrow, the sun was shining so brightly Artemis put her prophylactic brolly down.

"Huh," she said. "First you get thinner, now you've got the weather working for you. Looks like your luck really is changing."

• • •

Mother met us at the door.

"I'm sorry Father's not here to greet you. He's out—" and here she waved vaguely to the greater outdoors "—hunting something, I believe."

At sixty-two, Mother was still as stunning as ever in her pearl-gray suit and pumps, her Cristal champagne hair styled in an ultra contemporary, uneven cut that many far younger women would have had trouble pulling off, but on her looked perfect. Mother always prided herself on Artemis's many boyfriends saying the two women looked more like sisters than mother and daughter. As for me, at first Artemis's boyfriends always thought I was the hired help.

Mother squinted at me. Too vain for glasses, too squeamish for contacts, Mother could never quite see anything that was up close.

"My *God*, Diana! You're so much smaller!" Then she gleamed a smile at Artemis. "If you're not careful," she said wickedly, "Diana will wind up thinner than *you*."

"The garden looks great, Mum," I said, accepting her air kiss to my cheek.

"It's nothing." She waved. "So long as Father doesn't track

through it when he's trying to hunt things, the flowers seem to grow. Now, why don't you put your bags upstairs in your old room, and I'll set us out a nice tea. Cake, everyone?"

It was going to be a long week.

* * *

As it turned out, it both was and wasn't a long week. It was long in that it felt odd sleeping in the same room I'd slept in as a child, where nothing had been changed, not even the stuffed bears; I suppose I could have stayed with Artemis, but she claimed her place was too small, that she'd only need to work in the daytime, so I'd just be there alone all day; and anyway, would it really have been better spending the entire week with Artemis? And it was long in that I had to repeatedly explain to Mother that my body could not tolerate the rich foods she kept trying to force-feed me. And it was long in that I missed Dan and my new friends in Connecticut so much I was on the phone to him and Lise every day, trading "I love yous" with the former and trading concerns over Cindy's pregnancy with the latter as well as Lise's new concerns for her own sister, Sara, in Africa.

But it was a short week in that I was actually having fun in London for maybe the first time in my life. I was more confident now when I walked the streets, and, perhaps as a result, people behaved more kindly toward me. When I went shopping, I felt proud. Oh, I knew I still didn't look like most other people. But I did look *better*, and it was suddenly fun to see what fashionable clothes I could find in my size, rather than just buying any old ugly thing merely because it fit.

I was scheduled to leave on Sunday. Early Friday evening, the phone rang.

"It's for you," Mother said. "It's some loud person."

"Where are you?" Artemis shouted through the phone, presumably shouting to hear herself talk over the racket I could hear at her end.

"I'm here," I said, stating the obvious. "You just called me, so you must realize that here is where I am."

"Yes, but why aren't you *here?*" she shouted some more.

"Which here is your here?" I countered.

"My flat. Don't you remember me inviting you over here for a welcome-home, going-away party in your honor?"

"Nooooo," I said the word slowly. "I'm fairly certain I'd have remembered if you'd done that."

"Huh. Perhaps I only invited you in my head. Or maybe the sudden weight loss has compromised your memory? Whatever." I visualized her shaking it all off. "Just get over here as soon as you can…and wear something nice!"

I'm not quite sure why I went scurrying off to do Artemis's bidding. Perhaps it was the exciting prospect of a party? I'd never been much for parties before, always hiding in the corners in the hopes that no one would notice me; if they didn't see me, they couldn't say something unkind. But now I was thrilled, if a little scared, at the prospect of showing off the new me to Artemis's friends. And I was glad I'd done so much shopping since my arrival. Before, I'd have worn black for a party—so slimming, they always tell you, as though extra-extra-large anything can ever look slim—but now I opted for a white outfit I'd purchased the day before. It had palazzo pants and a tunic trimmed with gold. When I put it on, I felt like a Greek huntress straight from mythology, even if the pants were more Roman. I even had a gold circlet I arranged in my hair. When I thought about it, I realized I'd never felt so pretty in my life, not even on my wedding day.

* * *

The man who answered Artemis's door was tall, his thin body covered in a cutting-edge suit: black pants, white shirt, skinny black tie, and glittery gold jacket; the sort of thing you might see Rod Stewart in. His hair was long and blond, his dark eyes sparkling, and when his full lips parted in a smile, that smile was so wide and genuine, if I wasn't married already, I'd have given up my new palazzo pants to get him to smile at me like that again. Behind him, I could see Artemis on her couch, legs tucked to the side as she held court.

"Hello." The man kept smiling as he held out his hand. "I don't believe I've met *you* here before." He took the hand I offered, kissing it lightly on the back. In my whole life, no one had ever kissed my hand like that before.

"I'm Diana," I stammered the words out at last. "Artemis's sister."

"And I'm Dirk Peters," he said, "Artemis's fr—"

But he never got to finish, because it was then that I snatched my hand back from his and slapped him hard across the face.

"My God, Diana!" Artemis leapt from her couch. "I didn't invite you over here so you could beat up my friends!"

"I'm sorry," I started, but then corrected myself. "No, I'm *not* sorry. Your *friend* hurt my friend, badly, with his rejection letter to her. He deserved what I just gave him and worse. He'll be lucky if I don't hit him again several more times before the night is out."

Dirk had the back of his hand to his upper lip, which was starting to swell.

"That's right," he said, wagging the finger of his other hand as though he was just figuring something out. To my surprise, he was smiling, despite that I'd hit him. "You referred that American woman to me, the one who'd written her first novel. What was her name again?"

"Lise Barrett," I spoke through clenched teeth.

"Lise Barrett is lucky to have a friend like you."

I ignored that. "I'd think you'd at least have the decency to remember the names of the people whose lives you destroy."

"But there are so many and one loses track." He shrugged, not bothered in the slightest. "Tell me, is she revising now?"

"You must be joking," I said. "After your cruel e-mail, she destroyed the manuscript!"

"Oh no!" His horror was real, not the mock you might expect. "Why ever did she do that?"

"Because *you* told her it was rubbish!"

"But I only said that to make her work harder. I could tell she had the glimmerings of a strong talent, but you don't become more than just a glimmering by people telling you how good you are. Do you know that someone once rejected Charlotte Brontë over *Jane Eyre* with the old-world equivalent of 'Don't quit your day job'? And look what that did for her!"

"It doesn't matter anymore," I said. "She's given up on that book. She's started a new one."

"Oh, really?" he said, his smile coming back again.

• • •

Two hours later, I was surprised at what a good time I was having. In the past, Artemis's friends had been no more than civil to me; in fact, in our really young days, they'd been downright awful. But the group of people she had gathered at the party that night were more than kind. They kept complimenting me on my clothes, on my hair.

On the mantel over Artemis's fireplace, she had on display photos of her doing adventurous things on her exotic holidays, intermingled with family photos. At the center was a large one of her and me together. I'd always suspected she kept that photo on display because, compared to me in it, she looked even more gorgeous than she usually did. At one point, having allowed myself a rare glass of wine and feeling just a bit tipsy, I heard one of Artemis's friends who was regarding the picture say to her, "Isn't it wonderful how much better Diana looks now than she does there? Perhaps it's time you replaced it with a more up-to-date photo to do her justice?"

"Why bother?" Artemis said, not realizing I was standing behind her as she knocked back her own glass of wine. "She's only going to gain it all back."

I was about to speak up on my own behalf when I discovered I didn't have to. Sidling up to Artemis and her girlfriend, Dirk said, "I think you're jealous. Your sister's star is on the rise and you can't stand it."

"What are you talking about?" Artemis scoffed. "Her 'star is on the rise'? Rubbish."

"Oh, but it is," Dirk said. "Mark my words. My whole life has been devoted to spotting stars on the rise." He looked at the old picture of me. Then he turned to look straight at me. "And I know what I'm seeing."

The look of shock on Artemis's face was well worth the price of admission.

I left a short time after that, thanking Artemis for the lovely time, only half meaning it. When I got to the door, Dirk was there to hold it for me.

"I wonder if you'd do me a favor," he said, reaching out to gently touch my hair.

"And what would that be?"

"Your hair is beautiful, don't get me wrong. But that face? It's stunning. You shouldn't be hiding it behind all that hair. Let me take you to the salon tomorrow. My treat."

I'd always kept my hair long because, well, large women can look ridiculous with short hair, like a pinhead attached to a balloon body. But his smile was so persuasive, he'd stuck up to Artemis for me, and Dirk "the Jaguar" Peters, as I'd come to learn through Lise, was known for his eye.

"Why not?" I shrugged.

* * *

The next day I sat in the stylist's chair, hands over my face as Dirk stood behind me.

"Come on," he coaxed. "Look. I think you're going to like it."

At last, I peeked through my fingers and saw...

My God. It was like a whole different woman. The hair was much shorter now, cut at varying jagged short lengths, and the stylist had colored some strands lighter, some darker, so the whole was exciting to look at. It occurred to me that if I could only keep to the weight loss, someday I might be considered a pixie, a thing I thought I'd never be—not in this lifetime.

"What do you think?" Dirk smiled.

"I like it," I practically gasped the words out. How could I not like it? And then another thought occurred to me for the first time: I hadn't told Dan I was cutting my hair. What was Dan going to think?

But I didn't have time to worry about that, because Dirk was swiveling my chair around so that now I was facing him.

"I like it too," he said. "And you know what else I'd like? Once you go back to Connecticut, I'd like to plan a visit out there, perhaps see your friend Lise and talk to her about her new book." He paused. "Perhaps get to know you better." And then he leaned down and kissed me gently, first on my cheek and then on the lips.

It happened so quickly, I didn't think to turn away.

Sylvia

That night we'd had the get-together at Sylvia's Supper had been such a good night for me. I was so happy to find out I was cancer-free. I was so happy to be with those three women, thankful for their support. I was so happy, I was even nice to a customer. And oh what a good customer I picked to be nice to too.

So, OK, it wasn't me who was nice to the lady in the summer-squash raincoat. It was the others—Diana, Lise, and especially Cindy—who made sure she got everything she needed to solve her sudden food emergency. If they'd left it up to me, I'd have just said, "Can't you see we're having a private party here? The sign on the door says CLOSED. It wouldn't say CLOSED if I wanted to be OPEN!"

At the time, I'd been sort of miffed that they'd overridden me. But when I found myself two hundred dollars richer after the lady left, I could see where maybe it was a good thing to have people in my life who could occasionally save me from my worst instincts. And now, three weeks later, when the lady in the summer-squash raincoat came back—minus the summer squash but with a special friend in tow—I was really grateful for those three people in my life.

I was just pulling the tables in from the sidewalk. It had been a good day. The weather was glorious, warm with none of the humidity that would no doubt soon make its ugly appearance and stay with us through the rest of the spring and then summer, and the shop had been busy. Everyone wanted to eat lobster-salad sandwiches, it seemed, and the tables had been full all day.

"Is this Sylvia?" I heard a voice ask as I was repositioning the last table back inside.

I turned to see the speaker. Her white-blond hair was so short it made my own crop look long, and her eyes were like flint. Her body, so skinny in her filmy spring dress, made me wonder if she ever ate anything; and her shoes, impossibly high, made me wonder how she could walk.

"Remember me?" the woman next to her asked. It was the woman who had worn the summer-squash raincoat.

"Of course," I said. "I never forget a customer. What do you need? Another last-minute meal after closing time?"

"I love it!" the white-blond said. She wasn't talking to me, though. She was talking to her companion as if I wasn't there.

"This is Magda Riley," Summer-Squash Raincoat said, introducing us. "She's the important guest I had over that night I picked up supper here. You do know who Magda Riley is, don't you?"

"No." I crossed my arms. "Should I?"

Magda held out her hand, the nails of which were so long, I wondered how she ever got any work done. If she tried to pick her nose with one of those things, she'd probably puncture a hole straight through to her brain.

"This is such an honor," Magda said, taking my hand in both of hers and shaking it too many times.

"Pleased, I'm sure," I said, taking my hand back.

"I just loved everything about that meal you gave Sheila that night," Magda said.

I strained to remember what I'd given her. The shrimp, definitely, because I remembered wincing when Cindy called them "shrimps." But what had been so spectacular about the food I'd given her? It was just food.

"But what I really loved," Magda went on, "was some of the things Sheila told me you said."

"What did I say?" My eyes narrowed with suspicion.

"Oh, I don't remember exactly." Magda waved her hand. "Sheila said you were pretty rude about her coming in after closing hours, and then there was that thing about the veal."

"Oh, right," I said. "I probably said something not politically correct about not caring how veal is killed. Who are you? The food police?"

"Close," Sheila said. "She's a TV producer and her network is in the tank."

"I wouldn't say *in the tank*, per se," Magda sniffed. "But we are struggling."

"Everyone else has all those reality shows," Sheila said. "Magda doesn't want to be accused of being derivative, but the movies of the week they've been making haven't been exactly ratings successes, and everyone else's crime shows are better."

"So, I was thinking food. Right?" Magda said. "I mean, everyone has to eat. It's not like people are just going to stop eating anytime soon, right?"

Except for maybe her. She was so skinny I wanted to offer her a cookie.

"But Magda needed to meet you in person first," Sheila said.

"Wait a second," I said. "Meet me in person for what?"

"Before putting you on TV, of course," Magda said, as if I was stupid. "It doesn't matter how well you cook, you need personality to succeed on TV."

"Who said I want to be on TV?" I said.

"Who doesn't want to be on TV?" Sheila countered. "You could be the Martha Stewart of food."

"Martha Stewart is already the Martha Stewart of food," I pointed out. "At least she was in the beginning. It was only later on that she became the Martha Stewart of decorating. And prison."

"But she'll need a gimmick," Sheila said to Magda, ignoring me now. "Emeril's got his 'BAM!' Julia had her wine—"

"A gimmick?" I said. "Who says I want to do this in the first place anyway? And what kind of fucking gimmick? I'm Sylvia! I make supper!"

"That's it!" Magda snap-pointed at me.

"What's it?" I asked.

"You're rude," she said. "You're the rudest chef ever. People will eat it up."

"Just remember," Sheila added, "you can't say 'fucking' on TV."

"And when is all this supposed to happen, if it *does* happen?" I wanted to know.

"We'll bring in a camera crew to shoot a pilot—" Magda started.

"You want to shoot it *here?*" I cut her off.

But she ignored me.

"Then of course the network execs will have to sign off on it," she went on. "But, if all goes well, you could be a summer-replacement show."

"People would definitely rather watch *her*," Sheila spoke about me with certitude, "than that stupid show about the divorced woman with twelve kids."

"Is there really a show like that?" I asked.

"Shh," Sheila whispered. "I never should have said anything. Magda's very sensitive about it. It's on another network and that damn show is a huge hit."

* * *

I was so stunned after they left, saying they'd be in touch, it was like I'd been hit by the train. I was so stunned, I forgot to lock the door behind them or put up the CLOSED sign. Instead, wanting to do something normal, I'd called Cindy up to see how she was. I didn't want to make a nuisance of myself, but I'd been calling her every day since she told us her news about being pregnant. She'd been there for me during my breast cancer scare, and I wanted to be there for her now.

"I still don't know," she said. "I don't know what I want to do yet."

It's what she said every day, but each day I could hear the anxiety in her voice ratcheting up a little higher.

"Well, it's still early days, right?" I said. "What can you be? A month, a month and a half along? You still have time."

"I don't know," she said again. Then in a whisper, "Oh, shit. Eddie's home early. I gotta go."

I was sitting at one of the tables, trying to make sense of things, when I heard the tap at the glass. Looking up, I saw a slightly familiar face with coffee skin and black hair: it was Dr. Gupta. *How nice, I thought, he's such a well-mannered person, he's knocking first even though I don't have the CLOSED sign up.* Then it hit me. *Shit! Dr. Gupta! What would he be doing here?*

I hurried to the door, opened it.

"What is it?" I said. "What's wrong? Did some test I didn't even know about come back with bad results?"

"What?" He was puzzled. Then he looked mortified as recognition hit. "Oh no," he said. "I am so sorry. I suppose I should have phoned first. I was just in the neighborhood, and I thought I would stop by and see how you are doing."

That was odd. My surgeon made house calls?

No, of course not. Surgeons didn't do that. But what else could he possibly want? And then it struck me: this was a social call. When was the last time a man came to visit me who wasn't the mailman or some delivery guy? I couldn't remember. It had to have been back when Minnie and I were in college, lost back there somewhere in that long, dim hallway of dark memory. And how did I feel about this *particular* man being the first after such a long dry spell? The idea was scary and wonderful, all at once. But there was no time to think about that, because he was talking again.

"But then," he said, "when I saw you through the window, your face looked so sad and confused, I thought I should knock first so as not to intrude by just walking right in."

He was such a kind man, this man who'd cut into my breast and now had made a special visit to see how I was doing. And my shop was full of food. The least I could do was be gracious, for once in my life, and offer him something.

"Would you like some dinner, Dr. Gupta?" I offered, holding the door for him.

"Oh no," he said. "You need not go to the trouble. But make it Sunil, please. My name, that is. Perhaps you would like to talk for a bit, Ms. Goldsmith?"

It was weird. With the exception of Cindy and Lise and Diana—and of course Minnie when she was alive—it had been years, decades even, since anyone had asked me to talk to them.

"Make it Sylvia," I said.

And then, at his urging, I started talking. I told him about the crazy TV people. I told him about Cindy's problem without betraying her by naming her. It was so weird hearing myself tell it, mostly weird because, for the first time since Minnie died, I saw myself as a woman with a full, if peculiar, life. And not only that, I saw myself as a woman with real friends.

Cindy

Carly was lying in a ratty old lawn chair in the tiny front yard when I got there. She had on cutoff jean shorts and a pink baby tee, her eyes were closed as though she were asleep, and her face was tilted to catch the sun. Since it was Saturday afternoon, I'd figured it would be safe to come since both our parents would still be at work. I hated running into my parents there. All my father ever did was hassle me about my life, which was only slightly better than his other pastime: fighting with my mother.

I really wanted to talk to Carly, but she looked so peaceful lying there it seemed a shame to disturb her. I was debating whether to just kiss her on the forehead and go when she lazily opened one eye, squinting up at me.

"Don't go, Cin," she said. "I was just resting." Then she shivered, even though the day was still warm for April, wrapping her arms around her bare midriff as she straddled the chair and rose. "C'mon, it's freezing out here. Let's go inside."

Inside at my parents' house always depressed me. Nothing ever changed. There was the same furniture in the living room they'd bought when they'd moved in over twenty years ago: the same brown sectional sofa, the fake-wood coffee table with water stains on it, and even the fake plant in the corner with the heavy dust on the long leaves was the same. And the walls were barren. The few times Mom had tried to buy new furniture with money she'd saved from her own job, after paying the bills of course, Dad'd made her take the things back. "Why waste money," he'd say, cracking the tab on his Budweiser, "when what we have still works so fine?" And when she'd tried to hang a framed poster she bought at the print shop at the mall? "Art's for fancy people, Bev. It's not for people like us."

Carly led the way through to the kitchen. She opened the fridge, took the bottle of milk out, and drank straight from it before offering it to me.

I shook my head. The milk would probably be good for the baby inside me, if the expiration date wasn't past due, but I couldn't face swallowing anything right that minute. Then Carly followed the milk up by snagging a can of Diet Pepsi, and the idea of her drinking the one after the other caused my stomach to go into one of its increasingly regular threatening rumbles.

She sat down at the Formica kitchen table, and I settled across from her.

"You look great," I said. "You haven't looked this good since…"

"You were going to say 'before,' right?" she said with a hard-edged smile that softened quickly. "It's OK, Cin, you can say stuff like that to me. I'm doing better now."

"I can see that," I said, glad. "How's it going…here?" I said, indicating the house around us as if it were more person than place.

She pulled a face. "Put it like this," she said, "I can't wait to get out. The 'rents are driving me nuts."

"You must be better," I laughed.

"Nah," she said, as she made another face. "I couldn't wait to get out even when I still felt lousy all the time."

"Where would you go?" I asked. Not that I blamed her. Only back in that house for ten minutes, and *I* couldn't wait to get out again. Growing up, I'd never been able to understand how my mother stayed. I used to lay in bed at night, listening to them fight, my mother threatening to leave, my dad threatening to kill her if she did, my mom saying she didn't care but then finally crying, saying she couldn't leave us, meaning me and Carly, and saying she'd forgive him. I used to want to run down the stairs and scream at her, "Run! If you want to go, I'll pack for you!" But I couldn't do that. My dad would've killed me.

"I don't know," Carly said now, studying the ingredients list on her soda can. "I guess I'd need to find a job first. Even still, I'd need someone to share a place with."

I thought about Carly's friends, at least the ones I knew. They were the people who often got Carly into messes in the first place. If she stayed with one of them, she'd be back to drinking and drugs in no time; her moods would spiral down again, and she'd be back in what she laughingly referred to as "The Dark Place."

"You could stay with me," I offered. "It's not much, I know, but I've slept on the couch before. It's really comfortable. Or you could get a sleeping bag for the floor."

"No, thanks, Cin. Thanks, really, but no. If I stayed with you, I'd have to stay with Eddie too, like last time. I don't think I could take that."

I tried not to let my hurt show. Carly had been through a lot the last three months. Hell, she'd been through a lot her whole life. She couldn't help it if sometimes maybe she didn't have any tact. *Tact* being a word I'd learned about in one of the new classes I was taking on the computer to get my GED so I could take some college-level classes.

"How's old Eddie doing these days anyway?" Carly asked.

"Actually," I said, smiling and really meaning it, "he's doing great. We got this new computer—"

"*You* got a computer?"

"Well, actually, this woman I know gave it to me, a laptop. She said she didn't need it anymore and since I wanted to take some classes—"

"Omigod, you're taking *classes*?"

"You think it's dumb?"

She thought for a second. "No, I think it's great. I think it's really cool. What are you studying?"

"Right now I'm just catching up on all the classes I never finished in high school—math, science, you know the stuff. But after I get through with all that, OK, *this* you're going to think is really dumb," I said, suddenly feeling shy about it. "I want to be a social worker. I want to help women in trouble; you know, people like Mom."

"I don't think that's dumb at all, Cin."

"No?"

"No, I think it's the coolest thing I ever heard. But wait a second. What does Eddie think of all this? Does he *approve* of your going back to school?"

"Well, that's the thing," I said, unable to conceal my smile. "Eddie thinks I got the computer so he can download like a gazillion songs. He thinks it's the coolest thing I've ever done too!"

"Omigod!" Carly was laughing so hard, she could barely gasp the word out as she reached to high-five me. "Wait a second, though," she said. "What happens when he finds out?"

I shrugged. "He won't. Honestly, so long as he can download free music, he's happy. He's even trying to figure out how to set up one of those fan pages for the band."

"Too cool!" Cindy high-fived me again.

I was so happy in that moment, to be living that moment of sheer joy with her, but in the next the nausea hit me, harder than it had all day, and I had to wrench my hand from hers so I could make a mad dash for the bathroom.

The need to throw up was so immediate, I didn't even have time to close and lock the bathroom door behind me. I just hurled myself to the floor in front of the toilet, my new temple.

There were hurried footsteps down the hall, and then I felt Carly's soft hands, pulling my hair back out of the way for me. When I was done, when there was nothing left inside me, I turned over, resting my back against the cool wall of the tub, eyes closed.

"What's wrong with you?" Carly asked, still stroking my hair.

I didn't have the strength to lie to her. "I'm pregnant," I said. "Are you going to tell me that's the coolest thing you've ever heard too?"

She ignored my attempt at humor, or maybe it was irony; the class I was taking on the computer talked a lot about irony. "Does Eddie know?" she asked.

I shook my head. Then I opened my eyes. "I went to the doctor, got a prescription for those prenatal vitamins, just in case I keep it, but I haven't really decided yet."

"You're thinking of having an abortion?" she asked. Then she smiled ruefully. "I've had two."

And I'd had one.

When I was fifteen, I'd gotten pregnant. I'd actually wanted to have the baby, even though I realized I didn't love the guy, and he definitely didn't want me to have it. But things were so fucked up at home I figured that, even if my dad didn't kill me outright, it would only make everything worse for everybody.

"What do you *want* to do, Cin?" Carly asked.

I thought about how if I'd really wanted to get rid of it, I could have done so already. The doctor at the free clinic I'd gone to had been friendly enough. It hadn't seemed to matter to her one way or the other whether I accepted the prenatal vitamins or had an abortion, just so long as whatever I decided, it was what I really wanted to do.

"Would you think I'm crazy if I said I want to keep the baby, but that I'm not sure I'm ready yet to tell Eddie about it?"

The Party

RECOMMENDED READING:
Lise: *On Writing*, Stephen King
Diana: *Shopaholic and Sister*, Sophie Kinsella
Sylvia: *The Cloister Walk*, Kathleen Norris
Cindy: *Cold Sassy Tree*, Olive Ann Burns

Lise was cutting vegetables for the salad, trying not to splatter juice from the tomatoes onto her white Capri pants and matching top, while Tony was transferring beer and wine from the fridge into a giant cooler to take outside, when the first knock came.

"Your hair!" Lise squealed when she saw Diana. "Why didn't you say anything?" Then she turned to the man standing next to Diana. He had on khakis and a pink Oxford shirt and looked as though he was somehow missing his tie. Lise held out her hand. "Dan! Hi! Don't you just love her hair like this?"

"It was a shock at first," Dan said, his smile tight.

In fact, it had been more than a shock. When Diana had arrived home from London, Dan had been just shy of livid.

"How could you cut your hair without telling me first?" he'd said.

"I thought you were my husband," Diana had sniffed, "not my fashion consultant. If you don't like it, just say so."

"It's not that," Dan had said, on unfamiliar ground with his own wife. "But imagine this: Imagine if I came home one day from Japan with a mustache and beard, or maybe with my head shaved. Wouldn't you be just a little upset that I hadn't told you what I was going to do first, that I hadn't given you any warning?"

"I suppose," Diana had conceded.

"It's not really the hair that's the problem," Dan had said with a sigh. "In fact, it's beautiful. I can really see your face now in a way I never could before. It's that you keep changing things around— you schedule a major operation on your body, you hack off all your hair—without even thinking to discuss it with me first."

"I'm sorry," Diana had said, "but what would you have had me do? Call you up from the salon in London on my mobile and ask you to set up the webcam so I could have you look at pictures in hair magazines with me to see which style you think might look best?"

"Now that I've had time to get used to it," Dan told Lise now, "I think it looks beautiful." He held out a bottle to Lise. "Here. For your celebration."

"But I told everyone not to bring anything!" Lise protested.

"You've earned it," Dan said. "It's not every day a person can say she's finished a first draft on a first novel."

"Second novel, actually," Lise smiled ruefully. "The first became kindling."

"This is great," Tony said, reaching in with one hand to accept the champagne before Lise could turn it down again, and offering his other for a shake. "Tony, by the way. It's a bit small inside here, and with just the one bathroom and eight of us there might be a bit of a line for the facilities today, but the yard should certainly hold us all."

Tony was right. Despite the smallness of Lise's cottage, it sat on a full acre of land, and Tony and Lise had spent some time that Sunday morning arranging lawn chairs that were far enough away from the barbecue that people wouldn't get smoke in their eyes, setting up croquet in case anyone wanted to play, placing citronella candles in strategic areas to keep the mosquitoes away as night fell.

"Sounds like more of your guests are here," Dan said at the crunch of gravel on the drive.

Lise peered out the window over the sink. "Who's that gorgeous man with Sylvia?" she asked Diana.

"I dunno," Diana said, coming to stand beside her. "And why is he wearing a suit on Sunday?"

"I told her she could bring a guest," Lise said. "I told everyone that."

"You probably never expected Sylvia of all people to show up with a date, though, did you?" Diana said.

"But look at how pretty Sylvia looks," Lise said. "I've never seen her in a dress before."

"I didn't think she even *owned* a dress," Diana said.

The dress in question had a gauzy, mid-calf, wide jade skirt and an embroidered white peasant blouse that had been in fashion twenty years ago and suddenly was again. Sylvia had on a wide-brimmed straw hat over her short red hair, and she tottered up the drive in unaccustomed heeled sandals, a covered dish in her hand.

"Oh, Sylvia!" Lise said, holding the door open for her. "I especially didn't want *you* to make anything! It's like you're taking the cook's version of a busman's holiday."

"I have no idea what that means," Sylvia said. "But I was trying out some new recipes anyway—you know, for the show pilot—so I just figured I'd bring some samples along. Oh," she added, as though suddenly remembering she had someone with her, "and this is Sunil. Dr. Sunil Gupta."

"Please call me Sunny," he said, his smile wide. "Sylvia does."

"*Sunny?*" Lise and Diana mouthed their shock across to one another.

"Yoo-hoo!" Cindy's voice called through the door. "Sorry we're late, but I got us lost with the directions."

Like Lise, Cindy wore Capris, only hers were denim, and she had on a red tee, her long hair pulled back into a high ponytail that made her look even younger than usual. She held one open palm out to indicate the man at her side in a presenting gesture. He had on khakis so perfectly creased they looked as though someone had just snipped off the tags on the ride over, the white Oxford shirt looked just as crisp and new, and his Jesus hair was tied back in a neat ponytail.

"Everyone," Cindy took a deep breath, "this is Eddie."

* * *

"Why do all parties, no matter how much space there is to spread out, always wind up in the kitchen?" Diana asked.

"I don't know," Lise said. "I always figured it was a guy thing. Like maybe they're waiting for the food to come out of the oven, or so they can be right next to the beer in the fridge?"

"Maybe it is a guy thing," Sylvia said, "but Cindy seems to favor the kitchen too."

The three women were out on the lawn, listening to the sounds of boisterous chatter from those on the inside.

"And then I said," they heard Eddie say, "'I don't like blind people, because they can't drive cars!'"

The kitchen exploded with laughter.

"The men all seem to really like Eddie," Lise observed.

"It is funny, isn't it?" Diana said. "I mean, they're all so different from him. I don't know what I expected, really. In the beginning, when Cindy first told us about him, I thought he sounded charming. Then, as time went on, I started getting an odd feeling when she talked about him. And then there was her hesitancy to tell him about the baby, as though something weren't quite right there."

"I still don't like him," Sylvia said. "There's something not kosher about that guy."

"But he's so gorgeous," Diana said. "I can easily see why someone like Cindy would fall for him. Isn't he the kind of guy all young women dream about? A gorgeous guy who sings in a rock band?"

"Listen to them all laughing at his jokes," Lise added.

"Lise says you play in a rock band," they heard Tony say. "I always wished I had the guts to do that, put myself out there. It must be great."

"Oh, it is great, most of the time," Eddie said. "But sometimes? It sucks. There was one time, we were playing this club in Brewster and this guy, Mickey, was sitting in front of the stage. Everyone in Danbury knows Mickey. He's got these eyes that are so red, the cops might as well just arrest him every night, you know? Anyway, there

I am onstage, trying to sing, and every five minutes Mickey keeps yelling, 'You suck! We Break For Dogs'—that's the name of my band—'sucks!' I knew he didn't really mean it. I mean, he was just being Mickey, right? And the definition of Mickey is annoying. But who can sing with someone doing that? So finally, I leaned down from the stage, microphone in my hand, got right up in his face and screamed, 'Hey, Mickey!' Then I tilted the mic to him so the crowd could catch his stoned 'What?' before switching it back to myself and screaming, 'Get your own fucking rock 'n' roll band!'"

For a long moment afterward, there was dead silence in the kitchen. Then the room exploded in laughter.

"Oh, that is wonderful!" Sunny was heard to say. "Perhaps I should try that line on some of my patients who are always second-guessing me?"

"Or I could use that on the dean," Tony said. "He's always talking like he could teach classes better than any of his staff, if only he had time to teach them all."

"There's a man in Japan who's been giving me grief," Dan started to say.

On the lawn, Diana couldn't contain her glee. "What a perfect thing to say!" she laughed. "I'm going to try that out on Artemis the very next time she gets shirty with me about something. I'll just say, 'Artemis, you get your own fucking rock 'n' roll band!'"

"But she won't get it," Sylvia said. "There's no context."

"So?" Diana was still laughing. "It's the perfect all-purpose metaphor!"

"I'd love to hear you play sometime," Tony said to Eddie.

"Actually, I've got my guitar right in the car," Eddie said.

"Oh," Cindy said, "I don't think it's that kind of party—"

"What are you talking about?" Eddie said. "Every party needs music."

"I'd like to hear you too," Dan said. "Just don't tell me to get my own fucking rock 'n' roll band, OK?" he added, clapping Eddie on the shoulder.

Eddie got his guitar from the car while everyone gathered outside. As he started to sing—a ballad he'd written called "Cindy" that was somehow elegiac and aggressive all at the same time—the women stood off to one side. His eyes shined as he looked at Cindy, and she smiled back at him with pride before turning to Sylvia.

"So now you're dating your *doctor*?" Cindy whispered.

"We're not *dating*," Sylvia said. "We're just friends. So we spend a little time together. What's the big deal? And if I'm ever worried again that I might have breast cancer, I'll just find another doctor."

"Just friends," Diana laughed, "right."

"Do you see the way Sunny looks at you?" Lise said. "I remember when Tony and I were first together, he used to look at me like that."

"What do you mean 'used to'?" Sylvia said. "And anyway, cut it out. This isn't a date."

"That was incredible," Tony spoke into the silence after Eddie stopped playing. "Your voice is amazing."

"You should be on that show all my nurses watch," Sunny said. "You know the one I am talking about? Where everyone sings, but each week someone gets knocked off the show until there is only one person left standing?"

"You must mean *American Idol*," Dan said. "You're right. Eddie could easily win that thing."

"I don't think it's quite that easy," Eddie said, "and I wish, but there's an age limit. Still, I keep writing the producers letters, telling them they oughta change that, so you never know."

"Do you think the other men really like him?" Diana whispered to Lise. "They're all being so nice."

"*Overly* nice?" Lise questioned. Then she shook her head. "Tough to say. His stories *are* funny, and he does sing incredibly well."

The air took a sudden turn toward the chill as the sun dipped down below the tree line.

Tony clapped his hands together. "How about that champagne now?"

A moment later, he was handing out glasses and filling them.

"None for me, thanks," Cindy said.

"I don't know what's up with her," Eddie addressed the group at large. "She never used to not drink." He turned to Cindy. "Not even to toast your friend finishing her book?"

Cindy shook her head.

"It doesn't matter," Tony said with an easy smile. "You don't need to actually drink anything to take part in the spirit of a toast." He raised his glass as he looked at Lise, pride filling his eyes. "To Lise, for finishing her book!"

"To Lise!" everyone echoed back.

Sylvia

"It's not a date," I told Cindy.

"A man, a man you've been talking to on the phone every day, a man who stops by your shop regularly, a man who you took to Lise's party, *that man* asks you to go out to dinner with him—how can that not be a date?"

"It's just food," I said. "We're just two people who will be eating dinner in the same room together at the same time at the same table. Stop making such a *tsuris* about it."

"You need a new outfit for this tsuris."

"You don't even know what tsuris means."

"So? You still need a new outfit."

I was offended. "What's wrong with the clothes I've got?"

"I'll bet that skirt and peasant blouse you wore to Lise's are the only things remotely girly you own. I'm right, aren't I?"

"Of course you're right. What would I be doing with girly clothes?"

"My lunch break is at one. Put the CLOSED sign on the door and meet me outside the lingerie shop at one."

"I can't just close the shop during lunch. Lunch is the busiest hour of the day at Sylvia's Supper!"

"Look, you wouldn't have called me if you didn't really want my help. Just do it."

Two hours later I was on time waiting outside Midnight Scandals, as ordered, but apparently Cindy wasn't ready for me yet, so I went in. Of course I'd walked by the store many times in the past, but I'd never gone in; Minnie and I'd always bought our unmentionables at Sears.

Look at all that stuff! I thought. Enough red bras to outfit a hundred whorehouses, panties that left no mystery to the game of Hide 'n' Seek, scary-looking contraptions I could never figure out the proper wearing of, not in a million years. The purple wallpaper alone was enough to make me want to run away.

Cindy was behind the counter. She had on a black suit—I'd never seen her in her work clothes before—and she was talking to a severe-looking woman who was dressed the same.

"So I was thinking?" Cindy was saying to the other woman, her voice at least an octave higher than I'd ever heard her speak in before, with a too-bright smile on her face, and every line coming out as a perky question instead of the statements they should have been. "When I get back? I'll rearrange the front window?" Now Cindy was slinging her satchel over her shoulder. "I promise not to be late?"

I couldn't hear what the other woman said, but the tone sounded grouchy. Then Cindy saw me and smiled, a genuine smile, and started walking me out.

"Who was that woman?" I whispered out of the corner of my mouth.

"You mean Marlene? She's my manager."

"I didn't mean her. I meant who was that woman you were when you were talking to her? I've never seen you act like that before."

"You mean my blithe-spirit face?" She shrugged. "Doesn't everyone have a different face for work? Different faces for different areas of their lives?"

"No," I said. "I'm the same everywhere. I'd confuse myself too much if I ever tried to be different."

"Well, today you're going to be different, because today we're going to get you new clothes for your date."

"It's not a…!"

But she wasn't listening. She was a woman with a mission.

I tried leading us toward Sears, but she turned me in a one eighty and pointed me toward Macy's. "You can use my mall-employee discount card," she said. "You'll save twenty percent."

"Couldn't I use the same card at Sears?"

Again she ignored me.

In Macy's she was all business, holding up one outfit after another, inspecting each for perfection.

"You don't want to look like you're just wearing any old thing, but you also don't want to look like you've spent too much time on it," she said. "Know what I mean?"

"No," I said.

At last, not listening to my protests at all, she shoved me in a dressing stall with a straight-line aqua skirt and a white top that came down low in front and wrapped at the waist.

"This is too low cut," I said.

"It's perfect," she said. "You've got a gorgeous neckline. You should let it show more often. And that skirt? That color is going to look amazing with your hair."

A few minutes later, I had to admit she was right. Fifty years old, and I'd never looked so good.

"And you need gold sandals too," she said, "but flats. You looked like you were going to trip on those heels you wore to Lise's."

"Hey!"

Still ignoring me. After getting the sandals, she trapped me in the makeup department.

"Just enough to bring out her eyes and even out her skin tone," Cindy instructed the woman behind the counter. "And try to find a lip color that doesn't clash with her hair, but no frosteds. We're going for a matte look here."

I was beyond protesting, but I knew I'd never be able to duplicate what the counter lady was doing to my face.

New face in place, Cindy walked us back to Midnight Scandals.

"Well, thanks," I said, my new purchases filling my hands. "Even though it's not really a date."

She grabbed my hand and gave it a tug.

"What are you doing?" I said.

"I'm not done with you yet," she said, pulling me back into that purple emporium of bradom.

"But I already have underwear!" I was back to protesting. "I don't need any of this...*stuff*. We're just going to have salads, a main course, maybe dessert if we're not too full, but we're not going to sleep together!"

"Whether you sleep together or not is not the point. And it's not *about* need, or at least not that kind of need. It's about feeling pretty from the inside out. Really, I promise you, you'll have a much better time, and you'll feel much more confident if you're not wearing old granny underwear that hikes up to your neck."

"Hey!"

* * *

But as it turned out, Cindy was right, because when I walked into the restaurant and saw Sunny already waiting for me at the table, I felt pretty through and through.

When Sunny had called that afternoon to say he'd made reservations at La Finesse, I'd been surprised. Somehow, I'd been expecting something less fancy. I'd heard of the restaurant of course, but never been. It was all dark corners but with warm lighting, which was OK: if my food didn't look so hot, I'd never know it; if I didn't look so hot, maybe Sunny wouldn't notice that either.

I'd also told Sunny I'd drive myself, even though he'd offered to pick me up.

"How is the TV program progressing?" he asked, once the waitress had taken our drinks order: a scotch and soda for him, straight scotch for me.

"You should see these women!" I said, falling into the easy rhythm we always had while talking together on the phone, forgetting my own awkward feelings about being dressed up and having makeup on. "Especially Magda. I keep watching her running around—scurrying here, shouting something over there—and I keep finding myself wondering: Does she even *know* what she's doing?"

Sunny laughed, a joyful noise like water racing down a river. "Do you think the show will be ready in time for July?" he wondered.

"I don't know if they'll be ready," I said, "but I will. I mean, all I've got to do is cook, right?"

The waitress came back. Sunny ordered the braised sole with a side salad, while I asked for the lasagna and another scotch. Usually considered to be a cafeteria dish in Italy, I was surprised to see it on the menu of such an upscale restaurant, but then I noticed they had it all tarted up with truffles. It still seemed like a safe choice and anyway, I figured, who can mess up lasagna? But as soon as the waitress was gone, I began worrying, *I could mess it up. I could mess it up all over this white blouse.*

Then I told myself to stop worrying about such foolishness like trying to remain perfect looking. This was just two friends having dinner.

"Get this," I said, "they've finally settled on a name for the show."

"And it is?"

"*The Rude Chef!*"

There was that laugh again. I could happily drown in that laugh.

"Tell me about your sister," Sunny said, sobering. "You never say much about her."

No, I thought. This was supposed to be a nice social night out. If I began talking about Minnie now, I'd start thinking about what happened when we were both back in college, and I didn't want to be thinking about that, not now. Besides, I'd never told that story to anyone.

"No, no," I said softly, or at least as soft as my voice ever gets. "Every time we talk on the phone, all we ever do is talk about me. Tell me something about you for a change."

He shrugged. "What is to tell? My family came here when I was young, I am an only child, I never lost my accent. I am a surgeon, much to my mother's delight, and I dislike golf, much to my father's despair, and I am now forty-two years old."

He was eight years younger than me.

I looked inside my drink. If it were tea instead of scotch, I'd have tried to read the leaves. Oh well. At least the ice cubes were interesting.

"You must feel like you're out to dinner with your mother," I said, still lost in my ice.

"Hardly," he said, reaching across the table and gently tilting my chin up with his fingers. "I feel like I am out to dinner with a very beautiful woman who is most definitely and officially no longer my patient."

I moved my head so it was out of range of that gentle hand. "Tell me more," I said as our dinners arrived.

He picked up his fork, but then looked at me and waited. "How is your lasagna?" he asked.

I didn't want to touch it, sure I'd somehow drop the fork, splattering sauce-covered truffles all over myself. Gingerly, I picked up the fork, touched it to the sauce, and then touched the tine to the tip of my tongue.

"It's delicious," I said, even though inside I was thinking, *Oregano, basil, too much salt, a little red wine—big deal. I could make better.* "So?" I said. "You were about to tell me more. There must be more to you than surgery."

He settled back in his seat and sighed. "What else is there to say? I love this country, but after the events of 9/11, some of my patients left, accusing me, although not in so many words, of wanting to fly airplanes into skyscrapers to earn a few dozen virgins to call my own. Is that the sort of thing you have in mind?"

"That's awful!" I said.

"Indeed."

"Have you ever been married?" I asked.

"That is a sudden conversational shift," he said.

I waved my empty scotch glass. "Another one of these, and I'll start talking about politics and religion too."

"No," he laughed, although he didn't order me another scotch either. "I never married. Did you?"

"No."

"How come?"

"Because I was too busy being my sister's sister."

"And I never married because I was too busy studying and building my practice. I did not want a trophy wife, attractive as they might look, and by the time I was done studying and practicing, all the smart and interesting women I knew were divorced and bitter about it."

"You make it sound as though all the women in the world can

be distilled down into a few types."

"I would never try to distill you down to anything, Sylvia."

"May I interest you in some coffee or dessert?" the waitress asked.

"Yes," Sunny said.

"No," I said. "Check, please?"

"Another sudden conversational shift?" he asked.

"I can't think straight in here," I said. "I feel like I'm in a cave."

The waitress set the check down in front of Sunny, but when he reached for his wallet, I grabbed it. *Damn*, that was an expensive lasagna! Maybe if I transformed Sylvia's Supper so it looked like a cave, I could charge triple for things.

"What are you doing?" he asked as I reached for my purse.

"Paying my fair share," I said, counting out the bills. "Your fish was more than my lasagna, but I drank more than you so let's go fifty-fifty."

His smile was amused. "I can assure you, I paid off my student loan fifteen years ago, and I can afford to treat you to supper."

"And I can afford to pay my share. I thought we agreed: friends, right?"

"Are you scared at the idea of this being a date?" he asked.

"*Friends*," I said pointedly. "Right?"

Sunny sighed as he set down his half of the money. "Friends."

But when he walked me to my truck, even though he just pecked me on the cheek, my cheek didn't feel like friends afterward.

Cindy

The beat of the bass seemed to pound up through the cheap carpet on the floor, like my body was one big conductor with my feet taking the pounding from there right through to my brain, and the ice in my club soda had long since melted. I was seated at a small front-row table of the Bar None with all the other girlfriends and wives from Eddie's band. It was the last place in the world I wanted to be, feeling as I did, but Eddie wanted me there.

"You never come to the shows anymore," he'd said earlier that night when we were still back at home. "What do you have to do tonight that's more important?"

I had to study for my online classes, for one thing, and I had to get to bed early, for another, because the pregnancy was making me damn tired all the time. But I couldn't say either of those things.

"I'm not feeling so good," I'd said. "But maybe if I start feeling better, I'll call Donna and catch a ride over with her? Then you can always drive me home afterward."

"Oh, jeez," he'd said, his face clouding with concern. "I didn't know you were sick." He put his hand on my forehead. "You do feel warm."

I'd noticed the pregnancy made me warm, my temperature always running slightly higher than normal, but I couldn't say that either.

"Do you want me to stay home?" Eddie'd asked. "It is a little late to cancel the show, but—"

"I'll be fine," I'd said. "You go on ahead. Maybe I'll see you later."

But as soon as he left, I started feeling guilty. He was right: I almost never did go to the shows anymore. So I put on my glad rags—in this case cropped jeans and a green halter top, because I knew the bar would be too warm—and called Donna and came. Not quite two months' pregnant yet, my belly was still totally flat. But I could feel my body changing in subtle ways.

Now, despite the noise and the headache, I was glad I came.

As soon as Eddie'd seen me walk in with Donna, he stopped singing, motioning the other band members for silence.

He'd held the microphone close, addressing the audience, but his eyes were locked on me the whole while, compelling the room to follow his gaze. The men looked at me with curiosity, the women with envy.

"Now we're going to ratchet it up, folks, because my lady, the love of my life, is in the house."

And then they'd started to play again.

I'd been starting to take Eddie's dream of the big time for granted, starting to doubt it would ever happen. But that time he'd played and sang at Lise's party, I'd heard him through *their* ears, saw that what they were hearing was really good. And now I was hearing him through my own ears, like it was for the first time, and I heard they were right. There was no reason, other than chance and luck, that Eddie couldn't be as big as the greats. He could be like that lead singer for Coldplay. And if Eddie could be that guy, then maybe I could be like Gwyneth, only I would never name our baby Apple, whether it was a boy *or* girl. I felt a tingle of excitement inside me. Maybe I'd finally tell Eddie about the baby tonight.

The applause was deafening as the band finished their final set.

"I hate this part," Donna said, leaning in to me as she pointed to where the guys were coming off the stage, and I knew exactly what she was talking about. Immediately, they were engulfed by groupies. But the groupies all looked so young it was almost funny, like twelve-year-olds trying to look legal, and I wondered how they ever got by the bouncer at the door. I could see why Donna was bugged—her Ron, the keyboard player, had his neck encircled by eager young arms—but even though Eddie was listening politely enough to the young chickie who was bending his ear, I wasn't bothered, because: 1) even Carly had to admit that "You never have to worry about Eddie cheating on you, Cin, he's only got eyes for you"; 2) the young chickie had size thirty-eight breasts crammed into a thirty-four bra and Eddie always hated for girls to look sloppy; and 3) even as he was listening to her, I could see him looking around over her shoulder for me.

"Are you ready to go?" I asked when Eddie made it through the crowd, pulling my bag off the back of my chair and rising even as I spoke.

"What's the rush?" he said. I could see he was still feeling high from performing, high from the audience's response. He wasn't ready to go yet, and I couldn't really blame him. Who wouldn't want to bask in the glow of people endlessly telling you how great you are before heading off into the night?

With the show over, the audience started drifting back to the larger room where the bar was, and Eddie drifted with them. He probably wouldn't need to pay for his own drinks for the rest of the night. We girlfriends and wives started drifting back too.

In addition to the long bar that ran the length of the room, pockmarked by time and bottles slammed down in joy and anger, there were three pool tables and people were playing partners, it was that busy. Before I was with Eddie, I used to shoot a pretty good game. As I watched players take their turns shooting, I thought about which shots I'd take, how I'd set up the next shot, and I listened to the satisfying clack of ball against ball. I couldn't remember why I'd ever stopped.

One of the guys on the table closest to me was down to shooting the eight ball for his team, but it was blocked from the easiest pockets by the scattered balls of his opponents, who frankly sucked. "Bank it long," I said aloud without even thinking. "Cut straight between their three and their eleven and send it right back at yourself into the right corner."

The shooter looked over at me. He was real tall, a good six inches taller than Eddie. There was something about his features—his eyes, nose and mouth—that struck me as familiar. But his brown hair was shorter than any of the guys I knew, not to mention his easy confidence, and he had on a business shirt and tie, like he'd come from some office. He and his partner both looked out of place in the Bar None. "You think?" he said, and now his voice sounded slightly familiar too, hazel eyes flashing friendliness as he raised his Heineken to me in salute.

"I don't just think." I couldn't help but let a smile slip through. "I *know.*"

Without another word, he set his beer down, bent to the table, sized up the shot, and slammed that eight ball on a bank home straight to that right corner. I felt so good watching it go in, you'd think I'd made the shot myself.

"Play the next game with me?" he offered. He looked over at his partner. "He always needs to pee during rounds—no offense, Steve—and it takes forever for him to come back."

A short time ago I'd felt exhausted, all the noise and the pain in my head, but now my brain felt clear as a lake and I was excited too. I looked over to the bar where some girl was paying for Eddie's next drink. I knew I had nothing to worry about. Whatever problems I might have from time to time with Eddie, I knew he'd never cheat on me. Never had, never would. But I also knew he'd stay at the bar as long as the drinks were free. What could be the harm in playing one round? It'd be good to feel a cue in my hands again.

We beat the challengers easily. My partner put two balls in on the break, followed by two more good shots before woofing on an easy tap. One of our challengers made a tough bank but then got cocky and scratched, putting the cue ball in, and I cleared the table.

"We make a good team," my partner said. "Go again?"

"I don't think so," I said, propping my cue against the wall. "Isn't the guy you came with back from the bathroom yet?"

"So?" He smiled, shrugged. "He'll only be back there again in another few minutes."

"Maybe just one more then."

We won again. Tougher opponents, but still we won.

"We haven't even introduced ourselves yet," my partner said. "But maybe I should just call you Lucky?"

"It's Cindy," I said.

His eyes twinkled as he spoke. "Of course," he said, "I already knew that."

"Huh?"

"You really don't recognize me," he said, "do you? Have I changed that much?"

I squinted, as if, even though I didn't need glasses, the act of squinting would make me see him more clearly.

I squinted harder. Then:

"Omigod! *Porter*? Porter *Davis*?"

"In the flesh," he said simply.

But it was a far different flesh than the one I remembered. The Porter Davis I remembered had gone to high school with me. He'd been a band geek and a drama geek, with long stringy hair he wore so that a hank of it always covered one eye, like some old-time Hollywood actress trying to look mysterious. He'd always been tall, but even in high school he'd still carried a fair amount of puppy fat, nothing like the hard and lean look he had now. Oh, and back then he'd had a crush on me. Big time. And I'd just been considering going out with him, at least giving it a try just once, when Eddie came along; Eddie had been out of high school so long, he made being in high school seem like being from the wrong planet. Once Eddie came into my life, that was it for me and other guys. Still, it was great to see a face from the past. And it was even better to see that he was obviously doing so well.

Impulsively, I threw my arms around him, then quickly drew back, checking to see if Eddie was still talking to the girl at the bar: he was.

"It's just so good to see you," I said. "I can't believe how much you've changed."

"Well, it's been eight years since you left school, Cindy. I sure hope I've changed. Everyone does, don't they? Except for you, of course. You're still as pretty as ever."

I could feel the blush in my cheeks.

"God," he said, "I can't believe how good it is to see you." Then he laughed. "That's what you just said, wasn't it? But it is, it really is *good*, and I'd love to catch up with you, find out everything you've been doing. Do you think maybe you could give me your number so

I could call you sometime? Or, better yet, maybe we could go grab a bite to eat right now?"

I can't say I wasn't flattered. It had been, I don't even know how long, since a guy other than Eddie had shown any interest in me. And, certainly, no one who looked like Porter ever had. Still...

"Thanks," I said, "that's, um, very nice. But you see, I already have a boyfriend and—"

I felt the hand on my shoulder spinning me around before I even heard the words.

"What's going on here?" Eddie asked quietly.

Even though his words were quiet, I felt like there was an iceberg coming at me. I tried to smile.

"I was just shooting a game of pool while waiting for you. We were just—"

"What the *fuck* do you think you're doing?" Eddie screamed in my face.

"Hey, pal," Porter said, "back off."

"Back off?" Eddie said. "Back off? I don't fucking think so. What the hell you think you're doing, hitting on my girl?"

"Hey," Porter said again, "we were only playing a game of pool. I asked her out, she said no, that she had a boyfriend—which now I'm guessing is *you*—and that was that. No harm, no foul."

"I'll tell you what the harm is, *asshole*," Eddie said, snatching the cue out of Porter's hand. Eddie flipped the cue on its side so that he was holding an end in each hand as he pressed it into Porter's chest, pushing again and again with it until he had him backed up against the wall. "It's that you never should have even been looking at her in the first place."

Porter started to push back but he needn't have bothered because Eddie dropped the cue and grabbed my hand, hauling me out of there. "C'mon," he said.

"Hey, maybe you shouldn't drive with him when he's like this!" I heard Porter call after me, but I didn't turn back.

Out in the car, Eddie keyed up the engine and peeled out of the parking lot.

"Hey," I said, "aren't you going to at least help the guys load the equipment up?"

"Fucking assholes can do it themselves for a change," Eddie said. Then he pounded the wheel with his fist. "Damn! I've got to keep an eye on you every second. If I just look away once, just once, someone tries to snap you up."

"It wasn't like that," I tried to say. "It was just a game."

"Don't you get it, Cin? With guys like that, it's never just a game."

I looked out the side window, watching the night whiz by. How could I salvage the night? How could I bring Eddie down off his anger?

The car was really old, meaning there was no shift between us, so I undid my seatbelt and slowly slid over until I was next to him. Then I took my hand, traced it from the inside of his knee up his thigh until it came to the crease.

"What are you doing?" he said.

"I was just thinking," I said, "maybe when we get home we could…or maybe we could even pull over to the side of the road here?"

"What are you talking about?" he said. "You've got your period."

I *did?*

My hand froze.

"What do you mean?" I said.

"You don't think I keep track? I know exactly when you're going to get your period. You're like clockwork, every thirty-one days. A guy needs to keep track of these things so he can plan ahead, you know? You know how I hate wading through the red tide."

It was true. Except for when we were first together, Eddie never wanted to have sex when I had my period. Still, the idea that he counted the days in his head somehow creeped me out. But it also explained why last month, when I missed my first period, Eddie hadn't come near me that week, even though we usually had sex every day.

"I've been meaning to ask you, though," Eddie said, breaking into my thoughts. "Those little packages you usually leave in the garbage, I haven't seen those around lately. And your tits are getting bigger. What the hell is up with that?"

Lise

"Tea?"

"Yes, please, Dean."

I've always hated tea, but since I was being called on the carpet, I figured I might as well be sociable about it.

We were in the dean's house, in his study, the mid-May sun streaming through the Victorian windows, casting wide shadows of the frames across the Oriental carpet. As he poured tea from the silver service, I studied his face for signs of what was to come.

Dean Jones had a long oval face and blue eyes that were friendly more often than not, and a horseshoe of black hair rimming his shiny pate. He always wore a three-piece dark suit, whatever the weather, whatever the fashion, and had manicured nails that were prettier than mine. When he smiled, his teeth were more equine than human, and as he was smiling now, it was tough to discern just exactly what was coming my way.

"Milk?" he offered.

My dad always said that only sissies put milk in their tea, but I figured if the dean was going to take milk in his, I might as well go along for the ride; and if I was going to hate the tea anyway, I might as well hate it even more.

"Yes, please," I said again, re-crossing my legs where I sat on the brown leather sofa.

Done with his host duties, the dean took a seat on the sofa with me. He was being too friendly, I thought. This couldn't possibly be good.

He lifted his china cup and took a sip, nodding as though he approved. "You know, Lise," he spoke, "this could all have been so much easier if you'd simply set up a meeting with me when I first requested one back in April."

God, I'd forgotten all about that until he'd just mentioned it. What had been going on that day he'd sent the e-mail? Oh, right. I'd received that worrisome e-mail from Sara saying she was sick in Africa. And then, of course, there'd been the book. I was just too preoccupied to bother about the usual departmental bullshit.

"I'm sorry, sir," I said. "I was very busy at the time and—"

"Too busy to answer a request from your boss? You do realize, don't you, that I am in fact your boss?"

"Of course. It's just that—"

"What's going on with you, Lise?" And here he looked sincerely concerned. "Are your mother and father all right?"

"They're both fine," I said, "but my sister Sara—you know, the one who's in Africa—became very sick there. She wound up in a Nairobi hospital for a month."

This was true. I hadn't said anything to Diana, Cindy, and Sylvia about it on the day of the party—Diana knew about Sara initially becoming sick but not about what came after—because I hadn't wanted to ruin everyone's good moods. And I hadn't said anything since because I didn't want to worry anyone else when they all had their own problems, but I worried every day about Sara.

"Did they find out what was wrong with her?" he asked.

I shrugged. "A parasite. Anyway, she's out now. She says she's not as strong as she used to be, but she refused to come home. Sara's determined to finish out her time there, but thankfully she should be back in a few weeks."

"Still," he said, "what an ordeal for her to go through. For you, as well. It must have been very frustrating having someone you love in a hospital so far away."

I conceded that it was.

"I can see," he added, "how something like that could distract one from one's job."

"I never said it distracted me," I pointed out, "merely that I was worried about her."

"Is there something else going on with you, then? How are things with Tony?"

I sat up straight in my seat. "Ex*cuse* me?"

"Oh, come on," he laughed. "Everyone knows about you and Tony. Why, it's as obvious as Sally Markham's eternal crush on Phillip Exeter."

"Tony and I are fine, thanks," I said settling back. "There are no problems there."

"Then what else could be taking your mind from your work?" he said.

I could have told him that in addition to worrying about my sister, daily, I also worried about how Diana was coping with the fallout from losing a lot of weight quickly, that I was concerned about Cindy's pregnancy, and that I wondered if Sylvia saw how much she was starting to care for her former surgeon and where it was all going to lead for her. But I didn't think he'd care about them, nor did I imagine he would understand my concern for women who would seem to him to be relative strangers in my life, so instead I said, "Who said my mind isn't on my work?"

He set down his china cup and saucer, and then rose and walked over to his desk. Then he put on his reading half-glasses and picked up a folder I hadn't noticed before.

"I've got your student evaluations of you as a teacher here," he said.

That's right. In the e-mail he'd sent me back in April—that e-mail I'd unwisely ignored—he'd said something about one of my students leveling a complaint at me. At the time, I suppose I'd unconsciously assumed the complainant must be John Quayle, that bane of my teacherly existence, and that John Quayle was such an obvious pompous ass—although there were certainly enough professors in the department who were like that too, not to mention the dean himself—that no one would ever take his complaints too seriously. Each year there was at least one English major who caused problems for one of the professors in the department. That professor had never been me, but I guessed that after years without a single nuisance complaint, it was finally my turn.

"It's John Quayle, isn't it?" I said now.

The dean flipped through the folder. "It is John Quayle," he said. "It's also Danitra Jackson and Tiffany Amber and Brad Moffett. It's all of them, really."

"*What?*"

"It's true," he said. "Every student in your writing class complained about you. The gist is that you were wonderful in the beginning of the semester but, as time wore on, you grew increasingly distant. One even says that you graded her on something she never wrote. Here: '*My* story was about a woman of color trying to balance romance and career in the big city, but Professor Barrett wrote on my paper that the extended metaphor involving cows was pretentious and didn't quite work for her. I didn't have any *cows* in my story!'"

Oh no. I'd mixed my evaluations of Danitra's work up with John's. God only knows what I'd written on *his* paper.

"One or two complaints, I can understand," the dean said. "Every teacher gets those, although you never have. But all of them?" He removed his glasses. "So I ask you one last time: What is going on with you?"

"Well, I suppose I was spending a lot of time on the novel—"

"What novel?"

So I told him about the novel I'd written, how first I'd written one, tossed it out, then wrote another.

"But that's *wonderful* news!" he said, and suddenly I could see departmental dollar signs dancing in his head. Finally, I was going to deliver on the promise he'd seen in me when he first hired me.

"How can it be wonderful," I said, "when all my students say I'm doing such a lousy job?"

"Oh. That." He made a dismissive gesture at the folder. "So you had one semester's worth of less-than-stellar evaluations. I'm sure you'll make it up in the fall. Do you think all famous novelists who are also university professors are always able to perfectly compartmentalize their creative lives from their teaching lives?"

Famous novelist? I thought he was laying it on a bit thick, seeing success where there were no guarantees, making him sound naive. After all, I didn't even really have an agent yet. But then I saw it through his eyes: When he first hired me, straight out of Iowa, he'd thought I'd be the Next Big Thing. Was it really surprising, then, now that I'd actually shown signs of working on a novel after all these years, that in his own mind he'd see a fairy-tale ending even though there was little basis for it?

As to his question about whether other novel-writing professors can compartmentalize their lives, I honestly had no idea. But I did have another idea, and it came to me in one of those Joycean epiphanies I was always telling my students about. For the first time I saw clearly that I couldn't wear two hats at once. Maybe Joyce Carol Oates could go on spinning out book after book while teaching at Princeton, but it turned out I was more of an all-or-nothing woman than I'd ever imagined. I couldn't go on doing both novel writing and teaching. One of the two was always bound to suffer. And I knew now which one it was I *couldn't* afford to let suffer.

And I saw something else. The reason I'd never responded to his e-mail about there being a complaint; my thinking about everything other than teaching; my inattention even in the classroom—all of it was because my heart was no longer in my work, not *this* work. My heart was somewhere else.

I took a deep breath. "I'm sorry, Dean, I know this will come as a shock to you, but I won't be coming back here in the fall."

"*What?*"

It took a lot of explaining and soothing on my part. And I could see the dean fighting to hold on to his dream of having a successful novelist in residence; which, when you think about it, is very funny, since there was no guarantee I'd ever sell the book, nor that it would be successful. But at last I made him see that I could never really take a chance on the one while still trying to do justice to the other.

And then I was out in the sunshine, ecstatically happy until the thought struck me: for the first time in over a dozen years, I was out of a job.

Diana

I set off down the driveway, water bottle in hand, taking my time because it was that hard to breathe. It wasn't the walking that bothered me—I was used to that by now—but the humidity! If anyone had told me it got this humid this early in the season in Connecticut, I'd have stayed in London.

"Dress cool today," Dan had warned before leaving for work that morning. "It's supposed to hit ninety today."

"*Ninety?* But it's not even June yet!" What a hot spring it had been. "What sort of an insane country is this?"

"One that's affected by global warming, just like everywhere else."

"Then it wasn't always this bad?"

"Nope. When I was growing up, winter was winter, spring was spring. But now? It could be ninety today, sixty-five tomorrow."

As I walked through the neighborhood, shocked at how hot and humid it was even so late in the afternoon, I wished it could be tomorrow so that I'd have a chance at that sixty-five. I also wished it were an hour from now, so I could go back home and check my e-mail again. Usually I walked for thirty minutes, forty-five tops, but today I'd committed to a full hour just to get myself out of the house.

When I first started walking, as soon as I could get around following the surgery, I'd attracted funny looks from people in passing cars. Not that the streets in our sleepy neighborhood were so very busy, but any people who passed through all gave me funny looks. Could I blame them? I must have looked ridiculous, this incredibly obese woman walking for a few minutes a day, as though that could matter. It was not so different really than ordering a diet cola to go with your all-you-can-eat buffet. But as the days piled up, and I kept walking farther and farther, the pounds melted off. Now the people who passed, at least the ones I recognized as being regulars in the neighborhood, usually gave me a silent thumbs-up when they saw me with my water bottle. It made me feel proud and walk a little faster, as though I had my own private fan club cheering me on.

The scale that morning said I was now down sixty-five pounds. Sixty-five would have made a great weather forecast, but it made an even better weight-loss number. At the rate I was going, if I could only keep it up, sometime next month I'd break two hundred pounds for the first time since I was a young teenager.

Numbers, numbers, numbers!

Some days, I got sick of it. But what else was there? How many minutes walked, how many calories or fat grams in a bit of food, the numbers on the scale, how many pounds lost, the decreasing sizes on the clothes I tried on each week at the store—my whole life was reduced to bloody numbers.

I had to admit it: I was bored here, lonely too. Oh, sure, I had Lise and Cindy and Sylvia, but they all had jobs during the day, and they had busy lives and relationships. But what did I have? I had numbers and e-mail.

I'd confessed as much to Artemis on the phone that day, not about the e-mail but about the boredom.

"Why don't you get a job?" she'd suggested.

Of course, before Dan and moving to America, I'd had a job. I'd been a videographer. I shot all the high-fashion runway shows, a truly masochistic job for a fat woman to have. What I'd really wanted was to be a documentary filmmaker, shooting people who did peculiar, almost obsolete jobs. But when the BBC kept refusing all my attempts, and the only places that would even accept my short films were small festivals where the highest hope was that twenty people in a smoky room might actually view my short all the way through, I sought more lucrative work with my camera equipment. Then I saw the ad for shooting runway shows. Apparently the design houses, even though they're physically at the shows, like to go over the tapes later, seeing what works and what doesn't once they're removed from the adrenaline rush that are the shows themselves. At first it was exciting going to places like Milan and Paris, shooting film in posh rooms, being up close with famous people who most other people get no closer to than snaps in the fashion magazines or on the screens of their TVs. But the reality of it as time wore on, listening to women who weren't much bigger than an X-ray debate about whether they can afford to eat another celery stick before slipping into their Lagerfeld or Balenciaga was shockingly boring.

And, as I say, it was masochistic. But the money was excellent. As the years passed, I became in high demand as an editor, meaning the design houses preferred I send someone else to shoot, leaving me in the booth to cut and splice, which was fine by me. And the money improved yet again. When I first went over to editing, Artemis questioned it.

"Doesn't the person with the camera make more?" she'd asked.

"No," I'd responded, delighted for once to know something she didn't. "The editor makes much more. Firstly, the day rate is higher. Also, a cameraman might spend one day shooting something that takes the editor two weeks to cut."

But I didn't want to go back to that now. I didn't need to go back to that now.

"Dan makes so much money," I'd told Artemis, "we don't really need for me to have a job."

"It's not a matter of *need* in that sense. It's a matter that you need to do something more than sit around that house all day. Don't you ever miss having a job where you were in high demand and earned your own nice living?"

I thought about it and realized it was true. Despite the fairy-tale quality of my meeting Dan, followed by our whirlwind romance and marriage, it had been hard leaving behind something I'd worked so long and so hard at, a world where I was valued.

"Yes, but I wouldn't know how to start up a similar career over here, and I don't know what other kind of job I could get. I can't imagine it would look very good to Dan's colleagues. 'My wife is an investment counselor,' one of them would say. 'Mine is a veterinarian,' another would say. 'What does yours do?' 'Oh, she just got a job at the mall,' Dan would reply. Can you picture that?"

Artemis had admitted she could indeed picture that, conceding it would be just awful, then she'd rung off, but not before promising to put her mind to the idea of how to keep me from going stir crazy here.

Of course I did already have something to keep me from going stir crazy, at least part of the time, I thought as I trudged up the drive, having seen that the hour was up and I could now go inside. And that something was what also kept me from seeking out a job that would take me away from home all day. I had my e-mails, from Dirk. But of course I hadn't told Artemis that.

Inside, I set my empty water bottle down on the kitchen counter before doing my version of racing up the stairs. In the bedroom, I quickly looked at the computer screen, which I'd left on, but there were no new e-mails, unless of course you counted spam, which I didn't. I glanced at the clock. It would be eleven in the evening in England now. Where was he?

The first e-mail had been waiting for me when I'd arrived home from my transatlantic trip just a few short weeks ago.

> From: dirk.peters@dirkliterary.uk
> To: dananddiana@comcast.net
> It was such a pleasure meeting you. How does your husband like your new hair?

And then it had continued from there. The first day or two, there had been just the one e-mail—Dirk writing a one-liner to ask how I was doing, me replying—but then those e-mails began to multiply, like two rabbits left unattended. By the time the first week was out, Dirk was writing me enough times a day for Dan to comment on it.

"You must have made quite an impression on Artemis's friend," he'd said. "But isn't he a literary agent? And isn't Lise the one who wrote a book? Don't tell me he wants *you* to write a book too."

So then I took to deleting the string of e-mails between us before Dan came home from work at night, but one day I just got busy with something and forget to do it. Dan saw them again and commented again.

That was when I opened a new e-mail account. And I didn't tell Dan.

Dan and I used to share one account. It had just been simpler that way. There was nothing either of us didn't want the other to see. But now? It wasn't that there was anything *wrong* with the things Dirk wrote to me, and yet Dan had already noted the frequency, twice. Why ruffle him? Dan had so much on his mind all the time, what with work and everything.

The e-mails themselves were innocent enough: Dirk asking me how the weight loss was going, encouraging me, asking about what it was like growing up as Artemis's sister. He even had me e-mail him pictures of myself as I grew progressively smaller. Dirk had also asked to see Lise's new book, a request I'd forwarded on to her, only this time he was taking his time commenting on it. She'd told me she was sure he must hate it.

Where was he?

Then a new e-mail popped into my inbox and there he was.

From: dirk.peters@dirkliterary.uk
To: dianat@yahoo.com
Diana, luv, sorry I'm late. You would not *believe* how dull some of these literary dinners can be. Bloody fucking Booker. Why don't they just give the next twelve to McEwan and have done with it? Now, then, where were we? And what have you been up to while I was gone?

I pictured him ripping off the confining tie of his tux with one hand as he typed with the other. It made an attractive picture. Then I set my hands to the keys, and replied.

Memorial Day

Sailboats kept out of the way of speedboats trailing water skiers, a floating raft bobbed in the distance, and sunlight stippled the dark blue waves of Candlewood Lake. The small beach was already crowded with people taking early advantage of the long holiday weekend, and at the water's edge, a sullen boy in long navy trunks and a resiliently sunny girl in a glittery red, white, and blue one-piece suit were fighting over a Styrofoam noodle; it appeared the girl would win. Farther up the beach, four women sat on two large striped towels that had been placed together, a cooler and picnic basket between them. It was the Saturday morning of Memorial Day weekend, and Sylvia, Cindy, Lise, and Diana had managed to escape the real world for the time being, carving out a few hours together.

"Shouldn't you be working today?" Cindy asked Sylvia. Cindy's face was tilted up to catch the sun, her question lazily asked with no urgency or judgment.

"Advantage of being your own boss," Sylvia said. "I just put the sign on the door. It's an important day, Memorial Day, a day to remember those you've lost even if they weren't soldiers. People can just cook their own meals today if they want to eat."

"Just don't try that attitude every day," Lise advised, rubbing suntan lotion into her arm. "You might find yourself out of a job."

"Nah," Sylvia said. "I've got the TV show now. Or at least I will, once it's on."

"How's that going?" Diana asked. The other three were all in bathing suits—Cindy in a yellow polka dot bikini, Lise in a red tankini, and Sylvia in a navy suit that looked ten years old—but Diana had yet to take off the floral caftan she had covering hers.

"You'll know how it's going when you see me on TV," Sylvia said with a rare devilish smile. Then: "Some days I wonder if those TV people know what they're doing. But me, I just keep cooking." She turned to Lise. "You're a fine one to talk about being out of a job. I can't believe you just quit teaching. What did Tony say?"

Lisa gave a rueful grin. "Plenty."

"*Tony?*" Cindy opened eyes that were filled with shock. "But I'm sure everything he said was positive…right?"

Another grin, this time wry and tinged with resentment. "Not exactly. You'd think the man I've been sleeping with for the past few years would be supportive at least, but no such luck."

"I can't believe that!" Diana said. "What did he say?"

Lise tilted her head, considering. "I believe his exact words were, 'How the hell do you plan to pay your mortgage without a job?'"

"No!" Diana said.

"He has a point," Sylvia muttered.

"Yes," Lise countered Diana, ignoring Sylvia. "Believe me, I'm an adult. I have my financial bases covered. I just wish Tony would treat me like one. So I said, 'What's it to you? *You* don't pay my mortgage.' It just got better from there. Apparently, Tony always looked upon my writing as a hobby."

"So that's it?" Cindy asked. "You and Tony are breaking up?"

Lise looked at her strangely. "Of course not. It's just one fight. It'll all work out." Then she sighed. "But maybe he's right. Maybe it is just a hobby. I'm sure if the second book was any good, I'd have heard from Dirk Peters by now."

"Funny," Diana said, "Dirk hasn't mentioned your book lately."

Lise sat up straighter. "You've talked to him?"

Diana moved back a bit. "Not *talked*. We e-mail." Then in a quieter voice but with a certain pride she added, "Every day."

"Hey," Lise laughed, "you're not trying to steal my agent from me, are you? Not that he's *my* agent...yet."

"Of course not." Diana reddened. "We've just found that, well, we have a lot of things to talk about." She squinted up at the sun as though angry with it. "God, it's getting hot out."

"So take off that caftan," Sylvia suggested.

Slowly, like a virgin on her wedding night, Diana removed the outer garment to reveal a new black bathing suit. She was still a large woman, but she was much less large than she had been.

"Wow," Sylvia said, "you look fantastic. See? I was right. I told Cindy to get pregnant, I told Lise to write a book, and I told you to lose weight. Everybody listened to me and everything's working out great for everybody."

"Fat lot of good it's doing for me," Diana said.

"What does that mean?" Sylvia asked.

"It means Dan never even touches me anymore."

"What?" Cindy said.

"Oh, he touches me," Diana said brusquely. "I mean, it's not like he never kisses me good-bye. But we used to have sex nearly every day. Lately, though? It's like I have the plague or something. You'd think he'd want me more now, not less, wouldn't you?" She shook her head as though the shaking would make the thoughts go away. "I can't believe how hot it is already." She looked out at the water. "Do you think we might swim out to that raft over there?"

The lake was cool against their skin and the other three got to the floating wooden raft before Diana did. They waited then held it in place so she could climb on first. Once they were all aboard, Cindy spoke.

"How are things going with Sunny?" she asked Sylvia.

"How many times do I have to tell you? We're just friends."

"I never said you weren't friends. I just asked how things were going."

"Not good," Sylvia said.

"Oh, no!" Diana said. "What's wrong?"

"I think Sunny wants to be more than friends."

"And what's wrong with *that*?" Lise wanted to know.

Sylvia shrugged. "I don't know. Maybe I keep feeling like he must be putting me on. I mean, why would he want to be with me? I don't know. I guess I just keep thinking about Minnie."

"What does that have to do with anything?" Cindy asked.

Sylvia just shrugged again. Then: "I guess it's just Memorial Day, and I'm missing my sister."

"Wow," Cindy said after a moment, "it's so weird. It's like everyone is having man trouble except me."

Sylvia snorted so loud, it was impossible to ignore her.

"What's that supposed to mean?" Cindy said.

"You're not having *any* trouble with Eddie?" Sylvia said. "Like, none at all?"

Cindy looked confused. "Well, he did get mad at this guy I was shooting pool with a couple of weeks ago."

"He got mad at the guy just for shooting pool with you?" Sylvia said.

"Well, sure," Cindy said. "But that's just Eddie. Stuff like that just bothers him, I guess."

"It's not normal," Sylvia said, "for someone to get that mad over a pool game. And what was Eddie doing while you were shooting pool?"

"He was at the bar, having a drink with some girl who bought him one."

"Weren't you jealous?"

"No." Cindy shrugged. "Girls are always buying Eddie drinks after shows."

"And yet he felt like he had the right to get mad at you just for shooting pool?"

"Well, not just that." Cindy squirmed. "He was also mad because the guy asked me out. The guy was someone I used to know back in high school. He's always been really sweet. But I said no of course."

"And did he hear you say no?"

"Well, yeah. It was right before he attacked the guy. But can you blame him for getting jealous?"

"*God!*" Sylvia said, banging her hand down on the raft.

"What?" Cindy said.

"Why are you with that guy?"

"You mean Eddie?" Cindy was puzzled. "Because he's wonderful and he loves me. Because—"

"Yeah, yeah, I know all that. He hates blind people, and he thinks everyone should just get their own fucking rock 'n' roll bands. I get all that. That Eddie's a real great guy." Pause. "But why are you with him?"

Diana

From: dianat@yahoo.com
To: dirk.peters@dirkliterary.uk
I used to sit in movie houses watching *Flashdance*. I must have seen Jennifer Beals get hit by that bucket of water while she sat in that cabaret chair, must have seen her soar through the air and then dance on the judges' table in her legwarmers a hundred times. I used to walk down the streets of London hearing that soundtrack in my head as though it could possibly score my life:

"I can't have it all, now I'm dancin' for my life"

Even tore the necklines, tore the sleeves off my sweatshirts, and wore pink legwarmers. "You can dance right through your life!" As if any of that was going to happen; as if I was ever going to soar through the air. It was pathetic, really. Do you have any idea what it's like to go through your entire life knowing it doesn't matter what you do or what you accomplish, you'll never achieve your ideal?

D

I'd written it the previous night before going to bed, and now here was my response.

From: dirk.peters@dirkliterary.uk
To: dianat@yahoo.com
You wanted to be Jennifer Beals then? But don't you realize, D? Jennifer Beals wasn't even Jennifer

Beals! There was that other woman—what was her name again?—who it turned out did all the major dancing for her. Just like someone else did the singing for Natalie Wood in *West Side Story*. You know, it's funny when you think about it: all over the world people dream of being someone they see on the silver screen, but when you get right down to it, half the time it's someone else doing the parts they most want to be like. Don't long to be other people, D, just long to be more yourself.

D

P.S. I'm fairly certain the lyric is "I *can* have it all..." Or if it's not, it should be.

Hearing Dan's alarm go off, I shut off the computer. It was still so early in the morning that, once the glowing screen was off, the room went dark and I had to blink against it. Grabbing the new clothes I'd set out the night before, I went into the bathroom. Before stepping into the shower, however, I stepped on the scale, but first I closed my eyes.

For the past week, I'd been frozen at two hundred pounds, and it was making me feel crazy, not to mention worthless. *Come on, 199!* I'd tell myself. *Come on!* Was it so much to ask? Was I doomed to spend the rest of my life seeing that annoying two as the first digit in my weight? It wasn't fair! I was doing all the work: walking, eating properly. The day before I'd walked an extra hour in the heat and for dinner I'd only allowed myself a small green salad with lemon squeezed on top in place of dressing. I'd eaten that dinner at four-thirty in the afternoon, not allowing myself even a glass of water between then and bedtime. I wanted to see the scale move that badly.

If this had been my scale back in London, one of those old-fashioned ones with the moving needle, I'd have leaned over to the right as far as possible without falling off to take some of the weight off the scale, eyeballing the number through my left eye. That was always good for taking off a few quick pounds. But this bloody modern scale wouldn't let me do that. No matter where I moved on it, it always knew exactly what I weighed.

At last, I opened one eye, slowly, squinting down at the number beneath me.

199!

Yes! Yes!! *Yes!!!*

I stepped into the steaming shower, vowing not to eat more than a piece of fruit for breakfast, foregoing the usual dry toast, so that the scale wouldn't betray me by jumping back to 200 the next day. But who needed toast? I was jubilant.

I was a woman who weighed 199.

◦ ◦ ◦

Layla Kozinsky looked to be a woman who weighed ninety-nine. She also looked perfect in her pink polo shirt and matching miniskirt, with her long chestnut ponytail pulled through the gap in the back of her pink visor, pink leather gloves on her hands.

Richter was a sea of vivid green, the golf course spread out before us.

I'd met Robert, Layla's husband, before when he'd come to the house to work on something with Dan. Robert was one of Dan's vice presidents, one of those bald men with a slight paunch who wore it all with a confidence that said, "It doesn't matter what I look like, does it? I'm making so much money, *you'll* talk to me anyway."

Six months ago, I'd have never agreed to such an outing—a foursome for golf, a game I'd never played—but when Dan suggested it this time, I'd been game.

"But you'll need to take a few lessons first," Dan had cautioned. "I hate to put it like this, but golf is a sport that's very big on etiquette and it would be considered extremely bad form to have a total novice on the course. Would you mind terribly?"

I'd told Dan of course I wouldn't mind, but when the day for my first lesson with the golf pro arrived, I called in sick, preferring to go shopping, telling Dan when he'd called later that day that the first lesson had gone well. The idea of a strange man standing behind me, staring at my big butt as I tried to master my swing, was too much. And besides, how hard could golf be?

If nothing else, I'd figured golf would present a great opportunity to take up a new sport, and a great opportunity to buy new clothes for that sport in a lower size than I'd ever worn as an adult. Now, as I stood before Layla, who was her all pink glory, in my new belted tan trousers with my navy polo shirt tucked in, I was sorry I'd come.

"Diana," Robert said, pecking me on the cheek, "it's always good to see you."

"Dan," Layla said, her voice flowing out like liquid silver. Then she kissed him straight on the lips and linked arms with him before turning to me. "Diana, such a pleasure to finally meet. Where has Dan been hiding you?"

As if someone could hide a 200-pound wife. OK, 199. But still. I didn't hide easy.

"Is everyone ready to play?" Layla's voice glittered.

"I'm not sure…" I said vaguely, suddenly daunted at the idea of playing a game I didn't know anything about, really. Thankfully, Dan came to my rescue.

"This is Diana's first time playing with others," Dan said, "so perhaps I'd better help her a bit."

He set up that impossibly small ball on its even tinier tee, selected a club or an iron; I couldn't tell the two apart. Then he positioned my body and got his arms around me from behind as best he could, placing his hands over mine as he demonstrated how I was supposed to hit the ball.

I'm not sure what he had in mind for me, but I'm fairly certain it didn't involve striking the golfing instrument he'd given me into the ground and churning up dirt.

"When you used the phrase 'first time playing with others,'" Layla observed coolly, "I assumed you meant it was her first time playing *here*. I had no idea you meant it was her first time holding a club *anywhere*."

I resented Layla talking about me that way, as though I wasn't even there, like maybe I was a comical character she was watching on the TV, a character who couldn't hear her remarks. I also resented the intimacy with which she spoke to my husband.

And it only got better from there.

The men both hit the ball very nicely. Well, they would, wouldn't they? It being their game and all. Layla had elected to go last, and when it was her turn, her body became one fluid line as she swung upward, sending the ball soaring into the sky.

"Wow," Dan said enthusiastically, "that may not have been a hole in one, but it was pretty damn close."

"Do you remember when we played together at Trump International," Layla said, "and you bet me a hundred dollars I couldn't hit under par on the eleventh hole?"

"How could I forget?" Dan said. "That's a hundred dollars I'll never see again."

"Did you mind very much?" she teased.

"Not at all," Dan said. "It was a thrill watching you play that day."

She caressed the side of his neck with her iron, which I'd finally figured out was an iron since the whole thing was, well, iron. It was such an odd move for her to make, and I felt like she was trying to hook him with the thing, show possession.

"It's always thrilling," she said, "when we play together."

I wanted to snatch that iron out of her hand and smash it over her pink visor.

Robert and I might not have even been there. Oh, Dan was always very patient with me, helping me line up my shots when it was my turn, even though he must have realized how futile it was, and I suppose he may have been just a tad frustrated, since surely he must have realized I hadn't exactly made the most of the lessons he'd paid for. But the rest of the time? It was as though he and Layla were on a date, with Robert and me as chaperoning parents, trailing behind.

Robert, walking beside me, cleared his throat. "You mustn't mind them," he said with a nod of his head at the two beautiful people walking on ahead of us. "They're always like this when they're in the same room together or on the same golf course, as it were. Layla and Dan go way back."

"How far back do they go?"

"Let's see…I've been with Dan for ten years now, and Layla and I were already married when he hired me, so it's been ten years."

Ten years.

Dan and I had been married less than six months and hadn't known each other all that long before marrying. It was a drop in the bucket compared to how long he'd known Layla. Funny, but as the wife, you assume, based on your union, that you know your partner better than anyone else in the world. But the amount of time I'd known Dan, been with him, was nothing when taken against the history of *ten years.* Ten years of golfing together. Ten years of company parties. *Ten years.*

Even as I listened to them laughing ahead of us, I told myself it didn't matter. I was Dan's wife, not her, even if she was acting like it. Moreover, I had Dirk, didn't I, and his e-mails?

The June sun had risen higher in the cloudless sky, and I could no longer ignore the nausea of not eating anything much that morning, and not having had enough to drink. Damn, I should have brought my water bottle with me. Double damn, I should have worn a jaunty little visor like perfect Layla to keep the worst of the heat off of my face. Oh, well. Nothing for it now.

I stood before the ball and tee on the ninth hole getting dizzier by the minute. Beside me, as through a wall of water, I heard Dan's voice encouraging, "Come on, Diana, I know you can do it this time."

And I wanted to do it. I really wanted to do it for him.

I pulled the club back to the right, swung upward to the left, and felt the world spinning around me, never even knowing if I'd successfully hit the ball that time or not as the earth melted away and I blacked out.

Lise

I could never drive by the Fairfield train station without thinking of 9/11. Not long after that ineffably horrible event, the papers ran a picture of the commuter lot the following morning. It was empty, save for a few scattered cars—cars whose owners would never be coming home. At the time I'd imagined similar scenes in commuter lots all up and down the Metro North line.

A few months after 9/11, I attended a professional conference in Iowa that had professors from all over the country. Everyone was still talking about the tragedy all the time in those days, and yet for the first time I realized people processed it differently. Oh, to be sure, it was difficult for everybody. But in Connecticut, everyone I knew, if they didn't personally know someone who died that day, knew someone who lost someone. It was that close: just one degree of separation.

And the emotional devastation never got any better. In college, I'd taken a course in psychology where I'd learned all about systematic desensitization, the process through which people exposed to violence in the media become less sensitive as time goes on. And yet here was the thing: every time I saw pictures of those two towers coming down, even five years later, I didn't grow less sensitive, but more so. It got worse and worse, never better; it got harder to look at.

"Have you talked to Diana since that first call after she passed out at the golf course?" Tony asked.

"Every day," I said. "She promises she'll be careful to eat more, but I worry."

"Speaking of food, what do you think your folks will serve?" Tony asked.

"The usual," I said, looking out the window, breathing easier now that the train station had passed. "Or maybe they'll surprise us. One or the other."

My parents were having a picnic at the home I'd grown up in to honor Sara's safe arrival home from Africa.

Everyone else was already there, I could see from the cars lined up when we pulled into the drive: my parents, cousins, my father's family, and my mother's older sister Tess, ten years senior to Mom's sixty-two. I didn't recognize the emaciated bald woman who threw open the screen door, racing across the lawn toward the car before it was even stopped. But as I opened the passenger door and heard her shout "Lise!" I sure recognized that voice.

"Sara!" I shouted back, stunned, catching her up in my arms so that her feet came clear off the ground—she was that light. Then: "What happened to your hair?"

"Oh, that." She laughed. "After I got out of the hospital in Nairobi, I kept imagining there were bugs in my hair, so finally I just shaved it all off." She shrugged, smiled. "And then I just kept it that way."

I looked at her. Even without hair, she was beautiful, a constant laugh in her dark eyes. Her skin, though, had an unsettlingly uneven quality to the coloring, her face much darker than her scalp. The latter having been exposed to the African sun for a shorter duration.

"Come on," she said, after giving Tony a quick hug. "Everyone else is out back at the pool."

In the backyard, my dad was already manning the grill, with an unlit cigar clamped in his mouth, a Mets cap jammed low on his head, and his diamond pinkie ring glittering as he poked at whatever mystery meats he was cooking. Oh, sure, there were the usual hamburgers and hot dogs. But just for fun, every now and then my dad liked to throw something like venison steak into the mix without telling anybody. At least the rabbit I could always identify. "Princess," he said, tilting his cheek to receive a kiss.

"Art, do you need more rolls?" my mom screamed out the back door.

"How could I need more," my dad answered her without looking up, "when I haven't even served anything yet?"

. . .

Two hours later, and everyone had eaten so much food we were like a group of waddling ducks, funnel-fed grain for foie gras. Even Sara had managed to put away a surprising amount, although she'd eaten tentatively at first.

"More cake, anyone?" my mom offered.

"Give it a rest with the food, Ann," my dad said.

"I'll take another beer," Tony called out from the pool. Despite my mother's admonition that no one go swimming until at least thirty minutes after eating, Tony was already back in the water. "I'll stay on the chair raft, promise," he'd told her. "And if I tip over and sink? Maybe, just maybe, Lise will save me."

If it was OK for Tony to break the rules, then it was OK for the cousins, and they soon joined him. That left me with Sara, my parents, and Aunt Tess at the redwood table, under the umbrella.

Aunt Tess adjusted her bathing suit cover-up, a polyester floral thing with some seriously scary mutant-sized flowers, and leaned over, tapping Sara's wrist with one long gnarled finger to get her attention.

"Now that you've got Africa out of your system," she said, "what do you plan to do?"

"God, I barely just got home and it's Sunday," Sara said. "Do you want me to go out looking for work *today?*"

"Tomorrow would be nice," my dad said, adding, "I'm kidding!" when he saw the horrified look on Sara's face. "You know, though, your grandfather always said how important it was to have a steady paycheck."

It was true. Both sets of grandparents had inculcated my parents as children with the value of a dollar and the importance of saving for a rainy day. This advice had served my parents well: they had a large house in Fairfield, on which they'd long since paid for the mortgage, and they'd been able to pay for both daughters' college educations without anyone having to take out a loan. But none of that took away from the fact that it had been a bitch repeatedly getting subjected to "The Money Talk" growing up.

"I don't know yet what I'm going to do next." Sara shrugged. "Maybe go to work for Habitat for Humanity?"

"Oh," my dad snorted, "*that* sounds like something that'll come with a steady paycheck."

"At least the things Sara does constitute 'good works'," my mother said.

"What about you, Lise?" Sara turned to me. "What are you going to do now that you left your job?"

I'd been so busy missing and worrying about Sara the past year, I'd forgotten this about her: how good she'd always been at shifting the attention to me when the focusing light grew too hot for her. And of course I'd told her about my move in an e-mail right after I'd made the decision.

I just hadn't told my parents yet.

"What the hell's she talking about?" my dad said. "She's kidding, right?"

I felt all eyes on me.

"No," I said, "she's not. I gave notice at the university."

"Don't tell me you're going to become one of these charity workers too!" he said.

"No," I said evenly, "I quit so I could devote all my energies to revising the novel I've written."

"Oh, Lise." My mom's words dripped disappointment. "I thought you gave up on that silly dream ages ago."

"It's not silly," I said, "but it does require all my energy. I'll never make it if I'm working full time."

"When will the book be in stores?" Aunt Tess asked. "I can't wait to buy it. I love to read."

I was grateful for her enthusiasm, even if it was naïve.

"I'm afraid it doesn't work like that," I said. "It's not as easy as just writing the book and then—poof!—it's published and I'm John Grisham. Once I finish revising it, I'll need to find an agent. And if I can find an agent, then I'll have to hope and pray the agent can interest an editor who will then publish it."

"Sounds more complicated than I thought," she said. "Is that hard? Finding an agent?"

"I think usually it must be," I said. Then, despite my tendency to be cautious, I allowed myself to get a little excited as I spoke. "But a friend of mine, Diana Taylor, hooked me up with this literary agent in England. In the beginning he was dreadful, at least about the first novel. But then I wrote this second book and sent it off to him. For the longest time he was silent, but lately he's been e-mailing me about it and—"

"You never said you heard from Dirk Peters again," Tony interrupted from the pool.

"Sorry," I said. "You haven't shown much interest in my writing lately."

"Well, what did he say?"

"He said he likes it, mostly, but he says he wants…changes."

"What kind of —"

"Who cares about some Dirk Peters?" my dad said. "What I want to know is: How do you plan to pay the mortgage now that you're out of a job?"

"Exactly," my mom said. "It's not like novel writing is in any way 'good works,' not like what your sister does. At least if it was something like that…"

"That's what I wanted to know," Tony said, propelling the chair raft by lazily paddling the water. "How is she going to pay the mortgage? But she never has an answer."

* * *

Not long afterward, some of the others were piling into their cars, arms filled with aluminum-covered leftovers, when Aunt Tess came up to me and pulled me aside.

"You know," she said, "my father always said to get a good job and never quit that job until you have a new one lined up."

Not her too, I groaned inwardly.

"I believe I may have heard something like that somewhere before," I said, arms crossed.

"Hey," she said. "I was born during the Depression. Jobs weren't something to take lightly, certainly not good ones. But there was something else my dad taught me, two things really: one, always save ten percent of what you make; even if someone gives you ten cents, you save a penny."

"It sounds like great advice," I said, while inside I was thinking, *Who can afford to do that? No one I know does that.* "And what was the second thing?" I asked, more to be kind than out of any real interest. I always liked Aunt Tess. "You said your father taught you two things."

A devilish gleam entered her eye.

"The other thing my dad taught me was, never trust banks," she said.

"What are you saying, Aunt Tess?" I asked, my eyes narrowing because now she really did have my interest.

"I'm saying my father convinced my husband, your uncle, about his finance theories. When your uncle was still alive, he used to bury ten percent of everything we made in mason jars out in the backyard."

"You're telling me you've got a fortune in your backyard?"

"Of course not." She dismissed my ignorance with a wave. "After your uncle died, I dug it all up one night and put it in brown paper bags, then I put all the bags up on the top shelf of the closet in my bedroom. I was sick of not being able to have a garden."

"Just how much is in those paper bags?" I asked.

"Enough," she said, smiling with certitude. "Enough to last you a good long while, however long it takes to get your book published which, the good Lord willing, will be soon."

I couldn't believe she would do this for me. And, by the way, was she *crazy*? A part of me wondered what she did at night, alone with her money. Did she go through it, count it, turn small bills into bigger ones?

"But why, Aunt Tess?" I said. "Why would you give me some of your hard-earned savings? You and Uncle Henry saved it. That money should be yours."

"Why?" she echoed my question. Then she took my hand in hers. "Because I wish I'd had the nerve when I was younger to do what you're doing now. Saving ten percent and living safe is for the birds. Write your book, Lise. Write the best book you know how."

I hugged her.

"Thanks, Aunt Tess, but I don't need your help, not just yet."

"What do you mean?"

I could feel my eyes twinkle. "I've got my own jars filled with money in the backyard."

"You do?"

"Well, no. That was a metaphor. But I do have money saved, enough to last me a while."

"How long is a while?"

"Long enough to give myself a fair chance at this novel-writing thing."

She laughed. "But why didn't you tell Tony that? Or your parents? Get them off your back."

"Because, I'm tired of being treated like a child who can't be depended upon to think things through for herself like an adult. I'll bet if I were a thirty-seven-year-old *man*, everyone wouldn't be questioning my judgment at every turn. Tell me, if you were me, what would you do?"

Her laugh was practically a cackle. "I'd let them keep squirming." She paused, considering. "And I'd move my money to paper bags in the top of the closet."

Cindy

Six weeks after the night at the Bar None, I was home alone, trying to get the damn computer to work right, when there was a knock at the door. Eddie had another gig at the Bar None, but I'd pleaded out of going, saying I wasn't feeling well. In truth, I was feeling great. I'd had my monthly visit with the obstetrician that morning—I was twelve weeks' pregnant, if the OB's projections were correct—and heard my baby's heartbeat for the first time. It was so strong and it was amazing to think that now there wasn't just one heart, my own, beating within my body, but two.

I was so mad at the computer. One of the reasons I'd stayed home—well, aside from the fact that I simply did not want to go—was so I could get some work done for one of my classes. But the Internet link, which ran through the phone line, got interrupted by a prank call. And no matter how many times I tried to get back online, I kept getting a message on the screen saying that attempts to connect had failed. Damn technology! How was I supposed to work so I could get smart so I could leave behind my job at Midnight Scandals forever if I couldn't even access the Internet? And the help link was useless. Whatever that purple question mark was telling me, I didn't get it; I just could not be helped.

Knock, knock.

"I'm coming!" I shouted, reluctantly leaving the uncooperative computer behind to open the door and fly down the long interior flight of stairs from our apartment door to the door at the bottom that led to the sidewalk and the street outside.

I was in such a hurry to get back to what I'd been doing, or *trying* to do, that I didn't even bother to ask who it was. Maybe Eddie had forgotten his key? But that didn't make any sense. It was only ten o'clock at night. Eddie should just be starting his second set and wouldn't even be home for another two hours, probably three.

I flung open the door just as my caller was raising his hand to knock again.

"What are you doing here?" I said, seeing who it was. Not the friendliest greeting, I'll admit, but I was that stunned.

It was Porter.

"Can I come in?" he asked.

He was dressed differently than he had been the night I'd shot pool with him at the Bar None, the night Eddie got so mad. Instead of business clothes, he had on khakis with a button-down white shirt and loafers without socks on his feet. It was the kind of outfit Eddie hated seeing on other guys, calling them "preppies" or "yuppies" and claiming they were stuck up. It was the kind of outfit I'd talked him into wearing that day we'd gone to Lise's book-finishing celebration party.

My eyes narrowed. I was tempted to just turn him away, but I was desperate.

"Do you know anything about computers?" I asked.

• • •

Porter sat at my computer, completely at home with the mouse. I couldn't help but contrast it with the awkward look Eddie always had when he sat there trying to download music.

"It's usually just something simple," Porter said. "Did you try calling the help line?"

"No, should I?"

"Probably not." He shrugged. "Every time I call it takes forever to get through, and then they only reroute my call to some guy in India who says, 'And how may I make your day even better, sir?' That might sound racist, but that's exactly what happens."

He fiddled around some more, and when he still couldn't log on, he clicked the help link for troubleshooting.

"Um, Cindy?" he said.

"Yeah?"

"Did you check the phone first?"

"What?"

"The phone. Where is it?"

I showed him the wall phone in the kitchen. Even I could see that after the prank call earlier, when I'd replaced the phone, I hadn't put it completely on the hook. As he picked it up, I could hear the automated voice saying, "Please hang up and try again. If you need assistance…"

Carefully, Porter replaced the phone on the hook, and then picked it up to check for a dial tone before putting it down again.

"Problem solved," he said. "And you didn't even have to call India."

"Great," I said. "Now I can get back to work."

"Aren't you going to at least offer me a drink?" he said. "After all, I did put your phone back on the hook for you."

"What are you doing here?" I asked a second time. Maybe I should have been more gracious after he'd made it so I could use my computer once more, but he did only have to put the phone on the hook. It wasn't like he'd had to take it apart and put it back together again or anything like that.

He leaned back against the counter, arms loosely crossed like he had all the time in the world. It was funny, because if I'd gone to the apartment of someone I barely knew and that person asked me what I was doing there, I'd have gotten the hell out.

"Ever since that night at the Bar None," he said, "I haven't been able to stop thinking about you."

"You must have been doing a lot of thinking," I said, keeping my distance, "or you must lead a pretty empty life, because that was weeks ago."

But I might as well not have said anything, because Porter just kept on talking.

"There you were, this sharp, funny girl, just like I remembered you from back in high school. You could even shoot a good game of pool—something I didn't know about you back then. Then your boyfriend comes along and terrifies you, steals the light right out of your eyes, and spoils all the fun."

"I was not terrified of Eddie. It was just time to go."

"I would have gone after you. I was worried about what he might do. But I've read enough to know that sometimes, if people try to intervene, it only makes it worse for the victim afterward. Besides, when I called to you, you just ignored me and kept on walking."

"I'm not a victim. I don't know what you're talking about. It was just time to go, like I said. How did you find me here anyway?"

"I've been trying to find you since that night. I looked for a number, but you're not listed. Then I tried calling your old number and your dad answered, said you were living with Eddie when I asked after you. 'That scumbag,' were, I believe, his exact words, but he just hung up when I asked what your new number was. I've checked at the Bar None every weekend but haven't seen you or Eddie since. Then, when I saw Eddie walk into the Bar None tonight and you were not with him, I asked around if anyone knew where Eddie lived. It's amazing. Everyone at the Bar None knows Eddie. I figured while he was playing, it'd be safe for me to stop by here, see if you were really OK."

"What did you expect to find, me hacked to death in the freezer? Look at me." I held my arms out. "I'm fine. You might as well have saved yourself the time and stayed to listen to the band. Eddie's really good."

"No, he's not, Cindy. Eddie's not good in any way, shape, or form."

"Look, I've had about enough of you. You—"

"Why are you with that guy?"

"What?" The words stopped me cold. I'd heard those words somewhere before.

"I just don't get it," Porter said. "You've got everything going for you."

"No, I don't! How can you say that?"

"How can you not? You're sharp, you're funny, you're sweet, you play a mean game of stick, you're even great to look at—always have been. You've got everything going for you, even if you're the only one who can't see it. But Eddie? Eddie's just one mean son of a bitch. Anyone can see that. If he was a dog, someone would have to shoot him in the yard."

"Why are you with that guy?" Sylvia had asked me that the day we'd all gone to Candlewood Lake for our pre-Memorial Day picnic. At the time, I hadn't answered her. Well, I couldn't answer her. And I couldn't answer her because the question was all wrong. The question everyone should have been asking was, "Why is Eddie with you?"

Didn't any of them get it? Eddie was the smart one, not to mention drop-dead gorgeous. Eddie was the talented one, the one with ambition. I was lucky to have him, because who was I next to someone like that? I wasn't pretty like Diana, or smart like Lise, or talented like Sylvia with her cooking. I was just a dumb blonde who couldn't do any better than a job at Midnight Scandals. And if I ever lost Eddie, who would I be then? I'd be no one. I'd be alone. There wasn't another guy in the world who'd ever put up with me.

"Eddie is not a dog," I said. "You come by my home, uninvited. Sure, we used to be friends, once upon a time, and you fixed my computer problem for me and I thank you for that. But now you're insulting the guy I live with, the guy I *love*, and I'm asking you to leave."

"I just think you should think about what you're doing with your life. I think you should—"

"Get out," I said, grabbing him by the collar and pulling him toward the stairs. "Get out. Get out! Get *out!*"

"Fine, I'm going," he said, wrenching his collar from my grasp. "But do me a favor first." He reached into his pocket, pulled out some expensive-looking leather wallet from which he removed a business card, and then handed it to me. The card has his name, Porter Davis, and a number. "Look, if you ever need anything, anything at all—"

"Just go," I said. Then I closed the door.

● ● ●

I stood with my back to the door, fingering the card in my hand. I was madder than I'd been in forever.

How could they all be so wrong about Eddie? Oh, Lise and Diana hadn't said anything that day at Candlewood Lake, and their men had been nice enough the day of Lise's party. But maybe they were all thinking what Sylvia said. And then there was this Porter, straight-as-an-arrow Porter, showing up out of the blue, echoing Sylvia, butting his nose into my business.

I needed to show them all. I needed to show every one of them once and for all that they were wrong about Eddie, that he was the perfect guy for me.

But how?

Then it came to me: a party. Everyone else in the club had entertained the other members in their homes. Well, except for Sylvia, who'd had us all to her shop, which was practically the same thing. But none of them had ever been invited to a gathering at my apartment, which could maybe be why they doubted how good Eddie and I were together. They needed to come to our home and see us here together. I'd invite them all tomorrow, for the end of the month.

And I'd show them. I'd show them all.

Sylvia

"Cindy was here last night."

Lise and I were in my condo, sitting on the lavender sectional in the living room, drinking coffee with a shot of Kahlua in each cup, and snacking on éclairs I'd brought home from the shop. They'd be too old to serve to customers in the morning, but they were still fine now.

I didn't usually have visitors—OK, I *never* had visitors except for last night and today—but I hadn't felt like spending one more night by myself, rattling around in my fourteen hundred square feet: two bedrooms and bath up; half bath, living room, smaller dining room and ridiculously tiny kitchen down; and finished basement with the ping pong table on which Minnie and I used to hold marathon tournaments for two. I'd been to the graveyard after work that evening and sat on the grass by Minnie's stone, which was next to my parents—one day I'd lay next to them all—unable to take my eyes off the lonely etching: MINNIE GOLDSMITH, SISTER, 1965–2014.

As soon as I got home from the cemetery, I didn't know what to do with myself. Even the idea of fixing dinner wasn't attractive. So I ran through my short list of people to call: there was no way I was calling Sunny; Diana seemed to be increasingly self-involved, not that I wasn't happy with her weight loss, but it was all she talked about those days; and Cindy had just been there the night before, besides which she already had enough on her plate. That left Lise. I certainly wasn't going to call any of the TV people.

"What was Cindy here for?" Lise asked.

"She wanted me to teach her some simple recipes for this party she's having. I offered to do the cooking, but she said no, said she wanted to do it all herself, only she wasn't sure what foods went with what foods, and she said if I didn't help her, and I quote, 'I'll probably freak at the last minute and call Domino's.'" I couldn't hide my shudder. "Perish the thought."

"God, she's sweet. So, what did she finally decide to serve?"

"Who knows?" I shrugged. "I showed her maybe a half dozen different recipes, and she said she'd decide later, that she wanted to surprise me. But she kept confusing the paprika with the turmeric, so it should be interesting."

Lise laughed.

"Don't laugh," I told her. "You do realize this party is going to be a disaster, don't you?"

"Why would you say that?"

"Because it's true. Can't you see that? There's Cindy, letting herself get all excited, like this is going to be some kind of great party, like maybe it'll be exactly like the party you threw or something."

"And it's not?"

I snorted. "What's it that young people always say these days? Oh, right. Hel-*lo*! There's that little problem known as Eddie?"

"I still don't get it," Lise said. "I thought Eddie was mostly fine that one time we met him. I don't get why you had to be so hard on Cindy about him that day at Candlewood Lake."

"Do you think it's normal the way Cindy said Eddie reacted to her shooting pool with another guy?"

"Who asked her out."

"But she said no and Eddie knew it."

"No, maybe it's not exactly *normal*." For once, her tone turned judgmental. "But how would you like it if people criticized your choice in men?"

"What choice in men? I already told all you people, I'm cooling it with Sunny."

"You want to talk about something I don't get? *That's* something I don't get. Sunny's smart, he's respectful toward you, he's funny, he's handsome, he dresses nicely, he's *a doctor*—"

"Who the hell are you?" I tried to laugh. "My Jewish mother?"

"No, I'm just your *friend*, and as your friend I'm trying to figure out what's wrong with you."

"What's wrong with me? Nothing."

"Oh, no? Then way are you scared of intimacy?"

"Scared of…? What a crock-of-shit, new age, dumbass thing to say. I'm not scared of intimacy! I'm just fifty years old. I'm too old for all that dating nonsense. I'm too old to be dating, to have," I did that half-quote thing in the air with my fingers, "relationships."

"You're fifty years old, Sylvia! You're not *dead*."

"Oh, yeah? Who says?" Which, I'll grant, was a pretty dumbass thing to say on my part, but she had me riled.

Her expression softened. "You *are* scared of something," she said. "What are you scared of?"

What could I tell her—the truth? That I hadn't had sex in thirty years?

* * *

Back in college, when Minnie and I were both twenty, there'd been a fraternity party that Minnie went to without me. I was sick—strep, plus I never really liked to go to parties anyway—and even though Minnie said she didn't want to leave me, I insisted she go alone. I told her I'd just sleep the entire time she was gone, which I did, meaning I was sleeping while my sister was busy getting gang-raped. I woke to her crying on the twin bed across the room.

She'd been invited to the party by a friend of hers, or at least it was someone she *thought* was her friend. When she got there, it was mostly guys and just a few girls. She figured she was safe because it was her friend's frat house, right? And, being outgoing, Minnie had always been kind of a mascot of the place. But apparently some guy there was mad at her. I don't know. It was tough to get the story straight, she was crying that hard. But there was something about this one guy really liking her but then getting mad at her because one night she'd brought some other guy to a party. So, anyway, on this night, her friend got her really drunk—she swore it must have been spiked, that she didn't really drink that much—and then he said someone wanted to talk to her, and it turned out to be this guy who was really mad and the room was dark, and she tried to get away but then she heard noises and realized there were more people in the room and then she *really* tried to get away but she was just so dizzy and the room kept spinning and there were just too many of them and…and…and…

I tried to convince her to go to the cops but she said no way, she said no one would ever believe her, and even if they did, they would only blame *her*. And I saw it immediately: she was right. This was 1985, not that it would be that much easier on her now. But back then, people would definitely just say she'd gone to the party by herself, she'd been drunk, she went to the room by herself, she never screamed, she was asking for it. The semester before, a girl on our floor had been "trained"—that's the word guys used for what the rest of us called "gang-raped"—by some members of the hockey team. She hadn't kept quiet about it, made a real stink, even though she didn't press charges. Then one night, she was waiting in line in the cafeteria, talking to her roommate who was one of her loudest defenders. Some guys from the hockey team were a few places ahead of them in line, and I guess the girlfriend must have said something about them they didn't like, because one of the guys turned around and, pointing straight at her, said, "Watch it or you're next." Her face went dead white and anyone could see what she was thinking: they'd gotten away with it before, they'd get away with it again. Sure, there'd be some kind of slap-on-the-wrist disciplinary action taken. But in the end, they'd walk, more powerful than ever. It had started already. If you took a poll in the dorm, most would have said it was the girl's fault and that they felt sorry for the guys that the stupid bitch was giving them so much grief.

And it would have been the same for Minnie.

She made me promise I wouldn't go to the police on her behalf; she made me promise I'd never tell a soul what happened to her that night; she made me promise neither of us would ever go to any frat parties ever again.

And it was easy to promise her those things—I'd do anything, say anything, just to stop her crying—but it didn't end there. It started out so gradual at first, I barely noticed it. It started out with her not going out on a date when she was asked the next weekend, which seemed entirely understandable at the time, and grew from there until she slowly shut out men completely, except for relatives and service workers she couldn't avoid, like the mailman. Minnie had been so hurt, she never wanted to be hurt like that again.

And me? I went along for the ride.

Before Minnie's rape, I'd had the healthy sex life of any college student—we both did. They were experiences I'd enjoyed plenty at the time. And I even thought I was in love, once, but now I thought maybe that wasn't true at all; it was that very young, "I just want to be in love and you could be almost anyone," kind of thing, very different from the perplexing combination of giddiness and deeply mature longing I now secretly felt for Sunny.

Did Minnie make me go along for the ride? No. It's not like she made me or anything; it just turned out that way. Thirty years of living together like two Jewish nuns.

* * *

How was I supposed to get back on the horse again after thirty years?

I couldn't tell Lise all that. Not that she'd have laughed at me, I don't think. But she lived such a modern life, with her boyfriend and never getting married and everything, la-di-da, she'd never understand the decisions I'd made.

"Never mind that," I answered her now, figuring the best way to get people to stop talking about you is to ask them about themselves. "How are things going with the revisions? You said that Dirk's been e-mailing?"

"Dirk," she said, laughing and proving my point about people being easy to throw off the scent. "He keeps sending me all these ideas for revisions, some of which are contradictory, and keeps talking about the need to make the work 'more commercially viable.' But he also says that if I just listen to him, he's sure he can sell the book *and* get a lot of money for it."

"And that'll make you happy?"

"Well, sure. I mean, what would be greater than walking into a bookstore and seeing your name on the spine of a book?"

"I don't know," I said, popping the last bit of pastry in my mouth, "maybe fresher éclairs?"

But Lise didn't care about éclairs just then, fresh or not.

"Dirk is just, I don't know, like this Svengali character. And I guess maybe that should bother me, but it's just all so much fun. He tells me to make changes in certain areas of the book and—poof!— it's like it's a whole different book."

"And that's a good thing?"

She shrugged, not bothered.

"What does Tony make of all this?" I asked.

She made a face. "Don't ask. Ever since I quit the university, Tony hasn't exactly been a pillar of support." She shook it off, returning to her new favorite subject. "I was really disappointed. I thought Dirk was going to be coming to New York. He comes a few times a year to have lunches with editors and clients. But now Diana says he told her he's not going to New York this season, that instead he's waiting for the end of July when he's going to come for some big romance writers' conference in Atlanta."

I tried to stifle a yawn, hoping she wouldn't think me rude, but she caught it anyway. I wasn't bored, just suddenly tired, tired after remembering.

"I should go," she said, starting to rise.

"No, stay," I said quickly. I didn't really feel like talking anymore, but I also didn't want to go back to being alone just yet. I picked up the remote control. "Maybe we could just watch some TV?"

"OK." She settled back. "Sure."

I flipped it to the Food Network.

"How's the show coming?" she asked.

"I don't want to talk about those crazy people," I said. "You'll see the show along with everyone else in the country in July." Then, looking at the screen I said, "'Bam!' What the hell is it with that guy? 'Bam!' Who says that?"

The Second Party

RECOMMENDED READING:
Diana: *The Foursome*, Troon McAllister
Lise: *Misery*, Stephen King
Cindy: *Baby Proof*, Emily Giffin
Sylvia: *Chocolat*, Joanne Harris

Eddie woke late in the afternoon, hungover, to the smell of turkey in the apartment. It had been a late night the night before, playing a gig, and he could have been working that night as well if only Cindy hadn't insisted he stay home.

"What do you need me here for?" he'd asked her yesterday. "They're *your* friends."

"How would it look if you weren't here? Wouldn't it have been odd if, the day of Lise's party, everyone had shown up as couples and she was there all alone? C'mon, it'll be fun. It'll be something different to do."

"Fine. Then at least let me invite some of the guys over too."

"No," Cindy had said, putting her foot down in a rare act. "If your band comes over, it'll just turn into another jam session. Before the night is out, everyone'd be snorting coke and using all the spoons for instruments." On one occasion back when Cindy was still drinking, sometime the year before, she'd awoken from a night of partying with Eddie's band to find spoons all over her living room. It had taken her a while to figure out where they had come from, but then she'd had a flash of everyone using her spoons to play percussion along to Bruce Springsteen and Eddie's drummer trying to hang a spoon off his nose and failing. "I want to have a normal night, like other people have, with four couples getting together for good food and intelligent conversation."

Eddie had sneered at that last part, but in another rare act for the Cindy/Eddie household, he'd let her have her way.

Now Eddie struggled upward, sitting on the edge of the bed for a few minutes holding his head before rising and heading off to the shower. As he passed through the single room that constituted the living room and smaller dining room, he didn't look up, didn't take notice of the white Christmas lights with which Cindy had lined the ceilings, didn't take notice of Cindy herself sitting at the round table in the dining area doing something on the computer.

When he emerged twenty minutes later, chest damp, a tattered green towel wrapped around his hips, Cindy hurriedly turned off the computer.

"What the hell's all this?" he said, taking in the lights for the first time.

"I thought it would make the place look more festive. Don't you think it looks festive?"

"For December maybe," Eddie snorted. "Not June. And where's that turkey smell coming from? You didn't say anything yesterday about making a turkey."

"I changed my mind at the last minute. All those recipes Sylvia showed me, they just seemed too complicated. I figured, my mom always made a turkey on Thanksgiving—how hard can it be? You just stick it in the oven for a few hours and serve it."

Eddie wandered into the kitchen. A moment later he called out, "Are you sure this turkey's cooking? You've got the oven down awful low."

"It's a slow-cooking turkey. It's supposed to be low."

"How long's it been in here?"

"I don't know. An hour or two, maybe?"

"And what's this shit? Gluten free?" He came back in, holding a turquoise and yellow box.

"That's for Diana. You know how she had that surgery and she's still trying to lose weight?"

"That woman could lose fifty more pounds and she still wouldn't be skinny."

"That's not the point. The point *is* that she can't eat rich foods anymore, and the guy at the natural-food store I stopped in said this gluten-free pasta is low-glycemic, which I guess is supposed to be good for weight loss and stuff."

"Now you're going to specialty stores for this party?"

"It didn't cost that much," Cindy said. "It's just the one box."

"Whatever." Eddie took the box back to the kitchen, bored with the subject. "We got any beer in this place?"

"Look in the fridge," Cindy called back. "There should be some in the drawer on the lower right-hand side."

"*German* beer? I can't drink this imported shit. Where are my Buds?"

"You must've drank them all."

"Where the hell's the bottle opener? The damn cap doesn't even twist off."

* * *

A few hours later, Cindy was putting the finishing touches on her makeup in the bathroom. She was staying away from the heavy black eyeliner Eddie preferred to see her in, going for more of what in previous generations might have been referred to admiringly as "the Cover Girl look." Before doing the grocery shopping the day before, she'd stopped by the mall. Ignoring the stores she usually bought clothes from, she headed straight for J Crew where she spent half her paycheck on an outfit that included a tailored white shirt with ruffles and a long beige skirt that had a tiered effect and looked like something from Cowgirl Barbie's collection. Combined with the white shirt, though, it made Cindy feel confident, like she was selecting something that Lise might wear herself. On her feet she wore a pair of beige canvas flat slides.

"I thought you said this was supposed to be a party," Eddie said, slouching in the doorway, regarding her with a beer in his hands. "What are you dressing up for? Church?"

Cindy studied Eddie's reflection behind her in the mirror. He had on torn jeans and a Black Sabbath concert T-shirt that had seen better centuries.

She ignored what he'd said to her, instead saying, "What about wearing that outfit I bought you for Lise's party? You looked great in those khakis with the white shirt."

"No way," Eddie said. "I may have to put up with whatever that gluten shit is and German beer, but this is my home. I'll dress any way I want to."

"If you're not going to change, then maybe you could put some music on?"

"Now *that's* the first good idea you've had all day."

"I bought some new CDs," Cindy called after him. "They're next to the stereo."

The apartment being small and the living room already cramped with the sofa, La-Z-Boy chair, coffee table, end table, and TV meant the stereo was in the bedroom. The apartment being small meant it didn't matter because you could hear the stereo, loud, in every room in the place.

"Crap, Cindy!" Eddie yelled after just a few bars from the first CD on the pile. "I can't listen to this. What did you buy? *Muzak?*"

•   •   •

As it turned out, Eddie's instincts about what to wear were more on target than Cindy's. As the others arrived by twos, dressed on the downside of casual as though a memo had gone out that this was not the kind of place you wore your fancy or preppy clothes to, Eddie favored Cindy with a satisfied smile. If Sunny and Dan looked out of character in their stiff jeans, neither seemed the type to complain, and Tony was certainly at home in his. They were even more at home once they had beers in their hands.

"Why don't I help you in the kitchen?" Sylvia offered.

"No," Cindy said, speaking more sharply than she intended, holding up her hand. Then she softened. "Really. You're all our guests tonight. Let us wait on you for a change."

"Cindy, it is so wonderful to see you again," Sunny said, "and the food smells marvelous. You look marvelous as well. How is the ba—?"

He never got to say the second syllable because Sylvia kicked him in the shin.

"Is that turkey I'm smelling?" Sylvia said, sniffing the air. "At least let me peek in the kitchen. I promise I won't touch a thing."

Cindy led Sylvia to the kitchen. On the counter was a big glass bowl of fruit: strawberries, chunks of pineapple, cherries.

"These look delicious," Sylvia said, reaching out to steal a cherry.

"I bought an angel food cake for dessert," Cindy said. "I figured I could serve it with fudge sauce for anyone who wants it and Diana could have the fruit."

"That was very thoughtful."

"Is it hot in here?" Cindy asked. "It feels hot to me all of a sudden."

"Why not just open the door?"

In addition to the interior flight of stairs from the living room down to the street, there was another door in the kitchen, on the other side of which was a tiny deck and a flight of weathered wood stairs. The overhanging roof and the so-close-you-could-practically-touch-it building across the way meant that the deck didn't get any sun for growing flowers or sunbathing, but it was at least big enough for Eddie to go out and smoke on when he was drinking.

"Why didn't I think of that?" Cindy said, opening the door with a tight smile.

"Relax," Sylvia said, putting her hands on Cindy's shoulders. "You're having a party. This is supposed to be fun." She looked around the kitchen. "And everything looks, just," she turned her smile up another twenty watts, "great."

"I thought you said you were slowing things down with Sunny," Cindy said.

"I am. But you said everyone had to bring someone, and who else did I have to bring? Enough about me, though. Let's see what the others are doing."

"This place is really charming," Dan was saying as they entered the room. "I had a place like this when I was in college."

"What the hell's that supposed to mean?" Eddie said. "When are you talking about, like, before you won the lottery?"

"I'm sure Dan didn't mean—" Diana started to say.

"Your husband can't speak for himself? What kind of man lets his wife stick up for him?"

"Yes, of course he can," Diana said. "I only meant—"

"*I* only meant I really like your place," Dan said with an easy smile. "Nothing condescending intended." Then he clapped Eddie on the shoulder. "Get you another beer?"

"Yeah. Yeah, sure," Eddie said, allowing himself to be led away. "We're cool."

* * *

Eddie walked the floor of *his* apartment. He was looking for somewhere to settle down, get comfortable with his beer. But in every corner, there were people.

"Dirk says if I just make these last few changes, the book will be perfect," Lise said.

"Isn't that what Dirk said the last time?" Tony said.

Eddie walked on.

"I love that outfit," Cindy said.

"Thanks," Diana said. "I just bought it today."

"I think maybe I should go put the pasta on now," Cindy said. "Do you want something else to drink?"

Eddie walked on.

In another corner, Dan and Sunny talked baseball while Sylvia fiddled with the chips and dip Cindy'd brought out.

"Do you think the Mets will go all the way this year?" Dan asked.

Sunny laughed. "If they do, it will be a miracle."

Eddie downed the rest of his beer. Ugh. Backwash. Imported backwash.

Who the fuck were all these people? And what the fuck were they doing in my home?

Oh. Right. They were Cindy's friends. Cindy's *fancy* friends, even if they all were slumming it, wearing jeans that night.

Enough. Enough of the friends and enough of that god-awful Muzak.

Eddie went in the bedroom where he replaced one of Cindy's new CDs with an old Guns 'n' Roses tape. Ah, that was better. Then he passed through the living room, grabbed another beer from the fridge, and headed out onto the deck where he lit up.

"Nice party," a friendly voice said. "Thanks for having us."

Which one was that one? Oh, right. Lise. The big-shot writer. Say this for her: at least she was smoking too.

"My pleasure," Eddie said, blowing two streams of smoke out his nose.

Now the bitch would probably want to make small talk.

"How are Cindy's online classes going?"

"Say what?"

"Her online classes. I came here a few months ago to help her set up the computer Sylvia gave her. I was just wondering how the classes were going."

Eddie, ignoring the glass ashtray on the brown plastic parson's table, tossed his cigarette over the railing and went inside. Lise ground hers out in the ashtray before hurrying after him.

"Yo, Cindy," he said, catching her checking the turkey in the oven. The others had all followed her in. "What's this *bitch*," he yanked a thumb at Lise behind him, "talking about? You taking some classes you didn't tell me about?"

"Hey," Tony said, putting a protective arm around Lise's shoulders. "Watch your mouth."

Eddie stabbed a finger at him. "You watch your mouth, asshole. I wasn't talking to you." He turned to Cindy. "Well?"

"It's nothing, Eddie," Cindy said, tucking a stray hair behind her ear. "I'm just taking some classes. It's nothing."

"If it's nothing, then how come this is the first I'm hearing about it? You wanna explain that to me?"

Cindy sighed, and then tried on a smile. "It was going to be a surprise. I thought I could get my GED, and then maybe take a few college courses, learn something useful that would get me away from Midnight Scandals."

"Oh. Some surprise. And then what?" He grabbed her hard by the upper arm, so hard she couldn't move out of his grip. "You get your college diploma, and then maybe you leave me? Maybe you leave me for one of these *fancy* guys like all of your *fancy* friends?"

"It's not like that! It's—"

"Easy, Eddie," Dan said soothingly. "Let her go."

"If I need your help," Eddie said, "I'll ask for it."

"C'mon," Dan said. "This was supposed to be a party, remember? How about another beer? I sure could use one."

"Yeah." Eddie let go of Cindy's arm, ran his fingers through his hair. "Yeah, a beer'd be good."

"And maybe some food?" Diana suggested. "Perhaps we'll all feel better if we have something to eat?"

"That's a good idea," Cindy said. "Right. The food." Turning back to the oven, she lifted the turkey out and turned to the group with a smile. "Who wants to carve?"

Sunny stepped forward and reached for the knife. Shooting Sylvia a warm smile, he said, "I am told I have a nice touch with one of these."

"Save your talents for cutting into people," Eddie said, brushing by him. "My house. My woman. My turkey."

Eddie took the carving knife and fork from Cindy and put a big slice in the turkey, right down the middle.

"What the fuck?" he said. "This thing is all pink in here! It's raw!"

Cindy looked mortified. "Maybe if I just—"

But it was too late. Eddie had already picked up the bird in his bare hands and, striding to the back door, hurled it over the railing of the deck where it smashed into the neighbor's house. A light went on next door.

"Can you blame him?" Cindy said, forcing a laugh. "Who wants to eat raw turkey? When Eddie's right, he's right."

"Maybe the pasta?" Diana suggested.

"Of course," Cindy said, her smile taking on an air of desperation now as she lifted the lid. Then her face fell. "Oh, no."

"What is it?" Sylvia asked.

Eddie leaned over Cindy's shoulder. "What the hell is that shit? Is that your *gluten* pasta?" He stuck the same fork he'd used on the turkey into the gelatinous white stuff in the pot. He laughed, a nasty sound. "It looks like it melted on you." In an instant, the gluten pasta followed in the path of the turkey. "What the fuck is the matter with you?" he screamed in Cindy's face. "Can't you ever do anything right?"

Sunny stepped between them. "I do not like to interfere, but someone really needs to tell you that that is not the proper way to talk to a lady."

"Nobody asked you, you Middle Eastern motherfucker," Eddie said. Then he placed both hands against Sunny's chest and shoved.

"Don't you touch him!" Sylvia said, getting between them. "And he's not Middle Eastern, not that that would matter. He's from Southeast Asia, Pakistan." Sylvia put her hands on her hips. "You've laid hands on nearly everyone at this party. What are you going to do, hit me next? C'mon, tough guy. Everyone else may be scared to tell you what's what, but I—"

"*Get out!*" Cindy shouted. There were tears streaming down her face. "Don't you realize how much worse you're all making it?" She herded her guests toward the door, barely giving the women time to gather their purses. "Get out! Get out! *Get out!*"

In the kitchen, the bowl of fruit sat on the counter and the cherries gleamed.

Cindy

"Get out! Get out! *Get out!*" It seemed I was saying that a lot lately, seemed like it was all I *could* say.

But as soon as the others left, and I was alone with Eddie, and I saw the look on his face, I was sorry I'd done it. *Why* had I done it? At least if they'd stayed, even though things would probably have gotten ugly—or ugli*er*—at least I would have had backup. The sheer number of the others would have kept Eddie from…doing things.

So *why* had I done it?

But, then, it hadn't been the first time…

A few months before Carly's last stint in the hospital, she'd moved in with us for a week. She just couldn't take the 'rents ragging on her about her drinking and drugs anymore, and she said she just needed a place to get her shit together for a while. One day, Eddie and I'd been drinking all day. I didn't usually like to drink much, but something about having both Eddie and Carly under the same roof, something about the unseasonable warmth of the late October day, more like spring, made it feel OK to join in.

As the day wore on, though, Eddie's mood darkened. We were sitting at the little round dining room table. Eddie used to sit me down there when he wanted to have one of his little talks that always felt more like one of those criminal interrogations you see on TV except, in this case, Eddie was both good cop *and* bad cop. Eddie'd gone to the kitchen for another beer and to change the CD in the bedroom, and Carly got up from where she'd been trying to ignore our fighting on the couch and told me she was going out for a bit.

"Please don't go," I'd begged her in a hushed whisper. "I'll give you anything you want. You can come to Midnight Scandals tomorrow and pick out anything you want, and I'll pay for it. Only

just don't leave right now. I'm scared of what he'll do if you leave."
I know, it was crazy to bribe my own sister. But Carly hated being
around us when we argued.

So Carly had stayed, taking a chair at the table. I like to think she
did it because she was worried about me, but who knows? Carly was
pretty fucked up back then. It could have just been for free thongs.

When Eddie came back in and saw Carly at the table, things got
better for a while. We even laughed a bit. But maybe another hour
later, things started to escalate, I guess you'd call it. Eddie asked me
something personal—I don't even remember what it was now—and
I don't know why I said it, but I just said, "I can't answer that with
Carly sitting here."

Even though she'd been drinking right along with us, meaning
she was pretty drunk too, the look of confusion and betrayal on
Carly's face had been huge. I could see her mind saying, *You asked
me to stay here and protect you and now you're the one who's giving him the
opening to—*

"Yeah," Eddie'd turned to Carly, "what the fuck are you doing
sitting here? Don't you have anything better to do than listen in on
a couple's private conversation?"

Carly had risen from her seat, shot us a look of disgust that
seemed even more meant for me than for Eddie, grabbed a few
beers from the fridge, and was down the stairs like a light, the door
to the street slamming shut behind her. And, after she had gone,
things just got…worse. She'd moved out the next day, but not
before leaving me with a few words of Carly wisdom.

"I don't know what's wrong with you, Cin. It's like you set
yourself up. That whole thing yesterday, begging me to stay and
then making it so *of course* Eddie would ask me to go? And all week
long, I've seen you saying little things to Eddie; the kind of things
I'd never say to him because I know they'd just set him off. It's sick.
What are you getting out of all this? God, it's worse here than with
the 'rents."

And then she was really gone.

And now I'd sent away all my close friends—Sylvia, Lise,
Diana—and their men, the people who could have saved me.

In the kitchen, Eddie closed the space between us. Usually, if I was crying, Eddie would feel bad about whatever he was doing, at least after a while, and back off. It was only when I tried to stand up for myself that he really tried to take me down. But, hard as I was crying right then, he just kept coming at me.

He grabbed hold of my ponytail, yanking so hard my head snapped back.

"What did you think, you stupid little idiot? Did you really think you were going to have some kind of *fancy* evening with those *fancy* highbrow people?"

"It could have been nice, Eddie. It could be again." I squirmed to get out of his hold, but every time I squirmed, that hold just got tighter. "They're really nice. They're my friends."

"Those people aren't your *friends*! Don't you get it, Cin? They laugh at people like us." His face was an inch from mine. "They laugh at you. The only reason they want you around is so they can feel better about themselves. You're such a loser, that next to you they feel smart and successful and rich. That's why they keep you around."

"That's not true! They're my friends!"

"They're not your fucking friends!" He yanked harder. "And I'll tell you something else. You're not seeing them anymore."

"What? No! You can't tell me who I can and can't see!"

"Oh, no?"

Still holding onto my hair with one hand, he reached for the glass bowl on the counter with the other. Then he grabbed a handful of the cherries that I'd so carefully washed earlier in the day.

"No," I said. "What are you going to do?"

He hiked up the back of my skirt, the one I'd bought at J Crew, and put his hand under the waistband of my panties, shoving the cherries down against my skin. Then he kept his hand there, squishing the cherries against my openings until I was wet.

"See that, Cin? You and me are alike. We're trash. We're not like those people."

Then he lifted the front of my skirt, ripped off my panties, and finger-fucked me against the counter before dropping his own jeans and fucking me for real, the red juice from the cherries, pieces of skin from the fruit pressing between us.

God help me, I enjoyed it.

He held my legs wrapped around his waist as he thrust into me, talking in my ear.

"You love me, Cin, right? You love only me?"

"Yes, Eddie," I said into his shoulder, holding on, "only you."

. . .

I awoke the next morning to a hangover of self-hatred and the phone ringing and a note on Eddie's pillow where his head should have been. Picking up the note, I hurried to the other room to get the phone.

It was Carly.

"Hey! How'd the big party go last night?"

"It was great," I said. "Everyone had a nice time."

"That's wonderful! And here I was worried it wouldn't go well for some reason. Hey, I wanted to ask you something."

"Sure. Go ahead."

"Listen, the 'rents are starting to drive me up the wall again. Mom keeps getting on my case, Dad keeps getting on Mom, and I was just wondering: Do you think I could come stay with you again, just for a few days?"

I looked at the note in my hand.

Hey, Babe:

Sorry I had to go while you were still sleeping. You looked so beautiful lying there. Last night was great, huh? Ron called, said he wanted to jam all day today, so that's where I'll be, but I should be back in time for supper. Make something good, OK? Oh, and clean this place up. It looks like a dump!

"Hey, Carly, can I call you back in a little bit? I don't feel so good right now."

Twenty minutes later, I was getting out of the shower, having experienced my first bout of morning sickness of the day before stepping in, when the phone rang again. It was probably Eddie, calling to tell me he loved me or with specific instructions about dinner.

"Hello?"

"Is that asshole there?" It was Sylvia.

"No," I said, "and he's not an asshole. As a matter of fact, after everyone left last night, we made love."

"That's just the pregnancy hormones talking."

"What? And what do you know about pregnancy?"

"Ever since you told me you were pregnant, I've been reading up on it. Pregnancy makes women horny. It says so right in the book. It wasn't Eddie that was making you feel so good last night after we left. It was the pregnancy. When will he be back?"

"I don't know. I—"

"Pack your things. Pack everything you want to keep in this world. I'm coming to get you."

Diana

"What is *wrong* with Sylvia? Is she nuts?" I said.

I was on the phone with Lise, who had called to tell me about Sylvia taking in Cindy. Not only had she taken in Cindy, but apparently, she'd also taken in Cindy's troubled sister Carly.

The night of Cindy's party, Dan and I had discussed things in the car on the way home.

"I never guessed Eddie could be like that," Dan had said. "He seemed so nice the first time we met him."

"He did, but I suppose sometimes people can be deceiving. You know, the person you see in public is different than the person you see in private. Then, too, he was drinking much more tonight."

"What do you think would make Cindy stay with someone like that?"

"I haven't a clue," I'd said. "Perhaps she has self-esteem issues?"

The next morning, Cindy had still been on my mind, although there were a few other things encroaching on my thoughts again.

The good news? The scale said I weighed one hundred and ninety pounds. It was hard to believe at times, but if I just kept on doing what I was doing—putting one step in front of the other in my daily walks and downing one carrot after another, however much I hated carrots—in another month and a half I'd weigh one hundred pounds less than I had when I'd first started. For some people—tiny Sylvia came to mind—that would constitute their whole person.

More good news? There was another e-mail from Dirk. Well, there were e-mails from Dirk every day, but this particular e-mail was different. I'd mentioned to him about how bored I was starting to feel in Danbury; or, if not bored, then restless. I'd said I was thinking about looking for a job, but had no idea what around here might suit me. That was when I came up with my idea, or at least the germ of one. *Perhaps I could do some work for you*, I'd written. *Now, there's an intriguing idea*, he'd written back. But then he'd trailed off with one of those ellipsis things, and I had yet to pin him down on what exactly I could do for him. Still, I thought, wouldn't it be something if I, Diana Taylor, were somehow to align myself with a first-rate literary agency? If Dirk was known as the Jaguar, then perhaps one day I could be known as the Panther.

Of course, when I'd intimated as much to Artemis in a telephone conversation the next day, she'd laughed.

"The Panther? I don't know about that, Diana. Maybe you'd be 'The Ocelot'? Or possibly 'The Lemur'?"

"Never mind about that now," I'd hurried on, not wanting to let her hear how her words had hurt me. "There's something else I was hoping to get your feedback on."

Then I'd told her about Cindy and Eddie; how, except for Sylvia, we'd all mostly thought he was terrific at first with just a few minor reservations; how wrong we'd all been.

"Maybe it's the old break-up-to-make-up thing," Artemis had suggested. "Know what I mean?"

"No, I'm afraid I haven't a clue." Artemis had always had so much more experience with men than I had. I felt inadequate compared to her whenever the subject came up.

"Maybe the sex is wonderful. Maybe the periods of tension make it more so."

"But that's daft! Cindy's beautiful. She's sweet and she's kind. Why not pick a man who's her equal and have sex with him? Who would put up with a man treating her dreadfully just to get laid?"

"You'd be surprised."

"I have a theory."

"Do tell."

"Well, I don't know how to say this, but Cindy's...*different* than Sylvia and Lise and myself. And Eddie's...*different* than the other men."

"How so?"

"For one thing, neither of them has been to university. And

then, too, they live in a one-bedroom flat instead of a house or at least their own condo. Eddie sings in a band, Cindy works at the mall—"

"Diana, I'm shocked at you!"

"Whatever do you mean?"

"That's just such a classist thing to say. It's the sort of thing Mother would say! You're not honestly telling me that this Cindy friend of yours is in an abusive relationship just because she and her Eddie didn't read Homer at Cambridge or because he sings in a band instead of being a CEO like Dan, are you?"

"Well, when you put it like that…But I didn't mean—"

"Nobody ever does, do they? The fact of the matter is, women who live with CEOs are just as likely to get bashed around by their husbands as your friend is. The only difference is, you never read about it in the papers, and they get bigger presents as part of the makeup phase."

"So you're saying Cindy stays with Eddie because the making up is so good?"

"Of course. And I'm also saying I think it's very small-minded of you to assume that your friend Cindy's current situation has anything to do with her socioeconomic stature. It could just as easily be you as her. Only it's not."

That was something to think about.

"And here's something else," Artemis had gone on. "People looking at marriages from the outside—"

"But Cindy and Eddie aren't married."

"Whatever. People looking at other people's relationships from the outside only see a part of the picture. Speaking of pictures…"

"Were we? Speaking of pictures?"

"Of course we were, Diana. Don't you ever pay attention to me when I speak?"

Then Artemis told me about some man she'd been seeing, said there was a picture she was going to e-mail to me of the two of them together at a party, and to see what I thought.

As soon as she'd rung off, I did as she asked. Not because I so desperately wanted to see a picture of gorgeous Artemis with her latest gorgeous boyfriend. I didn't. But because I knew she'd only grill me about it the next time we talked. And if I made a slipup while describing him, a slipup revealing that I'd never looked? Say, if I commented how lovely his hair looked when in reality he was as bald as Vin Diesel on most days, Artemis would eat me alive.

As it turned out, Artemis's new boyfriend looked *exactly* like Vin Diesel, which I found out when I looked at the e-mail she'd sent me to the account I shared with Dan. It had been a long time since I'd checked that account, since the e-mails I received from Dirk came to the new account I'd created, but I saw now that there were several e-mails that had "Layla" as part of the e-mail address, and I knew exactly who those must be from. The temptation to read them was huge, I must say, but then I reminded myself how annoying it had been when Dan had mentioned Dirk's repeat e-mails to me in a suspicious-sounding way. And I did have Dirk. Thinking of him made me promptly switch to the other account to see if there was anything new from him.

> From: dirk.peters@dirkliterary.uk
> To: dianat@yahoo.com
> D,
> I've never known another woman like you…

• • •

And now here was Lise on the phone, and she wasn't at all agreeing with my assessment of Sylvia, that she was nuts for taking Cindy in, not like I would have expected Lise to have done.

Lise and I always agreed on nearly everything, so it came as something of a shock.

Then Lise said something strikingly similar to what Artemis had previously said about people looking at other people's relationships from the outside only ever seeing part of the picture. She went on to say, "They only see what the couple allows them to see, or maybe they only see what they want to see. But it's always more complicated than that. It's easy to judge. It's a lot less easy to understand."

"Fine," I said, growing tired of people casting me as someone who could only see things in blacks and whites. I could see grays too. "Whatever the true nature of the relationship between Cindy and Eddie, it *is* nuts, Sylvia interjecting herself in that way. She could get hurt. That Eddie is a maniac! It's only a matter of time before he figures out who Cindy is staying with, and then what might he do?"

"But how would he find out?" she wanted to know. "Chances are Cindy never even told him any of our last names. True, he was here that one time, and he did come by last night wanting to know if she was with me—"

"He was *there*? In your *house*?"

"Yes."

"Why didn't you say something earlier, for God's sakes?"

"Perhaps because as soon I answered the phone, you went off on your tear about Sylvia being nuts and I had to respond to that first." She sounded amused. "Besides, it wasn't anything I couldn't handle. And Tony was here."

"Well, what did you tell him?"

"I lied. I told him I had no idea where Cindy had gone to, said I hadn't talked to her at all. At least that part was true: I haven't talked to her, only Sylvia. He grumbled and yelled a bit afterward, but he did finally leave. Tony saw to that."

"But don't you see what I mean? Eddie's determined. Somehow he'll find her. And Danbury is so small."

"There are eighty thousand people here," she laughed. "That's hardly small."

"Well, that still doesn't make it London. And haven't you ever noticed how you keep running into the same people over and over again? The odds are Eddie will find Cindy. It's just a matter of time. And then what will happen?"

There was a long pause on the other end of the line. Then: "Why did you get us all together in the first place? When you put that ad in the bookstore newsletter."

"Come again?"

But she didn't answer that one. Instead she said, "I know, from what you've said, that your sister Artemis can be toxic. But I'm curious: What are you like when you talk to her?"

"What do you mean?"

"Do you ask her questions about what's going on with her? Or do you just talk about yourself, only to wind up disappointed when the response you get from her isn't totally up to your expectations?"

"I suppose the latter, but I'm still not sure I understand quite what it is you're getting at here."

"I suppose what I'm getting at," Lise said with a sigh, "is that relationships—and by 'relationships' here I don't mean just romantic relationships but all kinds of relationships—are as much about what you bring to the table as what the other person does. I think Sylvia sees that, maybe better than any of us. If you're always thinking about 'What's in this for me?' or 'How do I benefit?' or 'Can I get hurt by this somehow?' then life will always fall short for you."

Sylvia

If anyone thought I was nuts, they were probably right.

Not that long ago, I'd been feeling lonely rattling around my condo by myself. OK, I'd felt lonely ever since Minnie died. And now I was living my mother's old line of "Be careful what you ask for." What was I doing with not one but two young women sleeping in Minnie's old room? *Someone*, I thought, *should lock me away*.

Except I wasn't the one who should be locked away. That Eddie should be locked away, he was that crazy and mean. And Cindy should be locked away for putting up with him. Oh, and while we're locking people away, might as well throw Carly into the bargain too, just because.

The day after Cindy's party, when I'd gone to get her, riding in like the cavalry in the Sylvia's Supper van, I'd expected some resistance. Cindy had obviously been in denial about Eddie for a long time. Maybe she'd tell me she'd changed her mind about coming with me. After all, I'd only known Cindy for a matter of months. She'd been with Eddie for years. This couldn't have been the first time things got really bad. Maybe there was a history of things getting bad enough for her to begin the process of leaving, and then Eddie doing something at the last minute to win her back.

But when I got there, she was practically waiting at the door with one pathetic old suitcase packed.

"That's all you're taking?" I'd asked, surprised.

"I want the computer too. But I was scared to lift it myself because of, you know, the baby."

It was just a laptop. It didn't weigh much. But, I figured, with everything else that was going on with her, she probably wasn't thinking straight.

Four months pregnant and she was just beginning to show, but there was definitely a little bump there you couldn't miss. And yet, somehow, Eddie *had* missed that bump. Maybe Cindy wasn't the only one in denial?

So I'd disconnected the laptop and loaded it into the van along with her suitcase. We were driving away, heading toward the condo, and that's when she lays her bombshell on me. Only, her being Cindy, she'd done it in a tentative sort of way.

"Um, do you think maybe we could swing by my parents' house and pick something up first?"

"Sure. What do you need? More clothes?"

"Um, not exactly."

"Not exactly" turned out to be her whacked-out sister Carly who, considering what Cindy had gotten herself into with Eddie, maybe wasn't the most whacked-out Cox sister after all.

"What am I running here," I said, as Carly threw a duffel into the back of the van, climbing in after it, "Sylvia's Wayward Home for Girls?"

Carly had laughed, a clear tinkling sound, before addressing her sister like I wasn't there. "You're right. She's really funny."

"See?" Cindy had said, smiling for the first time that day. "Told you."

Great, I'd thought at the time. Somehow I'd got myself into a situation where I was going to have two young women, practically girls, under my roof. Girls who said things to each other like, "Told you." This was going to be just peachy.

And so we began. We worked out a schedule where Carly covered the shop for me briefly midmornings while I dropped Cindy off at Midnight Scandals, picking her up again at the end of the day. I made our meals, they cleaned up afterward—sort of—and everything was just peachy.

* * *

It took Eddie a little over two weeks to find out Cindy was staying with me, which could mean that he wasn't trying very hard or maybe he just wasn't all that bright.

Or maybe he was too busy barking up wrong trees.

Lise had told me he'd already shown up at her place, and then he'd showed up at Diana's; Diana's husband being a famous CEO and all, they weren't hard to find.

That just left me.

It stands to reason that he knew I was a caterer—it's the kind of seemingly innocent detail that Cindy or anyone would tell a boyfriend, just like Lise would tell Tony about Diana's weight-loss surgery or even I'd tell Sunny about Cindy being pregnant, only in my case making the mistake of forgetting to tell him *not* to say anything in front of Eddie about the baby—and from knowing that it'd be just a simple hop, skip, and a jump through the Yellow Pages and a look-see under "Caterers." In the greater Danbury area there's only one caterer with "Sylvia" as part of the business name and that would be me.

He showed up at the business one night just prior to closing, demanding to know where Cindy was. I lied, of course, and said I hadn't a clue. But I've never been the best of liars and maybe he sensed that because, the next night, as I was driving home, I saw a beat-up old car trailing me from two cars back. When I got to the condo, I made a dash for the door, locking it behind me.

"*Cin-DY! Cin-DY!*"

"Who the fuck does he think he is," I said, listening to him howl outside the door like a wolf howling up at the moon, "Stanley Kowalski?"

Carly laughed. I'll say this for Carly: she was a great audience. But Cindy wasn't laughing. No. She was peering out the slats in the mini blinds.

When she first heard him yelling, she looked scared, but then her expression softened and she walked toward the door.

"Don't let him in here!" I said. "I will *not* have that man in my home."

"Fine," she said, and now it sounded like she was actually angry at me. "Then I'll talk to him outside. I have to at least hear what he has to say."

Of course, Carly and I couldn't hear what he said, or what she said, not with the door closed. But we could certainly see through the crack in the blinds as Cindy walked outside, as Eddie handed her some flowers he was holding, as the two of them sat down on the stoop, as Eddie started to cry.

Seeing him cry like that, something in me softened too. I'd never seen a guy cry in my life, not unless it was in a movie. Maybe he was sincerely sorry for what he'd done?

"Just like Daddy and Mama," Carly said in a hushed voice at my side.

"What do you mean?" I looked at her.

"Every time Daddy would do something bad to Mama, every time he *still* does something bad, out come the flowers and the tears."

"How often does this happen?" I asked.

"Sometimes monthly, sometimes weekly, sometimes daily, sometimes as much as a few months will go by without an event. It all depends."

"On what?"

"On how bad things are."

"How bad is bad?"

"Drinking, hitting, beating, humiliating—mostly humiliating."

That thing that had softened for a minute? I felt it hardening right back up again as I glimpsed a pattern. I never took any psychology classes in college, but even someone like me, with little experience of men, could see exactly what Cindy was doing, *had* been doing: she was living what she knew. I wondered if Eddie had ever beat Cindy. There were never any signs of it, that I could see, but who knew what I wasn't seeing? Who knew what went on that she wasn't admitting, not even to herself?

Cindy and Eddie must have sat on that stoop a good half hour or more, Carly and me watching all the while. A part of me felt like it was wrong to watch. Cindy was, after all, an adult, had been one for a long time. She was old enough to make her own decisions and mistakes. But a part of me couldn't stop looking because I wanted to make sure, if he tried anything funny or bad, I'd be there to stop it.

But nothing bad happened. They just kept talking, even laughing occasionally, and when Cindy came back inside, Eddie having left peacefully, she had a smile on her face as she leaned back against the closed door, sniffing her flowers.

"Those are pretty flowers," I said, keeping my voice neutral.

"Aren't they gorgeous?" Cindy said.

"Oh, shit," Carly said. "She's going to get back together with the prick."

"Did I *say* that?" Cindy said.

"You didn't have to," Carly said. "I can see it in your eyes. So, tell me, what did schmucko say?"

As Cindy spoke, her eyes took on a misty quality. She told us how sorry Eddie was for everything, not just for being rude to her friends the night of the party she'd so looked forward to, but for every bad thing he'd ever done. He wanted to make amends. He'd even cleaned the apartment himself. If she wanted, he'd get a part-time job, in addition to the band, so maybe they could move up in the world a bit.

And, as she spoke, I felt myself going along for her ride. I *wanted* to believe Eddie could change for her. I *wanted* to believe she could still have a happily ever after with him, if that's what she wanted.

"He did say I'd have to give up the classes," she said. Then she shrugged as if it was nothing. "But that's only because he worries about me so much. He doesn't want me doing too much, working and trying to take classes at the same time."

I didn't say anything, and Carly, give her credit, didn't either. But we certainly did look at one another.

"He even apologized for the cherries," Cindy said.

"Cherries?" I said. "What cherries?"

Cindy never had told me before just what exactly happened after the night of her party, only something vague about them fighting, but she did now, making it sound like just another one of Eddie's amusing stories about getting a job because he didn't like blind people or telling people to get their own fucking rock 'n' roll bands. Finishing up, she said with a laugh, "That's funny, right? Isn't it? The whole thing with the cherries?"

"No," I said evenly, "it's not funny at all. In fact, it's the most degrading thing I've ever heard in my life."

She stiffened. "What do you know about men?" she said, obviously meaning to sting me, and it did. But I ignored the feeling of being stung.

"You should listen to me," I said. "I'm old enough to be your mother."

"Actually, if you want to get technical about it, you're *older* than my mother."

In the months since I'd met her, I had always felt older than her—stands to reason, right?—but I'd never felt *old*, not until that minute.

But it didn't matter. I had to push that feeling away too. Because I saw the future clearly now. Eddie hadn't worn her down tonight, not enough to make her go back with him right then and there. But give him time. He would.

I saw the future and I made a promise to myself.

I hadn't done right by Minnie. I hadn't been able to stop her from getting gang-raped, hadn't stopped her from throwing her life away when she was. And afterward, when she was dying, I hadn't been able to stop that either.

But Cindy was here and she was alive and I *could* do right by her. I had to.

Lise

I closed my checkbook. The July bills were paid and I felt that perverse satisfaction one feels after shelling out a few thousand dollars because at least I'd been able to do the shelling all on my own.

It had been nice of Aunt Tess, even though her own money-management plan was unorthodox, to offer to subsidize me while I got my writing career off the ground. But I was too old to have someone else support me. I'd lived fairly conservatively for the last decade or so, had a small nest on reserve in the bank; not in jars in the ground or in paper bags in the top of my closet. I'd be OK, at least in the short term. Still, it was nice to know the net was there should I ever need it.

I suppose I could have told Tony about my safety net, my parents too for that matter, to allay their fears that I was leaping into a financial void. But it just rankled too much: the idea that, old as I was, I couldn't make an adult decision about my future without others leaning over my shoulder, needling, "Are you sure you've thought all this out?"

And Aunt Tess had agreed with me: it was right to make them squirm.

I put the checkbook back in the drawer, got up, stretched, and then went to the kitchen to put some TV-watching snacks together.

"Those look good," Tony said a short time later, stealing a piece of melba toast with tapenade across the top. It wasn't exactly like I'd cooked anything: the toast came from a box, the tapenade from a jar.

"Diana is coming over to watch the debut of Sylvia's show," I said. "Remember, I told you?"

"Oh. Right. I think I'll go out."

"What does that mean?"

"It's just that, ever since you've met these women, they've started to slowly take over your life."

"They're my friends!"

"I know. But that doesn't mean *I* have to spend all my free time with them. Catch you later."

And he was gone, without even a kiss.

When Diana arrived, she had on white slacks with a red top and a jaunty red hat on her head.

"You look terrific," I said, meaning it.

"Thanks," she said, doing a little turn. "You like it?"

It got tiresome at times, always having to positively reinforce. I'd already said she looked good once, hadn't I? Why did I have to say it again? And it got tiresome always having to say, "Did you lose another pound?" and things like that. I liked Diana. I *loved* Diana. And it wasn't that I didn't want to see her succeed at her goals, because I did. But did it all have to be so all-consuming?

"Yes, I do," I said. "I like it very much."

"I just got it this morning," she said. "I'm glad you like it." She gave me a hug and that at least was good. Then she looked into the room behind me. "Where are Cindy and Sylvia?"

"They're not coming," I said, gesturing her into the living room where I already had the snacks set up on the coffee table in front of the TV. "Cindy wanted to stay home in case Eddie called, and Sylvia wanted to stay and keep an eye out, make sure Cindy didn't run off with Eddie."

"Oh dear."

"Agreed."

"Well," she said with a deep sigh, "I guess it's just the two of us then."

I understood her disappointment. Things had grown strained between us ever since that phone conversation in which I'd questioned her behavior toward her sister, Artemis. I hadn't intended to hurt Diana with my words, but I had meant them. Why always look at the failings in a relationship, sisters or otherwise, as being wholly the other person's fault?

I'd been giving a lot of thought to my relationship with my own sister lately. When she'd been gone, away, out of the country, I'd missed her so much. But now that she was back, she was just so...*Sara*. It's funny how when someone's gone, you think only of the good things they represent. But when they're in your face? All the old things start to rankle, all the old jealousies and petty competitiveness rear up again. I'd been inclined, all my life, to think it was her. But now I was beginning to wonder: Was it me?

"Tony's not around either?" Diana said, looking around as though she might find him under the couch. It made me sad to think that, close as we'd grown, she was now desperate to have at least one other person, any other person, there with us.

"Sorry," I said. "He went out." Then, because it's only natural when someone asks you about your man to ask about theirs, I asked, "How are things going with Dan?"

"Dan." She sniffed. "Do you know he's been getting e-mails all the time from this Layla person he's known since back before we met?"

"Are you jealous of her?"

"Of course not. I just don't see why she has to e-mail him practically every day."

"But don't you get e-mails from Dirk every day?"

As soon as the words were out of my mouth, I regretted them. Even though Diana had been the one to put me in touch with Dirk, for which I was grateful, she'd become weirdly competitive about it, as though she resented the time he spent on me.

She stiffened. "That's different."

"Here," I said, reaching for the remote and clicking on the TV. "Why don't we just watch the program? It's about to start."

"Welcome to the debut of *The Rude Chef*," the voice-over said. "*The Rude Chef* has been taped before a live studio audience."

"Oh my God! There's Sylvia!" Diana squealed, impulsively grabbing onto my hand, forgetting the differences between us. "She looks *fantastic!*"

"Her hair looks gorgeous, at least what I can see of it," I said. "But look at her apron and that toque. They're so big, she's practically swimming in them."

On the screen, Sylvia didn't say a word. Not one. She just got to work slicing and dicing. In front of her work area was a high semicircular counter, in front of which in turn were six barstools with people in the seats, both men and women. They looked like they were in Vegas getting ready for blackjack, and they all looked like they'd done this sort of thing before. I figured they were Sylvia's tasters.

"Isn't she supposed to be talking?" Diana asked me after a bit.

On television, just a half-minute of silence can seem like an eternity. Just watch any host try to fill airtime on a show that's run short. But *The Rude Chef* had been on for far longer than a half-minute and Sylvia had yet to say a word.

One of the tasters delicately cleared her throat as Sylvia threw some black and blue shells into a massive boiling pot. "Um, aren't you supposed to tell us what you're doing as you go?"

"Nobody said anything about that when they hired me," Sylvia said, not even moving her eyes up from her work. "I'm Sylvia. I'm making supper. What more do you want from me?"

The taster laughed nervously. "OK, Sylvia. But what *are* you cooking?"

"Herb steamed mussels with rice pilaf. Are you satisfied? I hope you're not allergic to shellfish. I'd hate to kill someone on my very first show."

"That looks good," Diana said a few moments later as Sylvia slapped bowls down in front of her tasters. "It's going well, I think, don't you?"

"But that one taster is right," I said. "Shouldn't Sylvia be talking more?"

"No," Diana said, "I'm starting to think it's better this way. If she talks less, then she can't offend everybody, right?"

Then we sat through a commercial break in which it was strongly suggested that we buy pharmaceuticals to prevent erectile dysfunction.

"What are you making now?" one of the male tasters asked when the program came back on.

"Asparagus and shellfish salad," Sylvia said.

"Are those mussels you're putting in there?" the woman taster who'd been so inquisitive before asked. "Isn't that a bit...redundant? And isn't that doing things in reverse order: giving us the main course and then throwing a salad at us?"

"I can throw a lot more than a salad at you," Sylvia suggested.

"You're not very nice, are you?" the woman sniffed.

"Of course I'm not nice. I'm the rude chef. It's what they pay me for. You want nice, go on that Nigella person's show."

"I'm not sure I want to know what she does for an encore," Diana said, as the show cut to another commercial break. "Do you think she'll try to serve them some form of mussels for dessert? And now I'm certain of it: she *definitely* does better when she doesn't talk."

Dessert had nothing to do with mussels and everything to do with ladyfingers.

"Oh dear *God!*" Diana said. "Did Sylvia just throw a ladyfinger at that woman?"

"You don't like the way I do things," Sylvia said, "get your own damn cooking show."

And then the food fight broke out.

"Is it just me," I asked, "or is this the strangest show you've ever seen?"

"For reality TV?" Diana shrugged. "I've seen stranger."

While the credits were still rolling, I went to call Sylvia. No matter how awful the show had been, she was my friend. It was my job to congratulate her on her success. But the phone rang against my hand just as I went to pick it up.

"Hello?"

"We have to do something." The voice, while still a masculine form of feminine, was hushed.

"Sylvia? I was just about to call you. Diana and I wanted to tell you how great the show—"

"Never mind that now. Who cares about the stupid show? We need to get Cindy out of town. And fast."

Road Trip

RECOMMENDED READING:
Cindy: *Grand Avenue*, Joy Fielding
Diana: *Margaret: The Last Real Princess*, Neal Botham
Sylvia: *Like Water for Chocolate*, Laura Esquivel
Lise: *Wonder Boys*, Michael Chabon

"I've booked us a house right on the Georgia coast!" Diana crowed into the phone, obviously pleased with herself.

"Isn't that taking a bit much on yourself?" Sylvia asked. "Deciding where we'll go without consulting anyone else first?"

"Do you have any idea how hard it is to get seaside lodging with four bedrooms at the last minute?" Diana's voice stiffened with offense. "Thank God the economy's so bad, and the most expensive places aren't all taken as the booking agent told me they would be in most seasons, or we might have had to settle for New Jersey." Then she brightened. "And it'll be perfect! A friend of mine is going to be there around the same time in Atlanta—"

"Wait a second. You booked this thinking the Georgia coast was near *Atlanta?*"

"You mean it's not?"

"Before Minnie got sick, we went to Scotland together and took one of those tours where you walk across the country in a week. But this is the United States, not Europe. And every state in the country isn't like Connecticut where you can throw a stone and hit New York. You're talking Georgia, for crying out loud. It's big!"

"Oh. I see."

"By the way, how were you planning on getting all of us down to the Georgia coast?"

Diana's tone lightened once more. "That's the best part! I've rented us one of those RVs!"

• • •

After checking e-mail one last time, Lise closed the lid on her laptop. She unplugged the machine and wound up the cord, tucking the whole in its special case. She put the encased laptop by the suitcase, already packed, on the bed. Then she unzipped the suitcase one last time to see if she was forgetting anything.

"Don't you think you're taking this friendship thing too far?" Tony said. He was slouched against the doorframe, arms crossed as he watched her move about the bedroom.

"No, I don't," Lise said, not bothering to look up as she squeezed a few more pairs of panties into the already overstuffed suitcase.

"Your own sister was sick in Africa, and you didn't go there."

"That was different."

"How so?"

"For one thing, it was still during the school year. I couldn't very well have just up and deserted my responsibilities mid semester."

"Why not? I'm sure the dean would have let you."

"Perhaps. But Sara was being well taken care of in the hospital. She didn't need me."

"So why do you have to go too? Why can't Sylvia and Diana take care of this on their own?"

"Sylvia says that for the intervention she's got planned to work—"

"God, I hate that psycho doublespeak. *Intervention.*"

"We should all be in on it."

"But she's not your sister. You've known Cindy for less than a year, barely more than six months, and you're running off to help her when you wouldn't even go to your own sister?"

"You keep saying that. But maybe who we're closest to isn't always about blood. Maybe it has something to do with who we choose."

"I thought you chose me."

"It's not about that *kind* of choosing! This has nothing to do with you!"

"Apparently not," Tony said. Then: "I may not be here when you get back."

"That's not surprising." Lise tried on a laugh. "You have your own place. It only seems like you live here because you're over here all the time."

"It's just too much, Lise. You quit your job without even discussing it with me first."

"It was *my* decision to make!"

"Half the time I don't even know what's going on between you and Dirk over that damn book."

"It's *my* book!"

"And now you're running off to Georgia to perform an... *intervention* for some woman you've known for less than a year, when the other two could just as easily do it without you."

"But I've already explained that—"

"It doesn't matter. What I meant before was that I may not be here as in I may no longer be a part of *us*."

Lise stiffened as she grabbed the suitcase handle in one hand, the laptop in the other.

"Then that'll be your choice," she said.

• • •

"You can't do this!" Magda screamed through the phone.

"Of course I can do this," Sylvia said evenly, clearly not bothered by being shouted at by her hysterical producer. "I've done it."

"But the show is a huge success! Did you see what Jonathan Dalrymple wrote in the *New York Post*? 'A food fight! It made me crazy when that one taster kept asking Sylvia to tell everyone what she was doing. All I could think was, oh, I'd actually watch a cooking show that didn't bother trying to teach me something. I don't want to learn. I'm just there for the food porn! And when the food started flying through the air? I actually caught some of it. And, let me tell you, that flung food was superb. I think Sylvia Goldsmith has a summer hit on her hands and I, for one, am now a devoted fan of *The Rude Chef.* Throw some more food at me, Sylvia baby. I'll eat it right up.'"

"I'm very happy for you," Sylvia said. "But we've already taped all six of the scheduled summer episodes. You don't need me here. I can just as easily watch myself on TV from Georgia as I can from Connecticut."

"But what about the publicity? The *Today Show* called. The *Today Show!* They want you to come on and do a live segment. I think they want you to throw food at Matt Lauer."

"And I'm sure me and Matt'd both find it a treat. Sorry, Magda. I've got more important things to do. I have a friend in need."

"But it's in your contract! It says you're required to fulfill any reasonable requests to do promotion for the show. I'd say the *Today Show* is a pretty reasonable request! We could sue you!"

"You really think so?" Sylvia's voice would have sounded just like steel if she weren't laughing. "If you're lucky, and the show continues being a hit, *maybe* I'll come back to you in the fall. But if you sue me now, my *fans* will eat you and your network alive."

* * *

"What do you think of these jeans?" Diana said, doing a more confident model's twirl than she'd formerly done. "They're called Tummy Tucks. They're the latest thing."

"They look great on you," Dan said from his position on the bed where he was lying on his side, head propped on his hand. "But you do realize it gets hot in Georgia in August, don't you?"

"Hot?"

"Much hotter than here."

"Oh. I see. Then perhaps these khaki shorts I bought yesterday? I didn't usually ever wear shorts. But lately I've started thinking, why not?"

"I'm sure whatever you wear, you'll look terrific."

"Thanks. Now where did I put that box with the new sandals?"

"I still can't believe you're going. How long will you be gone?"

"I booked the house for the whole month. I don't know if we'll stay that long, but at least the option's there if we decide to."

"So you might not even be back for Labor Day."

"Why? Is that a very important holiday for you?"

Dan just shook his head. "And how did you pay for all this? The house on the beach…that RV out front…the clothes."

Diana looked shocked. "Why, the same way I pay for everything. With one of the credit cards you gave me, of course."

Dan didn't say anything.

"You don't mind, do you? You've never minded before."

"No, of course it's not the money."

"Then what?"

"You've changed, Diana. These last several months, you've changed a lot."

Diana put her hands on her noticeably slimmer hips. "One would think you would like those changes. Most men would."

"Maybe I'm not most men."

"I don't know what that means. And I don't have time to figure it out now. If I don't leave soon, I'm going to be late to meet the girls."

"We can't have that, can we?"

Diana, hearing the sharpness of his tone, stopped what she was doing and looked at his face clearly for the first time. Finally registering the depth of his displeasure, she approached him and placed her hand against his cheek. "Come on," she said softly. "Can't you see how important this is to me? That I need to be there for my friend in her hour of need?"

"What I see is that we haven't been married for very long, not really, and now you're running off and, like with so many other things, this is a decision you made without even discussing it with me first."

"I'm sorry. Of course you're right. I should have." Diana glanced surreptitiously at her watch. "Oh, God! I really do have to—"

"Fine."

"Aren't you going to at least kiss me good-bye? Aren't you going to miss me?"

"I miss the woman I fell in love with," Dan said, "every day." Then he shook his head. "But, no. I don't think I'll miss the new you."

* * *

Sylvia lay in her bed with her head against Sunny's chest. They were both fully clothed.

"Do you think we're doing the right thing?" Sylvia asked again.

"Not only do I think you are doing the right thing, I think you are perhaps doing the *only* thing. What is more, I wholly endorse it."

Sylvia let out a sigh of relief.

"There is just one thing that still worries me," Sunny said. "What if Eddie comes after you? Things could get ugly."

"That's the whole point of leaving in the middle of the night. By the time he figures out we're gone, we'll be halfway to Georgia." She paused, considering the people she'd be traveling with. "We'll at least be across state lines."

"Cindy still does not know?"

"No. The others should be here soon. Then I'll wake her up. It feels funny lying here with you like this with Cindy and Carly in the other bedroom. It makes me feel like we're their parents."

"Speak for yourself." Sunny laughed. "I am not old enough to be their father. My mother would have killed me."

Sylvia swatted his shoulder.

"I shall miss you, Sylvia."

Sylvia sat up, gazed down at his face. "You'll be here when I get back?"

"Of course. I am your great good friend."

* * *

"But I can't just take off!" Cindy said, still wiping the residual sleep out of her eyes.

"Of course you can," Sylvia said.

"What about my job at Midnight Scandals?"

Sylvia snorted. "I thought you never liked that job anyway. This'll give you the perfect excuse to quit."

"Actually," Carly piped up, "I was thinking I could take over your job. I need work and you always said Marlene could never tell any of her sales help apart, that it didn't matter who was working there so long as the *D* cups stayed out of the *A*s because whenever they got mixed up, customers got all insecure and everything."

"What?" Cindy's eyes narrowed at her sister. "You're in on this too? Not that I'm even sure what *this* is."

"I have no idea what you're talking about," Carly said, her eyes going all innocent.

"But what about Eddie?" Cindy said. "He was going to come by tomorrow night. Or would that be tonight?"

"Oh, don't worry about Eddie," Carly said. "I can take care of him too."

Cindy turned to Lise. "What about the work on your book?"

Lise waved her laptop case in the air. "Nice thing about the modern era. A writer can write anywhere."

Cindy turned to Diana. "What about Dan? You've been married less than a year. Isn't he bothered by the idea of your leaving?"

"No," Diana spoke softly. "I don't think Dan's going to miss me at all."

"What about your TV show?" Cindy spun on Sylvia. "What about your business, Sylvia's Supper?"

"I told Magda the damn show could spin without me for a month," Sylvia said. "As for the business, I'll put a sign up on our way out of town: 'Gone fishing. See you in September…*maybe.*'"

"A *month*? September? But I can't go away for a whole month. What about my ob-gyn visits?"

"You just had your last one recently, didn't you?"

Cindy nodded.

"And everything was OK?"

Cindy nodded again.

"And you're still at the stage where you only go once a month anyway. The once-a-week stuff doesn't start until much later, right?"

"Yes, but—"

"So you'll be on time for your next appointment." Sylvia thought about it for a minute then shrugged. "Or maybe you'll be a little bit late."

"But—"

Sylvia placed her hands on Cindy's shoulders. "Look, when was the last time you went on a trip somewhere outside of Connecticut?"

Cindy didn't even have to consider that one but when she answered, she sounded just as surprised as the others looked. "Never."

"Then don't you think you owe it to yourself? Wouldn't it be great to go away with three girlfriends to have some wild fun before the baby comes and every second of your life changes?"

"I guess."

"I've got just two words for you then," Sylvia said. Then she screamed, "*Road trip!*"

Lise

"What are you doing?" Sylvia said as Diana moved to climb into the front passenger seat of the RV.

"What?" Diana looked perplexed.

"Aren't you driving?" Sylvia asked.

"God, no," Diana said. "I only drove it over here. But you can't expect me to drive it practically all the way down to the bottom of the United States. This isn't even my country! As you've so often pointed out, I haven't a clue as to the proper geography here."

"Don't look at me," Cindy said to Sylvia, climbing into the backseat. "I remember what a hard time you gave me that one time I drove you to the doctor's in your catering van."

"I'm with her," I said of Cindy, climbing in beside her.

"Great," Sylvia said, accepting the driver's position.

"Oh, come on," I said, trying to joke her out of her suddenly foul mood. "You're such a control freak, you'd hate it if anyone else drove."

"And that's supposed to make me feel better?" she said, keying the ignition. Then she turned to Diana beside her. "Tell me you at least got us a map."

"Well, of *course* I got us a map. But do you really need it? I thought you just took I-95 straight down."

"And I thought you said you didn't know where you're going. But, yeah, we could do that. Or we could take the scenic route, which would take longer."

"Does the scenic route take us by the ocean?" Cindy piped up.

"Uh, *yeah*," Sylvia said with a laugh that was not unkind. "That's why they call it the scenic route."

"I've never seen the ocean," Cindy said wistfully.

"You're kidding," I said.

"No. Well, one time Eddie took me to Seaside Park in Bridgeport, but I don't know if you'd count that."

"I wouldn't," Sylvia said, pulling out. "The scenic route it is."

· · ·

New York, New Jersey, Pennsylvania.

Each state took me farther away from Connecticut, farther from my breakup with Tony. I tried to tell myself that *back there* didn't matter, that if Tony really loved me he'd have been more supportive when I made the decision to leave my job, that he'd be more supportive now of my need to support Cindy.

As we drove, the sky began to lighten with the dawning of a new day. As we drove, Cindy snored softly beside me; before nodding off, she'd mentioned with a big yawn that the farther she got into the pregnancy, the more tired she was. As we drove on, I listened to Sylvia and Diana talking in the front seat.

Mostly, it was Diana doing the talking. Mostly, Diana was talking about her diet and weight loss.

"I'm a bit worried about this trip," Diana confessed.

"How so?" Sylvia asked.

"Well, at home it's easy for me to control what I eat. But here we'll be on vacation for possibly a whole month. We'll probably go out to eat three meals a day. How will I manage?"

"You'll do fine," Sylvia said patiently. "We're renting a house, right? I assume it will have a kitchen with refrigeration and cooking facilities. We can always bring food in a lot if you're that worried."

"I suppose," Diana said skeptically. "I just don't want to blow it after coming so far."

"You won't."

"About that house…"

"What about the house?"

"Well, I was going over the rental agreement and brochure again this morning and it appears I made a slight mistake. Well, two slight mistakes actually."

"What two slight mistakes?"

"For starters, the house isn't right on the beach, per se."

"How much not per se is it?"

"About four houses back from the ocean."

"Four houses? That's not so bad." Sylvia shrugged. "The walking will be good for Cindy. It'll be good for all of us. So what's the other slight mistake?"

"Well," Diana said with a little laugh, "I know you'll laugh at how I could possibly screw this up, but remember I told you there were four bedrooms? Well, there are only three."

"I'm not laughing."

"Yes, I can see that."

"So what were you thinking? Two women will share and two will have singles?"

"Exactly. I'm sure it will be fine."

"I'm too old to be living like a sorority sister," Sylvia said, "sharing a dorm room."

"So," Diana suggested, "perhaps you and I will have the singles and Lise and Cindy can bunk in together?"

We drove on toward Delaware and, as we drove, I wondered why I had ever liked Diana so much.

. . .

Delaware.

Cindy was awake now and Sylvia suggested stopping so Cindy could see the ocean. But when we got to Rehoboth Beach, the sky was so overcast with fog it was too hazy, like a scene from a post-nuclear movie.

"Let's push on to Maryland," Sylvia said. "Maybe the sun will be out there."

. . .

Maryland turned out to be much sunnier, and when we crossed into Ocean City, Sylvia saw a sign that made her let out a girlish squeal, or at least as girlish as a masculine-sounding voice could get.

"Parasailing! I've always wanted to go parasailing!"

The place with the advertisement was located on the bayside of Ocean City and, after Sylvia found a place to park the huge RV, we found somewhere to change into our suits.

Cindy, her tummy bulging slightly in her suit, settled down on a beach towel on the sand. Cindy had somehow managed to hide her pregnancy from Eddie—I suppose because she'd gained so little weight in the first trimester—but I was sure if he saw her now, he couldn't help knowing.

"Aren't you going to try it?" Sylvia asked.

"No, thanks," Cindy said with an easy smile, inhaling deeply. "It's enough just to be here, see the water, smell the air." She patted her belly. "And I don't think Junior would much like Mommy flying up in the air like that."

"Who's going first?" Sylvia asked.

I could see she was itching to go. "Why don't you?" I suggested. "You're the one who's been doing all the driving."

I didn't have to ask her twice.

I sat on the towel with Cindy and Diana, watching as the tiny boat took Sylvia out to the center of the bay. When she came back, exhilarated, it was my turn.

Once the boat had me out as far as Sylvia had gone, I was strapped into a tiny carriage seat and, almost instantly, I was soaring five hundred feet above the water. It was scary going up that fast but, once I got used to it, I didn't want the ride to end.

"Your turn," I said to Diana, when the fun was over.

"Oh no, I couldn't."

"Why not?"

"Look at me. I'm so big, I'd probably break the tow rope in two. If I don't die from the fall, they'll sue me for damaging their equipment."

"Don't be ridiculous," I said. "They take up people who weigh far more than you every day."

"Do you really think so?"

I was losing patience. "Just do it," I said.

When Diana returned, laughing so hard it was contagious, I was glad I'd insisted.

"That was marvelous," she said, throwing her arms around me. "For the first time in my life, I felt weightless! I wish I could do that every day."

It was funny. Even though Diana was a handful of years older than me, I always felt as though I were the older of us two. Now, as I felt her warm hug, I remembered again why I'd liked her so much in the first place, something I'd forgotten in recent weeks.

Maryland was such a happy place for us after the parasailing, we resolved to stay overnight and get an early start the next day.

• • •

Virginia, North Carolina, South Carolina.

By the time we got to the Georgia coast, what with stops for Cindy to empty her pregnant bladder and for the rest of us to eat, it was after dark again. As we pulled into the sandy driveway, there was a car already there on the concrete slab that served as the parking spot, a rental car. It was a black Jaguar. The beach house itself was raised a story above ground on large wooden piers, I guess in case of flooding. And, on the weathered wooden staircase leading up to the door, was a man with longish blond hair, dressed in inappropriate-for-the-beach business attire, who I recognized from the publishing trade magazines.

"Dirk!" Diana cried, hurrying over to the man in question who rose, enveloping her in a big hug.

"Diana! Let me look at you! You look even better than the last time I saw you, truly marvelous." He let go of her and turned to me. "And you must be Lise, my author. So wonderful to finally meet." Instead of accepting the hand I held out, he enveloped me in another one of his big hugs. "We've got a lot to talk about, my girl." Taking in the other two, and Cindy's belly, he said, "And you must be Cindy. And Sylvia, of course. I've seen *The Rude Chef*, and I'd know you anywhere."

Cindy looked stunned, as though she'd been hit by a truck,

which Dirk was in a way, while Sylvia settled for a terse, "Charmed. I'm sure."

"But, Dirk," Diana said, drawing his attention back to her. "What are you doing here?" Funny, even though she asked the question with an innocent expression, her eyes were almost too wide, *too* innocent. Did she invite him? Did she know ahead of time he'd be here?

"The conference is done as far as I'm concerned, so I thought I'd pop over to see you since you did say you were arriving today, but Tybee Island is a lot farther from Atlanta than I thought. Do you know it took me several hours to get here? I thought you'd never come! I don't suppose you mind putting an old Englishman up for a day or two or more?"

"No, of course not," Diana said, fumbling the key we'd picked up from the booking agent along the way into the lock. "There are three bedrooms, so we women will sleep two in each and you can have the third. I'm sure no one will mind."

As Dirk followed Diana in and Cindy followed them, Sylvia turned to me. "Great. Who let the fucking rooster in the henhouse?"

Diana

Dirk got the best of the three bedrooms.

It only seemed fair, since two were of equal size while the third was massive, and if two of us women had gotten that bedroom the other two would have been resentful.

I was hoping for Cindy—she was so easygoing—or even Sylvia. But Sylvia called first dibs on Cindy—they had that whole mother/daughter thing going on—so I got stuck with Lise.

Funny, to use the word "stuck" about the one woman in the three I'd formerly felt closest to, and yet that's exactly how I felt. The bedroom had one double bed, not even a queen or king. She'd probably hog all the sheets and spend whatever waking moments there were before sleep passing judgment on me.

As it were, she didn't hog all the sheets, but she did snore a bit. I suppose it was all that smoking she still did on the sly.

The rental house, despite only having three bedrooms for the five of us, turned out to be even better than expected. Sylvia quickly made herself at home cooking meals for everyone in the kitchen, and Cindy discovered the game room with a pool table, dartboard, and other amusements. Cindy looked a bit strange, bending over the table with her slight bulge of a belly to shoot against herself, but she seemed so at peace in those moments, we all volunteered to let her teach us how to play.

Funny thing about Cindy too: She didn't appear to grasp why we were all there, that it had to do with saving her. Instead, she seemed mystified every time she wondered aloud about calling Eddie and Sylvia suggested she wait until some nebulous "later." When was Sylvia planning on saying something?

Having Dirk there was a huge revelation. Even though I liked him when we met in London, and I really loved the e-mails we'd exchanged since, particularly the racier ones, I always thought he came across as spoiled and would have expected him to want us four women to wait on him hand and foot. And yet it wasn't like that at all. The first few days we were there, he made himself extremely useful: going back to the house to get more drinks for everyone when the cooler on the beach ran out, placing cushions under Cindy's feet when she complained of her ankles being swollen; he even offered to help Sylvia with the barbecue!

Which, of course, she refused.

But that didn't seem to deter Dirk in the slightest. If he couldn't offer practical services, he would question the others about their lives. I'd once read an article in a women's magazine that said one of the best ways to get others to like you is to ask questions about them, to show an interest in what interested them rather than nattering on about your own life. I'd never known if it really worked before, but it certainly appeared to be working for Dirk now. The—women that would include me—were eating out of his hands.

Well, except for Sylvia.

"He makes me feel like a bug under a microscope," I heard Sylvia say one night while she and Cindy were in the kitchen doing the dishes. "Why does he want to know about my sister? Why does he want to know about the TV show? And asking you about Eddie and the baby—the guy's a fucking sponge! What I'd like to know is, when he wrings his spongy self dry, what's going to come out?"

I would have made my presence known, leapt to Dirk's defense, but sweet Cindy saved me from it.

"What are you worried about," Cindy said with an easy laugh, "that he wants to write a book about us? He's just being nice."

Still, I saw that quarters were getting tight there for the five of us, and it was time I did something proactive to temporarily remove two of us from the equation.

* * *

"I was wondering," I said to Dirk, catching him alone on the deck that circled three sides of the upper story of the house, "what do you say to dinner out tonight?"

"Funny you should mention that. I just asked Lise the same thing. It's so hard to get any talking in about the book with everyone around all the time."

I'm sure my face must have fallen dramatically. But then I felt his hands on my shoulders.

"And of course," he said, "I was going to ask you to join us." Then he kissed me lightly on the lips. "I haven't had nearly enough time alone with you these past few days. After all, you're the reason I'm here in the first place, right?"

So, as twilight fell that night, I put on the best outfit I'd brought with me: all white and gold, echoing what I'd worn the first night I met the three other women in the bookstore, only this time the clothes I was wearing were designed to fit a woman approximately one hundred pounds lighter. I felt very good about myself until I saw Lise come out a few minutes later, also wearing white, only in her case it was a sarong-style dress and the woman in that dress was a good sixty pounds lighter than me. Suddenly, I wasn't feeling so keen anymore.

"Are my two ladies ready?" Dirk said, offering each of us an arm. Then to Sylvia and Cindy he said, "I suppose I should say don't wait up since I have a notion these beautiful women are going to keep me out very late tonight."

And then we were gone.

* * *

The restaurant was packed. We'd grown so isolated at the house, even though of course we saw other people on the beach each day, I'd forgotten there were a ton of other people vacationing too.

"I made reservations," Dirk said, "but it looks like there'll be a wait anyway. Shall we have a drink in the bar?"

The bar was crowded too, but a man with a wild case of sunburn gave up his seat when he saw Lise.

"No, thanks. I'll stand," she said when she saw there wouldn't be places for all of us, which, I suppose, was nice of her.

Once we had our drinks, Dirk turned to Lise.

"I'm really liking the changes you've made to the novel," he said, "but it doesn't feel as commercial as it did before. I think it would be a great big error if you tipped over too far into the literary."

"How so?" she said earnestly.

Dirk barked an amused laugh. "Oh, you know, all that politics you've included. Do you really think the average reader cares how the Swiss elect their presidents?"

"That's not literary," Lise said, "it's technical detail. And, anyway, I imagine the Swiss care how their officials are elected."

"*Well.* If you think your audience is the Swiss…"

"If you don't like the politics, and it's a political satire, then what do you like?"

"Well, I still like the part where she sleeps with both presidents on the same night. I like that part very much." He knocked back the rest of his drink. "Onward and upward. You'll get there. I'm sure by the time I'm done with you, your book will be perfect."

Whatever Lise murmured in response, I didn't hear it, but it practically sounded like a simper.

When we got to the table, the waitress having finally called our party's name, I could almost see Dirk debating whose chair to pull out first. The awkward moment went on so long, we finally just all sat.

"This sea air really improves one's appetite," Dirk announced, opening the heavy menu.

"I know what you mean," Lise said, following suit. "I may just have to order one of each." Then she proved her point by ordering for an appetizer the crab Louie, which sounded very fattening to me with all that sauce and made me resent her very much as I ate only the lettuce from my shrimp cocktail.

The drink from the bar, on top of which I was piling glass upon glass from the bottles of wine Dirk kept ordering, was going to my head. Their conversation, all about bloody damned books, swirled around me like just so many words. I kept trying to get a word of my own in edgewise, and Dirk was always encouraging whenever I did manage, but I couldn't shake the feeling of being a third wheel on someone else's date.

I said as much to Lise after he excused himself to use the bathroom.

"Do you think you could flirt any heavier?" I said.

Her eyes were a picture of innocence. "What are you talking about?" she said. "He's my agent."

"Well, there are three of us here. And you already have a boyfriend. Have you forgotten all about Tony?"

"Tony? I'm not *married* to Tony. Besides, I have the feeling Tony and I are finished. Have you forgotten about *Dan*?"

"Do you have to be so childish about it?"

"Do *you*?"

She had a point, I thought, but just barely.

I would like to say it got better from there, but it didn't. My resentment grew as she ordered shrimp with lobster sauce to my large green salad—hold the dressing—and intensified as she and Dirk split a large piece of something called Death By Chocolate as I drank one more glass of white wine.

Nor did it get better when we returned to the house. Sylvia and Cindy were already asleep. Cindy's pregnancy hormones no doubt kicking in, while Sylvia was used to going to bed early from running her catering business. So Lise and I silently resolved to see who could wait the other out with Dirk.

We retired to the game room with more wine, figuring if we made too much noise there, at least we'd be far enough away from the sleeping quarters we wouldn't disturb the others.

For a drowsy minute, I was sure Lise would outlast me, but then one of the many rich things she'd eaten for dinner must have kicked in, and, with a pained look on her face, she made fast for the bathroom.

No sooner was she gone, then Dirk sidled closer to me on the overstuffed sofa, draping his arm along the back.

"I was sure we'd never get a moment alone together," he said.

I burped; unladylike, I know. Then I said, "But I thought you liked Lise?" I was still feeling burned about dinner. "You could barely stop talking to her all evening."

"Of course I like Lise," he said easily. "She's my client, sort of, isn't she? But she's not close to me, not like you are." He tightened his arm around my shoulders.

I have to admit, it felt good. And it felt even better when he commenced nuzzling my neck. It had been a long time since Dan had nuzzled any part of me. Worrying that Lise might return soon and steal him away again, I sought to come up with something that would hold his attention.

"I was thinking," I said as Dirk nuzzled my neck.

"Yes?"

"All of my friends are so fascinating. I'll bet there're books in each of them, perhaps more than one. Lise, of course, is already working on hers. But perhaps Sylvia could do a cookbook tie-in to her show or possibly a memoir about losing her twin sister; that sort of thing is always popular. And then there's Cindy, who has the whole abused-girlfriend/single-mother/up-by-her-bootstraps thing down pat. Book her on that Oprah of yours, and, with that face of hers, she'd be worth a million pounds."

I had to pause so I could barely stifle a burp.

"I don't think it's quite that easy to get on Oprah," Dirk said.

"No? Perhaps not. But it would still be marketable, don't you think?"

"I suppose. People love reading about pretty people with problems. In fact, you could say there's a whole cottage industry around it: PPPs–Pretty People Problem books. What are you getting at?"

It was tough to concentrate at the moment—the neck nuzzling was that good—but I had to get my point across.

"It has to do," I said, "with what I once wrote you in an e-mail about me possibly doing some work for you. How'd you like me to be your talent scout? I could start with my friends…" Then I thought of something. "But don't you already have a thriving agency?" I said. "You probably wouldn't want my help."

"Of course I have a thriving agency." He laughed. "But I'm

pretty sure the Duchess of Windsor once said that one can never be too pushy or have too many successful clients. I'm always looking for new talent."

"Well, if you really think it's a good idea…"

He kissed me on the lips.

"If you really think I could be of service to you…"

I heard Lise's step just as the overabundance of wine attacked my own stomach, causing me to follow her precedence with a mad dash to the loo. As it turned out, the food got her, the wine got me.

I can't honestly say who won that night: Lise or me. Did he kiss her as he had done me, as I vomited up my chardonnay? She certainly seemed smug when I saw her the next morning at breakfast.

All I know is, by the time I got done tossing my lettuce in the loo, I was feeling too gross for anymore kissing. And when I woke briefly in the middle of the night because my mouth was dry as shoe leather, Lise was in bed beside me, snoring.

And her bloody feet were cold.

Sylvia

Here's the recipe, just in case you want to try it at home:

> 4 very different women
> 1 male "literary" agent
> 1 rental house with only three bedrooms
> Mix together liberally

Result? One recipe for disaster.

Remove the literary agent from the mix, and you've still got a disaster.

My advice? Don't try this at home. The recipe sucks.

My point? Nothing was turning out the way I'd planned. I'd had such high hopes for this trip, thinking that if we could just get Cindy out of Connecticut, if we could just come around her as a united group, we could find a way to make her see the light, make her see that it was best for her *and* her baby that she break from Eddie for good. But none of that was happening because two of our intervening triad—Lise and Diana—were too involved in playing out their own petty drama. And for what? Some fast-talking geek in a gold suit?

This is to say that even after Dirk left, streaking out of the sandy drive in his black Jaguar, things were just as tense, even more so, than when he'd been there. All my life, up until that past year, I'd avoided groups of women. Of course I'd avoided men too, because of Minnie, but I'd particularly avoided groups of women. There was a good reason for that. Put two women together for any length of time and they start fighting like a married couple. Put more than two women together for any length of time and they start fighting like a family.

A chill had grown up between Diana and Lise. Obviously, it had something to do with the Dirkster. I can't say it made a whole lot of sense to me. What woman in her right mind would want Mr. Smarm? And yet I was sure jealousy lay at the heart of the silent feud. But didn't Lise have Tony? Wasn't Diana married to Dan? Sure, they'd both alluded to problems with their men. Lise had told us Tony wasn't exactly supportive of her new career, while Diana had grown increasingly critical of Dan: he was never home; when he was home, he didn't have sex with her; blah blah blah, the things she'd told us all the way back on Memorial Day weekend, not to mention the night we left Connecticut when she said Dan wouldn't miss her. I'm not saying they shouldn't have felt the way they did, but from where I was sitting, those women didn't exactly represent bargains for their men. I know I'd encouraged Lise to just write her book, but I never told her to impulsively quit her job, and I could see where Tony might be put off by her doing so. It's one thing to say you're going after your dream and another thing to burn down all your bridges before you were even sure just what that dream was.

Lise herself was having doubts.

"All these changes Dirk keeps asking me to make," Lise said to me one overcast afternoon while Cindy was in the game room trying to teach Diana to shoot pool. "In the beginning, when I was first writing this book, I liked the feeling that I was writing my story for an audience of one: Dirk. But now? There are days when it doesn't even feel like it's my book anymore."

"I don't get it," I said. "I always thought people just wrote books and, if the writing was good enough, someone published it."

"You'd think, wouldn't you?" Lise said with a wry grin. "But Dirk always says that there are two kinds of agents: the kind that just take your work and turn it back out into the world again without so much as a comma changed, like a publishing revolving door; and then there are the other kind, the craftsmen who act as early editors, making sure the work is as near to perfect as possible before they'll submit it."

"So, Dirk's this second kind?" I said. "He has to put his fingerprints all over everything first?"

"Dirk…"

But then Diana came through, on her way to the kitchen to get another can of diet soda, and Lise shut up about Dirk.

It had gotten to the point where Lise and Diana would no longer talk to each other unless they absolutely had to. This meant that they'd barely say "Pass the salt, please" to each other at the dinner table. If I were a nicer person, I suppose I would have offered to switch rooms with one of them. But both of them were acting so loony, there was no way I was going to do that. And I suppose that, with Dirk gone, one of them could have moved into the bedroom he'd been using. But I'm guessing, for one of them to move out, it would have felt to both like admitting a defeat of their friendship. Me, I'd have just admitted defeat right away and jumped to clearer waters…not to mention the bigger bed.

I would have liked that bigger bed. And I also would have liked to be relieved of some of the cooking duties.

When we first got there, and for the first couple of weeks, I enjoyed it. It was fun shopping in stores where they had some different ingredients than I was used to working with at home, fun trying out new dishes. But after a while, I started feeling like not only was I the den mother to this dysfunctional family, I was also the chief cook and bottle washer too.

"Cook, cook, cook! That's all I seem to do around here," I said one night. "You'd think I was a caterer or something."

"Well, you *are* a caterer," Lise pointed out. But she took my point, and she and Cindy offered to cook dinner.

"I'm so glad we have some time, just the two of us, to talk," Diana said in a low voice as we sat on the deck, the other two doing God knows what with my kitchen inside.

I wasn't sure whether I wanted to encourage her or not. She probably just wanted to complain about Dan again or tell me all about the latest pound she'd lost; or, worse, talk about Dirk. Still, it didn't seem right to be rude.

"Oh yeah?" I said. "What'd you want to talk about?"

"I was wondering," she said, "have you ever considered putting the story of you and your sister down on paper? You could write about how the two of you lived, and then how she died. I'm sure it would make a fascinating tale."

"You mean, like, for other people to read?"

"Of course. What else would be the point?"

"God, no," I said. "I'd feel as though I was exploiting her."

Diana's face fell.

"I don't mean it's wrong for other people to do that sort of thing," I hurried to say. "People can do what they want. I'm just saying it'd be wrong for me."

"Oh. I see." Then she said, "What about a recipe book? The ratings for the taped episodes of *The Rude Chef* seem to be holding strong. You could maybe do one of those tie-in things, put together a collection of all your favorites, maybe jot the odd rude comment or two down with each one. I'm sure your fans would love it."

"A collection of my favorites?" Now, there was an idea with more appeal.

Still, I thought, *Books, books, books! First, everyone wants me to cook, cook, cook, and now everyone wants to talk to me about books, books, books.*

• • •

The only one who appeared untouched by the cold war that was now Diana and Lise, and the only one who wasn't coming to me to talk about books—maybe because she spent half the days with her nose buried in one romance novel or another—was Cindy. She just moved on, growing marginally bigger each week, seeming to be blithely unaware that we were all there because of her. She was so calm, in fact, I hated to burst the bubble around her by talking to her about what we'd come there to talk to her about. And so, the days piled up with nothing said.

But I did sneak calls to Carly every now and then whenever Cindy was otherwise occupied.

"How's it going?" I asked, on one such occasion.

"Good. I like working in the bra shop. At least it beats sitting around the house all day, and I get paid once a week." Pause. "Oh, and Eddie was here last night."

My grip on the phone tightened. "Eddie? What happened? What'd he want?"

"He wanted what he wants every time he comes by: for me to tell him where Cindy is, for Cindy to come back."

"You didn't tell him, did you?"

"Not a chance. The only problem was, this time he was really drunk. And, um, he hit on me toward the end. But I think it was because he was so drunk. Cindy and I look so much alike, he probably started thinking I was her."

"Oh shit! Are you OK?" I knew I never should have left Carly alone to deal with Eddie. If I'd been smart, I would have gone all FBI and moved her to a safe house first before we left.

"Of course!" She laughed. "You don't think that after everything I've lived through I'd have any trouble dealing with a tiny problem like Eddie, do you? I'm fine. I'm handling it. Everything'll be fine."

* * *

Lise's problems with Tony, Diana's problems with Dan, and Cindy's problems with Eddie—even if he wasn't immediately in the picture anymore, and no matter what Carly said, he was still a big problem. The only one of our happy foursome not having problems with her man was me, and maybe that was because I didn't think of Sunny as my man. He was, as he himself had pointed out, my "great good friend."

But that great good friend did call every night we were down in Georgia, checking up on me, checking up on everyone else.

When I told him how awkward our living arrangements had become, he even offered to come down. Maybe, he told me, his presence would defuse some of the tension everyone except Cindy was feeling.

"You can't do that," I objected. "You have patients who rely on you. You have appointments."

"Say the word," he said, "and I will be on the next flight. I can always get someone to cover me. Just say the word, Sylvia."

"The word is, no, thanks, Sunny. OK, so maybe that's

two words."

"Very well, then. But please feel free to reserve the right to change your mind at any time."

"Thanks. It's just this is something the four of us have to work out here on our own. It's not like I don't appreciate your offer, though. I do. In fact, I appreciate everything you do, calling me every day to check in and stuff."

"I am glad," he said. "It is nice to feel appreciated, and I am happy if it helps you. But, listen, Sylvia. When you get back home, we are going to need to talk. Much as I have enjoyed it, I do not want to go on being *just* great good friends anymore. It is not enough for me. It is time we take things up to the next level or consider saying good-bye."

OK, so maybe the other three weren't the only ones with man problems.

Cindy

People must think I'm stupid, I thought.

And why wouldn't they? After all, I'd always thought of myself that way, so why wouldn't everyone else?

I felt the damp sand squish between my toes as I walked closer to the surf. There was limited sun in the gray and white skies as I slowly lowered myself a few feet in front of the water. I ran the thick wet sand between my fingers, enjoying the ooze of it and, before I knew it, I was pushing the sand together, molding little piles of it into individual shapes.

A castle, I thought. *Why not build my own castle?*

It was easy at first, scooping out a great big circle for the moat. But when I tried to make more intricate details—rooms for my castle, a drawbridge to keep bad people out—castle building proved harder than I'd thought.

I was tempted to ask a child a little ways down if I could borrow her pail and shovel, but then realized how silly I'd look: a grown woman, asking to play with a kid's toys. So I pressed onward, going down to the sea to gather small amounts of water, which I brought back in my cupped hands, hoping to turn the sand within the moat into the consistency of something I could build with.

It took a lot of trips.

But, eventually, things started to stick.

While the sun continued its disappearing act, and a hot wind with an unusual under layer of chill came in, I built my rooms, my protective drawbridge finally in place.

Who would live in my castle? Me, of course. And, if it was going to be my castle, I might as well declare myself to be the queen. Then, across from the queen's bedroom, I constructed a room for my baby, a nursery for the princess. If I was fantasizing, I might as well make the baby a girl. I knew when people asked pregnant women if they wanted a boy or a girl, the right answer was supposed to be, "I don't care, just so long as it's healthy." And that was the main thing I cared about, but I was still sure I'd have a girl. With all the women who'd been around me lately—really, only women, except for Dirk before he left—it was like being at the center of a coven, all that female energy, and I could no more picture having a boy come out of me than I could a pig.

So now there were two people living in my castle: my baby and me.

I never let on to any of the others, but I was scared to have the baby. Sure, I'd wanted a baby, wanted to be pregnant. But now that I was, I was scared of everything. I was scared of my body changing, scared of actually delivering the baby, scared of everything that would follow once the baby was out in the world. Mostly, I was scared of being alone.

I'd always been thin, as paranoid of being fat as any other American girl I knew. It was distressing to think of my body getting bigger and bigger, even though I knew that wasn't what I was supposed to be thinking about now. I was supposed to be thinking about the health of the baby.

And I was, nearly all the time. At night I'd lie in bed, hand on my tummy, thinking the words only in my head because to say them aloud, even in a whisper, might wake Sylvia in the next bed: *Hey, you,* I'd mentally whisper to my baby, *are you OK in there? Am I doing everything right? Are you getting enough food? Enough sleep? Are you resting up for your big day?*

And how was the baby going to get out of my body? Oh, I knew how. I'd read some books, looked at articles on the Internet. I knew women had been having babies as long as there'd been women on the planet, some of them under much less ideal circumstances than the hospital birth I planned on for my baby, like the woman who gave birth up in a tree during a flood. Really, compared to that, what did I have to worry about? But I did worry. I worried about everything: the pain, how I'd deal with it.

More than that, though, more than anything else, I worried about what would come afterward: How would I take care of the baby once it was here? Would I do a good job?

Grabbing another handful of sand, I started making the queen's bedroom bigger, big enough for two.

Who else would move into my castle? Who would move into the queen's bedroom?

I pictured Eddie living with me there, the two of us married, Eddie somehow—even though he was over thirty—getting onto *American Idol* and winning it all.

"Hi, honey. I'm home," I heard Eddie say in my head.

"How was the tour?" I said back.

"It was great. We played a million places and rocked them all. But you know what? I missed you every second. I couldn't wait to get back home to you."

It was a nice dream. But was it possible? I knew the *American Idol* part'd never happen. But could Eddie and I still have a happily ever after?

People must think I'm stupid, I thought again. And by "people" here I meant Sylvia, Lise, and Diana. But, really, even if I was stupid about a lot of things, I wasn't nearly as stupid as they thought. Did they really think I didn't know they were up to something? Did they really think I thought this whole trip was just about the four of us spending some "quality time" together? Did they think I didn't notice how, every time I even hinted I might call Eddie, someone else would race to the phone first or say there wasn't enough time because they had some activity planned for all of us that simply could not wait?

Nobody could be that stupid. Not even me.

And yet I remained calm. I was the eye at the center of their storm.

I went back to my castle building, wondering if there was anyone else who could share the queen's room besides Eddie. I'd never thrown away Porter's business card. Even though I'd never called him, throwing away that card would have felt like throwing away the only smidgen of my past that had nothing to do with my fucked-up family and my fucked-up life with Eddie. Porter was that tiny ray from the past that still had the shine of girlish hope around it. What would it be like to have him share the queen's bedroom with me?

"Hi, honey. I'm home," Porter would say. "I made a killing today on Wall Street but every second I thought of you."

Stupid, I told myself. *You really are stupid.* Every fantasy I had, it was like something out of an old fifties sitcom. The next thing you know, I'd be offering to make my men martinis, helping them on with their quilted smoking jackets, and angling to get money out of them so I could buy myself a pretty hat.

I started making the queen's bedroom smaller again, taking some of the sand away.

"What are you doing?"

I turned to see Diana, crouching down next to my castle in the sand.

"What does it look like?" I said, going back to my work. "I've never made a sandcastle before. I figured I might as well make one just once before we have to go on back home."

We'd been there nearly a whole month. Surely, it'd be time to go home soon.

"It looks wonderful," she said brightly. "I particularly like that moat. But have you noticed the tide's coming in?"

I used my hand to shield my eyes against a sun that was no longer there and looked out at the wide sea, the big waves rising and crashing far out, bigger than I'd seen them since we'd been there; the smaller waves at the shore edged closer to my fortress. "It's OK," I said, trying to make a tower room stand up at the top of the castle. "I wasn't expecting it to last forever."

"I wanted to talk to you while the others aren't around," Diana said like we were the best of friends.

"What about?"

"I was wondering: You love to read romances so much." And here she leaned in closer. "Have you ever considered writing a book?"

I laughed, the first real laugh I'd felt come out of my body in a long time.

"God, no!" I said. "I'm not smart enough to make up a whole imagined story like that. That kind of thing's for other people."

"I wasn't talking about a made-up story," she said. "I was thinking you could write something about your current situation: you know, being pregnant, having a child by yourself, and perhaps something about what you've been through with Eddie."

I wrinkled my nose. "Don't think so," I said. Then I thought about what that would be like, being someone smart like Lise, living in my castle with my baby girl and writing stories about my life. I laughed again. "Who knows? Maybe. Someday."

"Sorry to interrupt," I heard Lise say, joining us. "But Sylvia's trying to decide what to do. There are reports on the radio of a fairly big storm coming this way, and she's not sure if we should leave for Connecticut today and try and beat it, or stay here and ride it out."

"I suppose we'd better head back," Diana said, rising to her feet and wiping her hands off on her swimsuit, "and help her decide."

I helped the others gather up our beach things and followed them on the walk back to the house.

At the far edge of the sand, I turned back for one last look. The wind had picked up and the sky had turned a sickly greenish color. Something was coming. Something big.

I lowered my gaze to the water's edge in time to see the first wave break over the moat surrounding my castle, washing my carefully built fortress away.

Blackout

RECOMMENDED READING:
Lise: *Best of Friends*, Cathy Kelly
Diana: *Outer Banks*, Anne Rivers Siddons
Sylvia: *Such Devoted Sisters*, Eileen Goudge
Cindy: *The Friendship Test*, Elizabeth Noble

"Where were you when the lights went out?" Diana tittered.

"What the hell does that mean?" Sylvia said.

"It's just that I've always wanted to say that, but it doesn't work when there's only two people, and it seems I've only ever been with one other person during blackouts. But this? It's like a drawing-room murder mystery. You know? 'Where were you when the lights went out?'"

"It's not at all like a drawing-room murder mystery," Sylvia said.

Sylvia had had the foresight to prepare one more cooked meal before the storm hit in earnest, knocking out the power, and the four women were seated at the dinner table, finishing up the remains of shrimp scampi by candlelight as the rain lashed against the windows and the howling wind battered the house.

"It would be nice," Cindy said, putting down her napkin, "if we could get through one meal together without someone bickering with someone else."

"Are you feeling OK?" Sylvia said. She put her hand on Cindy's forehead. "Is the baby OK?"

"I'm fine," Cindy said with a sigh. "The baby's fine. I'm just not in the mood to hear everyone else fighting tonight, that's all."

In the hours before the storm hit, they'd debated what to do. Sylvia had been for staying put. Diana had been for packing as quickly as possible and getting the hell out of there.

"And go where?" Sylvia had asked. "South? West? The storm's coming down from the northeast. We can't go home."

"Can't go home?"

"No, Thomas Wolfe," Lise had backed up Sylvia, "not tonight at least."

"Oh. I see."

"We'll have to just ride it out here," Sylvia had said, "and hope we don't all get swept away."

Now, as the flickering light from the candles danced shadows across their faces, Cindy's expression settled, as though a decision had been made.

"Never mind what I said about not fighting," she said.

"What do you mean?" Sylvia asked.

"Look, I know that ever since we got here, you all have been burning to talk to me about something but haven't been able to get up the nerve. So, as long as we're all stuck here together, you might as well have at it. If we all die together in this storm, you might not get another chance."

"How can you possibly be considering going back to Eddie?" Sylvia burst out with it.

"What are you talking about? Who said I was *definitely* going back to Eddie? And what business would it be of yours if I was?"

"It's our business," Sylvia said, "because we don't want to see you hurt anymore."

"But isn't that part of life? Doesn't everybody get hurt sometimes?"

"Not like you've been hurt."

"That's where you're wrong, though. Sure, Eddie and I have had our bad spells. But what couple doesn't? Look at Diana and Dan, Lise and Tony. You can't tell me they're not having their own problems too now. Dan's not sleeping with Diana, Tony's pissed at Lise for quitting her job and for coming on this trip, that Dirk guy seems to be getting in everyone's business. But are they going to give up? And, if not, why should I?"

"Because it's different," Sylvia said. "It's—"

"Maybe it's not," Lise said, cutting her off.

Sylvia's head spun toward her, an expression as much shocked as betrayed upon her face.

"Look," Lise said, squirming uncomfortably in her seat. "Maybe we're all wrong." She addressed Sylvia. "I know I said I'd go along with this. I know it's what we came down here for. But do you realize how... *hubristic* it is to sit in judgment of someone else's relationship? It's too easy to stand on the outside of a marriage, or any other kind of relationship, and say what the people in it should do. But who really knows? Would you want us to dissect your relationship with Sunny like we do Cindy's with Eddie?"

"I'm not sitting in judgment," Sylvia said. "I'm just—"

"I can't believe I'm going to agree with Lise," Diana said, "but I think she may be right. Perhaps it's time we just butt out. We can't know why two people stay together."

"Maybe not," Sylvia said, "but I know why they should come apart. Do you know what Eddie did to Cindy that night of the party, after she got rid of us?"

"No!" Cindy said. "Don't! I told you that in confidence. Stop!"

But Sylvia didn't stop. She told Lise and Diana about the bowl of cherries, about what Eddie had done with those cherries. Then she told the others how Eddie had told Cindy—commanded her—to give up her friends.

"I had no idea things were that bad," Lise said.

"That's the most horrible thing I've ever heard," Diana said. "Well, maybe not the *most* horrible. But it is awful. I've put up with an incredible amount of shit in my life, much of it from men, but I'd never stand for something like that."

Cindy was crying in earnest now, fat tears rolling out of her eyes and trailing down her cheeks. "I can't believe I trusted you!" she shrieked at Sylvia. "You make Eddie sound like the worst person in the world!"

Sylvia put her hand on Cindy's back and gently rubbed the space between her jutting shoulder blades. "You know what's the funny thing?" Sylvia spoke gently. "I actually feel sorry for Eddie; it's like he's his own fatal flaw, like he can't help but smash the good things around him, at least where you're concerned. So, no, I don't believe Eddie's the worst person in the world. I just think he's the worst person in the world for you."

"Why are you with Eddie?" Diana said softly. "We've asked the question before, but you've never answered. Why be with him in the first place? Why stay with him after all the things he's done?"

"Because," Cindy said through the tears, "who would I be without Eddie?" As she went on, it was as though she were reciting something she'd memorized, a mantra. "I'm not pretty like you, Diana. I'm not smart like Lise. I'm not talented like Sylvia is with her cooking. If I didn't have Eddie, what other man would ever have me?"

Sylvia laughed. "Oh, God," she said. "I'm sorry. I know it isn't funny but…" She grabbed one of the candlesticks. Then, placing a hand under Cindy's elbow, she lifted the other woman from her seat and led her to the bathroom where, by candlelight, she made Cindy look at herself in the mirror.

"Look at you," Sylvia said. "I don't know how you can't see it when everyone around you can. You're not just pretty. You're *beautiful.* You've got one of the most beautiful faces I've ever seen, and the pregnancy only makes you more so. And you are smart. You were smart enough to make me go to the doctor when I was too stupid to go. You're doing fantastic with your online classes. I just know that whatever you decide to do in life you'll be talented at it. If you'll only believe in yourself."

"You're nuts," Cindy said, but there was a slight smile breaking through the tears.

Sylvia laughed again. "Now *that* we know." She sobered. "But it doesn't make what I'm saying any less true."

They returned to the table where Lise and Diana had cleared the dinner dishes, setting out fresh peaches and a peach pie Sylvia had baked earlier in the day.

"Thanks for the pep talk," Cindy said, using a napkin to wipe the tear trails from her face with a vengeance. "Really. But it doesn't change anything. I'm pregnant with Eddie's child. I think it's time I told him. Maybe that'll change things."

"That's where you're wrong," Sylvia said. "Wrong, wrong, wrong." And now it appeared she was getting angry. "What do you think will change? Do you think you and Eddie will stop being bad together once there's a baby in the picture?"

"'Bad together'? You say it as though part of what's the matter with me and Eddie is my own fault."

"I don't know," Sylvia said, considering. "Maybe it is."

"I don't think it's helpful," Lise interjected, "to start blaming the victim."

"That's not what I'm doing," Sylvia said. "And who said anything about blaming the victim? Or even about Cindy being a victim? She's an adult. She may not have been when she first got together with Eddie, but she is now. She's made her own choices. She needs to learn how to choose differently."

"Thanks for talking about me in the—what do you call it?—third person? I'm sitting right here, thanks," Cindy said. "And you still haven't explained what you mean by 'bad together.' You think it's possible that Eddie might not act like this if I were a different person? If he were with a different woman?"

"Maybe," Sylvia said, considering that too. "I don't know. I just know that when the two of you are together, it's like a bad recipe."

This was a new idea to Cindy; the idea that she and Eddie were a recipe that didn't mix well, an equation that didn't add up.

"You know," Sylvia continued, "Carly told me all about your parents. She told me how, when she was living with you and Eddie for a while, you used to do things that she knew would piss Eddie off and that you should have known too. I'm not saying women should walk on eggshells in a relationship—or men, for that matter—but when you know someone long enough, you know what their hot-button issues are. You know that if you hit those buttons, you're going to wind up with a fight on your hands. And if the person whose buttons you're pushing happens to be of a violent nature, it's that much worse. Carly also told me about how, one time, you set it up so she'd have to get out of the apartment when Eddie was in a bad mood, almost like you wanted him to abuse you. And then I remembered how you'd done the same thing with us the night of the party, sending us away when our staying might have made a difference in the outcome."

Cindy opened her mouth to protest, but Sylvia talked right over her.

"Don't you see, Cindy? You're living your mother's life all over again. You're caught in a pattern, a cycle, and it has to stop."

"What are you saying?"

"I think you know what I'm saying. I think you've known it all along. You've known you were pregnant for—what?—almost five months now? In all that time, how could Eddie not have noticed? He's been in denial—maybe he doesn't want a kid, maybe he's never wanted a kid, or maybe he's just scared of change—but you've been in denial yourself. And, yet, deep down inside, subconsciously, you must have known that the idea of you and Eddie raising a child, together, was a bad one, that it would just repeat the cycle. Why else would you have never told him before now about the pregnancy? You need to *break* the cycle, Cindy. If you have this baby with Eddie, with Eddie as the father, it won't end well. If the baby is a boy, he'll learn by example that women are inferior and that abusing and demeaning them is the way to go. If the baby is a girl, she'll grow up to be like you and your mother, thinking that being abused somehow equates with love."

Cindy looked at her hands, and then she looked up at Sylvia. "What," she said, "are you proposing I should do?"

Sylvia took a deep breath. "I think you should tell Eddie you're pregnant." She paused. "And I think you should tell him the baby isn't his."

Sylvia

"I have supported you in everything ever since I have met you, Sylvia, but I cannot support you in this."

In the aftermath of the storm, during the long road back from Georgia to Connecticut, I'd managed to mostly convince the other three women of my wisdom on this subject. Sunny, on the other hand, was proving to be another matter entirely.

"It is simply not ethical," Sunny said now, as if the matter was that simple. We were seated on my bed, and, instead of a welcome-home kiss, I was being treated to a course in ethics. What a world.

Not to mention, a loud world.

From the other side of the door I could hear music pounding as Cindy and Carly listened to some show on TV.

"I just do not think it is right," Sunny said, "keeping from a man the knowledge that there is a baby in the world that is his."

"Eddie never even told her he wanted kids," I said.

"Does that matter? Why not give the man a chance?"

"Sunny, you *met* Eddie. Do you honestly think that guy you met—you remember, the drunk guy that insulted everyone in the room, picked fights with everyone, abused his girlfriend after everyone left—is going to change? That he's going to suddenly be Mr. Sober Diaper-Changing Dad?"

"What about the baby? Once the baby is born, you do not think he or she has the right to a father?"

"Sure, a *good* father. But not Eddie. Not someone who will abuse his or her mother and probably abuse the baby too. And what do you think things would be like after the baby's born? Do you think suddenly Eddie and Cindy's relationship will get better? That's a fairy tale."

"Says the woman who never had any children."

"Says the woman who *knows*. I may have never had any kids of my own, but I know what a strain children put on a marriage, even the best of marriages. Did you know that, statistically speaking, married couples who don't have kids but do have pets are likely to live the longest and happiest lives?"

He couldn't prevent a smile from escaping. "This," he said, "I did not know. Perhaps you should write up an article for the *New England Journal of Medicine*?"

I ignored his sarcasm. "Hey, people can always find statistics to back up whatever the point is that they want to make."

"Then," he said, "perhaps you and I should put it to the test by getting married and adopting a cat?"

I ignored that too.

"All I'm saying is," I said, "you don't have to be a parent yourself to observe these things. The child's-eye view I had growing up was plenty for me."

"Meaning?"

"Meaning my parents, by all accounts, were in love before Minnie and I were born. I'm not trying to say they were anything as bad as Cindy and Eddie afterward—far from it—but everything changed for them and, because they wound up with twins instead of a single baby, everything changed times two. Every single thing was something to disagree about. What to feed us, how much we should eat, should we be able to cross the street by ourselves, when could we go on our first date, should we pay for all or part of our college educations. My dad thought my mom was too rigid. My mom thought my dad was too lenient. Everyone always thinks that parents cry when their kids leave for college. But I swear, in our family, it was like the whole house heaved a sigh of relief. They loved us plenty, but they were glad to just finally go back to being themselves, a couple again. Now you take the same thing, you throw a baby into a relationship mix that is not working, and what do you think you'll wind up with?"

"At least Cindy is not having twins."

"Amen to that."

"But it is still wrong, Sylvia. You must know in your heart it is wrong."

"I know nothing of the kind."

Sunny got up off the bed and walked out of the room, gently closing the door behind him.

I collapsed back onto the bed and stared at the ceiling.

• • •

An hour later, there was a knock on my bedroom door. "Sylvia?" Carly poked her head in. "Sunny's back. He says he'd like to talk to you."

I rose from the bed and went out to meet him at the front door. On my way, I tossed an afghan in Cindy's direction. The girl needed to take better care of herself.

"Let's sit out here," I said to Sunny, indicating the front stoop. "It's a nice evening."

And it was a nice evening. The early September day had been hot, but now that it'd gone close to dark, the air felt much cooler, clean, as we sat and watched people arriving home late from work and cars coming and going.

Sunny took my hand in one of his and patted the top with his other hand.

"Explain it to me," he said. "Explain it so a simple doctor can understand. Tell me how this is going to work."

"It's like this," I said. "This plan of mine, it's the one way everyone has a chance of winding up happy: Cindy, the baby, maybe even Eddie. Maybe he'll learn from his mistakes, at least a little something. Maybe he won't take the next woman for granted as much as he did Cindy."

"'Everyone has a chance of winding up happy,'" he echoed. "You do realize you are playing God, do you not?"

"Sure," I said. "But that's what 'Sylvia' means in Australian: 'God'."

"Really?"

"No." I cuffed him on the shoulder. "I made that part up."

"But what about child support?" Sunny ran his fingers through his hair. "Every time you turn on the news, you see moms complaining about deadbeat dads. I would think you would want to enforce the rights of Cindy to have Eddie support a child who is half his."

"You know," I said, "it's funny, but I don't. It'd be one thing if Cindy wound up pregnant because of condom breakage or some such thing, but she planned to get pregnant, without Eddie's consent. So, no, I don't think Eddie owes the child one red cent."

"How will Cindy support the baby, then, on just one income and probably a low one at that? Most families these days need at least two."

"I'll take care of her and support her, the baby too, for as long as it takes."

Sunny let out a low whistle. "When you play God, you do not fool around, do you?"

"Yeah, well…"

"And who is going to support you, Atlas, while you are holding up the rest of the world?"

"I don't know. Carly?" I laughed at the idea, a quiet sound in the night. "I don't know."

We were silent for a time, watching the neighborhood. The younger kids should have been in bed already, on a school night no less, but the weather was too nice for parents to mind or object that they wanted to skateboard or toss the football around a little longer.

"It is very peaceful here," Sunny said. "When I first met you, I could not understand why you would want to live in a condo when you and your sister could have undoubtedly afforded a house. But I can see it now. You get to enjoy watching a lot of other people grow and change and just live, but at night, or whenever you want to, you can just close the door."

"Plus, I don't have to cut my own grass," I added.

A stray football came our way and Sunny retrieved it from the small patch of grass next to my stoop and tossed it back to a child's waiting arms.

"But," Sunny said, as though we'd been in the middle of

debating whatever point it was he was about to make, "how can you be so certain that, even if Eddie can be made to believe the baby is not his, he will not bother Cindy anymore?"

"His ego," I said with certainty. "Some men, if they loved the woman enough, it wouldn't matter whose child she was bearing. They'd still do anything to be with her. But a guy like Eddie with that fragile ego that he masks by strutting around like he's got the biggest ego in the world? No way."

On the outside, I spoke each word with nail-in-the-wall certainty. But inside? I was praying like crazy I was right.

"And what if you are wrong?" Sunny asked simply, as though reading my mind.

"Hey, we're all only human," I said. "Every single one of us makes mistakes."

Cindy

I got a job volunteering at a help hotline.

Not long after we returned from Georgia, I realized I just couldn't take sitting around Sylvia's condo every day while everyone else went about their jobs and their lives. Carly was doing great working for Marlene at Midnight Scandals. Carly'd just shown up for work the day after we left Connecticut, telling my boss I had to leave town on an emergency, and she turned out to be so good at selling underwear, even better than me, Marlene hadn't minded the switch at all. And, even if Carly hadn't worked out so good, now that I was really showing, I couldn't imagine Marlene would want me back working with her super skinny staff. Sylvia said that there were laws protecting pregnant women from discrimination, that no employer could turn me down just because I was obviously expecting a baby. And yet I couldn't believe that there were a lot of employers out there just dying to hire a pregnant lady whose chief job experience involved working at the mall. But volunteer work? People would take even me if I was free.

Listening to other people's problems, one after another for hours at a time, seemed like good training for the field I hoped to go into one day: social work. It was also what you might call illuminating. I'd always thought my problems were pretty big, but listening to what some other people were going through—serious depression, husbands and kids suddenly dying—made me realize that mine were not the worst problems in the world. Listening to other people also made me realize that some people don't know how good they have it. At least once a day I'd get a call from some hysterical person who was going through a problem that was the emotional equivalent to a broken fingernail. But then I'd have to stop myself from letting my exasperation show in my voice. I'd have to tell myself that the worst a person has experienced is the worst they know and that telling someone who just sprained their ankle that they shouldn't whine about it because there's a guy next door in a wheelchair who'll never walk again isn't very useful.

So I just kept doing my job and hoping on good days I was making things better, at least for someone in the world. I hoped on bad days that I wasn't making anyone want to go out and kill themselves.

• • •

Eddie and I had spoken on the phone nearly every day since we'd been back. I'd told him all about the trip—with the exception of that conversation during the storm—while he'd told me what was going on with the band. Every time we talked, he said he missed me and asked when he'd see me again. Finally, a day came when I felt I couldn't put it off any longer. I asked Sylvia if I could borrow her van for a few hours, and then I told Eddie to meet me at the Dunkin' Donuts on South Street, figuring neutral territory was best; plus, I was really craving a chocolate frosted donut with sprinkles.

When I'd still lived with Eddie, I'd been able to hide my pregnancy because I'd still been in my first trimester, but now I made sure to wear something that would reveal it the instant I walked in. As I arrived, though, I saw he wasn't there yet, and when I sat down on the swivel stool, the counter came over my belly.

All the way over, I hadn't known what to expect. I hadn't even known exactly what I was going to say. So I'd turned up the radio, distracting myself with the musical heartache of others.

When Eddie finally walked in, I was done eating my first donut—during which time I'd looked around me and wondered whoever thought pink and brown and orange would make a great color combination but then recognizing it had worked out pretty well for them—and halfway through the second.

"God," he said, settling down in a rush onto the stool next to mine, "of all times to get pulled over for a taillight being out. The whole time the cop was writing me out the ticket, I kept worrying you wouldn't be here when I got here."

"Hi, Eddie," I said.

"God, I'm such a jerk," he said. "I've been dying to see you forever, and then I come in here and the first thing I do is start jabbering about some traffic ticket." He grinned. "Hi, Cindy. That's how I should have started, right? Hi, Cindy. How are you?"

A part of me felt like just delaying the next moment forever. But it was just time now. It was well past time.

I swiveled in my stool, stood up, and rested my palm on my belly.

"This is how I am, Eddie," I said.

"Holy *shit!*" People always talk about receiving shocking news and how it nearly made them fall off their chair. You never really think that kind of thing happens in life, like someone slipping on a banana peel, but it must because that's what happened to Eddie. "Holy shit, Cindy!" Then the shock, more like horror, on his face disappeared and he actually grinned again, like he was the happiest man in the world. "My God, it all makes sense now! The reason you've been acting so fucked up these last few months—it's because of this." He couldn't keep his eyes off my belly. "But why didn't you say something? Why didn't you tell me?"

"I—"

"Oh, man, Cindy, if only I'd known, I could have helped you. You were probably too scared to tell me because you thought I'd be mad, but I could have helped you."

"Really? You'd have done that?"

"Of course. I could have found a doctor for you to get rid of it. But don't worry. It's not too late. I'm sure we can still find someone who will be willing to—"

Now it was my turn to be horrified. "I don't want to find that kind of doctor, Eddie! I want to keep this baby!"

"Listen," Eddie said, and I could see him struggling to remain calm as he took my hand, as we played out our little domestic drama in Dunkin' Donuts. "If you want to have a baby, sure, we can have one. Eventually. But now is just like the worse timing in the world. Things with the band have been really going good lately. We have more gigs than we can handle. I'm thinking if we can just go on the way we are for the next six months—"

"I'm really happy that things are going so well for you," I said. Then: "And it's OK you don't want this baby, because it's not yours anyway."

"What?"

"It's not your baby. It's someone else's."

"I don't believe you. You never would have slept with someone behind my back. No way."

"Of course I would have," I said, making it up as I went along. In my mind, I pictured someone like Porter, only I didn't say it was him, because God knows Eddie would have hunted him down and shot him like a dog if I had. Then, with the picture of Porter in my mind, I spun a story of hooking up with some guy one night when Eddie was out playing with the band. "He was great," I finished up. "I never saw him again but it was definitely worth it."

"You *slut!*" Eddie said. Then his hand was up so fast to hit me, the only thing in the room moving faster than it was my own as my hand shot out, stopping his at the wrist. God knows if Eddie'd wanted to, he could have easily broken my grip, done whatever he wanted to me. I think he was so stunned though, at the very idea of me resisting him, of fighting back, he didn't move a muscle.

I spoke each word distinctly, so there'd be no mistaking them. "You. Can't. Hit. Me. Any. More." Then, so there'd be no room for error at all, I added, "And don't call me anymore either. I don't love you, Eddie. It's time you moved on."

I let go of his wrist, calmly picked up my bag, and walked out, not looking back even once.

* * *

I got in the van and drove, not right back to Sylvia's. I just drove.

Walking out of there like that was the hardest thing I'd ever done. Telling Eddie I didn't love him anymore was pretty damn hard too.

People looking at what I did from the outside might say that what I did was wrong, lying to Eddie like that, and I hadn't even known for sure I was going to do it until the words came out of my mouth. Up until then, I'd still believed things could go either way. But life doesn't come in one size fits all, the same decisions working for everybody. Sylvia was right about what I needed to do, but for the wrong reasons. If I told Eddie the truth, eventually I'd lose myself in him again, even deeper than before. I had just enough strength to stand up to him that one time.

In the months since I'd moved out of our apartment, I'd felt myself changing; not huge changes, just a little bit at a time, but enough. If I went back to Eddie, it might be good in the beginning, but then it'd only get worse again. Because the problem had never been who Eddie was; the problem was who I was when I was with Eddie.

And I just couldn't bring a baby into that.

Still, I loved him, not in the same way I used to, but in brief glittering flashes, like when I'd remember his smile or the way he said certain things.

A few years back, when Prince Charles got married for the second time, the TV kept replaying clips from his first courtship and marriage. They particularly liked showing the one where, when Charles and Diana got engaged, some reporter asked him if he was in love and he said something like, "Of course. Whatever 'love' is." You could tell people laughed at that, like he was the stupidest person in the world. But I could kind of understand where he was coming from.

Love, like faith, wasn't something you could touch. It kept changing all the time, depending on the people and circumstances. You couldn't put it in a box. You couldn't describe it. It just was what it was. It was what I felt, more than anything in the world, for the baby inside me.

I drove on, terrified of the future, determined to put the past behind me.

Lise

September.

For as long as I could remember, September had been a time of new beginnings for me. From my early preschool days through my early twenties it had meant buying new school supplies and new clothes with the hope of the reinvention of myself that the fresh school year always brought. And in the dozen plus years since I'd ended my formal schooling, none of that had changed. I'd simply exchanged one side of the desk for the other, graduating from being a student of the educational system to becoming *the* educational system, each fall bringing fresh faces in the classroom, fresh even though they were predictable: the ones who arrived certain they knew everything already about writing and there was, therefore, nothing left for you to teach them, and the ones that arrived filled with the hope that you would somehow miraculously show them the way.

But that September was different, the first in memory.

All summer long, my giving up my professorship had been both real and unreal. On the real side was my sense of relief, freedom, and the idea that I would finally no longer be what I'd been for so long, would no longer have to do the same old things. I'd imagined that when September came my sense of liberation would be complete. But it had been unreal too, as though, until September came and went without me stepping foot inside a classroom, none of it would be final.

Now we were three weeks into September, and it was nothing like advance imagination had predicted.

It was final, felt final, but not in any way you could call good. My cottage was close enough to the campus that I could still see the rest of the world coming and going, and me no longer a part of it.

Like an amputee mourning an artificial limb, I missed my classroom, missed my students, the serious and the silly.

September was no longer a time of new beginnings for me. It was a time of endings.

Now that I was no longer student or teacher, who was I?

• • •

I'd returned from Georgia to an empty house and grass that had grown a foot tall in my absence. Not to mention dust all over everything. Never much of a nester, I needed to keep physically busy in order to prevent my mind from ranging too widely—about Tony's absence, which he'd foretold, us having not even spoken while I was away; about everything to do with the writing and publishing of books; and even about my friends, the troubled and the not so much—and quickly got to work setting my small world in order. The worst was the lawn, which felt like it should have required a machete rather than the push mower I normally used. That lawn became a metaphor for my life: all the distractions that needed to get hacked away before you could get down to the essence of the thing.

Once I beat the lawn back into submission, it still didn't feel like enough. Whereas before I had mown it the usual once a week—or, more typically, Tony had—I now felt a need to go at it at least twice a week in order to ensure that the horror I'd come home to didn't make a return.

That's where I was, mowing the lawn for the second time that week, when the phone calls started coming. The cell phone I'd clipped onto the back of my cutoff jeans shorts vibrated against my hip.

"I know it's late," Dirk's voiced chirped. Then he amended, "Well, it's late for me here, but I don't suppose it's late for you at all. Anyway, I just got home from a night out and saw in *Publishers Weekly* online edition that two of your former students—John Quayle and some Danitra person whose last name I don't recall—have both sold first novels."

"What?" I said dumbly. "Both of them?" I typically tried to be happy for my students' successes, but this was a bit much. Were they working on those books when they were my students?

"But don't you see? This is *wonderful* news! The headline begins 'Two Connecticut University Students…' and right away I recognized your college. We'll be able to use this to promote the *hell* out of you once we're ready to send your book out. Just think how attractive this will make you to editors. If you teach the kind of students that go on to make big book deals, how much better, they'll think, might your own writing be?"

John and Danitra?

Big book deals?

"Dirk, I have to go. I'm sorry, but I was in the middle of something important when you rang. We'll talk tomorrow."

I clicked off before he had time to say anything else, unable as yet to digest what I was feeling. Nor did I get a chance to before the cell phone buzzed again.

"Have you seen *Publishers Weekly* yet?"

It was Aunt Tess.

Ever since she'd offered to finance me, even though I hadn't taken her up on it, she'd had a vested interest in my career. She'd even subscribed to the print edition of *Publishers Weekly*—not an inconsiderable cost—saying that she wanted to be the first to read about my deal when my book finally sold.

"No, I haven't," I said, "but I did hear something about what you're about to tell me. To tell you the truth, I was trying to get the grass cut and I think I should—"

"Never mind that right now. Don't you want to hear about what your students have gone and done?"

Not really, I thought, but I couldn't say that.

"Apparently," she said, "this Danitra girl has written a literary novel that they say is like nothing anyone has ever seen."

Danitra had written a *literary* novel?

"The title," Aunt Tess went on, "is *Something About Bees*."

In spite of myself, I had to laugh at that. When I was still teaching, I'd told my students that as important as talent was to a writer these days, perhaps more important still was perseverance. The people who got published were the ones who kept putting one writing foot in front of the other, no matter what happened. And, I told them, as important as having talent and perseverance was, you couldn't beat a perfect title. What, after all, I would say, would have become of *The Great Gatsby* if Fitzgerald had been allowed his first impulse, which was to name the book *Trimalchio in West Egg*? I'd further told my students that there were even some books that were destined to be bestsellers by sheer virtue of certain words used in the titles that seemed to have a magical hold over readers: "diaries" was one, "light" was another, "secrets" was always a winner, and, for some inexplicable reason, "bees" were big.

Apparently, at least one of my students had absorbed my publishing wisdom, such as it was.

"And this John Quayle," Aunt Tess was saying. "It says here that he's written the first in a mystery series, set at a college in Connecticut, about a secret writers' club that solves their first case when their favorite professor is found murdered."

I suppose another person would have dwelt on that last part—John had written a wish-fulfillment book about my death?—but not me. All I took away from it was: John Quayle, Mr. I Am Such a Pompous Ass, was writing *genre* fiction?

"What do five and six figures mean?" Aunt Tess busted into my thoughts.

"In what context?" I asked.

"It says here that Danitra got mid-five figures for her book, while John got a low six for the first three in his series. What does that mean?"

"It means my students sold well," I said.

• • •

By the time the knock came at the door, the sun had long gone over the yardarm, as they say, and I was already well into my third tumbler of self-commiserating vodka. Bleagh. I hated the taste, but it was all I had in the house, and I'd been in no mood earlier to go out to the stores where I'd have to see actual people; now I was too drunk to go. The last time I drank straight vodka had been during my third year in college when a friend and I were too broke to buy beer, so instead we played backgammon for shots of a half bottle she borrowed from a neighbor.

Knock, knock.

"Coming!" I shouted again. Or at least, I thought I'd shouted it once already.

I picked myself up off the floor and dragged myself to the door. I swear to God, if it was someone selling magazine subscriptions, and if one of the subscriptions on offer was to *Publishers Weekly*, I'd shoot the person.

It wasn't someone selling magazine subscriptions, however. It was Tony, who I hadn't seen since I'd been back. Under one arm, he held a rolled-up copy of a magazine, and I could see enough of the corner of the cover to make out the distinctive "P" from *Publishers Weekly*. In his other arm, he carried a brown paper bag that had the look of the liquor store about it.

Seeing my expression as I looked at the magazine corner, he spoke. "I'm too late, aren't I? You already know."

I nodded.

He set the items down on the kitchen counter. "I wanted to be the first to tell you," he said. "This must be so hard for you, Lise."

I let him take me in his arms, silently blessing him for getting it. Sure, I was happy for my students and proud of their accomplishments. But I was a wreck because every time my students succeeded where all I'd ever done was fail, I died a little death.

Diana

I felt the tap on my shoulder before I heard the voice. It happened in that order because, once I felt the tap, I had to remove my headphones in order to hear the voice.

"Diana, I need to talk to you."

What wife ever wants to hear her husband speak *those* words?

I was on the treadmill, which I'd purchased after our return from Georgia and had it installed in our basement in front of the bank of mirrors I'd also purchased upon our return so I could watch myself work out. The weight loss had slowed down a bit in recent weeks, yet I could feel the glorious specter of one hundred and fifty pounds looming tantalizingly in my not-too-distant future. One hundred and fifty pounds might sound like a lot to some people, particularly petite people or little dogs, but I was tall enough, if I could just get to one hundred and fifty, I'd practically be thin.

It was keeping the motivation up that was the problem, not to mention busting through the plateaus I seemed to get stalled at more frequently as time wore on. I figured using the treadmill, which I could do almost endlessly so long as there was music coming through the headphones, would step up my metabolism. As for the mirrors, seeing myself reflected back wherever I was in the room, however I moved, would surely go a ways to improving motivation.

But now there was Dan intruding on my early-morning exercise solitude. We'd not talked much since my return. When I did think about that silence, it was with a dread, as though the silence itself portended something. Now that he had chosen to speak, however, I found myself reluctant to hear what he had to say.

As part of our honeymoon, Dan had taken me to Italy. There, in Rome, we'd gone to some sort of palace or parliament thing where there had been something called the Hall of Mirrors. Looking at Dan now in the mirror as I slowed the treadmill just enough so I could talk over its motor without shouting, I was reminded of that place. The only problem was, that place wasn't this place, nor were the reflective surfaces so grand.

"Can it wait fifteen minutes?" I said. "In fifteen minutes, it will have been a whole hour."

"No," Dan said, reaching out and turning the off switch on the treadmill. "It can't wait. I have to talk to you now."

"I see," I said, even though I didn't. I grabbed a workout towel I'd kept handy and draped it around my neck, but I didn't step off the treadmill. "What's this all about then?"

"Ever since you came home, I've been wanting to talk to you about something, something that's been troubling me for a long time. It's important."

I held up a hand. "Don't," I said. "I know what you're going to say."

"You do?"

"Yes. It's Layla, isn't it? I've seen on the computer how she writes you all the time. I haven't read any of the e-mails—I wouldn't do that—but I've seen this coming for a while. You're going to tell me you're having an affair with her, aren't you?"

"Layla?" Dan looked perplexed. "God, no! I wasn't going to tell you anything of the kind! Layla writes all the time, that's true, but it's only ever about stupid things: golf or what to get her husband for his birthday. But it's nothing like you're thinking!"

"What, then?" Even as I asked the question, I recognized how relieved his words made me feel. For so long now, I'd sensed something wrong between us, but I had felt a curious inertia about it that prevented me from taking any positive action. Now that I knew there was nothing between him and Layla—his expression was too earnestly shocked to doubt him—I gave an internal sigh, my greatest fears allayed. And now, having averted the worst, perhaps I could get back to my exercise. "What, then?" I prompted a second time.

"I know," Dan said with great care, "it's probably wrong and selfish of me to tell you. It's undoubtedly more to expiate my own guilt than out of a sense of honesty, but I find I've been losing sleep not being open with you, and I simply can't go on like this. While you were in Georgia, I slept with a woman."

"You *what?* But who? How?"

"The usual way you do those things." Dan gave a rueful laugh. "Well, except that I was drunk. She wasn't anyone you know. She wasn't anyone I know, really. She was just someone I picked up in a bar."

"You *bastard!*" I reached out a hand to strike him, but he grabbed my wrist.

"I wouldn't do that if I were you," he said. "It's not like you're wholly innocent in all of this."

"I have no idea what you mean. All I know is, Artemis was right about you. She warned me about you before we were married."

"Artemis." He snorted. "That's rich, bringing her into all this."

"She never understood why someone like you would want to marry someone like me in the first place. I didn't listen to her, but now look what's happened. What kind of man are you, Dan? When you married me, I was a fat cow. But look at me now! And yet now is when you choose to cheat on me. I don't understand. How could you have possibly loved the woman I was and yet not want me now?"

"It's because you've changed so, Diana. You're not the woman I married, not the woman I fell in love with. You were so different before. I'd had my fill of vain women by the time I met you. You were so funny, so smart and so sweet, I wouldn't have cared if you were twice as big as you were. But now? It's like you've become one of those vain women. All you care about is clothes and how you look—it's so hard to be around you!"

"Most women gain weight after the marriage. But I've managed—miraculously, I might add—to do the reverse. Any man would be happy with what I've accomplished."

"In case you've never noticed, I'm not any man. And, anyway, it's not like you're innocent."

"Yes, you've said that already. And I've told you: I have no idea what you mean."

"Wait here," he said.

I listened to his tread going all the way up to our bedroom at the top of the building, and then coming back down again.

When he returned, he had a large sheaf of papers in his hands. Before I could ask to see what he was holding, he let fly with them, sheets of paper raining down around us like some sort of sick ticker-tape parade. Bending over, I picked up one of the sheets. It was an e-mail printout, from Dirk to me. I picked up a few more, and then hurried to pick up the others, but there were too many of them. They were all either from Dirk to me or from me to Dirk. With a sick feeling in my stomach, judging from the quantity of pages scattered on the floor, I realized the sheer mass of it must represent our entire correspondence.

"How?" I said. "Why?"

"Do you think I'm stupid? I pay all the bills in this house. I pay for that damn computer upstairs. Did you think I didn't notice when you took out a new private e-mail account? I knew what you were doing. For God's sakes, I'm not you! I couldn't stop myself from reading them, every last word. You told him everything about yourself, every intimate detail. You told him everything about me, us, our lives together." He barked a harsh laugh. "You even gave him a running tally on your rapidly decreasing panty size! What man wouldn't want to hear about *that*?"

"If you've known all this time, why didn't you say something sooner?"

"I think maybe a part of me hoped you would stop on your own, that you'd see what you were doing, how wrong it was, and put an end to it. I mean, if I'd confronted you earlier, maybe you would have stopped, but it had no value to me, if you didn't see to do it on your own. It wouldn't have meant anything if you'd only stopped because you got *caught*."

"It's not the same," I said, "what you did and what I did."

"Oh, no? You're right. It's *worse*. I slept with one woman one night because I was drunk and stupid and lonely. But you were sober when you did all this. What's your excuse?"

"How can you possibly say that what I did was worse?"

"Because that's how it feels to me. How do you think I felt, day after day, month after month, playing voyeur to your growing closeness to another man? It ate me up inside. It *killed* me. All I did was fuck another woman, once. I'm not proud of what I did. But you? You gave your entire self to another man, every single day. If you didn't give your body too, it was only because there was an ocean between you."

"Dan, I'm sorry, truly. But you have no idea how lonely I was here!"

"Perhaps I don't," he conceded, nodding. "But if you were that lonely, Diana, then you should have come to *me*."

Then he turned and started from the room.

"Where are you going?" I said. "We're not done talking."

"Oh, yes, we are," he said, turning. "You know, it's funny, when I came down here to talk to you, to confess my one sin, I was wondering how you'd ever forgive me. I felt so guilty about what I'd done, it was all I could think about, and I still loved you so much. Until the words were spoken aloud, though, I don't think I realized just how angry I am, how hurt. And now that we've had this chance to...*talk*," he surveyed the sheets of paper all around us with disgust, "the question I have is: How will I ever forgive you?"

And then he was gone.

I turned to my own reflection in the mirror. Then I picked up one of the weights from a small set I'd bought and smashed the looking glass.

The Third Party

RECOMMENDED READING:
Sylvia: *The Idea of Pakistan*, Stephen P. Cohen
Cindy: *Black and Blue*, Anna Quindlen
Lise: *A Long Way Down*, Nick Hornby
Diana: *Smashed: Story of a Drunken Girlhood*, Koren Zailckas

"Surprise!"

Diana certainly was surprised.

When Lise had phoned, inviting her and Dan to dinner, that's what she'd expected: dinner. Perhaps Lise wanted to pump her for information about Dirk. Or maybe she wanted to mend fences. But what Diana hadn't expected, most emphatically not, was a surprise birthday party in her honor. There was Lise, of course. There was Cindy and Carly. There was Sylvia and even Sunny, the only man in the room. Balloons were everywhere and, on the table in the kitchen where Diana had entered through the back door, was a huge cake with white, pink, and green frosting. Diana guessed that Sylvia had baked it herself and she further guessed that Sylvia had baked it using Splenda, rather than real sugar, for her sake.

"What's all this?" Diana asked.

"You didn't imagine we'd let your birthday pass without a celebration, did you?" Lise said. Then she glanced over Diana's shoulder as though the mere act of glancing would produce another person there. "Where's Dan? Is he still in the car?"

"He's not coming. Dan moved out. He cheated on me, and then he moved out!" Diana burst into tears.

. . .

"Perhaps I should go," Sunny whispered to Sylvia, as she made herself at home in Lise's kitchen, checking on the food in the oven, while the others sat in the living room. "Diana is so upset, it might be better if it were just you women here with her."

"Pish-tosh," Sylvia said. "You stay. You're always such a calming influence; you're practically an honorary woman."

"Oh, now there is a sentence designed to make a man feel good about his manhood."

"Never mind," she said, shoving a serving plate of hors d'oeuvres and a stack of happy birthday cocktail napkins into his hands. "If you don't want to be a woman, then make like a waiter and let them all sexually harass you."

"This just gets better all the time," Sunny said, but, after devouring one of the chicken satay skewers, he obeyed.

. . .

"I don't want to discuss it," Diana was saying defensively. "All I will say is, this is the reward I get for leaving my job, leaving my home, leaving my family, leaving my whole damn country and coming here: a husband who cheats on me and then walks out." She turned to Lise. "What about you?" she asked accusingly. "Where's Tony tonight?"

"I don't know," Lise said, clearly taken aback. "I saw him once since we've been back, when he came over to show me something in *Publishers Weekly* about a couple of my former students getting book deals. It was really nice, actually. Everyone else it seemed was calling me up that day to tell me about it and they were all acting as though I should be purely happy about it. Of course I was happy about it, but by no means purely. Tony was the only one who got that. As I say, it was very nice. But since then?" She shrugged. "I've hardly seen him at all."

"See?" Diana said, knocking back the rest of her chardonnay. "It's not that easy to hold onto a man, is it?"

"I wouldn't know," Lise said. "I've never tried to hold onto one."

Diana pointed a finger. "And there's your problem right there."

Lise forced a bright smile. "More drinks, anyone?" She got no takers but left the room anyway, saying, "Maybe one for me then."

. . .

"I know Dan left her," Lise hissed to Sylvia, the other woman having followed her into the kitchen, "but does she have to take it out on me?"

Sylvia thought about it for a minute. "Maybe she does." Then she smiled. "And, hey, look on the bright side. At least if she's taking it out on you, she can't take it out on me."

"Oh, you're a big help."

. . .

"How's the new job going?" Diana asked.

"Do you mean mine or hers?" Carly asked, indicating Cindy.

"Either. Both. It doesn't matter."

"I don't know," Carly said. "I guess it's OK. It's kind of fun seeing what people buy to wear under all their clothes. But sometimes using that tape measure gets a bit squicky. Women ask you to size them, then they get all weird when they realize sizing them actually involves putting a tape measure around their breasts."

"Mine's going great," Cindy said, "except for some of the really sad people who call or the ones who don't really have problems. After the baby comes, I'd like to stay home the first few months, but then I want to see if I can maybe find a job like this that pays."

"Ah," Diana said. "The baby. Speaking of which, how is old Eddie these days? Have you heard any more from him?"

"No," Cindy said. "Sylvia was right. As soon as I told him the baby wasn't his, he vanished."

"Our Sylvia," Diana said, smiling, but there was an edge to it. "She's always right about everything, isn't she?"

"I think so," Sunny said, patting Sylvia's knee.

"You two have quite the nice setup, don't you?" Diana said. "Sylvia cooks, Sunny's on the scene in case Sylvia ever has another health crisis involving her breasts, and no one ever has to have sex with anyone else."

Sylvia snatched Diana's wineglass, halfway to her lips, out of her hand. "You know, eating dinner fashionably late is overrated. I say we eat now."

. . .

But dinner didn't help. For starters, Diana wouldn't eat anything, claiming she didn't need the extra calories on top of the wine. Then, when Sylvia tried to switch them all over to coffee, Diana simply got up and opened another bottle of wine herself.

"It is my birthday, after all," she said, pouring a full glass. She swirled the pale liquid around, staring at it as though it might suddenly turn into tea leaves that she could then read. "I still don't understand why Dan got so upset about the e-mails from Dirk."

"E-mails from Dirk?" Lise echoed.

"E-mails *from* Dirk, e-mails *to* Dirk—what's the difference?"

"What were the e-mails about?"

"Everything. Life, him, me. Everything."

"Just how many e-mails are we talking about?" Sylvia asked.

"Dunno. Twenty, thirty, maybe."

"Since you first met him back in April?"

"No. A day."

"*A day?*" Cindy's eyebrows shot up.

"Yes," Diana said huffily. "Twenty to thirty a day. Each."

"Oh, man," Carly said. "What were you thinking of? Did you think your husband wouldn't *mind* when he found out?"

"So what exactly are you saying," Diana boomed, "that *I'm* at fault here? That just because I was conducting a private correspondence with a friend, it justifies Dan up and cheating on me with some watery tart he met at the pub?"

"No one's talking about fault," Cindy said soothingly.

"Of course not," Lise said. Then she winced. "But twenty to thirty e-mails a day? That does sound a bit obsessive."

"What were you," Sylvia asked, "out of your fucking mind?"

. . .

Diana cornered Sylvia in the kitchen.

"Look, I'm sorry for what I said before about you and Sunny not sleeping together. It wasn't very politic of me." She held up a hand. "And there's no need for you to apologize for asking me if I'm out of my fucking mind. I've already forgiven you. I know you didn't mean it."

"Oh, but I did."

Lise came in and reached into a cabinet to get out plates for the cake. Diana ignored her and kept talking to Sylvia.

"I see. Well. Be that as it may, how are things going with the book?"

"Book? What book?"

"The one you were going to write about your sister. No, that wasn't it. The cookbook you were going to write to tie in with the TV program. What's going on with the program these days anyway?"

"I've told Magda I want a hiatus. Maybe I'll agree to go back on the air again in January as a midseason replacement." She shrugged. "I haven't decided yet."

"I can see why you'd be unsure."

"And why is that?"

"Well, it was hardly the best program to ever go on the tube, you know. You must admit, throwing food at audience members can only take you so far. But this is really wonderful news! You'll be able to devote all your energies to the little cookbook. Well, except for when you're running your little catering business, that is."

"I never said I'd write any cookbook."

"But I thought you said—"

"I said I'd think about it. I thought about it and I decided no."

"But you can't! You can't say no!"

"No? Gee, that's funny. I thought I just did."

"Oh." Diana shook her head morosely. "Dirk isn't going to like that at all."

"Dirk?" Lise said. "What does Sylvia writing a cookbook have to do with Dirk?"

• • •

Diana squeezed in between Cindy and Carly on the couch, addressing Cindy as though they were in a bubble, the only two people there. Not even bothering to whisper, she said, "So, how's the book going? You know, the one you were going to write about being a struggling single mother, even though you're not a mother technically yet, or some such rot?"

"I have been keeping a diary," Cindy confided. "And I really do have you to thank for that. Putting my feelings down on paper has really helped me organize my thoughts about the future."

"A diary? Yes, I can see where that could be good. The whole idea of diaries is very marketable, I think. You know, *The Princess Diaries*, Anne Frank. When do you think you'll have something to show Dirk?"

"Show Dirk? Oh, no. I'm not writing this for anyone else's eyes. It's just for me. It's too personal. I'd be embarrassed to have anyone else read it."

"But what good does that do me?" Diana said. "If Sylvia refuses to write a cookbook and now you're writing something you won't let anyone read—"

"Excuse me," Lise cut in, "but first you get upset about Sylvia not writing, now you're upset about Cindy not showing you what she's written, and you keep mentioning Dirk—just what the hell is going on? You're not...*pimping books* for him, are you?"

"I resent that," Diana said.

"You can resent it all you like, but you'd better answer my question just the same."

"I don't need to sit here and take this," Diana said, struggling to pull herself out of the sofa.

"Don't go," Cindy said. "We haven't even had any cake yet."

"And I don't *want* any bloody cake! Even if you put Splenda in it, it's still loaded with white flour, terrible carbs. White flour is *death!*"

"At least have some coffee," Cindy tried again.

"No, thank you." Diana was on her feet now, wobbly but upright. "This is a fine reward I get for bringing all of you together.

Three women, and not one of you will write a book for me. Well, Lise is writing a book, but she was already doing *that.*" She eyed Carly and Sunny consideringly, with a flash of hope that just as quickly receded. "Nah. Who wants to read about a girl working in a bra emporium or a surgeon who hangs out with a group of women?" She grabbed her purse, headed for the door. "Someone should shoot me for thinking up The Sisters Club in the first place!"

"The *Sisters* Club?" Sylvia said. She looked at the others. "What's she talking about?"

"*She,*" Diana said imperiously, "or, rather, I, only put that ad in the bookstore newsletter last January because I wanted to find other women with whom I could be like sisters. I thought it would be great if women whose sisters weren't on the scene or who were otherwise emotionally unavailable were to come together to fulfill the sister function in each other's lives and support one another—you know, through thick and thin." She barked a laugh. "Fat joke, that. You supported me through thick just fine. But thin? Not so much."

Sylvia looked at the others again. "Does anyone know what she's talking about?"

"It doesn't matter." Diana sniffed haughtily. "Because it's all gone horribly wrong. Nothing has turned out the way I planned it!"

Diana

I woke to the mother of all hangovers.

Crap. What had I done?

The late-morning sun, streaming through the blinds, which I'd neglected to draw the night before, assaulted my eyelids, revealing the still-empty space in the bed beside me.

Husbandless, I relived the night before at Lise's house. Had I really said all those awful things to my friends? How could I have done such a thing when they'd been so kind as to throw me a surprise party? I dimly remembered blurting out that stuff about The Sisters Club. What a fool they all must think I was. And how, I wondered, had I ever made it home, when I'd obviously been too drunk to drive?

Then I remembered: Sunny. I'd been fumbling the key in the lock of my car when Sunny caught up with me in the driveway.

"Sylvia insists I am to drive you home," he'd said in that funny formal way of his.

"Sylvia can stick it up her arse," I'd responded, the height of graciousness.

"That does not sound like something she would find pleasurable. Still, I request you give me your keys."

I'd tried to resist, but was surprised at how insistent Sunny could be when he put his mind to it.

"But if you drive me home in my car," I'd said after relenting, "how will you get home again?"

"I will take a cab. Let it be an adventure for me."

It humbled me now to think that, after I'd been so horrible, Sylvia still cared enough about my well-being to have Sunny drive me home. He was lucky I didn't barf on him.

I groaned. I should never have thought that word: "barf." *I suppose that's what I get*, I told myself, *for drinking my dinner.*

No sooner did I feel remorseful about Sylvia, however, than I felt resentment. How could they have all let me down that way? They—Sylvia and Cindy—had said they were going to write books for me. Or at least I'd told Dirk I could get them to do it. Now what was I going to do?

Dirk. The name appeared in my mind as a life raft. I had lost my husband. I had probably lost my friends. But at least I still had Dirk.

I looked at the bedside clock and did the math. It would be early evening in London right now. Scrambling for the phone, I punched in the number I'd committed to memory.

Dirk had given me his numbers—home, work, and cell—not long after his first e-mail to me all those months ago. But, in the intervening time period, I'd rarely allowed myself to use them, not wanting Dan to see any of Dirk's numbers on the phone bill. But Dan was gone now, probably for good. What did it matter any longer?

"Hello, luv," Dirk answered on the third ring. "I'm on my way out to a party and was going to let voice mail pick this up, but then I saw it was you. What's going on?"

I pictured him in a tux, doing last-minute adjustments to his tie. It was a nice picture.

"It was my birthday yesterday," I said, feeling stupid and needy, but needing to hear someone say something pleasant to me all the same.

"Well, happy birthday, then! Did you do anything fun to celebrate?"

"Not exactly. Lise threw a party for me, but I think I may have alienated everyone."

"Does 'everyone' include Sylvia and Cindy?"

I nodded, then realized he couldn't see me through the phone. "Yes."

"That can't be good."

"No. No, it's not. That's why I was calling you. I was hoping you could cheer me up."

"I'm always good for that, but I am in a bit of a rush. Don't want to miss the canapés, you know. Perhaps we could do the short version, then? Let's see...You're beautiful, smart, and sexy. How am I doing?"

"Great, so far." I laughed. "Keep going."

"Sorry. 'Fraid it's all I've got right now. Maybe I could call you when I get home? I really should be—"

"I have something to tell you." Well, I had to say *something*, didn't I, to keep him on the line?

"And what might that be?"

And now that I'd said that, I had to pony up with something he'd find important.

"Remember how I offered to act as sort of a pre-agent for you, getting Sylvia and Cindy to write memoirs or something? Well, it doesn't look like that's on. Seems that"—I tried on a tinkling laugh here—"suddenly no one wants to write memoirs anymore these days."

Even as I was speaking, I sensed I was saying the wrong thing. And, if my own limited instincts weren't enough, the sound of Dirk's voice, fishwifing at me, certainly clued me in.

"What?"

I suppose I should have guessed he'd be a bit disappointed.

"I'm sure you must be a bit disappointed, but—"

"You don't know the half of it," he said.

I recalled Dirk being cruel to Lise in his first e-mail to her, but in all my dealings with him, he'd only ever been kind, charming, and supportive. I'd have never guessed he could turn such a derisive tone on me.

"Listen, Diana, I don't have time for this kind of shit right now. Canapés are awaiting, you know? So, here's what you're going to do: you're going to write a memoir."

"What?" Now it was my turn to be shocked. "I'm not a writer! I can't write a memoir!"

"Course you can. Easiest thing in the world. You just write down a few true things, and then make up a bunch of stuff. Everyone does it."

"I'm not everyone!"

"No? You could have fooled me. And I'm not playing around here."

"But what would I write about? There's nothing in my life that people would be even remotely interested in."

"Oh, no? You're a classic success story. You could call it *Fat Girl Thin*. People love to read about lardos losing a ton of weight. We'd rake in a fortune."

There weren't enough words to express the horror I felt at what he was suggesting I do, so I let it go with one word: "No."

"I wouldn't say no so quickly if I were you."

"No?"

"No. Do you have any idea how popular weight-loss accounts are? And you, you're gorgeous. Even when you were a total cow, you were gorgeous. If you start writing now, you'll be done by the time you're thin enough to make the story really worth selling. On the cover of *Fat Girl Thin*, we'll put a copy of that old picture of you as a fattie Artemis has in her flat, only we'll crop her out of it of course, and on the back we'll do a picture of the new slim and elegant you you'll soon be. Everyone will find it inspirational. They'll tell themselves, 'If *she* can do it, and she looked so much worse than I do...' We'll both make a fortune! Now if you'll just stop and think..."

But I didn't stop and think, at least not on Dirk's behalf. Instead I shouted at him, "What's wrong with you? Are you *crazy*? I would never write a book like that!"

And then I heard a sound I never expected to hear: laughter.

"What's so funny?" I asked.

"You," he said between gasps. "Can't you tell when someone's having you on?"

"What are you talking about?"

"I never asked you to get your friends to write books—that was all your idea!"

"Then you weren't really mad before?"

"Course not. I was joking." He laughed some more. "And I certainly never expected you'd take me seriously about writing a memoir. *Fat Girl Thin*!" Then: "Although..."

For the first time, I could hear the scorn he had for me in his voice.

"Dirk, what have you been doing with me all these months?"

"Playing, of course. Haven't you?"

I thought about what he'd said that night at Artemis's party, the first time I'd met him, when I said I would have thought he'd have the decency to remember the names of the people whose lives he destroyed, and he replied, "But there are so many, and one loses track."

When I hung up the phone, he was still laughing.

I sat on the edge of the bed, stunned. I couldn't believe what I'd just heard. Dirk had been toying with me all along. But how was that possible? How could I have missed that? I'd trusted him, told him every intimate detail of my life. And for what?

Even though I had the thermostat in the house set on low heat against the early October coolness of the mornings, I felt a chill I couldn't shake. I felt so empty, naked. Most of all, I felt alone.

I reached for the phone, set it back on the hook before picking it up again, preparing to dial. I needed to talk to someone, anyone. I couldn't confess the shame of what Dirk had done to me, but I needed to talk to someone, anyone, even if it was just about the weather.

But who was there for me to call?

Lise? Sylvia? Cindy?

They wouldn't want to hear from me, not after the hurtful way I'd behaved the night before. Would any of them ever want to speak to me again?

I thought back to when I'd first got the idea to get a group of women together and back to our first meeting. I'd had such high hopes. I would replace my dysfunctional relationship with my real sister, Artemis, for functional relationships with three women I shared no blood with. As the months went on, I felt us growing closer. Then, when we were in Georgia, I'd sensed that closeness start to unravel because Lise and I could no longer get along, we were too busy competing over Dirk. *Fucking Dirk.* And now? Now it seemed to me that the whole thing had unraveled completely. Or maybe I was wrong. Maybe there was still a group of close women here, but they numbered three while I stood apart.

My whole world was gone. Dan, Lise, Sylvia, and Cindy, and Dirk, who, as it turned out, had never been a real part of that world at all. I was more alone than I could ever remember feeling in my life. How had I gotten here? More importantly, how would I ever find the road back?

Not wanting to dwell on those painful thoughts any longer, I went to do what had been a discouraging act for me for most of my life but what was now the only reassuring act I had left: I weighed myself.

I stared down at the numbers between my feet, tears blurring my eyes. Then I jumped off the scale and hauled it outside for the trash collector to take away.

Who bloody well cared what I weighed anymore?

Lise

"Hello?"

"I'm sure I'm the last person you want to hear from right now, but I had to call you."

"No, Diana, you're not the *last* person I want to hear from," I said, and meant it. If she were Sara, calling to say she'd just been awarded the Nobel Peace Prize, she'd have been the last person I'd want to hear from. Sibling rivalry had been riding high in the Barrett family of late. Sara had been banging up houses right and left with Habitat for Humanity down in the Dominican Republic, while I had yet to sell my book. "Now, then, maybe if I were Sylvia or Cindy you'd be the last person I'd want to hear from."

"It's that bad, isn't it?" she said. And then, before I could respond, she went on, "Of course it's that bad. That was awful what I did to them, and you were right: I *was* pimping for Dirk. As a matter of fact, Dirk is the reason I'm calling you today."

"Dirk? What about Dirk?"

"He's not what he appears to be, Lise. As your friend, I feel the need to warn you about him."

"I don't know what you mean."

"Last week I had the most awful conversation with him. Afterward, I tried calling Artemis about it, only it took her a while to get back to me. Apparently she'd been on holiday in Spain."

"I'm glad to hear your sister takes nice vacations, but I don't know what any of this has to do with me."

"You know all that stuff from the trade magazines about Dirk being the Jaguar?"

"Of course. He's supposed to be one of the most revered and cutthroat agents in the world. His deals are legendary."

"His *old* deals were legendary. But tell me: How many deals of his have you read about lately?"

I racked my brains but couldn't think of any. After admitting as much, I said, "That doesn't mean anything, though. Every deal doesn't get reported in the trades. With hundreds of thousands of new books being published every year worldwide that'd be impossible."

"Perhaps. But how many agents go by the Jaguar? You'd think you'd hear something, wouldn't you?"

"Why don't you get to the point, Diana?"

"Artemis says that the scuttlebutt going around London is that the whole the Jaguar stuff is just smoke and mirrors. She says Dirk is just coasting on his laurels. He did make a few big deals, huge deals, early on in his career, but then he overspent on big-ticket items and invested his money unwisely. According to Artemis, he's become a bottom-feeder, spends all his time trying to poach other agents' clients and making dicey deals that smack of questionable business ethics or"—she hesitated for a moment—"trying to put together pie-in-the-sky schemes like weight-loss memoirs. Artemis says that, in literary circles, he's not revered as the Jaguar anymore. On the contrary, behind his back they refer to him now, laughingly, as the Tabby."

"The Tabby?"

"I know. It's awful, isn't it?"

"Yes, it is awful," I said, agreeing with her, only not about what she might have thought. "I think it's awful that you've become such a petty and bitter person now that you've made a hash of things with Dan, and I'm guessing you've made a hash of things with Dirk too, so you have nothing better to do with your time than try to interfere with my business relationship with Dirk. I suppose you think that, just because you're not happy, no one else has a right to be either."

"But that's not it at all! I was calling you as your friend! Not only is he…the Tabby, but he's also turned out to be a sadistic prick! I wanted to save you from being hurt by Dirk, as I've been!"

"The only thing you need to save, Diana, is your words. I don't want to hear them anymore."

"But—"

Too late for her. I'd hung up.

"What was that all about?" Tony asked.

"Diana." I sighed. "I don't know what's wrong with that woman. When I first met her back in January, I thought she was one of the sweetest women I'd ever met in my life. But now? How can one person change so much?"

"People do change, Lise. You should know that by now. It's part of life. Of course, they never change when you want them to."

I'd invited Tony over to spend his lunch break between classes with me. I'd even made lunch.

The last month or so had brought a revelation. Whereas in previous years I'd had no problems spending the summer months with my motor running on idle, now that we were full into fall and I was home every day as part of my job, being a full-time, at-home writer wasn't all it was cracked up to be. In truth, it was damn lonely. Most days, since my friends worked and it had long since become too cool to go swim in my parents' pool every day, I didn't see a soul unless I had errands to run, and I'd even started getting weird about that. I was quickly learning that having a job that kept you in the house all day was just a short hop, skip, and jump away from agoraphobia.

People have this glamorous view of writers, where we spend all our nights at book publishing parties sipping Cristal with Gore Vidal and James Patterson. Or maybe they have a lazy view, where we spend our days in bunny slippers and feather boa robes, eating bonbons while watching soap operas and pecking away at the old Olivetti during commercial breaks. Nothing could be further from the truth.

That's not to say much writing got done those days.

Most days I spent with my bottom plastered to the chair in front of the computer. Not writing, I visited online forums for writers that only made me more depressed because other people seemed to be producing things and selling things when I was doing neither. Not writing, I spent an extraordinary amount of time playing online games like Sudoku or Word Whomp, the latter being a Boggle sort of game, but only for one person at a time and with beavers involved. At least I think they were beavers. They could have been gophers. It'd gotten to the point where I was developing carpal tunnel syndrome, not from working on my book, but from whomping those damn words. I'd once read an interview with a successful author who was quoted as saying, "The more successful I get, the bigger my butt." Me, I was accomplishing the latter without ever having the privilege of the former.

So, since Tony had been so nice and supportive when I learned John and Danitra had sold their books, when the loneliness became too much—when I was tempted to go to Super Stop & Shop, not because I needed anything but just so I could chat with the item checkout workers—I'd turned to him for lunch companionship and he'd graciously accepted.

The phone rang again.

"It's probably just Diana again," I said. "I'll just let the machine take it."

But it wasn't Diana. Instead, I heard Dirk's voice booming, "Lise, if you're there, pick up! I've got some *wonderful* news for you!"

"Sorry," I apologized to Tony, "I'd better take this." Then to Dirk I said, "I'm here. What's the news?"

"Earlier today I had the most marvelous conversation with an editor who read your book."

"I didn't even realize you'd submitted it to anyone," I said, not daring to let myself hope or dream about what this call could mean.

"Sorry, I suppose I should have told you first, but it was one of those spur-of-the-moment, cocktail-party things a few nights ago. Anyway, she read it and loved it, and she has only a few minor reservations."

"What sort of reservations?"

"Well, she thinks—and I must say, I agree with her—that the book isn't quite commercial enough as it stands now."

"Not commercial enough?" I tried to think back on the book in question, but Dirk had already had me make so many revisions to it, it was mostly all a muddle. I did recall removing all literary allusions. Oh, and at Dirk's suggestion, I'd added a cat.

"Look, Lise, she's really keen on the book in so many ways. This is no time to pull any *author* crap."

"I wasn't—"

"The book needs to be bigger than it is now. It needs—I don't know—a murder or two, or something."

"But it's not a mystery."

"Now, why did I know you were going to say that?" He laughed. "No worries. The editor and I have it all planned out."

"You do?"

"Oh, yes. We're going to put you in touch with a book doctor—more like a ghostwriter, really—someone who can whip this mess you've written into shape."

He was right. The book as it stood now *was* a mess, which was why it was a muddle to me, but it was a mess because Dirk'd had me rewrite it every five seconds. Besides which...

"But if a ghostwriter works on it, even if my name winds up on the cover, it won't really be my book anymore, will it?"

"Oh, come on." And now he sounded exasperated. "You're not a schoolgirl. You can't possibly be that naïve. People do it all the time. Well," he considered, "perhaps not with fiction quite so much. But nonfiction? Publishers would have cows if every politician and celeb who signed on to write a book announced they wanted to write the books themselves!"

I tried to process what I was hearing. Dirk was telling me there was an editor who wanted my book, but only if I turned over the book he'd molded more than I had and let some other person write it instead.

"If this editor has a ghostwriter whose work she admires," I asked, "why not just let the ghostwriter pen a whole book?"

"Oh, that'd be way too much work. It's a lot like building a house, you know. You see, you've already banged up the basic structure, which is a lot of work. Now you just need to let someone else move in and decorate the place for you."

He'd said, "You see," but I didn't see much at all. And what little I did see, I didn't like.

"No," I said.

"What do you mean, no?"

"I won't do it."

"But you've already come this far! It's only one tiny step farther you need to take."

But I could see that I'd already come too far. As it stood now, the book only felt half mine. If I did what Dirk suggested, it wouldn't be mine at all.

"I'm sorry, Dirk. I know you've put a lot of time into this—"

"You don't know the half of it!" His voice had turned ugly, a sneering thing. "So, what are you going to do? Go back to writing about sunsets and Middle East strife? Anyone can describe a sunset. But not many people can make others laugh *and* think. With the proper ghostwriter you could become—"

"I'll take my chances," I cut him off. "I want to go back to writing about sunsets and Middle East strife. Maybe I'll find a way to do it that's never been done before. Maybe I'll find a way to write what I want *and* make people laugh and think. Good-bye, Dirk."

Cindy

"The baby's due in two and a half months, and I need someone to be my Lamaze coach."

"What does a Lamaze coach do?" Sylvia asked.

"Go to Lamaze classes with me at the hospital, and then be with me in the labor and delivery room when the baby is born so I won't have to do it all alone."

"Sounds like a great thing. Who are you going to ask?"

"You."

You always hear people talking about laughing so hard or being so shocked at something that they spit whatever they were drinking at the time out of their mouths, but I'd never actually seen it done until that night.

"Oh, jeez," Sylvia said, handing me a napkin to wipe the coffee from my maternity blouse, "I'm sorry."

"Don't sweat it," I said. "I'm sure when the baby comes, I'll get spit up on with a lot worse things than coffee."

"Look," Sylvia said carefully, "don't get me wrong, I'm flattered that you asked me. How could I not be? But isn't there someone else you'd rather ask? What about Carly?"

"Carly is doing much better these days. Anyone can see that. But you never can tell with Carly. I don't want to put too much pressure on her now that she's doing so good. Plus, she's been putting in so much overtime at Midnight Scandals and that'll only increase once we head into the holiday season, she'll probably be in the middle of some giant bra sale when I go into labor."

"What about your mother? Don't you think she might be offended that you asked me instead of her?"

"You only say that because you've never met my mother." I

snorted. "If a train was coming down the tracks, rather than pushing me out of the way and risk getting hit herself, my mother'd watch me get hit, and then tell everyone what a lousy day she just had."

"God," she said, "how'd you ever avoid turning into the biggest jerk the world has ever seen?"

I smiled. "I have a few good friends," I said. "At least now I do."

"You do," she said, obviously warming with eagerness to the idea, "you really do. What about one of those other friends, then?"

I shook my head.

"Lise?" she suggested.

I shook my head.

"Diana?" she suggested.

I shook my head harder. Even though Lise had told us how nice Diana had been in trying to warn her about Dirk, I still didn't want her. I knew who I wanted. But, apparently, maybe she didn't want me.

"Maybe an old girlfriend?" she suggested. "Maybe a teacher from back in high school?"

"You're really starting to get desperate here," I said, forcing a laugh that didn't feel genuine. "Who are you going to suggest next? The mailman? The neighbor's cat?"

Sylvia winced. "It's not like *that*," she said. "But this is a big decision to make. I just want to make sure you make the right decision."

"I have made the right decision," I said. "I want you."

"How do you know I'd even be good at this…Lamaze stuff?"

"You'll be perfect," I said, covering one of her hands with one of mine.

"Crap." She got up to refill her coffee cup. But before she turned away, I could have sworn I saw a tear in her eye. "I knew I should never have asked you to move in."

. . .

"I think they all think we're lesbians," I whispered, being quick to add, "not that there's anything wrong with that."

Sylvia surveyed the other students in the Lamaze class: five other couples, all paired off boy/girl.

"So?" she said. "Better that than they think I'm your mother."

"I just didn't expect to feel this out of place," I said. "The only woman without a man with her, you know?"

"Shh," she said. "I'm trying to learn something here."

As the night wore on, a night that included breathing exercises and a video, a part of me regretted my decision. Sylvia, it turned out, was a drill sergeant.

"Breathe in low, shallow spurts," she told me. "Do it again. You don't want them"—and here she indicated a tall redheaded woman to the left of us and her short spouse—"to be better at this than we are, do you?"

"This is not a competitive sport," I huffed between breaths.

"I don't care," she said. "I want us to be *the best*."

Some of her enthusiasm disappeared, however, as we watched the video of an enormously pregnant woman straining to give birth.

"I'm glad they don't give us popcorn and candy with this thing," Sylvia whispered. "Who thought of this?"

"Who thought of what?"

"Having babies like this. If human beings have to procreate, shouldn't there be a better way? It's gross. How's she going to get a baby out of there?"

"Oh, you're a big help," I said. "It's beautiful." That's what I said to her, but inside I was scared to death. How *was* I going to get a baby out of there? "Having a baby is going to be a piece of cake. Speaking of cake, I'm hungry. Can we go get dessert after this?"

"Jeez," Sylvia said, unable to tear her eyes away from the screen as the baby's head appeared between the woman's legs, "how can you think of food at a time like this?"

* * *

But I could always think of food those days, no matter what was going on, and I said as much to Sylvia as we walked out of the hospital and into the crisp night.

"You really want cake?" she said. "After that?"

"No."

"I didn't think so."

"I want ice cream instead."

"But it's cold out."

"I still want it."

So she took me to an ice cream shop where we just made it in as the last customers before closing time since all the local shops closed pretty early once the summer season was over. I ordered a dish of mint chocolate-chip ice cream with double hot fudge sauce, which I ate out in the van since the owners looked anxious to close up shop. I set the ice cream dish down on the dashboard and did up the buttons on my coat, a clown-like coat like the one Jacqueline Kennedy wore on the campaign trail with Jack that I'd picked up at a thrift store.

"Would you like some?" I took up my dish and held out a spoonful. To be honest, I wanted every last bite for myself, but it only seemed right to share.

After what she'd seen back in the Lamaze class, her face was a sickly shade, not as green as my ice cream, but definitely in the same color family.

"I think I'll pass," she said.

We ate in silence for a while; or, at least, I ate.

"What were you like before Eddie?" Sylvia asked.

"Where did that come from?"

"Natural curiosity." She shrugged. "I was just wondering what you used to be like when you were younger, back before you met him."

"I don't know." Now it was my turn to shrug. "I guess I was like most girls, wanting to meet the guy who would be the one."

"So how come you never go out at night?"

"What do you mean? I'm out now, aren't I?"

"You're having ice cream in a van with your Lamaze coach. I'd hardly say that qualifies as a wild night on the town."

"What do you expect me to do? Go out to bars and shoot pool?"

"Sure. So long as you don't drink any alcohol, why not? You're certainly not going to meet any new guys sitting around the condo, watching TV with me and Carly every night."

"Oh, right." I laughed. I patted my belly bulge, and then scooped up another spoonful of green ice cream and fudge. "I'm sure there are just a whole ton of eligible guys out there right now who'd want to be with me."

"Who's Porter?" she asked suddenly, right smack out of the blue.

"Excuse me?"

"Porter. Whenever I clean your room, I see that business card stuck in the corner of the mirror over the dresser. It says Porter Davis on it. You've kept it up there all these months, so I was naturally wondering who he was."

It's embarrassing to admit but true: Sylvia did regularly clean the room I shared with Carly. In the beginning we tried to do it ourselves, but when Sylvia discovered we never vacuumed under the beds, she took over the dusting and vacuuming, saying she was worried the dust bunnies would give the baby asthma even before the baby was born.

"I should have thrown that thing away a long time ago," I said, realizing even as I said it that she thought it was significant somehow that I hadn't. "That day you came to take me away from the apartment I shared with Eddie, things moved so fast, I just grabbed whatever I laid hands on, and when I got to your place, I guess I put everything away just as quickly and then forgot all about it."

"Oh, really? So, who is he?"

There were times when you just knew Sylvia wouldn't accept "None of your damn business" for an answer, so I told her all about the first night I'd met Porter at the Bar None.

Then I told her about the time he'd stopped by the apartment I used to share with Eddie because he'd been worried about me.

"He tracked you down?" she asked.

"I guess you could put it that way."

"But isn't that kind of...stalkerish?"

"I could see where you'd think that," I said, "and I even thought that myself at the time. But, no, it wasn't like that at all. You know how sometimes you're someplace public, like the library or Super Stop & Shop, and you see something happen, something that's wrong? Maybe it's a mother slapping her kid in a way that makes you realize that kid is getting a lot worse when he gets home. Maybe it's some guy being truly awful to his girlfriend. And you think to yourself, 'I wish I was still in grade school and believed in things like making a citizen's arrest. I wish I was brave enough to just *act*, to do something to keep life from turning into a complete disaster for another human being.'"

"I guess so," she said.

"Well, that's what it was like. At least that's what I think now. Porter, in that one night, saw the train of my life getting ready to fly right off the railroad tracks and, by showing up at my place, *by finding me*, he was doing what he could to keep that from happening. He was being the Good Samaritan. Plus, it wasn't like he was a total stranger acting that way. I knew him back in high school. We used to be friends, sort of, back when we were young."

"So," she said, "this Porter—is he cute?"

I laughed so hard, I thought I was going to pee myself right there. It was just so strange having Sylvia ask me if Porter was cute or not, like she and I were two teenagers talking about the guys we had crushes on.

"I don't know," I said, feeling the hilarity subside as a wave of sadness came rolling in. "I guess."

Sylvia had asked earlier what I'd been like as a young girl. Sure, I'd had hopes and dreams just like anybody else. But then, somewhere along the way, those hopes and dreams had fallen by the side of the road. How would I ever get back to that person I used to be? That person, but only better. A person who hoped and dreamed and wasn't totally naïve.

"It's OK to be happy, you know," she said.

But I was tired of thinking about me.

"What about you and Sunny?" I asked.

Sylvia

How the hell did that happen? One minute we're talking about her, the next we're talking about me.

"You say it's OK to be happy," she said.

"And it is. You know, some women go through life thinking the definition of a good relationship is high drama. I don't know where they get that idea. Maybe they get it from stupid TV talk shows. But they think that, unless they're fighting with the guy, unless there's high drama every second, it's not a real relationship. It's not a romance. All I'm saying is, it's OK to go for the good guy. It's OK to go for the guy who can make you happy, rather than the one who's always making you miserable."

"And all *I'm* saying is: What about Sunny? He's, like, the greatest guy who ever lived, even if Diana did corner me at that party at Lise's and ask me if I didn't think he was a bit like Yoko Ono, being around all the time, and that he'd break the Beatles—meaning us up."

I had to laugh at that, the image of Sunny as Yoko Ono. "Diana was pretty drunk that night, wasn't she?" I said.

"She was. But that's not the point."

"Which is?" I said, which I probably shouldn't have since I probably didn't want to hear whatever she was going to tell me.

"Sunny's so terrific, if the idea of the two of us together wasn't totally ridiculous, I'd go for him myself. But you? You've *got* Sunny, you've had him for months now. And what do you do? You treat him like he's your sister. You haven't even slept with the guy yet!"

"Hey!" I was outraged. Then I was curious. "And how do you know that anyway?"

"Because," she said patiently, "the walls in the condo are very thin. You never go over to Sunny's place, he always comes over to yours; he even goes into your bedroom, but Carly and I never hear any spring action."

"Hey!" I said again. "What I do in my bedroom is none of your business."

"Maybe not. But your happiness *is* my business."

"So, you think two people can't have a platonic relationship and still be happy?"

"The way Sunny's in love with you? No. No, Sylvia, I don't think he can be happy with you like that. Not forever." She set down her ice cream dish, long empty. When she spoke again, her words were softer. "What is it, Sylvia? What is it with you? Is it so hard to believe a man could love you, want you like that?"

And right there in the van, outside of the closed ice cream shop, I told her the one thing I'd never told anybody. I told her about Minnie.

• • •

"I think that's the saddest story I ever heard," Cindy said when I finished, wiping her eyes.

"Thanks," I said, at a loss as to what to say in response. People's pity always made me uncomfortable. "It was a long time ago."

"That's what I don't get, though. It didn't even happen to you and you've—what?—taken a vow of celibacy all this time?"

"Hey, I'm Jewish," I said, trying to make light of it. "We don't take vows of celibacy. We just don't have sex."

"But it's such a *huge* part of life! How can you just give it up like that? And for so long!"

"I don't know," I said. "I guess that, initially, I did it out of some sort of sense of solidarity with Minnie. If she'd been hurt, if she was going to renounce fun, then so was I. I never meant for it to go on forever. But once you start doing a thing—or maybe *not* doing it—it becomes habit."

"I don't know, Sylvia." She shook her head. "Can't you break the habit? What are you going to do? Go to your grave a virgin?"

"I'm not a virgin," I muttered. "I just haven't had sex in thirty years."

"Shoot," she said. "You should call up Sunny right now, have him meet us at home so you guys can do it before the damn thing falls off from lack of use."

"That's not funny," I said through gritted teeth.

"No, I suppose you're right. It's not funny at all. It's sad. You paid your debt to Minnie; you were the best sister in the world to her, you stood by her, you lived your life the way *she* wanted to live hers, just so she wouldn't feel alone. Even if," she added, "that way of life does smack of enabling."

Jeez. She was a fine one to talk about enabling.

"Minnie's dead," Cindy said, "but you're alive. You have a right to be happy. You have a right to be as happy in this world as you can possibly be."

"Hey, I'm the one who's supposed to tell *you* how to live your life."

"What we have is called friendship." She smiled in the dark. "It goes both ways."

Happy, I thought. *What was happy?*

I thought over my life; or, I thought over it as quickly as you can when you're sitting in a van and the pregnant lady sitting next to you probably has to pee soon.

When Minnie was alive, I'd been happy. Even if other people, looking at it from the outside, would call our life together "enabling," we were happy in our own weird way. And since then? This last year?

So much had happened since January: the business really got going, the TV show, my new girlfriends, Sunny. There had been moments that weren't always perfect, and some had been downright lousy, but most of it had been good. What did I want, though?

I saw now what I didn't want: I didn't want to go back to doing the TV show. There was a reason I'd been dragging my feet about answering Magda's repeat phone calls, and it was that I didn't want what she had to offer. Sure, she could give me lots of money and even fame. She could probably make me rich. But I didn't want that, not that way. What I wanted was to just keep cooking, feeding a few people at a time, and never worrying about hair and makeup unless I was going to see Sunny.

Sunny. I wasn't ready to think about him just now.

But my friends? I was very happy with my friends. Things with Diana may have gotten off track a bit, but I'd always be grateful to her for being the one who brought Lise into my life, not to mention Cindy. I never told Cindy—I don't know why; maybe I didn't want her to take me for granted—but having her under my roof, having her to care for had been one of the two greatest things to happen to me since Minnie died.

And the other of the two greatest things? It was Sunny, of course.

"I'll make you a deal," Cindy said. "On Halloween, we'll dress up and go out. And I'll even call Porter and invite him, but only if you agree to finally tell Sunny your secret. Soon."

Halloween

RECOMMENDED READING:
Diana: *Between Sisters*, Kristin Hannah
Lise: *Angelmonster*, Veronica Bennett
Cindy: *The Bitch Posse*, Martha O'Connor
Sylvia: *Love and Meatballs*, Susan Volland

Chalk Is Cheap was hopping, cobwebs were festooned from the rafters, and the vampire was cute.

"Cindy?" the vampire said, going up to the clown who was bent down low over the pool table to take a shot. The clown had on a voluminous white satin costume with big green pompoms for buttons. On her face she wore circus makeup, but she'd refused to put the red mop wig on. When she straightened up, it became obvious that the illusion of size was all costume and that the woman beneath the costume was very slim.

"No," the clown smiled. "I'm Carly, her sister."

"Wow," the vampire said. "Even with the makeup, you look just like her."

"I get that all the time," Carly said, still smiling. Then she jerked her head to indicate two tables that had been pushed together behind her. "The clown you're looking for is over there."

The women hadn't gotten there until after nine, mostly arriving in separate cars. Cindy was the one who had found out about the Halloween party at Chalk Is Cheap, which she'd read about in the paper.

"It'll be fun," she'd said. "They have pool tables there and everything, and they're even having a contest for best costume. The mayor is supposed to be the judge, and at midnight they're going to announce the winner. The prize is—get this!—round-trip tickets for four to Bermuda and a week there in a fancy hotel."

"Georgia was enough vacation for me for one year, thanks," Sylvia had said. "But, sure, I'll go. The only thing is, can we go late? At the condo we get about two hundred trick-or-treaters a year. I swear they bus them in! Even though I don't have kids of my own, and even though the kids'll get plenty of candy anyway, I always feel like a dirtbag of a neighbor if I'm not there to do my part."

So Sylvia and Sunny, with the help of Cindy and Carly, had spent the first portion of the evening handing out candy to little princesses and little Harry Potters. Then they'd all piled into Sylvia's van, where they met up with Lise and Diana, who'd each come in their own cars.

Now the vampire looked over at the tables that Carly had indicated. He saw an older woman with short red hair dressed as a surgeon; a caramel-skinned man dressed as a waitress, muscular arms coming out of white cap sleeves; a woman with short black and red spiky hair dressed up in a costume he couldn't quite make sense of: there was a black cape with leaves and twigs all over it—there was even a fake squirrel pinned to her shoulder—and autumn-colored makeup on her face including a leaf painted on one cheek; a tall woman in a Dorothy costume, complete with a red pigtailed wig and sparkly red slippers on her feet, that sat off to the side a bit as though she were part of the group but only just barely; and, between the surgeon and the leaf lady, another clown in a white satin suit with long blond hair.

"You're Porter, right?" Carly asked the vampire.

He nodded. "Cindy said to look for the blonde in the clown costume."

"I know," Carly said. "And I was going to go as something else, but then I couldn't think of anything else that was really good. I mean, Lise"—she indicated the leaf lady—"said she was going as autumn. She's a whole season! How can anyone compete with that? So I decided to just go as a clown too." Then she gave him a nudge. "Go on. Say hello. They won't bite. Well, the others might, but Cindy won't."

The vampire slowly approached the table, like people do when approaching a group where they only know one of the people there.

"You made it!" Cindy's eyes lit up when she saw him. "I didn't think you would come."

"Of course I came," Porter said.

Cindy rose to greet him, and, with the table no longer covering her midsection, it was clear she filled out her costume in a way Carly didn't fill out hers.

"Wow," Porter said, "things have really changed since the last time I saw you."

"It's yours," Cindy said, patting her belly.

Porter's eyes widened.

"I'm kidding, of course," Cindy said with a loud laugh. "Kidding!" Then her voice softened to a point where it was almost wistful, like someone dreaming of a world—a normal world—that would never exist for her. "Of course, it's not yours. How could it be? I mean, *duh*."

Porter still hadn't said anything.

"I'm sorry," Cindy said. "I guess I should have told you on the phone. But it's just so awkward, you know? What do you say? 'Hi, I know we haven't seen each other in a long time, so would you like to get together and, oh, by the way, I'm very pregnant.' If you want to leave, I'll understand."

"No." Porter shook his head. "I don't want to leave. It's just surprising, that's all."

"Here," Cindy said, "let me introduce you to everyone."

But after introductions had been made, and Sunny had pulled up an extra chair for Porter, there was silence.

"So," Sylvia said, breaking the silence, "a vampire. It's not like you don't see a million of those on Halloween, but somehow on you, it looks original."

"Thanks," Porter said eagerly, obviously relieved to be talking about something innocuous. "I actually haven't dressed up for Halloween in years. In fact, the last time I dressed up, I wore this costume."

"Oh?" Sylvia said. "Do tell."

"It was the fall after I graduated from college. I was at a party in Milford with this girl I was seeing at the time. I don't even remember now what I ever saw in her, because all we ever seemed to do was fight. Anyway, we were at this costume party, and we got in this huge fight and all I wanted to do was get out of there. But the fight was so bad, I didn't even want to leave with her. Only problem was, she was the one driving. So I walked up to the parkway, still wearing my vampire costume, with a tallboy in each hand. But Milford, as you must know, is quite a walk from Danbury. So when I saw this caterpillar on the side of the road after walking the curve of the parkway for an angry mile, I hot-wired it, and I guess you could say I stole it."

"You stole a caterpillar?" Diana asked. "But I don't understand. You stole one of those crawling little wormlike things that later turns into a butterfly?"

"No," Porter said. "A caterpillar is a construction vehicle. It's a huge yellow track-type tractor with giant bands around the wheels. This one had a glass cab on top. Anyway, there I was driving down the middle of the Merritt Parkway—"

"With your vampire cape flying behind you," Cindy put in, laughing.

"Exactly," Porter said, "with my vampire cape flying behind me. I had one tallboy between my legs for later and one in my hand. Let me tell you, it wasn't easy driving that thing while trying to drink a beer. I could only go maybe a few miles an hour. I was lucky, though. The cop who pulled me over, when I explained about the fight with my girlfriend, told me that his wife'd just left him. We commiserated. He didn't arrest me or even give me a ticket, but he did confiscate the tallboys and the caterpillar."

By now Cindy was laughing so hard, she was holding her sides. "Oh," she said, "it's just the picture: a vampire slowly riding a caterpillar down the middle of the Merritt!"

"I don't like blind people because they can't drive cars," Sylvia said to Cindy.

Cindy sobered up instantly.

Porter looked puzzled at the non sequitur. "I'm going up to the bar to get a drink," he said. "Can I get anyone anything?"

"I'll take another club soda," Diana said. Then she explained. "I'm on alcoholic probation. I made a bit of a jackass of myself one night."

The others passed.

As soon as he was gone, Sylvia turned to the others. "What do we have here? Another Eddie on our hands?"

"That's exactly what I thought," Lise said. "Fighting with his old girlfriend, drunken revelry…"

"Not to mention the caterpillar," Diana put in.

"Do you think perhaps you might be jumping to conclusions?" Sunny said.

"We're overprotective," Sylvia said, "with good reason. So sue us."

"The poor man was clearly just trying to make conversation."

"Maybe that's not a chance we're willing to take."

"I don't think—" Cindy started to say, but she was interrupted by Porter's return.

"One of the nice things about being tall," he said, sitting down, "is bartenders always see you." He looked at the group. "You did hear the part where I said that happened a while ago, didn't you?" he asked. "I don't do stupid things like that anymore. I don't get in drunken fights with women. I don't go out with women I fight with. And the only way I'd ever steal another vehicle is, oh, I don't know, if some woman went into labor and I had to rush her to the hospital."

The women breathed a collective sigh of relief. Whatever else Porter might be, and no one really knew yet, at least he wasn't an Eddie.

"What about your costumes?" Porter looked at Sylvia and Sunny. "You two make a rather original pair."

"I am her and she is me," Sunny said. "It is our *Wuthering Heights* moment."

"Except I'm not a waitress," Sylvia said. "I'm a caterer."

"This is true," Sunny said. "But if I wore the suit of a chef and a toque, it would have been boring." He turned to Sylvia. "Would you care to dance, Dr. Goldsmith?"

When the surgeon and waitress were gone, Lise turned to Cindy. "Do you want to shoot some pool? Isn't that one of the reasons you wanted to come here? To shoot a few games before the baby comes?"

"I don't think so," Cindy said. "It seemed like a good idea at the time." She made a face. "But now that I'm here, I realize I'm way too big to play now. Just the sheer size of me would probably throw my whole game off; and if I bent over the table, I'd probably need help getting up again. Do me a favor?" She looked wistful again. "You and Diana play, so I can at least watch. Go on. I showed you how when we were down in Georgia."

• • •

"I'm afraid I'm not very good at this," Diana said, holding her pool cue. "Would you mind breaking?"

Lise shot, sinking the seven on the break but scratching.

"Have you heard from Dan?" Lise asked as they played.

"We talk," Diana said. "We talk about what to do about the future. But nothing's been resolved. I'm not sure how it will be. But never mind about me. What's going on with you and Tony? Anything?"

"We're friends now," Lise said. "We do friend-type things together. Maybe that's what we should have been in the first place."

"Look, Lise, I wanted to say…"

Lise had been about to take a shot and stopped. "Yes?"

"Just, thank you for inviting me to join you all tonight. The house is so far back from the road, I doubt I would have gotten any trick-or-treaters, and it would have just been me there all night, alone. It was very kind of you to ask me."

"I owed you," Lise said simply.

"For what?"

"For trying to warn me about Dirk. I didn't listen. I *should* have listened—but I still owe you."

"I'm not surprised you didn't believe me," Diana allowed. "I'd made a big hash of things with everyone."

"All water under the bridge now."

"Is it? That's funny, because I still feel on the outside of things, looking in."

* * *

The mayor arrived just before midnight. People were beginning to think he'd never show up and that the Bermuda prize wouldn't be awarded. But then he was there, glad-handing people as he worked the room, studying each costume.

When he was done, the owner helped him up onto the bar, from where the mayor made his announcement.

"The winner for best costume and the winner of the trip to Bermuda is…the clown!"

The room filled with muttering.

"I can't believe it," Lise said. "I spent *two hours* putting this thing together with a glue gun. I'm a whole season! How can a clown win?"

"Which clown?" someone shouted.

"*That* clown," the mayor said, pointing to a woman that no one in the group had noticed before.

Cindy and Carly turned to one another, mouths open, but it was Carly who spoke first.

"Hey," she said, "what's that clown got that we don't?"

Cindy

I didn't allow myself to think much about Porter. When I did, I told myself he didn't walk straight out the door again at Chalk Is Cheap because he was too polite. I told myself it didn't mean anything that he'd slow danced with me after that other damn clown won the trip to Bermuda because he felt sorry for me. I told myself he'd asked for my new number at the end of the night, again because he was being polite. I told myself he kissed me right before he left because that's what people do.

I told myself maybe he'd be better off with Carly than me, and she'd certainly be better off with him.

• • •

Now that Sylvia was my Lamaze coach, she insisted on going to all the doctor's visits with me to my ob-gyn. And, when she did, she brought along a list of questions to ask.

"Cindy says she's noticed small bumps that appear to somehow be rhythmic with her uterus," Sylvia said to Dr. Carter. "Is that normal?"

Dr. Carter was about halfway between my age and Sylvia's and, for a doctor, she wore a lot of bling.

"Perfectly normal, Ms. Goldsmith," she said. "That sort of thing is usually caused by the baby having hiccoughs. There's no cause for alarm."

"Cindy says she's experiencing increasing contractions. In the beginning they felt like practice, but she says these seem like they mean business."

"That's a great sign. It means her body is getting ready for labor.

If this *wasn't* happening now, I'd be worried. Cindy's right on track to have her baby in about eight weeks."

"Cindy's having trouble sleeping at night."

"Good. That's Mother Nature's way of preparing her for life with a new baby. If she was still sleeping eight hours straight through, it'd be an awfully rude awakening once the baby comes and she's woken up every two hours for the first few weeks. Of course, sometimes sleep is disturbed by the prospective mother worrying."

"Worrying? About what?"

"Worrying about the health of the baby, worrying about the ordeal of labor, worrying about parenting once the baby is born." Dr. Carter looked at me. "Are you worrying a lot about those things these days, Cindy?"

"Thank you," I said, from my prone position on the examining table. "It's very nice of one of you to finally talk to me as though I'm in the room. And of course I'm worried about those things you said—all of them! I'd have to be insane not to worry about those things."

Dr. Carter laughed. "You're going to do great, Cindy."

"Easy for you to say. You're not the one with the sore back who's running to the bathroom to pee every forty-five minutes."

"What about that, Doctor?" Sylvia asked. "Is all that soreness and peeing normal?"

"Before you go, I'll give Cindy some exercises she can do to alleviate the back pain. And if she limits her fluids before retiring, it should minimize the amount of times she gets up to go to the bathroom during the night at least. Really, Ms. Goldsmith,"—and here Dr. Carter took one of Sylvia's hands in both of hers—"Cindy is doing just great. Everything is proceeding as well as it possibly can. Honestly, she's young, she's healthy, and there haven't been any serious complications with this pregnancy; and while I'm no fortune-teller, there's no reason to imagine there will be."

Sylvia and I shared a look. The idea of my pregnancy having progressed with no serious complications—when you thought about Eddie, Eddie, and, well, *Eddie*—made us both bust out laughing so hard, Dr. Carter must've thought we were nuts.

• • •

Sylvia's condo had a basement level. At the foot of the stairs there was a small room with a desk in it in which she did some of the accounting work for her business. Off that room were two doorways, one an open doorway to the laundry room. Sylvia liked to say that before Carly and I moved in, that room got hardly any use at all. But now the machines ran at least once a day. She added, "When the baby comes, they'll be going twenty-four seven. It'll be like a Laundromat in here!" The other doorway had an actual door in it that led to the largest room down there. Previously, Sylvia had used it for storage, but now she'd cleaned it out.

"When the baby comes, it'll be too crowded if you and Carly and the baby are all in the same room. We can move Carly down here."

"But there are only two tiny windows at the top of the wall right under the ceiling," I objected. "All she'll be able to see of the outside world is other people's feet walking by."

"True. But it's the biggest room in the place. We can put a queen-size bed in here. There's even room for a big couch. That way, she can watch TV down here all she wants to when you're upstairs taking care of the baby."

I thought Carly would feel offended, like she was being displaced, but she was thrilled.

"No offense, Cin," she said, "but you snore at night. *Loud.* I'm going to love it down there. It'll be like living on my own, except I won't be alone."

With Carly installed in the basement, it was time to turn my bedroom into a nursery that I could share with the baby. The only problem was, no one'd let me do anything.

"I'm not going to go into labor if I screw in a nail to put together the crib or get on a ladder to hang up a mobile," I objected.

"I'm not taking any chances," Sylvia said. "You sit."

There were a lot of beautiful things waiting for the baby; things I'd never dreamed I'd have for her, things I couldn't afford.

Instead of having a regular baby shower, the other women'd taken me shopping. They told me to pick out whatever I needed, whatever I wanted for the baby.

And Diana had paid for it all.

"I don't have unlimited use of Dan's credit cards anymore," she said with a laugh she was obviously trying to keep light, but it wasn't. "Still, he did leave me with one with a reasonable limit for shopping."

"But don't you need to spend that money on yourself?" I said. "I mean, as you keep getting thinner, won't you need to buy new clothes?"

"So I'll tighten my belt a little bit." This time her laugh was genuine. "Do you think it'll really destroy me to look sloppy for a bit?"

And so I had a beautiful high-gloss white dresser for the baby, filled with gorgeous tiny clothes. The women had insisted on some neutral colors since I'd refused to find out the sex of the baby, while I'd in turn insisted on a lot of pink since I was sure the baby'd be a girl.

Sylvia had been willing enough to go along with my belief in my baby's girlhood, enough so that she'd painted the room the palest pink imaginable, putting up the most darling Cinderella border along the top of the walls.

"If it is a boy," she said, "you and the baby can have my room while I quickly redo this place."

"You're not going to have to," I said, turning in awed circles as I surveyed her work. "It's so beautiful in here, it's like a dream."

"It's not a dream," she said. "You're wide awake."

"But you put so much work into this, you and Carly. It's all so permanent. And yet, who knows how long we'll be here? I can't go on imposing on you forever, and who knows what the future'll bring?"

Sylvia's voice was even deeper than usual when she spoke. "I know I won't have you forever," she said, "but as long as you're here, this is your home."

"Thank you," I said simply, because there weren't enough words to express my gratitude.

Sylvia looked around the room: at the crib, at the changing table, and at the glider chair with footrest where I'd one day breastfeed my baby.

"Are you ever sorry," she asked, "that Eddie's not part of the picture?"

"God, no," I said. "Sure, there are moments when I miss him. But then I think what it'd be really like—the baby waking up at two in the morning, Eddie screaming at me to shut up the baby, little stuff like that—and I don't miss that lost future at all."

• • •

"Why don't you give Porter a call? Here's his card."

"What are you talking about?" Carly said to me, pushing away my hand with the card in it. "I'm not calling Porter. God, Cindy, you can be so high school at times. What do you want me to do, call him up to see if he still likes you?"

"I didn't mean that. I meant you could call him for you. He's single, you're single—you two'd make a great pair."

"I never realized that coupledom was as easy as two single people getting together, so thanks for pointing that out. But… Porter? Eeuw!"

"What do you mean, 'eeuw'? Porter's very nice. He's nice and he's sweet and he's funny and he's smart and he's handsome and he's got a good job—"

"And he's totally not my type. What are you, nuts, Cindy?"

"Yeah," said Sylvia, walking into the room, "what are you, nuts, Cindy?"

"I was only trying to—"

"Set me up with some guy who's crazy about you," Carly cut me off. "No, thank you."

"What do you mean, crazy about me?"

"Anyone can see it," they both said at the same time.

"At the very least," Sylvia added, "he's very fond of you. You should call him. You should accept his calls when he phones, rather than always telling me to tell him you're in the shower. How many showers can one woman take?"

"You're a fine one to be giving advice," I told her. "You still haven't resolved things with Sunny."

"I'm getting to it. I'm getting to it. Stop rushing me. And while you're busy not rushing me, you might think about calling Porter."

"I'll think about it."

"Really," Sylvia said, "you should just do it. So much of life is: Did you get on the plane or didn't you? It's time to get on the plane."

Diana

I was glad to have had the opportunity and the privilege of helping Cindy buy things for her baby, but I still didn't feel as though I was a complete part of things. I didn't feel a complete part of my friends, of my family, and I certainly didn't feel a complete part of anything with Dan. I was just a woman, albeit an increasingly thin woman, living in a big house. Alone.

. . .

And then Artemis came to town.

Artemis, in all her artemisal glory.

She had on a pink suit and matching pumps, even though, in just another fortnight's time, the calendar would tick us over into winter.

"What are you doing here?" I asked.

"Some conversations don't work over the phone or in e-mail. Some conversations require a face-to-face meeting. I've come to save you from yourself," she said grandly. Then she amended, "Or at least talk some sense into you."

"Who are you supposed to be, George Hamilton?" I asked, surveying the vast array of suitcases around her. Was that an honest-to-God hatbox? Was she moving in? "And how long do you imagine talking some sense into me will take?"

She consulted her watch. "Half a day, perhaps? Maybe a touch more? If we work quickly, I can get back to New York City by tomorrow. Surely you don't expect me to spend an entire week in *Danbury*, do you? Do you have any idea how long it took me to get here? A half dozen or so hours on the plane, then, once I landed, imagine my horror when I realized it would take me over another hour to get to you! I certainly wasn't going to take the train or, worse, a bus. So I hired a car and driver. That's him over there." She turned, switching on her highest-wattage smile as she did so and giving the liveried driver a white-gloved wave. "Could you pay him for me?" she said through her brilliant smile. "And while you're paying him, could I borrow your shower? I need to wash the airplane out of my hair. *God,* I can't believe you live so far from civilization."

It was the most words anyone had spoken to me in days. And, in its own awful way, it was wonderful.

"You look fantastic," I said, meaning it.

"Thanks," she said, peering at me over the top of her Jackie O sunglasses, "so do you. But, my God, Diana, you're thin. I know you kept e-mailing me and phoning me with the numbers as you lost, but it's nothing like seeing the change in person." Then: "I can't believe it's so cold here, rainy too. And here I was, expecting a relief from the dismal London weather."

"It is November in New England," I pointed out.

"Might as well be Old England if the weather's going to be like that. And here I thought everywhere in the United States was like Texas."

Artemis went into the house while I went to pay the driver.

"Your sister," he said, "is she really royalty? She said the reason she couldn't pay me up front was that, as a member of the royal family, she's not allowed to carry cash."

"She's a distant member," I said, "but she is, by marriage of course. Princess Artemis, that's her."

"God, but your sister is quite a woman. I didn't believe half the things she told me but, by the end of the ride, I felt as though *I* should be paying *her.*"

* * *

A half hour later, Artemis sat at the island in my kitchen on a high stool, her glorious hair covered by a towel she wore turban style.

"Tea, Diana? I come all this way, and you serve me *tea?* The least you could do is put something a little alcoholic in it. Your tea has always, frankly, sucked."

After I'd placed a bottle of whiskey on the table before her, she consulted her watch again. "Time's a-wasting. So let's cut to the chase here, as you no doubt say now that you're living down here on the prairie."

"I don't—"

"You must reconcile with Dan. You must throw yourself at his mercy; if he still has any left, that is."

"But you never even liked Dan!"

"You're right. I didn't like Dan. I was suspicious of him. I was certain he was using you in some way. But no man would react the way he has to what you've done, if he didn't deep-down love you. E-mail. I swear, it's ruined more marriages than happy hour ever did! If technology keeps accelerating the way it has been, people will need to get divorced from each other before they've even bothered to get married."

"But Dan cheated on me. And he didn't cheat on me in e-mail; he cheated on me in the flesh."

"True. And I understand how it must hurt you. But don't you realize that, in a very real sense, what you did was far worse than what Dan did? He made one mistake, an accident practically. But you? With open eyes, you carried on an e-mail affair—and with *Dirk* of all people! God, Diana, if you're going to wreck your marriage, at least wreck it with someone who's worth wrecking it for."

"But I don't understand."

"Fine. Then I'll repeat myself. I said, 'True. And I understand—'"

"No, I get that part, thanks. I maybe even agree with it...now. But what I don't get is: Why? Why, Artemis? Why would you come all this way to try to save me, to save my marriage? You've never even liked me before!"

"You're joking, aren't you? I've always *loved* you, Diana. More, I respected you enough to treat you like I treat everyone else— horribly. No free ride for being my sister. No free ride for being fat. The rest of the world treated you like you had some sort of handicap, always tiptoeing around as if, were they to speak within your hearing the words they said behind your back, it might kill you.

But I always accorded you the same dignity I would to anyone else, and thus I treated you horribly. Still will, if given half the chance. Don't think that now that you're practically thin, I'll let you off the hook."

"You know," I said, "in a sick sort of way, that's the nicest thing you've ever said to me."

"Thanks. And now that we're feeling all cozy and sisterly here, it's time I tell you the truth."

Uh-oh.

"Ever since you've had that weight-loss surgery," she said, "you've turned into a thin monster."

"A *thin* monster?"

"Yes, a thin monster. All you talk about is how much weight you've lost, what foods you're eating and not eating, what the scale says in the morning, and what size clothes you're buying."

"And that makes me a monster?"

"When you care more about the numbers on your scale than what's going on in the rest of the world? When you care more about how you look in clothes than you do about the feelings of flesh-and-blood people? When you're so desperate for attention that you turn to a prat like Dirk when you have a good man like Dan? When you focus on what you look like and how much you weigh, the outward appearance of yourself, to the exclusion of all else? Then, yes, I'd say that makes you a monster. A thin monster. And it has to stop."

I told her about throwing out the scale.

"That's a terrific first step," she conceded, "and while it's difficult to believe you thought to do so on your own without my guidance, I'm glad you've done it. You need to stop defining yourself by a number, no matter if that number is high or low, it must stop."

Funny how quickly Artemis could make my temper shoot from zero to one hundred. But, honestly.

"You're a fine one to talk!" I practically shouted at her. "All your life you've been the thin one! You have no idea what it's been like for me."

"Why don't you tell me, then?" she said coolly.

"Do you have any idea what it's like, choosing not to go to the gynecologist for your yearly physical, risking cervical cancer because you know that if you *do* go, they'll insist on weighing you, and when they do that, all they'll want to talk about the entire time you're there is how fat you are and what's to be done about it?"

"I'm sorry, Diana, that trips to the gyno have been a trial for you. But do you honestly think the rest of us *like* going? Do you think I like lying there, legs in the stirrups, wondering why the man who has his finger up my bum hole ever thought to go into that as a specialty in the first place? No one likes going to the gyno, whatever the reason!"

Then Artemis did a thing she'd never done before. She reached across the table and cupped my face in both her hands.

"You must stop, Diana, before you throw your life away in addition to throwing Dan away. You're not the person you used to be before. You need to let it go."

"But who will I be," I asked, "if I stop defining myself by what I look like? By what I weigh?"

She let my face go, and then settled back onto her stool.

"You'll be a human being," she said, "a person." She shrugged. "You'll be Diana."

Sylvia

Dear Sunny,

I'm writing to you at Cindy's suggestion. Well, really, she didn't actually tell me to write to you. She told me to talk to you, but this is one conversation I just can't have with you face-to-face.

I have a secret, something I've told only one other person in the last three decades, and that only recently. Thirty years ago, my twin sister was gang-raped while we were both in college. I'm not quite sure how it happened—not the rape; I know how that happened because Minnie told me. I mean I'm not sure how it happened that Minnie decided afterward to give up sex for the rest of her life and I somehow followed suit, but there you have it: I am, in essence, like a virgin. That's a good one, isn't it? The Virgin Sylvia? It's like the greatest story never told, now told. Or maybe it's not funny. In fact, I know it's not funny. But it is what it is.

I know this is a lot to burden you with, but I also know that you've been wondering all these months why I wanted to keep our relationship platonic, why I didn't want to, um, consummate things.

I guess what I'm trying to say is that I'm ready now. But now I'm not sure if you're ready; ready, that is, to be with a woman who basically has no experience; or, what experience she has had, it's all so long ago, she's practically forgotten what you're supposed to do with all those body parts.

OK, I'm rambling here. Bottom line? If you want to find out what we'd be like together, if you're brave enough to go ahead with this, and you're not laughing as you read every word, then come by and see me tonight after work. If you don't show up, I'll understand completely. No matter what, we will always be great good friends.

Love,
Sylvia

I folded the two sheets of paper, placed them in the envelope, licked the envelope shut, and, closing the shop up for an hour, I went across town and delivered the letter to Sunny's receptionist.

* * *

The rest of the day moved slowly, even though I was busy. Thanksgiving was still two weeks away, but already people were coming in to place their orders for turkeys of all sizes and oyster stuffing and cranberry relish and pumpkin pie. I made a great pumpkin pie.

When I got home that night and put my key in the lock, I told myself not to expect anything. I made dinner for the girls—chicken pot pie, because all Cindy wanted was comfort foods these days—and insisted on doing the dishes myself just to keep busy.

Seven o'clock, eight o'clock, nine.

I left the girls in the living room watching TV, and went to lay down on the bed with the shirt and skirt I'd worn to work that day and the flip-flops I always wore around the house still on. Sunny wasn't coming. He must have read my stupid letter, laughed at my foolishness, and then thrown the letter away.

So that was that.

All of the pent-up anxiety of waiting for something that wasn't going to happen must've finally gotten to me, because I dozed off. I awoke to a soft knock at the door. Looking at the alarm clock, I saw that it was ten.

"Sylvia?" Cindy poked her head in. Her eyes were sleepy, like maybe she'd dozed off in front of the TV herself. "Sunny's here. Should I send him in or tell him you're sleeping?"

I rose to a sitting position, my feet dangling over the side of the bed. Then I took a deep breath. "Send him in," I said.

"OK," she said, yawning. "I think I'm going to hit the hay, Carly too. 'Night."

"'Night."

She shut the door on her way out. A minute later, there was another tap.

"Come in," I said, my words practically a croak, I was that nervous. Sunny was such a gentleman. He was probably coming to tell me in person that he didn't want me. I took another breath.

And then he was there in my room.

"I thought you weren't coming," was the first thing I said.

"How could I not?" he countered. Then, as though reciting something in school, he said, "'The robbed that smiles steals something from the thief.'"

"That's beautiful," I said. "What does it mean?"

"It means that even if someone has harmed you, if you go on to have a happy life anyway, in spite of that harm, then you have achieved your own revenge. Someone—some *ones*—once took something from your sister and, in the process, managed to rob you of something as well. It is time for you to have that happy life, Sylvia." He paused. "The quote is from *Othello*, act V, scene III. It is one of the reasons I took so long getting here. I was trying to find the exact quote."

In Sunny's hands, he held a brown paper bag. I watched as he reached into the bag and pulled out handful after handful of white votive candles, which he arranged on my dresser and night table. Then he reached into the bag again, this time coming out with handful after handful of rose petals, which he scattered on my bed. He was so serious about it all, I almost laughed.

"What are you doing?" I asked.

"I am trying to create a moment," he said, lighting the candles before turning off the lights. "I must say, it is not so easy, creating a moment knowing there are other people in the house."

Then he knelt at my feet, gently removed my flip-flops, and kissed the feet that had stood thousands of hours in the shop.

"What are you doing?" I asked again. It seemed, suddenly, like they were the only words I knew how to say anymore.

"I am going to resurrect the girl in you," he said. "The woman, as well."

He took my hands in his and raised me to my feet. I felt unsteady until he placed his arms around me, lightly kissed my neck, and then my lips. When he started to lift my shirt, I stopped him.

"I can do that myself," I said.

When I was standing before him in just my bra and skirt, I felt as though I might have been naked.

"I'm not sure if I'm ready for this," I said with a nervous laugh as he slid one bra strap off my shoulder.

"Oh, I think you are ready," he said, kissing the place where the strap had been.

"No," I said, pushing him away, "I'm really not. You're probably expecting me to look all great once you get this bra off me, but I won't."

"I understand all about gravity," he said gravely.

I had to laugh at that. Hands on hips, I said, "I'll thank you to know that gravity has not become my enemy…yet." Then I felt nervousness overtake me again. "It's just that I have this scar, see, that no one's ever seen before, not like this."

"I know all about that scar," he said, reaching around me and, with surgical precision, unhooking my bra. "I put it there."

He kissed the scar he'd created by cutting into me, all those months ago.

He started to unzip my skirt.

"I'm anxious," I said, "the nervous kind of anxious."

"You think *you* have anxiety?" He laughed softly. "It is an awesome responsibility to be entrusted with making love to a woman who has not been made love to in thirty years. And yet, here I stand, with that woman, the kind of quick-witted woman who will probably laugh if what I am carrying between my legs is not impressive enough, and *you* are anxious?"

But in the end, I didn't laugh.

Not to put too fine a point on it, but my doctor, as it turned out, was *hung*.

He kissed every part of my body, as though I were a temple he had come to worship at. And when he rose above me, with the flower petals all around me on the bed, the candlelight from the moment he had created flickering across that beautiful and familiar face, for once in my life I was at a loss for words.

"You, Sylvia," he said, "are a goddess."

I had thought, when I'd imagined this previously, that it would hurt, that this was one bike a person couldn't get back onto after such a long dry spell and have the ride go smoothly.

But it wasn't like that at all.

As he slid inside me, I felt him penetrating my entire being. And, as he began to move inside me, I felt a long groan coming out of me, a sound I'd never made before.

"Shh." He smiled, placing one finger on my lips. "You will wake the kids."

* * *

Afterward, I lay with him, his arms twined around me, my arms twined around him.

"I love you, Sylvia," he said to the top of my head. "You are not only my great good friend. You are the love of my life."

"I love you, Sunny."

Lise

"Can I get you a glass of wine?" Tony asked.

"Please."

We were at his place, a rare thing. He'd called up, inviting me to dinner, a rarer thing since Tony was even worse at cooking than I was.

Tony lived in a cottage, not dissimilar to my own in terms of size, yet he was better at nesting than I was, meaning the place was filled with overstuffed furniture, comfy chenille throws in forest and cream and burgundy to cuddle up in on a cold night—like this one—and the sea-green walls were covered with silver frames, not framing photographs of famous authors he'd met or awards he'd won, but rather letters he'd received from students over the years.

"Here you go," he said, handing me a glass of Shiraz. "I'll just go check on the steaks."

Since I'd been there last, Tony had invested in an outdoor grill, and, as he headed out the door, he threw on a parka over his Oxford shirt and jeans.

While he was gone, I wondered what he'd invited me for. Rather than using the dining room table, or even the one in the kitchen, he'd set our places at the pink marble-top coffee table, on which he'd already put out the salad and fresh rolls, not far from the fire that roared in the fieldstone fireplace. Near his own place setting, he had a brown paper wrapped package, approximately eight inches by eleven, tied with a string.

"Just the way you like it," he said, coming back in, carrying a platter with two steaks in one hand, another platter with baked potatoes still in their aluminum casings in the other.

"The perfect man meal," I said, after he took off his parka, as we both settled down on the pillows he'd put on the floor in front of the table, "meat, potatoes, and a salad just in case your mother has X-ray vision and can see what you're eating. Are we having strawberry shortcake for dessert? Or apple pie ala mode, maybe?"

"If you behave yourself," he said with a smile, considering, "perhaps both."

The food was excellent.

When I'd still worked at the university, there'd always been someone to eat with, if I wanted to, every day. But lately I'd had to content myself with three squares all on my own, all cooked by myself too. I'd forgotten how pleasurable it was to have someone else do all the work, and then place the food in front of me with the simple command: "Eat."

I was so intent on my eating, I was halfway through my potato, melted butter pooling in the creases, before I asked, "What's in the package?"

He ignored me. "I've been wondering," he said, spearing a piece of meat, "what do you want out of life?"

"Oh, God." I groaned and then laughed. "If I'd known you were going to want to have a philosophical discussion, I'd have gone to McDonald's by myself instead."

"I'm serious, though. Do you miss teaching?"

"I do," I acknowledged. "I didn't think I would, but I do. Every day."

"Enough to give up writing?"

"Not that much," I said, making a face.

"It was a shame," he said, "what happened with Dirk."

"Yes," I said, "it was a huge waste of time, but I did learn a few things."

"Such as?"

"It's funny," I said, between chewing, "but sometimes, things happen that cause you to learn as much about what you *don't* want to be as a writer as what you do want."

"Tell me about it," he said, but not in the sarcastic or flip way the mere words might indicate. He really did want to know.

"OK," I said, taking another sip of wine. "I learned that

I don't want my writing to be written by committee. After Dirk, I've had enough of agents who want to play Svengali. If I'm ever lucky enough to land another agent, I'll only make positive changes that make sense to me or lateral changes: changes that please the other person but don't affect the integrity of the book. No more running around like Chicken Little, though, making endless changes, even conflicting changes, just because some agent—or any other publishing professional—keeps telling me the sky is falling."

"Good. Sounds like a metaphor for life. More wine?"

"Please." I held out my glass. "I also don't want to write stupid books, empty books that have nothing to say."

"Also good. But if you're not going to do what you've been doing these past few months, then what are you going to do? What kind of book *do* you want to write?"

I took a deep breath. "I want to write something more like the book I wrote first, the one I burned after Dirk said those awful things about it, only I want to do it without all the overwritten parts. I think now, when I let myself think about it, that it wasn't such a bad book after all. It just needed a lot of work. I was too quick to think that, just because I had a first draft, I was good to go. I also wish I hadn't been so quick to burn it, delete the file, and throw away the disk. If only I'd saved it, I might be able to look at it again with fresh eyes. Maybe I'd be able to see now what's needed to fix it."

I set down my fork and knife, ravenous hunger gone, too empty at the thought of my foolishness to want to fill the vacant space with something as relatively insignificant as food.

"I know it wasn't the greatest book in the world," I went on. "And I don't even aspire to *write* the greatest book in the world. But that book did say something, however small, about the way we human beings live our lives. If only it was still here," I finished, staring at the flames, reminiscent of different flames on a different night. "If only I didn't destroy it."

"Would you ever consider going back to teaching part time?" he said, switching gears. "Maybe just one class a semester? I happen to know Dean would love to have you back, on any terms. He may have gotten complaints about you last year, but the new professor is a total dud. Add to that, the cachet the school has accrued from your students turning around and selling their own books."

"A few months ago, I'd have given you an uncategorical no. But now? I miss my classroom. I miss helping other writers settle on what kind of writers they want to be. I miss *people*! If only I could find a way to strike a balance: teach a little and still get the writing in. If only I hadn't—"

"Please don't say again if only you hadn't destroyed your book."

I laughed at myself. "You're right," I admitted ruefully. "The whining of coulda, woulda, shoulda does get old, doesn't it?"

"No," he said, "listening to you doesn't get old. But you didn't destroy it."

"What?" I sat up.

"Well, OK, technically, you did destroy it. But it's not gone."

"Tony, tell me what you're talking about. Tell me what you're talking about before I hit you."

"It's right here," he said, patting the package that had been sitting beside his plate all during our meal.

"But how?"

"That night after you burned it, after you deleted it and threw out the disk, while you were sleeping the sleep of the damned and the depressed, I went and rescued it from your hard drive. I hope you don't mind that, or that I've since read it. It's quite good, actually. Overwritten in parts, true. I think you'll know how to fix that now, though."

"But why?" I was stunned. "Why would you do that for me when you never believed in my writing in the first place?" I thought about that for a second. "And why would you wait so long to tell me?"

"I did it because writers who destroy their work always live to regret it, or they die and then the world regrets it. And no, I never said I didn't believe in your writing. What I didn't want was for you to go off half-cocked like, well, Chicken Little. I thought you should have more of a plan first, one involving more than quitting your job and saying, 'Today I will become a writer.' What can I say?" He shrugged, evidently mildly embarrassed. "I'm a man. Even when it comes to something as abstract as creativity, we deal in absolutes. You want to talk about it; I want to fix it. Man. Woman. Even our body parts are different." He laughed, I think as much at himself as at me, maybe at us. "Finally, I waited until now because I needed to make sure you were ready to go back to what you started and make it better. I needed to be sure you wouldn't just destroy it again. So, what do you say? Teach one class a semester and make your book as good as you can make it?"

In the very best Jo March tradition, I flew at his head.

Thanksgiving

RECOMMENDED READING:
Cindy: *Family Planning*, Elizabeth Letts
Diana: *My Sister's Keeper*, Jodi Picoult
Sylvia: *The Food of Love*, Anthony Capella
Lise: *The Art of Dramatic Writing*, Lajos Egri

"Do you know what one of the students said the new creative writing professor told them?" Dean Jones asked his wife as he carved into their turkey for two.

"No," she said, swirling the sherry in her glass, "but I'm sure you're about to tell me."

He ignored her bored expression.

"He said she told them they needed to become a perfect blend of Charles Dickens and Danielle Steel if they wanted to succeed in the current publishing climate. God, I miss Lise Barrett."

"I know, dear, I know."

* * *

"What are these little round things doing in the cranberry sauce?" Art Barrett asked his wife.

"Sara gave me the recipe and told me to make it," Ann Barrett said. "Sara wanted us to have an all-natural Thanksgiving, even though she's not with us this year."

"Don't you have any of that stuff in the can?"

"No. Sara made me promise to donate it to a food drive. First she wanted me to just throw it out, but then she changed her mind, saying it would be wasteful."

"Lise," Art said, "promise me that, whatever else you do, you won't be like your sister, at least not totally."

"I promise, Dad."

"Are you really considering going back to work at the university?"

"Part time? Yes, I'm considering it."

"Good. I'll bet Tony here had something to do with that."

Tony held up his hands. "I'm innocent."

"Lise," Aunt Tess said, "could you help me get more stuffing from the kitchen?"

"But we already have—"

Aunt Tess kicked her. "We need more. Without any decent cranberry sauce, your father will need thirds."

Once Lise had followed Aunt Tess into the kitchen, Aunt Tess turned on her.

"So?" she said. "Tony's here. You're here. Do I hear wedding bells?"

"Aunt Tess! We only just got back together!"

"So? I've still got that cash in paper bags at the top of my closet, if you need any help with the wedding!"

* * *

Eddie picked at his turkey. One of his band mates had invited him over to eat dinner with him and his wife.

"I'm thinking," said Eddie, "that maybe we should all just move to Europe. You know, if we went somewhere where no one knows us, maybe we could reinvent ourselves as younger. Then we could be like, I don't know, European Idols or something."

* * *

"Mom," Porter said, passing the three-bean salad, "there's this girl I met." He cleared his throat. "Actually, I met her a while ago, back in high school, but now I've met her again."

"A girl? A nice girl?"

"A very nice girl." He cleared his throat again. "Only thing is, there's something a little bit different about her…"

* * *

Richard Cox was drinking his dinner while the rest of his family was eating theirs.

"One daughter knocked up, the other working in a bra shop." He turned to his wife. "This is all *your* fault."

"How is it my fault?"

"If you'd been a better role model, they wouldn't be such losers."

"Maybe if you didn't treat me like crap—"

"How do I treat you like crap? Look at this place! I treat you like a queen!"

Carly put her head close to Cindy's. "Let's get out of here," she whispered.

"But wouldn't that be rude," Cindy whispered back, "to leave before dessert?"

"Nah. They won't even notice."

* * *

Magda Riley ate her frozen dinner as she sat in front of her TV table watching television; or, to put it more properly, watching the competition on television.

"Fucking Sylvia Goldsmith," she muttered. "That stupid bitch could've made me a mint."

* * *

Minnie Goldsmith, wherever she was, smiled.

* * *

"I can't believe you made dinner for me," Sylvia said. "It's like a cook's holiday."

"You deserve a holiday," Sunny said. "Although, I must say, I am not as good of a cook as you."

"It sure is quiet here without the girls."

"Do you mind that so very much?"

Sylvia thought about it. "No," she finally said. "It's just different."

"I was thinking, perhaps you would like to move in together."

"I think we'd get a bit crowded here, don't you? When the baby comes, there'll be five of us."

"I wasn't thinking about here necessarily. I was thinking about my place."

"But what about Cindy? She needs me right now. I can't just sell the place out from under her."

"Who said anything about that? So you stay here and help her for as long as she needs you, and then you move in with me. You own this place outright, do you not?"

Sylvia nodded.

"So turn it over to her and Carly and come to me."

. . .

"*Fucking* Americans," Dirk Peters said. "Just because they go on holiday they expect the rest of the world to as well. Might as well have not even bothered getting up this morning for all the work I got done today."

. . .

"Tell me again," Artemis's father said, "why your mother and I had to come over to your place and eat turkey even though it's not our holiday? I don't even like turkey. I'd certainly never shoot one. Way too easy. I'd much rather shoot a falcon."

"We're doing this," Artemis said through gritted teeth, "to honor Diana, *your daughter*, and her new life." She raised her glass. "To Diana."

* * *

Diana knocked on the door to Dan's hotel room, massive picnic basket in hand.

"I'm glad you decided not to go to your mother and sister's place in Michigan this year," she said when he answered the door.

"Travel's hellish this time of year," he admitted. "It was good to have an excuse not to."

"And I'm glad," Diana said, "you agreed to let me cook you a meal and bring it over."

"A man's got to eat."

"Yes, I know that. But if you didn't want me to come, you could have gone out to eat or had room service send you up something, right? Aargh, I'm doing this all wrong." She took a moment before speaking again. "I guess what I came here to say, what I'm *trying* to say, is that I'm very sorry for everything. I'm sorry for what I did, *and* I'm sorry for what you did. I know the way back into your heart isn't through your stomach." She laughed at the picnic basket she was carrying. "And I know it's not through your bed."

"Well," he raised his eyebrows at her, "we could see if it is."

But she went on, registering his willingness to make a joke, but needing to say what she'd come there to say all the same.

"Look," she said, "I know we can't just suddenly go back to where we were before this all happened. I've changed. You've changed. Who we are and the things we've done have changed each other. But we have to start somewhere. And maybe if we do, maybe someday we'll find ourselves at a better place than the place we were at before. At the very least, we can try."

"At the very least," Dan said, "we can try."

* * *

All over the city of Danbury that day, people gave thanks; if not necessarily for the families they had, then for the families they had created.

RECOMMENDED READING:
Lise: *The Color of Light*, William Goldman
Diana: *Gods in Alabama*, Joshilyn Jackson
Sylvia: *Tender at the Bone*, Ruth Reichl
Cindy: *The Cat Who Came for Christmas*, Cleveland Amory

Lise

We were all at Sylvia's for Christmas Eve dinner. Her dining room table, with extra leaves in it to accommodate the nine of us, nearly filled the entire room, and I was in the kitchen helping her. Cindy's due date had been two days previous, and the doctor had told her that morning that the baby was fine, just a little late.

"Funny," I said, "the two of us doing all the Christmas work when we're Jewish."

Sylvia nearly dropped the pot she was holding. "*You're* Jewish too? How come you never said anything?"

I shrugged. "I guess it never came up in conversation," I said. I peeked my head around the corner and took in the view of the living room where the others—Dan and Diana, Tony, Sunny, Carly, Cindy and Porter—were seated on chairs, on the couch, on the floor. In particular, I looked at Cindy and Porter.

"Is having a man the answer to everything?" I asked.

Sylvia bent down to peek around the corner too so that her head was beneath mine. Instinctively, she knew what I meant.

"Well, not if you're a lesbian," she said. "But having someone to love? A husband, a wife, a friend, a sister? I think it's a big part of what we're put here for. Otherwise, what's the point?"

Maybe, I thought, I was finally really ready to ask Tony to marry me.

Diana

I looked around the table Sylvia had put together for all of us: the long red and green candles inside their glass domes, the food lovingly prepared, and the people. And, as I looked, I felt the closeness of us once more; not so tight as to be restricting, but a closeness that bound us together like the strands of a whole just the same.

I reached for Dan's hand beneath the tablecloth and held on tight.

Sylvia

Sunny helped me do the dishes. He washed, saying it was more important that my hands stay nice than his, while I dried.

"Have you thought," he said, "about my proposal?"

"Which proposal is that?"

"The one where, after you see Cindy settled, you move in with me?"

"Yes," I said. "It sounds like a good plan."

"Good. Then, if you are going to move in with me anyway"—and here he dropped to one knee, removing a ring from his pocket without even wiping the soapsuds from his hands first—"how about agreeing to be my wife?"

Cindy

Even though it was freezing out, after dinner Porter and I sat out on Sylvia's stoop, staring up at the clear December night sky.

"I can't believe," I said, "that you want to date me, given everything."

"It's not like it's the first time I've wanted to date you. It's only that it's the first time I've wanted to date you when you've actually, maybe wanted to date me too."

"I guess. But I was too stupid when we knew each other before. And now," I looked down at my huge belly, "well, I'm hardly a bargain."

"Look at it this way," he said, rubbing my hands to keep them warm. "I've dated plenty of girls who seemed to have no baggage who then turned out to be nothing but baggage. At least this way, it's been as bad as it can get—violent boyfriend, etcetera, etcetera—going in."

"Oh, thanks," I said, cuffing him lightly on the shoulder. "That makes me feel *real* good."

"We're just kind of dating," he said. "It's not like the whole entire future has to be decided tonight."

"True," I said. Then I thought of something. "Hey," I said playfully, "at least you know I'm fertile. You know, just in case we ever get married. Kidding. *Kidding!*"

The Club

Sometimes in stories, people get beaten to death, they lose the baby, they never change, they never find love, or, if they do find it, they lose it because they don't know what to do with it; the manuscript stays burned and sadness ensues.

But those stories aren't this story.

That's not to say that the lives of these four women, from this moment forward, will be without pain or suffering. They are human. They will know plenty. They will love, and, because they love, they will know great tragedy. They will all die. They will grow old, they will get sick, one will die only after everyone she's ever loved has died first.

But right now, before we spin away from them, as we look at them in this moment, today, they are happy. We can let them have that.

. . .

Cindy went into labor.

It happened later on that night, long after everyone had left. Still, despite the late hour, before leaving for the hospital, Sylvia phoned Lise and Diana to tell them.

As Cindy labored, Sylvia at her side, Diana and Lise and Carly paced the waiting room.

"I don't think I can do this!" Cindy said to Sylvia at one point through gritted teeth as another contraction hit her.

"Of course you can do it," Sylvia said, her arm steady behind Cindy's back. Sylvia always had Cindy's back. "It's what you came here to do."

Three hours later, Carly and Lise and Diana came in to meet Cindy's new baby.

"This is *wonderful!*" Diana said, surveying the results of what she'd started all those months ago. "Today it really feels as though we *are* The Sisters Club."

Sylvia looked at her sharply.

"Oops, sorry," Diana said, looking embarrassed. "I just—"

"It's fine," Sylvia said. "I was just thinking how much I agree with you right now. Yes. Yes, it does feel like that."

Lise looked at the baby, wrapped in the hospital-issue receiving blanket, that Cindy was holding.

"She's beautiful," Lise said. "Have you picked out a name yet?"

Cindy looked at her daughter, not even needing to look at the others because she felt their love all around her—the love of the sister she was born with, and the love of the sisters she'd chosen—and spoke one word:

"Sylvia."

Lauren Baratz-Logsted is the author of over 25 books for adults, teens and children, which have been published in 15 countries. She lives in Danbury, CT, with her husband, daughter and cat. You can read more about her life and work at **www.laurenbaratzlogsted.com** or follow her on Twitter **@LaurenBaratzL**.

The Thin Pink Line: A Jane Taylor Novel

Jane Taylor is a slightly sociopathic Londoner who wants marriage and a baby in the worst way, and she's willing to go to over-the-top lengths to achieve her dream. When Jane thinks she's pregnant she tells everyone. When it turns out to be a false alarm, she assumes she'll just get pregnant, no one the wiser. But when that doesn't happen, well, of course she does what no one in her right mind would do: Jane decides to fake an entire pregnancy!

Crossing the Line: A Jane Taylor Novel

In the madcap sequel to the international hit comedy THE THIN PINK LINE, London editor Jane Taylor is at it again, only this time, there's a baby involved. Having—SPOILER ALERT!—found a baby on a church doorstep at the end of the previous book, Jane is forced to come clean with all the people in her world when it turns out that the baby is a different skin color than everyone had expected Jane's baby to be. As Jane fights to keep the baby, battling Social Services and taking on anyone who seeks to get in her path, what kind of mother will Jane prove to be?

Only one thing's for certain: no matter how much kinder and gentler she is now, she is still and will always be crazy Jane.

The Bro-Magnet: A Johnny Smith Novel

Poor Johnny Smith.

At age 33, the house painter has been a best man a whopping eight times, when all he's ever really wanted is to be a groom. But despite being everyone's favorite dude, Johnny has yet to find The One. Or even anyone. So when he meets high-powered District Attorney Helen Troy, and falls for her hard, he follows the advice of family and friends. Since Helen seems to hate sports, Johnny pretends he does too. No more Jets. No more Mets. At least not in public. He redecorates his condo. He gets a cat. He takes up watching soap operas. Anything he thinks will earn him Helen, Johnny is willing to do. There's just one hitch: If he does finally win her heart, who will he be?

Isn't It Bro-Mantic?: A Johnny Smith Novel

What happens after Happily Ever After? That's what Johnny Smith is about to find out. Having wooed—and won!—the girl of his dreams in The Bro-Magnet, he is ready to take on married life. Finally, Johnny will be the groom. But right off the bat, during the honeymoon, things start to go wrong. And it only gets worse when the newlyweds return home to their new house in Connecticut. Different taste in pets, interior design, friends. Too much togetherness. Jealousy. Nothing is easy, given that neither Johnny nor his wife has ever even had a roommate since college. Can this couple, still so in love, share a home without driving each other crazy?

wrinkled,
water damage
WPA Mar/16

CPSIA information can be obtained at www.ICGtesting.com
Printed in the USA
LVOW07s1612170915

454593LV00008B/819/P